William Horwood is the author of the bestselling Duncton Wood series and Wolves of Time books, among many others. He has also written an inspiring memoir, *The Boy with No Shoes*. William has worked as a teacher, in recruitment and as a journalist and he is now a full-time writer living in Oxford.

Find out more about the author at: www.williamhorwood.co.uk

BY WILLIAM HORWOOD

The Duncton Chronicles
Duncton Wood
Duncton Quest
Duncton Found

The Book of Silence
Duncton Tales
Duncton Rising
Duncton Stone

The Wolves of Time
Journeys to the Heartland
Seekers at the Wulf Rock

Tales of the Willows
The Willows in Winter
Toad Triumphant
The Willows and Beyond
The Willows at Christmas

Other works
The Stonor Eagles
Callanish
Skallagrigg
The Boy with No Shoes (Memoir)

The Hyddenworld Novels
Hyddenworld: Spring
Awakening
Harvest
Winter

HARVEST

WILLIAM HORWOOD

PAN BOOKS

First published 2012 by Macmillan

This edition published 2013 by Pan Books
an imprint of Pan Macmillan, a division of Macmillan Publishers Limited
Pan Macmillan, 20 New Wharf Road, London N1 9RR
Basingstoke and Oxford
Associated companies throughout the world
www.panmacmillan.com

ISBN 978-0-330-46170-2

A CIP catalogue record for this book is available from the British Library.

Typeset by SetSystems Ltd, Saffron Walden, Essex
Printed and bound by CPI Group (UK) Ltd, Croydon, CR0 4YY

Visit **www.panmacmillan.com** to read more about all our books
and to buy them. You will also find features, author interviews and
news of any author events, and you can sign up for e-newsletters
so that you're always first to hear about our new releases.

HARVEST

PROLOGUE

I t was August, time of the first harvest.

Right across the Hyddenworld folk were busy gathering their crops.

By day they collected such fruit and grain, fungi and herbs as ripened early.

By twilight they processed and stored it.

By night they lit their festive fires and sang and danced their thanks to Mother Earth.

At such times strangers were welcome at the communal fire. They brought news of the world beyond and shed light on old doubts and fears and new worries.

Then, as the night deepened, and folk became responsive to the lilting word, the tale-tellers came to the communal fire, and the old folk too, passing on traditions and wisdom that reached into the hearts of all who heard.

There are surely very few gatherings at harvest time that do not give thanks to the Mirror-of-All, in which hydden live their lives as reflections – living, moving, loving, dying as if they are real but knowing in truth that life itself is as insubstantial as a passing mist.

Now here, now swiftly gone, yet so often filled with matters trivial and small that hydden forget that now – *now* – is all they truly have. The past is but remembrance of reflections gone, the future but fleeting hopes and dreams of things that may never even find their way to the Mirror's light. Of these things tellers warn.

Often at these moments by the fire, one or other of the speakers will express for all the greatest fear of hydden everywhere: that the day might come when the Mirror cracks and all that ever was and might have been will be gone forever, eternally forgotten.

Few hydden can live long with such dread.

They can hear the threat of it, told as a story, and dwell on its awfulness, but only as long as it takes to stoke the fire, re-fill a cannikin with a sustaining brew and welcome another to the circle, shoulder to comforting shoulder, watching in silence as the sparks rise to the stars, while they wait for a new speaker to offer diversion and a brighter prospect.

If a tale-teller is known to be good, or a stranger comes to the circle with that quiet, rough confidence and grace that gives promise they have something new worth saying, or an old tale that might be newly told, he or she may be asked to speak.

There are a few tales and wisdoms which have a very special place.

No one asks for these to be told but, rather, hints at them obliquely, in the hope that one among the company who may not yet have spoken will finally speak up and talk of things others most want and need to hear at times of doubt.

Such moments, which happen when the night is deep and the fire warms a hydden's heart, so that utterance seems to come out of the Universe as if it is the Mirror speaking, are precious indeed. Such tale-tellers bless the company they keep, but their coming and going are unpredictable.

Whole decades may pass before a hydden village is honoured by the presence of such a wanderer. When it happens it usually does so for a reason. Perhaps in gratitude for good things past; perhaps as a warning against shadows yet to come.

Which is why one tale before all others is a favourite at such times, for it carries in its being both light and dark, warning and celebration. It feeds the mind even as it stirs the heart.

It is the tale of Beornamund, greatest of the CraftLords or makers of objects of power. He was founder of Brum, former capital of Englalond and still the stronghold of that which all true hydden love and fight for – freedom of the spirit and liberty of the individual.

His story is one of love lost in the mortal world but found again in the immortal one; of an object made of such perfection that it took to itself the Fires of the Universe and the colours of the seasons; and of a quest or quests to save mortal kind, whether human or hydden, towards which its folly in abusing the very Earth itself is surely leading.

That's a tale worth hearing and it's one oft-told at harvest time when folk reflect upon the oldest truth and the simplest: each one of us must reap what we sow, for good and ill and good again, just as great Beornamund did.

Though oft-heard, it is a tale rarely told well enough. It needs a teller who has plumbed the depths of life itself to bring back truths that have meaning for us all.

I

THREE TRAVELLERS

In the third week of August a rumour, strange and wonderful, spread across southern Englalond, that sea-bound place of mists and mysteries which lies in the far north-western corner of the Hyddenworld.

It told of three hydden who were travelling incognito, pursued by soldiers of the Fyrd, the fearsome army of the Empire which had subdued the country decades before. They were rarely seen and when they were they kept themselves to themselves, making camp in the shelter of isolated knolls, or on the holy ground of tumuli and other such burial places, or in the shade of a deep valley.

Their identity was known to every hydden in the land but their names were rarely spoken, out of reverence to the dangerous mission they were on and because none who loved liberty and freedom, and cherished the Earth, would ever risk leading the Fyrd to them.

Their starting point had been White Horse Hill in Berkshire, that much was known. Their destination was almost certainly Brum, city of freedom.

The quickest and easiest route was north and westward, by way of the old pilgrim road that leads to Waseley Hill where Beornamund once had his foundry. From there it is but an hour or two to Brum itself.

But the Fyrd patrolled that road and the three had been forced westward along green roads and river ways, the Fyrd close behind. From time to time they had called into a village along the way, for provisions and perhaps for company. None asked their names, though all knew them.

None asked their destination, though any could guess it.

Not a hydden ventured to ask their purpose, for to speak it might be to spoil it.

They said little, but were not taciturn.

They were well enough, but seemed weary with the weight of their wyrd or destiny.

There was the light of prophecy and purpose about them and it was said that miracles happened in their wake: a sick child became well, a dumb boy spoke again, a blind wyf saw, angry neighbours learnt to laugh once more.

Folk hoped the three might come their way and they prayed that if the harvest feast was set in their village they would eat and, when the fire was lit and stories told, the travellers would join the circle in the dark.

Then, if the Mirror willed it, and all were hushed, and things were put in the right way and all was good, perhaps one or other of those famed travellers might say a word, speak a wisdom or tell a tale.

'Would they?'

'They might.'

'Would they tell the greatest tale?'

'Not if you ask 'em, no. But if the wyrd's with us all and the stars are right and the fires good, then one or other of them might be moved to talk of Beornamund.'

Such was the rumour, such the hope.

Not least because that worrisome year, in Englalond as elsewhere, folk had lost confidence in their Mother Earth.

She who had been abundant through so many generations was no longer so.

She who was once benign was angry now.

She who had been friend had turned enemy.

The first harvest celebrations were muted and reluctant as if no one wanted to tempt providence. Strange unseasonal weather from Springtime on, unusual earth tremors and a collective unease and malaise among hydden folk ever since had made them jumpy and insecure.

It did not help that the human world had been even harder hit by the destructive Earth events than the hydden one. Some towns and even cities had been half destroyed, road and rail disrupted and the humans were in the grip of fear, of violence and of death.

A panic had seemed to seize the humans at the end of July and they fled from the south of Englalond to the north, or to the Continent, from lowland vales to the high passes of the Pennines and Cumbria, Wales and the borderland with Scotland, believing they might find sanctuary there. Indeed, though August was barely halfway through, many were already counting the days to the last and greatest of the harvest celebrations, which takes place on November Eve and is called Samhain.

They watched the fields and sky with worried faces; they tasted the water of lake and river with dubious tongues; and they poked and sifted, sniffed and hearkened close to the moist and shifting humus in the woods, saying, 'If we can only get through to the last day of October with all the crops safe in and stored, then perhaps . . . then maybe . . . *maybe* we might have a chance to survive this winter.'

'Aye, neighbour, if we can, but only if! For winters that follow such an ominous harvest time as this are usually bad.'

'Ssh! Say that not! Things may be late and all distorted, but at least the harvests have started and that's . . .'

'Yes, at least that's . . . that's . . .'

'Good? Is it not good?'

The other shifted about, hunched his head to right and left, wrinkled his brow and squinted at the still and silent trees whose leaves were already withering, and kicked the ground before answering.

'Perhaps it is,' he finally said grudgingly, 'perhaps it's not. The best I'd say is 'tis better than "bad".'

'Not good then?'

'Not quite bad!'

This gloomy exchange might have been heard in any of a thousand hydden villages in Englalond that month. But in reality it took place one mid-August evening on the outskirts of the hydden village of Cleeve. A pretty enough place which sits on the west and steeper side of the Cotswold Hills, overlooking the human city of Cheltenham, where it sprawls westward across the valley of the River Severn towards the great river itself, untidy, noisy, over-lit and generally polluting, as such cities are.

The talk might have continued and become gloomier still had not one of the villagers suddenly started and, grasping the arm of the other, whispered hoarsely, 'By all that's blessed in the Mirror, look what's coming down the hill!'

The other stared, his eyes disbelieving and then filled with excitement.

'Is it them and coming right towards us!?'

'I think it might be, brother.'

'Shall we scarper?'

'No, we stand our ground. Let 'em come right up to us if they will so we can see their garb and faces and know for sure.'

Three travellers, two males and a female, had appeared off Cleeve Hill and were making their way towards them with the slow but rhythmic gait of those who have journeyed far that day and need a rest.

'Hale and well met!' cried one of them, a well-made youth of nineteen or twenty who portered a sizeable 'sac with ease and carried a hefty stave. He was open-faced but serious, dark of hair and eyes, and he carried himself with authority. His stave was unusual, being anciently carved down its length, the facets and curls catching the fading light of the sky so that it shimmered as wind does through the leaves of a copper beech.

'Greetings to you too!' cried out one of the villagers as they eyed the other two.

Each was as striking and personable, though in different ways. One was a female, about the same age as the first male, fair and handsome but with weary pallor and tired eyes that suggested she had suffered a recent trial or tribulation. She wore a spousal ring of woven twine, newly threaded through with the fragrant stems of balsam and thyme, which suggested her union to one of the males was born in poverty or haste.

The second male was unusually tall, red-haired, freckled and hazel-eyed. He wore poorly made trews of dark fustian, leather boots with different-coloured laces and a blue kerchief round his neck. It had been a warm day and he wore no hose. His thin, white legs were as freckled as his face and the backs of his hands. He stood lop-sided because his portersac, which was even larger than that carried by the other male, was ill-packed and poorly balanced. Its many pockets were filled to overflowing with objects of mainly human origin: a roll of black plastic bin bags could be seen, a spanner, the top end of a split cane fishing rod, a half-used church candle, green string, wire coat hangers. A cooking pan dangled from one of the 'sac's straps, a small brass whistle from the other. His jerkin, which was strung, not buttoned, was open nearly to his waist. A thin rectangular object as long as a forefinger, as wide as a thumb, hung from a thin thread of gold about his neck. It was part glass, part mother-of-pearl, reflecting light as well as absorbing it.

Yet it was not this strange, sweet disarray of his person which finally held the eye but the expression on his face. It was alert, enquiring, challenging and abstracted, like one who has been thinking deeply about one thing when his attention has been drawn unwillingly to another.

They had a dog as well, a cross between a Labrador and red setter that settled at the tall one's feet awhile, before, growing bored, he dashed off into nearby woods.

One thing was certain: their youth, their pleasant manner, their peaceable and friendly approach showed they were no threat.

But this was more certain still: these three were the most famous hydden in all Englalond and there they were, bold as brass, making fair greeting.

'You seek bed and board?' ventured the other villager before adding diffidently, 'It be our festive night and your arrival is well timed! The bonfire has been long since made and all are welcome, provided they come with good intent and bring a peck or two of news from other parts.'

It was the female who answered and she did so with a polite shake of the head.

'That's courteous,' she said matter-of-factly, 'but all we seek is a place to pitch our camp, take sup and rest our heads.'

'That's well too,' they replied. 'The visitors' ground is across that field by the old oak tree. There's flowing water, a stove and shelter from the wind and none will disturb you. But if you're minded . . .'

'This is Cleeve, I take it?' said the tall one, breaking in abruptly. 'Can you say how far it is to Abbey Mortaine?'

'Too far to make before dark,' said the first villager, 'and it bain't a place I'd go just now and nor should any sensible traveller.'

They looked questioningly at him.

'Fyrd,' he said. 'Came here questing, didn't find what they sought and went on their way the day 'formidden.'

'What were they seeking?'

'Didn't say, but we knew,' said one meaningfully.

'Daredn't ask, but we mis-told,' added the other, winking.

The first of the travellers laughed.

'Meaning what?' he said.

'We'm said that them they sought had passed this way and they'd just missed 'em.'

'Did you say which way "they" went?' asked the female.

'Southerly, in a hurry, like they were on the run.'

'And which way did the Fyrd go?'

'Southerly, Cleeve folk being good at the honest lie!'

There was more laughter.

'Anything more?'

One of the villagers shrugged.

'Embellishment's no bad thing. One of the Fyrd asked if them fugitives stated their destination so one of us, meaning me, said they surely had.'

'Which was where?'

The villager winked again and smiled broadly. 'I told 'em that you . . . I mean the ones they sought, were heading for the centre of the Universe and were in a hurry for they had to be there by Samhain.'

It was meant as a joke, for all knew that the Centre of the Universe was the Mirror itself and Samhain was a long way off, being the last day of October. But as he repeated it a strange thing happened.

The stave of the first traveller who had spoken shimmered, a sudden gust of wind harried the trees nearby and the evening darkened as if time had shifted into night.

'Well then,' said one of the villagers nervously, 'we'd best leave you to settle in. You're welcome to join the feast later if you've a mind for it.'

With that they left the travellers to it, without a backward glance lest the three decided not to stay.

As they went, one said to another, 'Now that's a strange question from the tall one who, if I'm not mistaken, must be . . .'

'No, don't speak his name! 'Tis indeed most strange to ask the way to Abbey Mortaine when there's nary living there but mean spirits and old choristers!'

News of the arrival of the three young travellers in Cleeve spread fast and, despite the fall of darkness, far beyond the village. It was already full of visitors from places roundabout, there for the festival. From the descriptions given by the two who first met them, and further discreet investigation from afar, there was little doubt who the new visitors were.

Not that anyone actually said so, but it seemed plain enough. No wonder folk sent runners out to their own communities to say who had come and that there was a chance, though no doubt a slim one, that that night, by the communal fire in Cleeve, if it was in the wyrd or destiny of things, three heroes of the Hyddenworld might honour the company with their presence and maybe share a tale or two of their own.

'Are you serious? They're in Cleeve right *now*?!'

'They are, seen 'em myself and they looks like what folk say they look like: one tall and gangly-legged, one strong with the famous stave that shows his proper rank and one a female, who must surely be . . .'

'Ssh! Speak *that* not, lest mal-destiny or Fyrd get to know of it. You say they're there now and might attend the feast?'

'I do and they might. Bring the kinder, for this could be a night none will ever forget.'

'Should we bring gifts?'

'No, better not. Best to pretend we don't know who they are. Best not to tell the kinder except to say that important people are about, very important, the like of which they may never have a chance to meet again.'

From Woodmancote and Southam folk came hurrying, from Slades and Longwood and the old fort on Nottingham Hill; from Postlip and the Common, and those places beyond that rarely venture over the hill to Cleeve – the lads in Corndean, the good folk of Humblebee and old folk from Winchcombe, they came too.

Then in the late hour, burdened by their sick and lame, and by kinder sad and ill, one with a head swollen with water and pain, and a fair girl of three whose limbs grew awry and old Gretton of Greenfield, carrying his wife on his back in hope she might be healed of furrowed tongue. Even Old Annie, who lost a child and never recovered, came a-crawling out of Saxilberry as the fire deepened and the stories began.

All of these hurt ones and maybe the healthy too, hoping to find healing in the weave of the words of such great strangers should they decide to speak.

'As for you young ones, if you must stay up so late, you'd better be as quiet as mice and good as well-fed voles.'

Wide eyes, whispers, stomachs full, the feasting over, the singing dying now, the dancing to tuble and 'bag only occasional, the jokes and japes quietening, as a night hush fell and someone stoked the fire.

A hush then and a hope that the strangers would come from over the field, slipping in among them all, to listen awhile, to nod their heads, to smile and let their hearts move with the story-flow until someone of them, if their wyrd made it so and it was in the Mirror's reflection, offered to speak.

That was the hope of all, but not a body there who said it.

Say it and it might never happen.

Hope it and it might.

2

OLD FRIENDS,
NEW QUEST

The three travellers whose arrival had brought such excitement
and anticipation to Cleeve were more famous than they knew,
and with good reason. No wonder their reputation preceded
them.

The sturdy one with the stave that transformed light to something
magical was Jack, Stavemeister of Brum.

The female was Katherine, human-born. When she first came
into the Hyddenworld folk thought she was the Shield Maiden, the
vengeful warrior of the Universe, come to punish mortal kind for
its many wrongs against the Earth. They were wrong but not far
wrong. It had been the wyrd of she and Jack to meet and fall in
love. The result of their union was an extraordinary but disturbing child named Judith. It was she who was the Shield Maiden, born
less than four months before, which was why Katherine looked drawn
and tired.

But where was Judith now?

The answer was a tale any hydden would want to hear if Katherine
could be persuaded to tell it. As it was, what had happened to their
daughter had been in its way so shocking, so far beyond the normality
of things, that she had said nothing about it since the beginning of
August despite the attempts of both Jack and Stort to get her to
unburden herself.

Now she was tired and wan, not her former self at all. It was for that reason that Jack had brought them into a village, in the hope that some company at harvest-time would lift her spirits.

The tallest and oldest was Bedwyn Stort, scholar and scrivener, traveller and inventor, loved far and wide for his courage in helping others before himself. He was held in awe because it was now known that more than any other it was his responsibility to fulfil a quest set in motion fifteen hundred years before by Beornamund the CraftLord.

If Stort and his friends succeeded, then all might be well across the Earth again. If he failed, then mortalkind faced extinction.

No wonder folk in Cleeve and thereabout wanted to hear one of them speak.

In fact they might have left when they were told that the Fyrd had come calling but when they heard they had been sent on a wild goose chase to the south they decided to stay.

'It means it'll be safe to go to Abbey Mortaine,' said Stort, 'if only we can find an easy way to get there. It can't be more than ten miles off but we're too tired to head back up into the hills in the dark.'

They had hoped to reach the Abbey some days before but, as so often on their trek from White Horse Hill since the start of the month, the Fyrd had got in the way. It was Stort's job to route-find, Jack's to act as defender of them both, with Katherine a stout fighter too and normally a stable presence.

They did not use the visitors' site but returned to higher ground, overlooking the village. Jack felt they were more secure, for it gave them a view of things. As he had expected, Katherine was reluctant to join the festivities, though they could see the bonfire and hear the singing and the harvest dance.

It was a welcome and unusual sight, for as their name suggests hydden normally stay out of sight.

They had got their name millennia before, in the days when regular communication with humans was coming to an end. Though these two strands of mortal kind came from a common ancestor, time and inclination had made them separate.

Humans are giants by another name. To the hydden they are aggressive, acquisitive, clumsy and fearsome. More than that, as their numbers grew, they displaced their hydden cousins who, at only three feet high, could not easily resist them. It proved easier to learn to make themselves scarce, to seem as the fox does, or the deer, or the plump fish in a stream: nearly invisible.

It was then that the hydden became known as such, the word 'hydden' meaning just what it looks like in the old language.

Gradually the humans began to forget them and learnt, without knowing it, *not* to see them. The hydden became a memory that turned to a myth and story of little folk told in many ways in many lands. Folk who were magical and fey, or malign and mischievous. Until the time came when no humans knew them at all and most believed that the little folk were make-believe.

It was an outcome that protected the hydden from human aggression, which ran amok in the centuries following. The hydden went to extraordinary lengths to stay unseen. Their humbles or homes were underground or in places humans could not reach. Their settlements were far from those of humans. There the hyddening arts developed to such a degree that a hydden was better than a deer at staying unseen and faster than a snake to disappear.

Then, in the nineteenth century, with the human industrial revolution, something extraordinary happened.

Humans began to create buildings and structures within which, or between which, were spaces which they themselves could not see or easily visit. Sewers, conduits for water, ducts for service pipes, the undercrofts and footings of buildings, streams and even rivers built over, the interstices of factories where no human ever went.

These places the enterprising hydden soon colonized, finding it easy to remain unseen. So it was that urban hydden came into being, for the pickings were good from wasteful humans and the structures sound and often very long term.

There came a time when scarcely a human city in the world did not have its counterpart in the Hyddenworld.

One of the oldest of these was Brum in Englalond, always its capital before the Empire sent the Fyrd to occupy and control that ancient land. They turned London into their garrison and sought to sideline rebellious Brum.

As human settlements spread and the first villages turned to towns and gradually some of those to cities, the humans lost touch with all that the hydden held dear: the elements of nature, the movement of the stars, the diurnal rhythms of the seas, even the beginning and ending of the seasons, for Spring starts earlier than most humans realize, and Summer flees before they know it. Then, too, Autumn is a mystery to them, and when Winter or Samhain begins on the last night of October and November dawns they run shivering to their houses, light artificial fires, escape the dark with electric light and lose the benefits of the most sacred time of the year, when darkness descends and all things fall still to give space for thought and healing, worship and renewing.

These things the hydden knew.

So they were not surprised when the humans so far forgot their once-close companionship with hydden that even when, by some unhappy chance, they were brought face to face with a hydden, alive or dead, they quite literally could not believe their eyes. If alive they said they must be 'seeing things'; if dead, then the only explanation was that it was a dwarf, a freak, and inexplicable.

But the appearance of bonfires in the open, like the one now at Cleeve, was something else again. The violent earth events of recent months had so far disrupted human life that even the most elementary of precautions against the humans seeing hydden were being ignored.

In a world of fear and disarray such as now beset the humans, who among them was going to investigate a fire up in the hills? It might be dangerous to do so. It must certainly be made by humans up to no good. No, turn the other way, pretend it is not seen, flee to places of greater safety.

Even so, the Cleeve fire was bigger than they had ever seen before and as the evening wore on Bedwyn Stort spent long minutes staring at it.

'I never thought the day would come so soon in my lifetime,' he said, 'when hydden could be so sure that humans would not venture to find them that they would dare light such a fire as that in the open air.'

He said this grimly and with little pleasure.

'Which said,' he continued, 'I am inclined to wander over and join them to see if I can find someone who knows a privy way to Abbey Mortaine. We should go there soon, while the way is clear of Fyrd.'

'If it is clear,' said Jack. 'But they're never far away. Maybe one patrol has been sent in the wrong direction but we can't be sure there won't be others round the Abbey.'

'No reason why they should be,' said Katherine. 'No one in the whole of the Hyddenworld but Stort would think such an out of the way place would be worth a visit, let alone at a dangerous time like this.'

She said it affectionately and without any hint that they should not go there.

Stort was more than a scrivener and scholar; he was, in his quirky way, a seer too. Twelve years before, when she and Jack were six and Stort only eleven, he had led his mentor Master Brief of Brum and some others on what had seemed a pointless journey south-west of Brum because he sensed they would be needed.

They were.

On a night of rain, on an obscure piece of road where no one could have guessed Katherine's father would be driving the car, he crashed and died. Her mother was badly hurt and Jack hauled Katherine clear though he himself was badly burnt. Stort's adult friends were more than witnesses. Without their help Jack and Clare, her mother, would have died of their injuries.

There were other occasions when Stort proved himself able to be in the right place at the right time without any reason to be there beyond instinct. More than that, he sometimes seemed to see things before they happened.

So when, soon after leaving White Horse Hill two weeks before, he suddenly announced that there was wyrd in their need to go westward to avoid the Fyrd, and that the Abbey was a place they must go to, neither Katherine nor Jack questioned it.

But naturally they wondered why.

'It's a place well known to scholars as the source in medieval times of certain manuscripts including early musical notation.'

'That's no reason to go there now,' Jack had said. 'We need to get to Brum.'

Stort had frowned, shaken his head and begun to hum. He did that when he was thinking.

'The Abbey Mortaine,' he eventually explained, 'is also illustrated on one of the panels in the Chamber of Seasons in Brum.'

'So are many places, I should think,' said Katherine.

The Chamber was in the official residence of Lord Festoon, the High Ealdor of Brum. It was one of several extraordinary creations by the nineteenth-century hydden architect, scholar and lutenist, ā Faroün. It showed the full cycle of the four seasons with strange doors embossed with the name of each of them in turn. These doors were rusty and stiff with time. Until Jack, Katherine and Lord Festoon had reason to escape the Chamber, the door of Spring had never been fully opened. That door, at least, had had the magical quality of taking those who passed through it to where they needed to be, which was not exactly on the other side: it was somewhere else and at a slightly different time.

Festoon had rarely let others into the Chamber before and, as far as Jack and Stort knew, had never done so since. But the images of the seasons, which ran continuously round the octagonal Chamber, were known and had been studied, not least by Master Brief, an expert on ā Faroün.

Stort, too, had studied them. There was a different version of it, a very strange one, in the Library in Brum, in the form of a richly wrought embroidery, believed to have been made by the architect himself, which was the size of a large dining table, perhaps six or seven feet by four. It, too, had strange qualities, the most striking of which was that the threads and appliqué used in its making were so lustrous, and the imagery so complex and convoluted, that it seemed the landscapes and characters and the light that illuminated them moved and changed before a viewer's eyes.

It was these images to which Stort had referred when announcing his desire to visit the Abbey.

'You see,' he had declared, 'the Abbey is shown in the section relating to the month of August, which is now. Evidence enough to convince me that going there should be part of our present quest.'

The nature of the quest itself was by then well known to every hydden alive. It was to find a gem made by Beornamund . . . or sort of made. Made accidentally, along with three others which together constituted a gem for each of the seasons. Stort had found the gem of Spring on the last night of that season. It had been stolen from Brum by the Emperor of the Hyddenworld and Brief had been killed trying to protect it. Nothing daunted, during the Summer just past Stort and Jack had retrieved it, along with the gem of Summer.

Now the season of harvests had begun and Stort and his friends were in pursuit of the gem of Autumn. That was why they were heading back to Brum where, they had guessed, the quest for the gem should really begin.

'So what is the significance of Abbey Mortaine?' Jack and Katherine asked.

Stort shrugged.

'Nothing complicated. Master Brief went there two decades ago but did not find what he was looking for, which was a medieval musical instrument called a Quinterne. It was for that the notations were made. It was said by those who heard it that it was capable, in the right circumstances, of making a sound as beautiful as *musica universalis*.'

'The Music of the Spheres,' said Katherine.

Jack looked puzzled.

'*Musica* is the sound of the harmony of the Universe,' she explained, 'the sound the reflections in the Mirror make as they come and go, the singing and the raging of the stars, the sound of everything as one.'

'Ah!' said Jack, not quite getting it.

'Which of course,' added Stort without expression, 'mortal kind cannot actually hear in its purest form. Except, I suppose, in special circumstances of which I know nothing.'

'So how can a musical instrument make such a sound if it can't be heard?'

Stort had shrugged again.

'I don't know any more than you do but Brief believed it existed and might be found and because of its importance among the images in the embroidery, he argued that it was connected with the gem of Autumn.'

'But if he never found it, why should you? If it now exists at all.'

'I just feel we will,' said Stort simply.

Which, in the end, had been enough for Jack then as it was now. Stort had saved his life once by following his instinct. If it led him now towards an artefact that probably no longer existed, Jack was not going to argue.

Now Stort wanted to follow his instincts again and join the festivities, even though he was as tired as they were.

'But if you'd prefer to sleep then let us stay right where we are.'

They hesitated and finally it was Katherine who made the decision, to the surprise of both of them.

'Come on, let's go. We need a break and I could do with a good brew before I go to sleep!'

They put something warm over their jerkins and made their way through the darkness towards the fire's glow.

A hundred heads in silhouette, brief glances of pleasure as they came, room made for each one of them but separately: Jack with the two villagers they had first met, Katherine with a group of wyf and kinder, as seemed the custom in Cleeve, and Stort backaway, watching, alone for a time until the man who had borne his wyf on his back for a healing came from one side and Annie from another, quiet for once, at peace in Stort's goodly presence.

'Evening!' he cried out cheerfully.

The evening had truly begun.

3

THE GREATEST TALE

I t was Katherine, not one of the villagers, who finally prompted Stort to tell a tale or two of famous people he knew in Brum who were only names to the folk of Cleeve: of his mentor Brief, Master Scrivener, wise and good; of Mister Pike, a fearsome stave fighter who was in charge of law and order; and Barklice, Chief Verderer of the city, reputed to be more skilled in the arts of hyddening than anyone alive.

'Aye, I met 'im once myself,' called out a pedlar of festive candles, 'and that was a hydden could make himself scarce and unseen in the blink of an eye. Saw him last on meadowland near Cheam, not a bush in sight for a hundred miles and the next thing he was gone like he never was.'

'Be it true, Mister Stort,' asked another, a burly lad from Humblebee, 'that Mister Pike's as good with the stave as they say?'

Stort replied, 'I'm the wrong one to ask that question since we have in our midst none other than the Stavemeister of Brum himself, Mister Jack.'

They all knew that was so, the lad as well, and had hoped Stort would oblige by bringing Jack into their circle of story.

'Tell us the greatest fight you ever had, sir!' someone asked.

Jack grinned and replied, 'I can tell you the greatest fight I ever lost! And that was in defence of Katherine here, who was taken from the human world by fighters from Brum before they knew us as friends. They were former Fyrd, who knew the shadow arts, which turn a hydden cold and freeze his mind so he's helpless and in their power.

'I did my best to rescue her as she was forced sinister round the tree henge of Woolstone but . . . but . . .'

'I could see him,' said Katherine, 'but it was as if my voice was frozen too and I knew he mustn't try to get me, but either he didn't understand or didn't care. The next thing I knew was that the shadows were round me and him going to be hurt and . . .'

The listeners craned forward as her voice quietened, feeling the remembered terror with her. The silence was such that even the slightest sigh and crackle in the dying fire at their feet could be heard.

'Well, I did my best,' said Jack, 'and entered the circle and tried to get to her but it was no good and I was losing. They advanced on me to finish me off when there came spiralling out of the darkness from the dexter side of the henge, which is the side of truth, as you may know, a carved stave the like of which I had never seen. It caught the light of the stars to itself, sending it out like showers of blinding light which beat the shadow fighters back. When I dropped the stave it leapt right off the ground back into my hand! It saved my life but they took Katherine away before I could do more. So I lost that fight but lived to tell this tale.'

'And get her love as well!' called out Old Annie, which was the first time she had ever got a laugh in Cleeve.

'What happened to the stave?'

Jack seemed uncertain how to reply.

Then he said, 'The late Master Brief, who Stort mentioned, held the office of Stavemeister. He was there in the henge with Barklice and Pike and it was he who threw the stave to me to use. A test, I expect. When he died earlier this year the honour of being Stavemeister fell to me.'

He paused, turned round and took up a stave from the ground behind him.

'This is that stave,' he said.

He held it up and it caught the light of the fire and the stars above as he had said, and the silvery moon as well.

'Watch, but don't move,' he said quietly, 'for if you do you might get a knock on the head.'

Then he pulled back his arm, the stave in his hand, and hurled it high over the fire into the dark.

They heard it go, a whirling of sound.

'Don't move,' he repeated warningly, standing up, 'but listen!'

The sound of its flight suddenly ceased but they did not hear it fall to the ground. Instead, after a short pause, they heard it coming back. It reappeared in the firelight, a trail of light behind it, curved right round the company, turning end on end as it went, missing a head here, a leg there and sending embers flying before Jack held it once more.

'By the way,' he said in the awed silence that followed, 'I would advise anyone here against trying to pick it up. It has a habit of thumping anyone but its owner.'

There was a brief silence before some bright spark said, 'If that's the case, Master Jack, why didn't it thump you in the henge that night of the shadows?'

'It knew I was Brief's heir. That was his test. Luckily I passed!'

The night turned into a telling indeed.

It was one of the folk from Woodmancote who raised the inevitable, in a roundabout way. She made the point that some tales have more of a message than others, but which did the travellers think had the greatest message of all?

Everyone waited with bated breath for Mister Stort to take the bait. He did.

'I imagine,' he said, 'that you are thinking of the much-loved tale of Beornamund?'

'She may be at that,' said another.

'Which, no doubt,' continued Stort in all innocence, 'someone here has already told this evening?'

There was a murmur which was meant to make clear that no one had and they all hoped Stort now would.

But he knew the game as well as they did and said, 'I will say this of the true message in Beornamund's story of the gems, a subject much discussed by scholars in Brum, living and dead. It is simple enough. The story tells us that our future is ours to make or break. It is in our own hands.'

He was silent and the disappointment at this short statement was palpable.

Jack laughed.

'Go on Stort, tell us the tale. You were raised in Brum so you ought to know it.'

He needed no further prompting but did not spin it out for he was tired now and sensed they all were.

'You all know that Beornamund, who lived fifteen hundred years ago in Mercia in central Englalond, loved Imbolc. In the old language that name means Spring.'

He told how Imbolc died in a flood before their love had time to live through its natural course of Summer, Autumn and Winter. Beornamund blamed the gods. Gods to which different hydden at different times give different names but which are generally known as the Mirror-of-All.

In his anger Beornamund made a sphere of crystal and metal of such perfection that when he hurled it into the sky in defiance and fury it gathered to itself something of the Fires of the Universe and the colours of all four seasons.

The gods saw it and were afraid, fearing that what he had done had power to destroy all life. They caused the sphere to be broken into a hundred thousand pieces, which fell back to Earth like an exquisite rain, falling lightly where Beornamund stood, cooling his ire, putting wisdom in his heart and mind before they disappeared like mist.

But a lost love does not rest easy.

The sphere was broken but not quite destroyed.

Four pieces remained, each an uncut gem which held the ancient fire still and across whose surface ran the colours of one of the seasons.

He found three of the gems but not the first, which was Spring.

Seeing his sorrow and remorse for what he had done – for a hydden should not blame his gods for the wyrd of things – they sent Imbolc back to him at the end of his long and productive life, during which he made many things of wondrous beauty in payment for his youthful pride.

She came in half-mortal, half-spectral form, upon the White Horse, which some say is the Mirror itself, made corporeal. Perhaps it is.

It came to the old and nearly blind Beornamund, bearing his beloved on its back, and he understood at once what he must do and why.

In a single night he made a pendant of the purest gold into which he set the three gems he had found: Summer, time of abundance; Autumn, time of harvest; Winter, time of terrible renewal.

He left another setting empty and in the centre placed an orb of quartz and in the centre of that a roundel of jet.

The pendant was attached to a chain which he put around Imbolc's neck. It was this action which transformed her into the Peace-Weaver, doomed to wander the Earth for fifteen hundred years bringing calm and resolution to mortal kind, as best she could, until one by one the three gems fell from the pendant with the passing of the three remaining seasons of her long life.

Some say that each gem lost was a reminder to Beornamund that even his great skills could not make something that could withstand the Scythe of Time. Only when that lesson was learnt and the Peace Maiden's journey was done might she join him at last in immortality, his time of punishment and separation served, their love requited in the stars.

Such is the story told of Beornamund at harvest time, and at every other season come to that, though with embellishment here and new fancy there, and a whole cast of characters along the way as suits a teller's time and circumstance.

'Make new brew!' one will then cry.

'Bake new brot for the nourishing stew!' another commands.

'Put logs on the fire, tuck the kinder in bed, let the strangers now be known as friends!' each says to his neighbour.

It is then, the harvest night now deep but no adult yet yielding to the temptation of sleep, that the prophecies are spoken which arise from the CraftLord's tale.

These come as answers to four simple questions.

Will the lost gems, including that of Spring which Beornamund himself never found, be rediscovered?

If so, by whom?

And where?

Finally . . . what will happen next?

The different answers have through time merged into accepted prophecy overladen with one stark truth which stems from the certainty that the gems contain the Fires of the Universe and reflect the colours of the seasons. Meaning, they will be found when they are needed because the fires are waning and the colours are fading, which reflect – repeat, *reflect* – that a time will come when the Mirror will crack.

The wise ones long believed that the gems would be found by mortals – whether hydden or human or both none knew – at a time of great threat which would be marked by the birth of the Peace-Weaver's successor, the fearsome Shield Maiden. Their task was to find and give her the pendant Beornamund had made, which she would wear until each of the lost gems was put into the settings from which it had been lost or, in the case of the first, Spring, had never been placed.

Failure to find and return the gems before the end of their respective season would bring down upon mortal kind her wrath and that of the Earth she wandered. The destruction was nearly unstoppable and would be worse than a mortal mind could imagine.

The prophecies also said that three individuals in particular would lead the search and discovery and return of the gems to the Shield Maiden. One would be human, one hydden and the last a 'giant-born' or an individual born to a hydden but whose wyrd it was to grow to human size. A monster in one world, an alien in the other.

These were the key prophecies that sustained the spirit of hydden through the centuries and comforted each succeeding generation when they grew fearful that one day the Mirror would crack.

Such was the tale Bedwyn Stort told that night, his audience rapt and appreciative.

'But you've left it hanging in the air, Mister Stort!'

'And you bain't told it quite to the end as we've heard it.'

They were not going to let him go without telling the worst and the best.

The worst was what folk across the Hyddenworld had seen with their own eyes: that the Earth had inflicted tremors and quakes all over and the harvests were bad because of it. In short, the Mirror might already be cracking.

'Yes,' said Stort, the fire now barely a glow, 'I think it might.'

As for the best, as the gathering saw it, it was that Stort himself had found the lost gem of Spring. If it was true.

'Is it? Did you?' asked his increasingly bold audience.

'I did,' said Stort sombrely, adding firmly, 'but that isn't a tale I want to tell now.'

'But that means there's hope, don't it?'

'It does. Even more so that Jack here helped me find the gem of Summer too . . .'

Jack grimaced and said, '. . . and *that's* also a tale best told another time.'

They rose, hoping to escape.

'And now, sirs, what now?' the crowd persisted. 'Must you find the gem of Autumn like the prophecies say?'

'We must. That is the quest we are upon.'

'And will you?'

Another pause.

'Will you?'

A final lull, the time of tales surely near its end.

'We will try,' said Stort quietly. 'We will try very hard to find it. Which reminds me, I was hoping that someone here might tell me an easy way to Abbey Mortaine.'

Twenty people offered to at once and surrounded Stort and Jack to tell them how to make that trek.

Yet that was not quite the end.

Apart from Annie, it had been the males who asked the questions and told the tales.

Now, as people began to leave, a couple of females approached Katherine shyly.

'Be it true, like we've heard, that you did bear the Shield Maiden?'

'It's true.'

'Tell us, if you will. Tell us about her birth.'

'Well, I don't know . . .'

'It was on May Day Eve, they say . . .'

'It was.'

'Tell us.'

So she did, while Stort and Jack talked to the males.

Quietly, wyf to wyf, a telling of Judith's birth in the henge at Woolstone, overwatched by White Horse Hill, a night of destiny and love.

'A good birth then.'

'A good one,' she agreed. 'But afterwards, that was not so good.'

'Tell us. Babbies and birthing, new life, the oldest pain: they're the tales that are greatest of all, my dear.'

A hand touched her arm, another her cheek, a third rested on her shoulder.

'You're tired out aren't you, through and through?'

'She wasn't an ordinary child. She . . . she . . .' Katherine tried to speak. She had never talked of it before, not the guilt she felt for Judith's growing pain, nor the void that her rapid growth and departure two weeks before had left in her heart.

'She may have been the Shield Maiden, but Judith was also my daughter. She was born to pain and then was gone to fulfil her task as Shield Maiden. I know she's alive but it feels like she died and I don't know how to get her back.'

It was raw and it hurt and it went deeper than almost all of them understood.

Until Annie came forward and said, 'I know, child, I know. The loss don't ever seem to want to go away until suddenly it's gone. Which one day it be. It weren't your fault and who knows the life she'll live in the Mirror's light one day, who knows?'

She smiled on Katherine that same lovely smile that folk in those parts had not ever seen until earlier that night. Is was a kind of miracle.

She put her old arms round Katherine and let her weep.

'One day the pain will go for you as well, my dear, for all life is blessed by the Mirror's light. Did you see the White Horse?'

Katherine nodded.

'Then you'll be all right. The greatest tale is that of each one of us. Remember that, my dear.'

4
WYRD DECISION

They intended to leave for Abbey Mortaine early the next day but it was not in the wyrd of things that they did.

For one thing, Stort's dog Georg had disappeared, not for the first time.

Stort called him 'Georg with no E' because that was the way his name was spelt on the collar he still wore. He had been an abandoned dog, once owned by a human. The previous month Georg had defended Stort from attack by a pack of feral dogs in Germany while he and Jack were recovering the gem of Spring from the Imperial Headquarters in Bochum. The dog had hung around ever since, companionable and protective, and returned to Englalond with them, as faithful to Stort as any mongrel hound could be.

But he came and went as he pleased and that morning he had gone.

What also made them hesitate about going to the Abbey, despite Stort's belief that the secret it held about the Quinterne would help them in their quest for the gem of Autumn, were new reports of Fyrd being seen north and east of Cleeve, the direction they wanted to go.

But there was something more immediate.

There was a slight earth tremor in the night, barely enough to wake anyone, though Katherine felt it. Then, in the morning, their camp struck and their 'sacs packed and ready, another strong tremor was felt. It was enough to bring down some humbles in Cleeve and to send the ashes of the remnant bonfire into the air, where they hung oddly, making people cough, before a violent wind rushed down Cleeve Hill in the wake of these earth movements and blew them westward.

Was it a sign?

Katherine thought so.

Her mood was sombre for she was drained from her time with the wyfkin the night before.

Jack and Stort felt her mood but did not understand it and she made no attempt to explain. Perhaps one of the wyfs was right when she said that 'fellows were dim' when it came to the aftermath of babbies and birthing.

The tremor came and went, the wind after it, and Katherine wanted to go on west to the Vale of the Severn, away from the Cotswolds.

But they hesitated, making the excuse that it was Georg they were waiting for.

At noon, when he did not come back, Jack made the decision for them all.

'I'm not going to risk us getting caught by the Fyrd by back-tracking to the Abbey,' he said, 'especially if Katherine wants to go a different way. Our wyrd has taken us westward ever since we left White Horse Hill and we'd best trust it. The Abbey must wait.'

Stort hummed and ha'd but not for long. It was not in his nature to argue against others' decisions if they were well meant and reasonable. He could see the bleakness in Katherine's eyes and appreciate Jack's overwhelming desire to protect them all. That was *his* nature. In any case, Stort's interests were so many that if one opportunity was lost, he soon made another appear.

'I am not entirely unhappy about this,' he declared, a few minutes after they had said goodbye to their hosts and were striding westward along the green road once more, 'though when I tell you what is in store for us, historically and scholastically speaking, I fear you may not be best pleased.'

'Enlighten us,' said Jack drolly.

It was one of the intense pleasures, and occasional great irritations, of travelling with Brum's best-known scholar, that he knew a great deal about nearly everything and was not slow to pass his knowledge on.

'This route circles Cheltenham to the north, which means that we'll be heading directly towards Half Steeple, whose reputation – in cartographic and etymological terms – precedes it. It may strike you as a rather odd name considering that its human church has only ever had one steeple and that it was built before the year 1349.'

'So?' prompted Jack. 'What's the significance of that?'

The day was a warm one, the sky blue in parts and they caught wider and wider glimpses of the great vale beneath them as they dropped down through the glades on the scarp side of the hill and the trees were behind them.

'I mean to say it was never rebuilt, it has never been "half a steeple", though there is one view, dismissed by most, that it gained that name in medieval times because money ran out when the steeple was incomplete and the job not finished until years later.

'In fact, as I said, the steeple predates the year I mentioned, which is the year in which two things happened: one odd, the other seemingly miraculous, both involving Half Steeple.'

Katherine perked up. She was always open to Stort's quirky facts and histories.

'Why, goodness me,' cried Stort, 'if I'm not mistaken there's Half Steeple now!'

They paused to take breath and gain a second wind, leaning on their staves as they did so.

They could see, framed by two great horse chestnut trees whose leaves were reddened with mite, the Severn Valley below them, stretching away to west and north. Part of Cheltenham lay immediately off to the left, but it was the flat vale which drew their eye and a solitary steeple in the far distance rising from the buildings of the town with a strip of dark beyond, which looked like the River Severn itself.

'You see, it's all there, not just half of it!' he said, pointing his stave towards it. 'The odd thing I mentioned is that an early poet of Englalond penned some lines which describe a terrible vision of destruction of two human settlements; one can be identified as Half Steeple, whose name the poem includes. Which is very strange indeed when you consider that at the time of writing steeples were unknown in Englalond and the word was borrowed from the Frisian. In short, we may believe it was a vision of the future or some future event. It may or may not be significant that no hydden has ever built his humble in that particular location and I am myself reluctant to go too near it. It's a purely human settlement.'

Jack pondered this with a puzzled frown.

'And the other settlement?' asked Katherine. 'Which presumably suffered destruction or will do, if the poet is right? What was its name?'

'Brum,' said Stort shortly. 'The poem seems to predict its future destruction.'

They walked on in silence as the path flattened out and they faced the long trek across the vale, Half Steeple now out of sight.

Jack said, 'And what was the miracle?'

'I mentioned the year 1349,' said Stort sombrely. 'Do you know its significance for Englalond?'

They shook their heads.

'It is the year when the Black Death devastated our land, killing seven out of ten humans and hydden. Few places escaped it south of Brum.'

'And Half Steeple?'

'That was the miracle. Not a single inhabitant within its city walls suffered the plague. All lived. It was claimed it survived because one of its citizens, human of course, made a pact with what they call the Devil.'

'He or she or it doesn't exist,' said Katherine.

'Maybe not. Nor evil, perhaps,' said Stort. 'But darkness does and the utter darkness of extinction too, which is what happens when the Mirror cracks and cannot be repaired. Our mission, I believe.'

'What was this pact that was made?'

'That Half Steeple would be spared until the end of time.'

'Seems a good deal to me,' said Jack.

'And me,' added Katherine.

'But supposing time ends sooner than we think? Supposing time is ending now? Has it not occurred to you that the strange shifts in time associated with the earth tremors – a lost minute here, a strange hour there – which I myself have noted and put down to a faulty timepiece, and which we saw earlier this year in Brum, might be due to the breakdown in time? Could it be that the process has begun? I think it may have and that is why the gem of Spring made its presence known to me and we were able to recover that of Summer. That is why the

Shield Maiden was born, painful as that has been for both of you. That is why our mission now to find a third gem and get it to her is so important.'

Hours later they reached a bluff a mile to the south of Half Steeple, the wide slowly flowing grey water of the Severn to their left. Over the river to the north, not too far distant, was the dark rise of the Malvern Hills.

'The Severn Valley may be our easiest route north,' said Jack, 'but that means Fyrd patrols will be hard to miss.'

Stort agreed and said, 'The Malverns have a grim reputation but . . . well . . . they seem a better and safer option.'

'Grim?' said Katherine.

Stort welcomed the question but Jack held up his hand.

'Don't tempt him, Katherine, it'll be another dark tale to make us feel threatened and gloomy.'

'I was only going to say that it is said there are monsters of a . . .'

'Please don't,' said Jack, laughing.

'Of a rather fanciful yet interesting kind in those hills.'

The sun came out and glistened on the pale yellow stone of Half Steeple's spire and red-brick houses.

Jack asked, 'This poet, did he offer any other information?'

He sounded ironic but Stort looked very serious. He was gazing across at a group of trees on their side of Half Steeple. They were filled with rooks which rose and fell above the branches, fighting each other, their caws harsh on the breeze.

'He did,' said Stort, 'though the script is unclear and the translation difficult. But he seemed to suggest that the end of days would come when time ended and the "hroc" or rook flew backwards over Englalond.'

Jack followed his gaze and said, 'Well, they're not doing that today, and I doubt they ever could.'

Katherine suddenly stood up and asked, 'So, do you two want to know *my* preference about which way to go?'

They turned to her and then south-westward, as she did. The sun caught her fair hair and turned it gold and made her eyes shine. But it also showed her fatigue and recent strain.

'I'd like to forget all the things we're meant to be doing, the great quest we're meant to be on and ignore the way our wyrd keeps leading us. I want to turn south and head instead for the West Country and . . . and . . .'

They barely had time to register this unexpected announcement when a shimmer of light shot among them. A tremble in the trees sent a hiss among their leaves; a ripple of water shot across the current of the river and sent a vole scurrying from its hole on the far side.

It felt like a moment when time was no more. It was cold and menacing. It felt as if they had missed a heartbeat and something might have been lost that was irrecoverable.

It felt like the moment of death and Katherine put a hand to her mouth and stepped back. At once they both went to her side. Jack put his arm out to support her. Stort stared at her intensely, then across the river, then south-westward, as she had been doing.

He shook his head, puzzled and perplexed. Then he pulled out his chronometer and stared at it with a frown.

He tapped its glass, put it to his ear and stared again.

'It's nothing,' said Katherine, 'just a dream. There's no reason . . . there's no need to go.'

'No,' said Stort sharply. 'No reason at all to travel to a region where time, it is said, stands still.'

Yet that was the way they stayed facing awhile until they felt an urgency in the need to get back to Brum. Even Katherine felt that, despite her sudden whim.

'It's Brum by the direct route or the Malverns,' said Jack.

'Toss a coin,' said Katherine.

'Throw a straw to the fickle wind and see which way it blows,' said Jack.

Which is what Stort did, the breeze whirling the straw out of his hand high over their heads before it was carried off to west and north towards the river.

'It seems we're to cross the Severn and continue by way of the Malverns, after all, Mirror help us,' he said quietly as if it was something he had feared might happen all along. 'Let's go.'

Right on cue, as if Stort's quiet instruction was a loud command, Georg appeared out of the trees behind them and raced headlong towards the bridge.

5

IN AN ANCIENT FOREST

By the time Bedwyn Stort and the others had found a place to camp for the night up on the Malverns, it was late and rapidly getting dark. Even Georg was tired, settling down to sleep without even sniffing about or looking for food.

The hills were indeed bare, shorn of all trees and shrubs by humans centuries before, and grazed by sheep ever since. Only when they stumbled on a remnant of the ancient forest, down a forgotten gully, did the travellers take shelter among some stunted trees where a stream offered a supply of good water.

The place had a drifting, uneasy air, as if spirits came and went in search of what they could not find. They discovered the skeletons of two dead sheep, both so desiccated they no longer gave off the rank smell of death, just the odour of abandonment.

There were signs of humans being there – a dry-stone wall, a fallen post, litter such as wrappers and cola cans hurled by human ramblers from the paths above. Hydden did not litter.

It made a sorry sort of site, barely horizontal, yet it had a certain timelessness as if it was a place to stop and not move on. Their small fire sent up heavy soporific smoke which, though there was a wind above, hung about the old trees like wraiths unwilling, or unable, to move on.

The place might feel uneasy but it stilled and slowed them and, tired though they all were, there was still much on their minds that had been left unsaid through the days past, perhaps waiting for such a time and place as this.

So they sat close and talked.

Each had something different weighing on their mind; yet each recognized they had a common cause.

Jack thought it was just his duties as Stavemeister to Brum that troubled him. In fact, he didn't know why he felt it but he thought that back there by the Severn they had made a wrong turn.

'The mission I was charged with was fulfilled,' he said, 'to help you get the gems of Spring and Summer to the Shield Maiden, but when we later met our friends from Brum on White Horse Hill, I was still too sick from what had happened to give them a full and proper account of things they need to know.'

'I did that.' said Stort.

'I'm sure you did, but there are things you will have missed, in particular the strength and disposition of the Fyrd as we saw them then. Since we came back . . .'

The mission had been to travel to the Hyddenworld's Imperial City of Bochum, in North-West Germany, and win back a precious gem that had been murderously stolen from Brum by the Emperor's agent Witold Slew.

Jack had touched the gem, and a second one, which it was unwise for mortals ever to do, and Jack's illness was of the mind as much as of the body and it had nothing to do with his duty to Brum. In Bochum he had met his mother for the first time since his birth, but it was for moments only. That had eaten at him since and awoken emotions and yearnings he could not lay to rest.

'It makes me wonder,' he had said later, to Katherine, when he was still sick and speaking openly about such things, 'who my father was.'

'Maybe he . . .' she said.

'Maybe I don't care,' he said savagely.

'No, Jack,' she had replied, 'maybe you're not ready.'

The mission had aged and sickened Jack, and the trek across Englalond since had been in the nature of respite and recovery.

But he was still Stavemeister and as giant-born he was a protector of place and people. Now he was finding strength to face these responsibilities again.

'Since we came back and ran into all these Fyrd, it's become obvious that the Empire is preparing the ground for an invasion of Englalond and an attack on Brum to recover the gems,' he said now. 'That's why we must get to Brum as quickly as we can, to warn of the danger it is in '

Katherine's talk by the fire that night expressed different concerns, but these too would surely affect them all.

In that same instant, just three months before, the child of Jack and Katherine was born. Her name was Judith and it was her dread wyrd to be the Shield Maiden.

Her malaise and fatigue arose because her child Judith the Shield Maiden was doomed to live an entire mortal life of three score years and ten, from birth to death, in just nine months, from the first day of Summer to the last day of Winter. Which is to say from May 1st of the present year to February 1st of the one coming.

It meant that her days and years passed in a different and crueller timeframe than anyone else's. She aged in days and months, not years and decades. Within three days of her birth she was a year old, within a week nearly three years. Her body was racked by growing pain and each scream, each torment, each dreadful bewildering moment of stretched, torn, anguished growth was a hot knife turning in her mother's breast.

But there was something worse, the loss and separation when Judith left home at the beginning of August. By then she was a full-grown woman, already older than her mother and father, angry, tormented, not yet knowing the nature of her brief task upon the Earth but for one thing: if by then she had not been given the golden pendant Beornamund had made, the gems of Spring and Summer with it, she would wreak havoc on the Earth and those she loved. But no sooner had Stort fulfilled that part of their quest than the new one for the gem of Autumn arose.

Meanwhile, no wonder Katherine felt loss for a daughter who grew too fast, and guilt that she could not succour her better. No wonder she sought escape earlier that day with thoughts of the West Country.

No wonder the Mirror had chosen her to be mother of one so important to the Universe as Judith. No one else could have been found to carry the child with such love, to tend her despite all pain and now to desire to set forth, though so hurt and half-broken, for a time-bound quest for the next gem of Autumn.

'Whether I'll be able to keep up with you or help in any way at all, I doubt,' she said by the smouldering fire, 'but I'm here, and I miss Judith, and I hurt, but I'd not really choose to be anywhere else.'

Jack smiled and held her close while Stort said what he had to.

His concern was something else entirely, though it enmeshed itself in all his journeying, whether of body, mind or spirit. It was not something he spoke of easily, even to his closest friends.

Perhaps only to Mister Barklice, Chief Verderer of Brum, had Stort opened his heart fully on the subject of love and, more particularly, his seeming inability to find it. Not the pure and simple love of friends which Stort had the knack of engendering in all who knew him, for his innocence, his natural generosity and his selfless courage on their behalf – so frequently and modestly demonstrated in acts great and small. Such love he could make sense of and acknowledge.

No, the kind of love that he and Barklice endlessly debated and chewed at, like companionable dogs at a meaty but awkwardly shaped bone on which the best bits were annoyingly just out of reach, was that between a male and a female. Love of the grand, universal kind which caused the stars to shine brighter, the moon to orbit the Earth more swiftly and the sun's rays to carry their joyous warmth to a hydden's innermost being.

This kind of love had been something at once alluring, alarming and elusive to Bedwyn Stort until quite suddenly, but days before embarking on the journey they were now on, it had descended upon him with all the force of a hammer blow from Beornamund himself.

Unfortunately for Stort, as with so many innocent but hapless lovers before him, the subject of his passion was unavailable to him. He might as well have fallen in love with a female in permanent residence on a far distant planet as she upon whom his thoughts now dwelt. His chosen beloved was none other than Judith herself, fierce and unhappy bearer of the gems of Beornamund, an immortal in the making, who now and forever was surely not a being who could love an ordinary mortal. Or rather, if she did, which had seemed unlikely, could never say so – any more than he himself could.

This hopeless passion had begun simply enough but from the first it knocked him sideways and left him utterly bewildered.

Katherine fell pregnant, Stort, an innocent in word and deed, had contrived to fall in love with her unborn child when Katherine had placed his hand on her belly and he felt Judith's first movements.

The love was pure and deep, something universal, as if, in new life, new birth and the journey of the Shield Maiden, Stort had discovered not only that he could love, but that he might dare hope he was loved in return.

It was, of course, impossible. A mortal, even a rather special one like him, cannot hope for such love to be returned. And yet . . . yet . . .

It seemed to be.

In Stort alone did Judith the Shield Maiden find release from pain. In his faith in her, in his unsullied love, his courage before her and boldness in being his own self – and finally in his being the one who could and did place Beornamund's pendant round her neck as she mounted the White Horse, and then affixed the gems of Spring and Summer in their rightful settings – all that made her love him, though she could not say so.

Only now, just over two weeks later, sitting by a fire in a gully with his friends, he dared speak of his love and his impossible yearnings and conclude, 'My dearest friends, parents of the one I love, I do not have any expectation in all of this. Except to hope that in her dark times, as she ages and grows old and in pain once more, she will know, always know, that she was, she is and always will be loved by me. Know in the very stars! Know in the wondrous music of the Universe! Know through every twist and turn of time itself. So there it is . . . there it is . . .'

Such were the different thoughts and feelings expressed by those three that night in the shadows of an ancient forest.

As the fire guttered, each turned to the others and bade goodnight and lay still and silent until the last ember ceased to glow, and such few stars as they could see through the rough thicket above their heads were obscured by rolling cloud.

'Goodnight, Katherine.'

'Goodnight, my love.'

'Goodnight, Stort.'

'Goodnight.'

Later, when darkness had descended: 'Stort? You awake?'

It was Jack speaking, Katherine stirring in his arms.

'I am.'

'What was the monster that you said lives in these hills?'

Jack's voice was light, Stort's reply was serious.

'It is called the Scythe of Time. Trust me, it's better if it remains a myth and does not become real to us.'

The trees bent close and the darkness deepened as they slept and grew thick and resonant, filling with the shadow lives of other times.

They woke refreshed after a night without incident or any evidence of 'monsters', let alone scythes. They struck camp early and were ready to move with first light.

It was Jack's habit to check that it was safe to depart. The coast may have been clear the night before when they dropped down into the gully, but who knew who might have appeared above overnight?

It was as well he did.

'Fyrd!' he whispered, after a quick reconnaissance. 'Searching in force on the slopes above. For us, I think. Those patrols we nearly ran into yesterday may have caught sight or scent of us in some way.'

He decided that the safest thing was to stay just where they were until the patrols moved on.

'They've dug themselves in,' he reported later. 'I suggest we do the same.'

'Anyway,' said Katherine with feeling, 'we all need a rest.'

Jack grinned.

'Another night or two in this dank old forest should prove one way or another whether your monster's still alive, Stort, or died several centuries ago.'

They moved lower down the gully, to a place overhung with rocks and bent old trees that were half dead and covered in ivy. No Fyrd were going to find them there.

Later, Stort was the first to bed himself down again, soon followed by the other two and Georg. Time drifted, day became night again and rest was theirs at last.

6

EMPTY HOUSE

Two days later at eleven in the morning, seventy miles away in Woolstone House, in the lee of White Horse Hill from where Stort and the others had originally begun their new quest, two phones began ringing. They were the old-fashioned black Bakelite kind, one in a study downstairs, the other on the landing upstairs. Their sound was solid, sonorous, and as antiquated as the way they looked.

The house itself was a vast rambling structure, parts dating back to the fifteenth century and the contents ranging from an old oak pew that was even older, to nineteenth-century fenders round the coal fires, cracked twentieth-century linoleum on the bathroom floor and a twenty first century computer sitting on an office desk of indeterminate age.

The house was not quite tidy, nor quite chaotic, but aesthetically it was a complete mess. Yet it had about it the sense of a proper home, in which people had lived modestly but lovingly and enjoyed the many books, the poorly hung prints on the walls, the occasional oil painting of an ancestor, and outdoor pursuits such as gardening, walking and – judging from the weathered chairs and benches in the equally rambling garden – simply sitting still with a tea or whisky to enjoy the unmown lawns, mature trees and distant prospect of the White Horse galloping from left to right across the scarp face of the steep chalk hill that rose like a wall a third of a mile to the south.

The persistent ringing of the telephones echoed around the house and brought from the first-floor bathroom a sigh of discontent and then a mild swear word as it continued. Finally there was the wet pad, pad, pad of dripping feet, first on lino then on the thin and faded carpet of the upstairs corridor.

Yet when Arthur Foale finally got within reach of the upstairs phone, a towel around his ample waist, he did not pick up, but let the ringing continue. Instead, with water still running down his back and stomach, his shins and calves, forming wet patches at his feet, he just stood still.

He was a man in mourning and maybe he thought the call was not for him but for his late wife. Or, if it was not for his wife then it was *about* her, and he had no wish to take any more of those kind of calls either.

Whatever the reason, he let the phone ring until it stopped and stayed just where he was as the echoes died away into the cobwebs and far corners of their home, which was now his alone with no one to see him standing there, dripping, cold and, just then, rather sad.

The worst thing about a once-busy home where all the former inhabitants but one have gone is not so much the silence as the fact that nothing moves unless the last person left standing moves it. In fact nothing happens unless he or she makes it happen.

But for a phone-call, or a knock at the door, or an aeroplane droning overhead in the night as they sometimes did over Woolstone, taking supplies to a war zone, or a disaster, or bringing back the military dead of some other activity connected with any one of the several military bases in those parts.

Margaret had died a month before, and in the busy days following, Arthur had thought he had informed all her friends. It turned out they had been many and more varied than he had realized. Now he was tired of conversations that began with him saying, 'I'm very sorry, but Margaret has . . .'

Arthur was portly, heavily bearded, an aged but still vigorous bear who looked like he still had teeth and claws if he ever needed them.

The phone began ringing again, upstairs and down. He glowered at his feet, scratched his moist belly, and continued to stay where he was.

Why should he move?

What had he to do?

Which direction might he go which had meaning or purpose?

So he stood and listened to the phone, waiting for its ringing to end once more so he could chase the last of the echoing sound round the house in which he – no, which *they* – had lived and loved for fifty years.

'I daresay it's for you, my dear,' he murmured, bewildered as he was by grief and struggling now to find a reason for continuing on the road alone.

To his side was a wide staircase whose shallow, elegant steps, covered in a worn runner with loose-looking brass rods holding it in place, turned down around corners to the ground floor below. Vertically above it, another floor-height up, were damp-stained walls of peeling paper which ended with a window-light. An old woven cord used for opening and closing it was loosely attached to a brass tie on a nearby wall. It was half-rotten and they had been afraid to use it for several years, fearing that it might break and they would not be able to repair it, or ever close the heavy window-light and then open it again.

'Catch 22,' as Margaret had been in the habit of saying as she ascended the stairs in stormy weather, eyeing the cord as it blew about in the draught, drops of rain falling faintly on her head.

'Humph!' replied Arthur, who did not read the same books as she did and had never heard of Joseph Heller. He preferred archaeological journals to novels. 'Catch 22' might be to do with fishing, as far as he was concerned.

It was not the second time that morning that the phone had rung, but the third. Each time it seemed to do so with more irritating insistence and for a longer time.

This time, when it finally ended and the last echo had fled, Arthur sighed, frowned, and, urging himself to move, he turned and retraced his own wet footsteps to the bathroom.

'Bloody silly,' he murmured as he dried himself.

Then, 'Must make some tea.'

Then, '. . . Must mow damn lawns.'

Then, apparently irrelevantly since it was August, but it had been his wife who managed the house and she knew to buy early and save money, 'Must order coal.'

Adding, moments later, 'Don't know the supplier's name. Bugger.'

Finally, dry now but still mumbling to himself, he padded back to their room to dress, stood still and said, 'She never could iron shirts, so she never did, quite right. Stupid thought. Must iron another, this one's creased.'

Arthur was in mourning for Margaret; he felt grief, he was sad, but in no way was he depressed. He missed her hugely but when death came she had wanted it and he had the great compensation that they had lived a full, rich love. More so, in some ways, than they had had the right to expect. In fact, the most potent and persistent part of the grief was not for Margaret at all, but for three other people who had dominated their lives that summer, before she died, and who were now all gone too.

Arthur Foale, former Professor of Astral Archaeology at Cambridge, was the adoptive father of Katherine and, unofficially, of Jack. The way they had come into the lives of Margaret and himself, who were childless, was a miracle in his view. Katherine was six at the time. Her father was killed in the same car crash that left her mother Clare chronically injured and in which, by circumstances strange and some-how inexplicable, the six-year-old Jack had been travelling too.

The father got his wife out but died in the attempt to free his daughter. It was Jack, always exceptionally strong, who rescued her unharmed, though he sustained appalling third-degree burns to his back and neck.

Arthur and Margaret took Clare and Katherine into their home; Jack reappeared ten years later in the year Clare died. The two youngsters, as Arthur thought of them, were old enough to fall in love, which they did.

Arthur had already found a way to explore the Hyddenworld using the tree henge at the bottom of his garden as a portal. He was unsurprised to discover that Jack was something special, a giant-born from Germany. When Katherine was abducted into the Hyddenworld by the Fyrd, the Imperial army of its Emperor Slaeke Sinistral, Jack was able to invoke the hydden part of himself and use the same portal to follow her into the Hyddenworld.

It was the beginning of a long-prophesied quest for the gems of the sixth-century CraftLord Beornamund.

Later, Katherine gave birth to their child in the henge in Woolstone, and that marked the return of the couple – and Judith – to the human world and the summer just past with Arthur and the ailing Margaret. It was a happy and extraordinary time in which Arthur had forged a close grandfather-like relationship with Judith, a child in pain and like no other, who grew to adulthood in three months before she mounted the White Horse and was gone, as were her parents on a different path, all back into the Hyddenworld.

No wonder Arthur suffered their loss so keenly.

They had, in different ways, given meaning to his life. So really he had suffered the loss of four people, not one. It was hardly surprising that, now Margaret was gone and he was free of his pact never to show interest in such things as the Chimes, or latterly, in the Hyddenworld, he should now begin to do so.

It was inevitable perhaps that he was beginning to think that the direction he must also take was into the Hyddenworld.

As he continued his morning routine, he caught sight of the White Horse up on Uffington Hill and, smiling, sat down on their bed, his shirt still unbuttoned, to study the hill. They had chosen the room and positioned the bed for just that view. She had died staring at it as he held her hand. He unconsciously reached his hand behind him now to where she had been then as he looked through their window towards where he hoped she now was.

'Riding the Horse,' she used to say, 'that's what we'll all end up doing one day, Arthur, riding the Horse.'

Only someone who had known Margaret and the English language intimately over many years would have understood that she spoke the word 'horse' with the subtle emphasis of a capital 'H'.

As did he.

Neither was a Christian; they believed in many gods, and the White Horse was the greatest of all.

'If he is a god,' said Arthur.

'If he's a she,' she replied with tart ambiguity.

Arthur Foale was seventy and a good, kind man whose loneliness was tempered by gratitude that it was she who had gone first, he who could and would find the way forward alone. When, some years before, he had ventured into the Hyddenworld, the first human to rediscover how to do so for hundreds of years, she had suffered his absence terribly. He swore that he would never return to the Hyddenworld while she was alive.

Now she was gone and, though he could bear it and would survive, he already knew what his new direction was. He wanted to go back to the Hyddenworld. He wanted to understand the true meaning of the White Horse, if it had one.

'Of course it damn well does!' he muttered.

The phone began ringing yet again, this time within easy reach.

'Bloody thing,' he said.

He ignored it and remained on the bed, looking at the White Horse and trying to think up a plan for the day. Until she died, his days were always full. Now she was gone, they seemed endlessly empty.

Margaret would not have approved of him doing nothing much for too long, certainly not all the way past midday.

'Arthur,' she would have said, 'if you've nothing better to do, go and tend your tomatoes.'

He nodded at the thought, finished dressing and went downstairs to make a pot of tea.

August is a good month for tomatoes and this year they have done particularly well he found himself intoning in his mind.

'Sound like a gardening programme,' he muttered.

Gardening was something they enjoyed together but did separately. Margaret had inherited an entire walled vegetable garden for her produce. But as age had crept up on her, the area she used became ever smaller. Age, lack of energy and declining appetites for the preserves she used to make were the causes.

Arthur, regardless, carried on growing his tomatoes down in the nice out-of-the-way sunny spot between the tree henge at the bottom of the garden and an area they called the Chimes. Down there he did not have to worry about being watched by the ghosts of generations of professional gardeners who went back to Elizabethan times. When he first came to the garden he found tomatoes already growing there, planted by a child or a bird perhaps. He just carried on.

The henge, too, seemed to have been started before he came along. He had simply cleared trees and bushes that were in the way, and planted new trees to complete the circle. Five decades on it looked and felt as if it had been there forever, high trees all around and a wide, nearly circular area of grass in the middle, hushed even in the strongest winds, magical in its power, the place where he learnt to journey into the Hyddenworld.

Hushed but never silent; there was the never-ending sound of wind in the trees, however soft, and the eternal music of the nearby Chimes.

The Chimes were slivers of glass that hung from threads in the thick shrubs, catching the inconstant breeze to make a near-constant sound, a music which he, and anyone else who heard it, could guess came from a world beyond. Perhaps, even, the Universe. How the Chimes first came to be there, or where they came from, he did not know. Their origin and nature was a mystery. They never made the same sound twice, nor even, when he looked closely, did they ever seem to be the same chimes in quite the same places. But it was hard to tell. There were too many to remember and the ever-shifting leaves and branches of the shrubs made them impossible to count.

'What are they?' he had asked when he first came to Woolstone House in his long-ago courting days. He was a physicist at Cambridge then, Margaret studying medieval literature at Oxford. They met at a summer dig at an Anglo-Saxon site in Essex in the early 1960s.

'What are the Chimes?' she had repeated with a smile. 'Better never to ask, Arthur. Some things are best left free of scientific inquiry.'

'But not to ask is to negate my purpose in life, which *is* inquiry,' he had replied a little pompously.

'Trust me about the Chimes,' she had replied, reaching her hand to his then-still-shaven chin, 'and I will never seek to stop your inquiries on anything else . . .'

It was, in her gentle way, a marriage proposal and he had accepted it with a smile, and had trusted her, always, as he did still.

That single restraint had given him strange energy ever since. God, the Universe and Everything had all been fair game to his research but he let the Chimes be. They and the sound they made were a sacred space. He accepted them without further questioning, though just occasionally he dared wonder what they were.

Such thoughts, and the music of the Chimes itself, had been a comfort in the days since Margaret's death. They were a comfort now as, opening the conservatory doors, a tray of tea things in his hand, he headed into the garden and what he only then realized was a lovely, warm, sunny day.

He placed his tray of tea and biscuits in the shade of the Chimes and let their music play around him as he sat in the chair he kept there. The sharp scent of his ripening tomatoes relaxed him and . . .

'Damn phones!' he said aloud, the earlier ringing still jangling his nerves.

He let the Chimes claim him. Peace descended, his earlier sadness all gone, his smile returned. He drank the tea until the pot grew cold. He got up, he made his way slowly back to the house, he pottered about, not doing much as he continued to try to find his way through the straits of sadness and the thickets of loss.

Occasionally he glared at the phone, or scowled at it. Twice he mouthed mock insults at it, making himself smile as Margaret would have done.

'It's a damn nuisance.'

'It's communication, Arthur, and it's necessary, so stop swearing at it.'

Yet, as, later, he sat brooding, his curiosity had been aroused. It was unlikely that different people were calling all at the same time. No, it was the same person. But who?

Arthur suddenly remembered something Margaret had shown him but never tried: call back.

Hmmm.

Maybe not.

Maybe just check the number?

Maybe go and see if there was a message?

Maybe just stay right where he was.

The phone began ringing again. He was too late to pick up but he dialled the number to find out who had called. And he saw a message had been left.

'Humph!'

Frowning and reluctant, holding the phone a little way from his ear as if in disgust, he listened to the message.

It was from the person in the world he least wished to speak to.

A former student, Erich Bohr was now director of one of NASA's research agencies in an area in which Arthur was a world authority. Bohr was also a Special Adviser to the President of the United States in aspects of astronomy and the cosmos that might have military implications.

Arthur knew perfectly well why Bohr was calling him so insistently here in the outback of Woolstone in England; he wanted something only Arthur had: access to the Hyddenworld.

'The question is, why now?' he said aloud.

He went straight to his computer and online to see if he could find out. He had only to see the headlines to know why Bohr had called.

'Oh, dear God,' said Arthur Foale, appalled. 'Oh dear God.'

7

THE SCYTHE OF TIME

At dusk that same day the Fyrd finally gave up waiting for Stort and the others to show up. They never found their hiding place.

'If they're not up there tomorrow morning, we're moving on,' said Jack.

But they left suddenly and much sooner, while it was still pitch-black, startled awake by sudden violent noise at which Georg was already up and growling.

They heard a menacing hissing and sighing, and the rending of tree trunks and branches living and dead, and Stort said urgently, 'That's the Scythe of Time . . . we must flee this place. *Now!*'

They struck camp in silence, without a word, each to their task. In a few moments they were dressed, their portersacs packed, their bedrolls secure, staves in hand.

'Follow me,' Stort ordered them, 'and you too, Georg.'

The dog ran ahead of them.

'*Georg!*'

But he was gone.

'Stort, slow down, I can't see you,' whispered Jack, his hand strong on his stave, ready.

'Then hold on to my 'sac!'

'I'm doing the same behind you, Jack,' said Katherine.

'Right,' cried Stort, for the hiss-whisper and loud destruction of trees was getting nearer and louder by the moment. 'Let's go!'

Together, struggling up the gully, with the horrible sense that the noise and rending of the trees and vegetation was fast on their heels, they made for the bare slopes above. They hoped that the monstrous thing would not follow where there were no trees.

But it was not like that.

There were no stars, no moon, only a bitter, unseasonal wind. Nothing at all to guide them on their way but for occasional glimpses of the twinkling lights of human settlements in the vale far below, which were no use at all.

'I can light a lantern,' said Jack.

'No!' said Stort. 'No time. If the Scythe catches us up we'll be lost forever. *Come on!*'

That was easier said than done.

The high fell that had been so bare when they arrived was not so now. As the three hurried on in the darkness they began crashing into gnarled and thorny branches that shouldn't have been there, their jerkins and 'sacs getting caught in thickets, their hose torn to tatters by brambles, tight branches of trees they could not see arching overhead, banging hard into their foreheads, grabbing their staves. On and on, as if they were in an ancient forest and followed by ancient beasts which rent the very trees behind them, and would tear them apart too if they caught up with them, and scatter their limbs aside.

'We'll make faster progress if I do make a light,' gasped Jack after half an hour of trekking to what felt like nowhere.

'Try it,' conceded Stort, whose breaths were short and wheezy, 'but be quick . . .'

The hissing and sighing crowded in on them, the breaking of root and branch deafening their ears as the wind-blown leaves stung their eyes and faces like hail.

'Hurry!' cried Katherine.

Jack's first lucifer blew straight out.

His second shone briefly, showing only the alarm in his eyes, and died.

At his third, a nearby tree lost patience and whipped a branch like savage fingers down on his head, against his chest and scattered the lucifers to the wind.

Katherine fell one way, Stort moved forward another and Jack went a third, while the hiss-sigh Scythe came on, the screams of dying trees behind them and to their sides, the claws of branches, the savage upended hooks of roots grabbing their arms and pinning them to their sides, tripping them up, pinning them down.

'Jack!'

'Where are you?'

'Stort?'

'I can't see you.'

'Kather . . . ine!'

Somehow they came back together, clasping each other in the murk, blood on hands and faces, clothes in tatters, 'sacs half-torn or half-cut from their backs. Silence fell but for a whispering all around them, so they did not know which way to turn.

Jack's hand was on Katherine's arm, her hand on Stort's. He stood shoulder to shoulder with Jack. Friends as one.

'We're stronger together,' whispered Stort, 'that's why it's abated.'

'What is it, exactly?' murmured Jack. 'If I knew, maybe I could protect you both from it, though my stave's gone dead. Look!'

They looked as best they could in the near-darkness of the night. Normally his stave had a shine or shimmer where it caught the light, however faint, sometimes of a single star, but now there was nothing. They could not even see the stave.

'Scholars have spilt much ink over the definition of this phenomenon,' said Stort. 'It is not unique to the Malverns, but for reasons unknown it manifests itself very powerfully here.'

'So if we stay like this, in a closed circle, we're keeping it at bay?' said Katherine.

'A distinct possibility,' said Stort, 'but not for the reason you think. It is, I believe, a manifestation of collective thought and actions through time. Hills such as these, perhaps *particularly* these, have been stripped of life by generations of humans and, I fear, hydden. We have taken from the Earth and not given back. We did not harvest, we stole and diminished our world forever. The Scythe may be our own thoughts of shame and guilt at what we've done, resurrecting long-lost trees only to have them scythed down again.'

'Not us,' said Jack, 'but our ancestors.'

'In the Mirror, Jack, we are them as well, for all reflections meld to one. The Scythe is not good or bad, nor in any way judgemental. It is what has been; it is what has become. It rages along at the very edge of the future, which is why, if we cannot find escape from it now, it will consume us. We will cut ourselves down with our own thoughts.'

The hissing began again, circling them, still giving them no direction of escape.

'But . . .' murmured Stort.

'What?' said Jack.

'It has been reported of the Scythe that those who experience it sometimes disappear, as if cut down and carried into a different time from their own. There was one report, in a seventeenth-century manuscript which . . .'

He stopped abruptly.

The hissing was growing louder and more specific in location – not far in front of them.

'Which *what*!?'

'Which said that one hydden in a company of, well, um, three actually, was suddenly gone with the shards.'

'Shards?' repeated Jack looking about in the swirling darkness for a clear sign of the danger they heard so clearly. 'What are *they*, for Mirror's sake?'

In his movement his hand slipped from Katherine and hers from Stort. Stort, too, turned, and the circle was broken.

The hissing immediately turned into a roar once more and refocused some yards behind Jack, from where it started to advance, the trees thick again about them, mounting up so hugely that panic overtook them and they could not even move.

Their throats dried, their hearts hammered, their feet were heavy weights too great to lift from the ground. Even their arms were paralysed and their hands, so that they were unable to raise their staves to defend themselves. The so-far-unseen Scythe swung and re-formed to something visible. It manifested as a razor-thin slit of steely light in the sky, that looked so sharp it would turn to slivers whatever it touched, so vast it seemed to reach to the ends of the Universe. The sight of it overwhelmed them with fear.

They tried to cry out but no words came.

Their hearts stilled, their eyes were wide with terror, their last moments come.

It was then, from the corner of their eyes, they caught a movement of russet light through the old trees, accompanied by a drumming of paws. Then out of the roar of the night the growing bark of a dog. Georg appeared, teeth bared and nostrils flared, to take a stance in front of Stort, the others a foot or two behind.

He dropped his head, his tail stiff and straight, his growl turned deep as if it now came from the Earth Herself. He lowered his whole body and began to advance towards the great thing that threatened them. With each slow, deliberate forward step he took, the Scythe squirmed and retreated, thinning in the sky, the ice-blue fading towards white. They felt their limbs relax, their panic going.

Georg advanced further still and they saw that the Scythe, though less than it had been, seemed now to be swirling as a mist to something more, like some creature that has suffered a brief setback in a fight and is gathering its strength to strike again.

'Georg!' rasped Stort, his voice returning.

But the dog did not turn back. He growled more, his pace increased as if going for the kill, he began to run into the line of the Scythe's terrible curve.

'*Georg!*' they cried as one. 'Come back!'

The hissing turned to a sucking, sighing sound, the Scythe retreated far into the night sky until it was barely visible at all and then it roared its rage. It swung suddenly back towards the Earth, its colour turning to that of blood, its size now spreading right across the dreadful sky. Its hiss was a sound so vile they raised their hands to block their ears.

They saw Georg stop and go back on his haunches.

He seemed to stare at the great thing coming down towards him and around him, and to think, his head to one side. He seemed to see something that puzzled him. He looked back at Stort, his eyes all hazel and russet and filled with love.

Then he turned back and stood up to face the blade of light, puny and helpless before its size and speed, and he barked a savage bark, and he growled, and as he did the blade cut through him.

Hish . . . it went right through his flesh and *hish* . . . and *hish* . . . again and again.

Georg's body slivered to a thousand shards of exquisite light, which held his shape for a brief moment before they whirled away in different directions, like a pack of cards scattered by a gale-force wind. In among the gnarled trees of the ancient hill, cutting as they went, a hundred thousand shining facets of what he had been passed before their eyes and out of sight.

His last growl was a slice as well, melding into the Scythe sound, distorting it to something that was more gentle for a moment: his final offering, making the Scythe pull back for a few moments to give them time to flee once more.

They started running towards the nascent light of day, fighting, struggling through the thick, black trees. Running for their lives again.

Still there was forest where none should have been, for they were atop the hill, the ground falling away on either side on a stretch they had seen when they first arrived, which before was devoid of any vegetation but close-cropped sward. Then at last a shaft of light on the eastern horizon and they saw dawn begin to rise. Suddenly Stort stopped.

'What are you doing? Come *on*!' cried Jack.

'What I am doing is forgetting that I am a scientist, or at least an inquirer!' he shouted in Jack's ear. 'At the end of this you'll ask me again what it was and unless I put myself to the test I'll never be able to do more than offer you theories. We may never have this chance again.'

'For Mirror's sake, Stort!' cried Jack and Katherine, running back to his side. It was for this kind of courage of his they loved and admired him, shown so often before, demonstrated again now. They stood and faced as one whatever it was that manifested behind them.

They saw the dim forms of old bent and broken trees, the branches and twigs that had grabbed at them as they ran, though now bent upwards in pleading supplication, as if the trees were bent and distorted mortal forms, begging not to be cut down.

Then they saw it again and with it the vast form that wielded it. Beyond the trees, dark as the darkest sky, grey in parts, a thin curving line, like a smooth black cloud curving across the sky with an arctic sun that caught its bottom edge with the only light: vast, as powerful as the Earth herself, legs like black tornados against black sky, arms and hands whole mountain ranges, body a great storm, head malevolent as it swept back what seemed to be the Scythe – *whish* – and brought it curving, murderous and final, back down again but nearer still – *hisssss* . . .

Jack had seen enough.

It seemed real enough to him and he had no intention of letting anyone disappear that night. He grabbed each of them, turned them, and pushed them onward so that once more they ran and ran.

'But Georg is left behind!' cried Stort.

'Georg may have saved our lives,' replied Jack, 'and I've a feeling he can look after himself.'

The ground changed to something else that should not have been there up on the hill tops: a sizeable stream.

They tumbled headlong in, one after another, and now instead of running, were swimming for their lives towards a far bank they could not quite see. Cold, wet, gulping in water with their breaths, coughing, helping each other, the Scythe of Time breaking up the water behind them in huge waves, sending spray and spumes of foam right over them.

Until, as suddenly as they had woken into pitch-black night, they were on dry land once more and the shadows of the frightening forest fell away.

'Where are we?' wondered Katherine, circling round. 'If that's the Severn then it's flowing in the wrong direction . . . It should be going from left to right.'

One thing was certain: they were now in meadowland. A glance at the sun corrected their mistake at once. In their blind chase over the Malverns they had become confused, thinking east was west and north, south.

Behind them, which meant eastward, was a motorway.

'The M5,' said Jack.

In front, or westward, the wide, marshy river.

'The Severn,' said Stort.

'Which means,' concluded Katherine, 'that that "stream" we swam over in the dark . . .'

They eyed the wide river and the distant rise of the Malverns and shook their heads in wonder and surprise.

'But that's twenty miles at least . . .'

'More like twenty-five . . .'

Whatever the Scythe had been trying to do, what it had actually done was to drive them back to where they had been four days before.

'We know the hour,' said Stort quietly, 'but what day is it?'

'Should be a . . . Tuesday,' said Katherine, the only one who scrivened a daily journal.

'Hmmm,' muttered Stort, 'should be, but might not be. Time does not feel as if it is behaving as it should. Soon after our journey from White Horse Hill began, did I not say that Abbey Mortaine should be our first destination? I did! We survived the Scythe of Time by collective effort, each of us encouraging the other on, none of us letting one of us stop for long. Scholars have assumed the Scythe is a monster, if only of the mind. But supposing it's there to guide us in some way, to make us face what we don't want to?'

'Meaning?'

'Meaning that the Scythe has got us back to where we were meant to be before fear took us in the wrong direction,' said Jack ruefully. 'Maybe we *should* have gone to Abbey Mortaine in the first place and not let ourselves be diverted by worries of the Fyrd or anything else. Those villagers in Cleeve told us how to get to the Abbey easily and safely.'

Again Stort remembered Georg and he looked suddenly bereft. 'Georg with no E,' he murmured. 'I don't think he's coming back, not in this life.'

'He loved you, Stort. He must have thought he was saving you,' said Katherine.

They stood in silence, in memory of his courageous end.

Then Stort frowned, as he often did when some new thought or insight came to him. '"In this life",' he repeated in a hollow, distant voice, his mind elsewhere. He fingered the chime that hung from his neck.

'The shards,' he whispered, 'he became one of them, or rather many of them. Is that the secret of the Scythe's purpose and of the Chimes? Might Georg have gone to save us somewhere else?'

'You said that it stops on the very edge of the future, meaning it doesn't go on into it,' said Katherine.

'Or,' observed Jack, who generally preferred more practical discussions but was engaged with this one, 'we really have a choice as to whether or not we go forward into it . . .'

'Or back into the past,' added Stort excitedly.

'Or stay right where we are,' said Katherine.

'Whatever!' said Jack. 'Maybe time is not so much chronological but kind of all over the place simultaneously, all mixed up, and all we do . . .'

'Go on,' said Stort.

'All we do is choose,' said Katherine. 'Like we choose to go through the portals between the hydden and human worlds. Or like we choose whether to stand here and talk or continue along this green road?'

Stort shook his head as they all started walking.

'No,' he said, 'not a choice as simple as sitting still or walking. More the choices we continually make about where our lives are going.'

'. . . and maybe,' said Jack quietly, concluding the thought he had begun, 'we have far more choices in place and time than we think. Including going back, if not in time, then on our route. So now, Abbey Mortaine? Agreed?'

He did not wait for an answer but strode on ahead, sturdy and strong, his stave alive again and magnificent in the morning light.

8

FOR HIS PROTECTION

What Arthur found out so quickly on the internet was that there had been several sudden catastrophic Earth incidents spread across the continents in the few hours before Bohr's calls.

A township in Cape Town had been swallowed whole in the space of a few minutes and ten thousand lives lost when a fault opened suddenly and then closed as quickly again. A village in the foothills of the Himalayas of north India slid *uphill* into a reservoir, leaving two hundred and fifty-eight people dead. In central Germany, the town of Rinteln had been inundated by the River Weser on whose banks it stood, for no reason that had any climatological or other explanation. Two thousand lives lost.

There were many other smaller such incidents in the hours following.

Bohr had stopped calling as suddenly as he had begun because, Arthur guessed, he had been swamped with duties arising from what was happening worldwide.

In many of the newspapers, and in graphic television footage too, the incidents were initially referred to as 'seismic' despite the fact that many of them were not. Or at least, they did not have the character-istics of earthquakes or other Earth movements: they were very sudden, came without warning and in some cases, as in the Cape Town incident, the Earth's surface was only briefly displaced before its parts moved together again.

No wonder that very soon reference was being made to the Angry Earth and notions that the Earth was 'fighting back'.

Of more interest to Arthur was the relationship between what was happening in the Cosmos and these incidents, and he had no doubt at all that that was the focus of Bohr's and NASA's interest too. In particular, Arthur suspected, any recorded fractures or displacements of time, such as happened when anyone, hydden or human, moved between the two worlds.

For that reason it was a strange and unwelcome overnight news story following Bohr's unanswered calls, concerning an otherwise relatively minor 'seismic' incident in Moss, a suburb of Oslo, Norway, that put into Arthur a deep sense of foreboding.

Again, the Earth had shifted. Again, lives were lost. But this time the reports included reference to the bodies of three oddly dressed dwarfs being found, along with 'unusual medieval-style artefacts', as the *International Herald Tribune* website put it. Arthur had little doubt these were hydden and he was only glad that the rest of world news was still so shocking that the incident was soon forgotten.

Although communications had been disrupted worldwide – another reason Bohr might not have called again – Arthur was able to get through to another ex-student of his and ask him to make discreet enquiries about what had happened in Moss.

The answer was unexpected.

What had begun as a normal exercise for the rescue services, though a tragic one, had been taken over by Norway's NORDSS, its military security service.

The whole of Moss and what had been found there was off-limits.

Worse, for Arthur, was a brief additional message later that afternoon: 'Don't know if there's a link! Guess who flew in to Oslo this morning according to an unofficial blog I read? Our friend Bohr! Be warned!'

An hour later Arthur's phone rang in that especially insistent and accusatory way he imagined it adopted when he was expecting to find someone unpleasant at the other end of the line.

He decided not to pick it up that time but trawl through various specialist sites on the web so that, when he let Bohr catch up with him, he would be as up to speed on what was going on in the astral-archaeological and cosmological worlds as it was possible to be without access to official sources, except discreetly.

✳

He took a break at three and sat in the garden. His mind had drifted back to Margaret, then to Jack and Katherine and finally their daughter Judith. He was surprised to realize he missed her more than anyone.

'Judith,' he said, sitting up, her name a million memories: her coming three months before, like her going at the start of August, and everything between, a wondrous, alarming mystery.

Margaret had loved her.

He loved her.

And her parents, Jack and Katherine, they loved her too, so far as it was possible to love a child of the skies, of prophecy, of the elements and of the Universe, who grew from infant to adulthood in three months and whose life moved between the hydden and the human worlds and warped itself through the vales of time as well.

Now she, he was certain, *would* come back.

They had bonded as a real grandfather and granddaughter might have done: deeply, eternally, with a love and trust and good humour that is free of the responsibilities of closer family ties like those of parents and siblings, yet sharing something of both. A natural, familial love, pure and simple, made all the more wonderful to him because the others had understood and applauded it.

In her last days with them, when they holidayed in the Borderland of England and Scotland, Judith had taken him on a personal tour of the desolate Kielder country to show him how mortals ruined the Earth. By mortals she meant humans. It was done on her timescale, not his. A two-year journey passed in a few hours. He had flown through skies and dwelt for a time in water at the bottom of a reservoir. He had not expected anyone else to have believed what had happened, not even Margaret.

Why had he, of all physicists, been so privileged to travel through time and relativity as he had? For that was what it had been.

He did not know.

Had it really happened?

Arthur was sure it had and it meant that he could relate to Judith's between-world experiences and understand a little of how it was that time to her was not the same as it was to ordinary mortals.

The last time she spoke to him was by the henge, when she whispered, 'Arthur, I think the Chimes may be everything.'

It was a thought which, now Margaret had passed on and he felt free of the promise he had made, he dared to begin to examine.

The Chimes are everything.

'What does that mean?' he asked himself again and again.

The phone, so blessedly silent for an hour, rang suddenly, worse than before.

'Bloody thing,' said Arthur.

As he did there was a *beep-beep* from the kitchen. A text on the mobile he almost never used, which he had left charging for days, last used to check the time, when he discovered its battery had run out.

He had heard other texts come in, though none today. He looked towards the house furtively.

He went on up to it, hoping the ringing would die, which it did. He stood staring at the phone in his study, willing it not to ring again, which wish it ignored.

It rang again, horribly loud and he finally went to pick it up.

But even as his hand was on it he heard – incredulously, because he never had visitors – a car on the gravel at the front of the house and the *clunk, clunk* of a car door opening. No, doors plural, meaning at least two people had come to visit him.

Who the hell can they be? He shook his head, sighed, let go of the phone and went to answer the door.

Before he reached it, a dark shape loomed at the frosted glass, reached out and thumped the knocker, *bang-bang-bang*.

'Yes?' said Arthur as he opened the door.

He stood amazed and alarmed.

It was a man in a military uniform with a briefcase.

Another, of lesser rank, stood by the solid and expensive-looking vehicle on his drive. It had a discreet RAF logo on the front bumper.

Neither man was smiling, but nor did they look unpleasant.

Just neat, shining, solid and very purposeful.

Well, Arthur told himself, ducking to check that the car had no passengers, *at least they are not Erich Bohr.*

The one at the door was holding a mobile in his hand and Arthur was not sure if he had just spoken into it or was offering it to him.

'Professor Foale?'

'Er . . . yes?'

'You are not picking up, sir.'

'Er, no, I suppose I'm not.'

'Just a moment, sir.'

The officer pressed buttons on his phone. The soldier by the car, Arthur noticed for the first time, was armed.

The shiny car showed up the general dilapidation of the driveway and house and the two neat military men made Arthur look like a retired professor who, more or less, had just got out of bed.

Which, more or less, he was.

The officer spoke into the mobile, which looked sleek and slippery in his big square hand, 'I have him here, sir,' he said and proffered the phone to Arthur.

He shook his head, and said, 'I do not speak on mobiles. They hurt my ears. Who is it?'

'Dr Erich Bohr, sir.'

Arthur looked weary and muttered, 'I suppose . . . well . . . Oh God, give it to me, then.'

Bohr was not a man to put on hold, not without some sort of explanation.

He took the mobile, held it with difficulty, and shoved it near but not onto his ear.

'Bohr?'

'Arthur?'

'Yes.'

'Cells hurt my ears too,' he said. 'Pick up that damn antique phone of yours. We need to talk.'

'Er, yes. I will.'

'Now!'

'With two military personnel looming over me, one of whom is armed, that *does* seem to be the most sensible course of action, Erich.'

His house phones began ringing almost at once.

He handed back the mobile, trying to switch it off and failing.

'Leave that to me, Professor. Just take the call, *please*.'

Arthur retreated to his study, his heart thumping, and picked up his phone.

'I'm here,' he said reluctantly.

Dr Erich Bohr, Chair of NASA's Earth Enterprise, replied in his quick, clipped way, 'I've been expecting *you* to call me. You've seen the news, I take it?'

It was a statement not a question.

'Which particular bit of it?'

There was a pause.

'The *events*.'

'Yes . . . but I have not been very active of late . . . and I'm afraid Margaret died.'

There was a pause as Bohr slowly registered that Margaret's death deserved a few words of regret before he got down to business. He uttered them, though without much conviction.

Arthur acknowledged that he had, but without any gratitude.

What was now clear to Bohr was that Arthur Foale, who was possibly the most informed person in the world on the history of Earth's seismic events, was not going to yield easily to Bohr's usual hectoring approach.

He changed tack, trying to sound charming, and talked a little of the events of the past twenty-four hours and how mystified everyone was. He did not mention the incident in Moss, Norway, and nor did Arthur.

Bohr now told him of incidents not covered by news in the public media.

In Austria a mountainside had collapsed without warning, killing over a hundred people working on a tracking station. In the Tasman Sea three large container ships had been swallowed in calm seas, all hands lost. In Tunisia an oasis around which hundreds of market traders and their customers were doing business sank into the sands, taking people, livestock, everything down with it.

'Anything in England?' asked Arthur finally.

He knew there had been, but nothing serious, not even the various Earth movements that had happened in the Summer, in Birmingham, among other places.

'I'll send you a list by email. I presume you are on email?'

'I am, though . . . er, just a moment . . .'

He detected movement in the room above his head, which was his bedroom; and in the conservatory.

He put down the phone and went to inspect.

The officer who had knocked on the front door was in the hall; a different man he had not seen before was in the conservatory and someone else entirely in the garden.

'Dammit,' growled Arthur, going upstairs.

His bedroom door was wide open, a man who was not the driver of the vehicle was poking about, making five visitors in all.

'What are you doing?' Arthur demanded.

'It's for your own protection, sir,' said the man blandly.

Arthur guessed at once it was a lie, but played the game.

'From whom, exactly?'

'That will be explained, I expect,' replied the man.

Arthur swore, went back down the stairs, glowered at the officer and picked up the phone again. But his mind was on something else entirely. If they were searching his house there was only one thing they could be looking for. True, some of his archaeological work had been on Ministry of Defence sites, which made his cartographic records subject to the Official Secrets Act. But that wasn't it. Erich Bohr was one of the very few people in the world who knew that Arthur had researched something else entirely, something so odd that people would consider him half-mad for even thinking it a proper topic for research. Yet it was something which, if his theory proved correct, would need to be more secret still.

Arthur Foale had been trying to find out if certain evidence concerning the hydden and the Hyddenworld was true. He had once made the mistake of telling Bohr that the only way to prove it was to find a way into the Hyddenworld and he foolishly hinted that he nearly had.

Ever since then Bohr had asked about it, and when Arthur did finally work out what the portals to the Hyddenworld were, and how they worked, he knew that Bohr would hear the lie in his replies.

Arthur was sure he had.

Now he wanted the full story because somehow or other Bohr, who was nobody's fool, believed that the present global crisis might have a solution in, of all places, the Hyddenworld. In which, Arthur feared, he might well be right.

On these matters Arthur had hidden his records in a ruined outhouse where he was confident they would not be found.

'What's going on, Bohr?' he asked.

'There'll be a full explanation. Have you had any messages from . . . anyone else?'

'No.'

'Emails?'

'Don't read 'em.'

'Texts?'

'I've had texts but . . .' he hesitated because he was embarrassed. 'Margaret did all that, not me. I'm not even sure I know how to access them.'

'Do you mind if we . . . ?'

'Just another moment,' said Arthur.

He headed towards the kitchen where the mobile was and saw the officer already going that way himself. He picked up the mobile before Arthur could get to it.

'This your mobile, sir?'

'Yes.'

'Do you mind . . . ?'

'Help yourself.'

The officer scrolled through his texts, found what he was looking for, opened it, shook his head slightly and spoke into the discreet wire speaker at his mouth.

'They've been in touch, sir,' he said.

He listened.

Then, 'Yes, sir.'

Then, to Arthur, 'Dr Bohr would be grateful if you could return to your study and pick up again . . .'

Bohr was brief and to the point.

'I'm sorry, Arthur, but you'll have to go with those people. Well, they're our people really. It's for your own protection. I am going to have to convene a meeting.'

'Where?'

'You're the lucky one. The rest will have to fly in. RAF Croughton. I think you know it.'

Arthur did.

One of his remits while at Cambridge had been to oversee digs on various archaeological sites that emerged from time to time on land controlled by the Ministry of Defence. Some settlement features and a henge outline had been found at Croughton, and since it was only twenty miles up the road he had run the dig himself.

'Who else is coming?'

Bohr reeled off a list of names at rapid fire speed.

'Anton Boucher of Météo-France; Ira Aldridge of the Pacific Northwest Seismographic Network; Dr Felix Nusbaum of the Israeli Astronomical Association . . .'

Arthur grunted. Nusbaum was a former pupil.

'Aleman of the IASPE?'

'Yes, Miguel is coming. So is Tom Gould of the National Oceanic and Atmospheric Administration, whom you worked with in Oregon and . . .'

A brief pause before Bohr started again.

It was no less than a roll-call of the world's top researchers into global Earth events, seismic, meteorological and those that might be a function of, or influenced by, matters cosmological and temporal.

Arthur thought for a moment but said nothing. What was interesting was who was missing: the Chinese and the Russians. So this was political and the people Bohr feared might get to him first were, as he would have put it, on the other side. Not good.

'What is the purpose of the meeting?' he asked.

'To review the pattern and progress of events so far. To consider alternatives to the more mainstream approaches my colleagues in other disciplines are taking which, I fear, have not produced anything useful yet. And . . .'

He hesitated and Arthur thought he knew why.

'Tell me, Bohr, are you speaking from Norway?'

'Perhaps.'

'From Moss?'

The silence was vast and deep.

'Yes. Arthur . . . we are going to have to talk about the Hyddenworld.'

'Why?'

'Because we have to examine all options open to us.'

Arthur felt an absolute chill. If Bohr and his kind ever entered the Hyddenworld it would lead to disaster.

'And now?'

'Others may wish to get to you, Arthur, and that our respective governments cannot allow. Therefore for your own safety . . .'

'When?'

'Almost immediately.'

'I need time to get things together that may be needed.'

'We can give you time for that, of course.'

'And you're taking me to RAF Croughton?'

He needed the confirmation but he regretted the question the moment he asked it. He did not want Bohr to pick up on the fact that he liked the idea of going to that location. Bohr would want to know why.

'Yeees . . . any reason you ask?'

Arthur affected a self-deprecatory laugh.

'My bladder,' he said. 'But if the journey's only twenty miles or so I think I can manage.'

It was well done and Bohr seemed satisfied.

'How long will the meeting go on – hours, days?'

Bohr murmured a vague reply.

'When will you be there, Erich?'

But the line was already dead.

It's time to get myself back into the Hyddenworld, Arthur told himself, hoping he might be able to avoid the trip to Croughton.

'We'd like to leave by 1900 hours, sir' said the officer, looming now at his study door.

'Do *you* know how long this meeting is scheduled for?' Arthur asked.

'As long as it takes, I should think, sir. So, is 1900 hours good?'

'Yes,' said Arthur politely. 'Thank you.'

9

IN THE ABBEY GROUNDS

The route to Abbey Mortaine was a circuitous one, following an abandoned railway line. But it was safe, with good cover, until it opened out near the village of Coldrick.

As they neared it, down a valley to their right, a quacking and flapping over a nearby field drew their attention to the unusual sight of mallard flying about in evident distress. Usually they fly straight off in one direction or another, not over a river in bewilderment.

The river itself was a small one, but quite deep, and ran under the low bridge which carried the railway line over it and then down to the village and beyond.

They spied another odd sight: a hydden sitting quietly on the riverbank, his portersac to one side, his stave to the other, his feet dangling aimlessly in the water.

He was in his mid-thirties, rather roughly and dirtily dressed, and he looked around at them without interest when they approached, his face pale and bewildered.

It was only after they had plied him with food and drink and gained his trust, that he was able and willing to talk.

'Notice anything?' he said.

'Such as . . . ?' asked Jack.

'Fowl, the water surface and a frightened pike.'

Katherine said they had noticed that some mallard had been behaving nervously.

'Correct,' said the hydden, 'well noticed, madam! What else?'

'Nothing . . .' said Jack slowly.

'There was a bubbling up: don't see that often, down in the village; and a sucking down. Don't see that neither. Now, that's not a good sign is it? And then the pike . . .'

'What about it?' asked Stort, interested.

The hydden did not immediately answer. He was thickset with powerful arms and big hands, the nails thick and stumpy and black with grime

'Name's Dodd, no more, no less. No "Mister" for me. Plain Dodd will do. You can see my occupation from my portable grinding stone and my calloused hands!'

'You're a knife-grinder?' guessed Jack.

Dodd nodded.

'That and sharpener of fish hooks, repairer of brot-tins, maker of kettle spouts and such like things. Metal's got a way with it that I understand. Came this way three days ago, heading north, like you. Aiming for Brum. Can't say I ever knew there was a hydden community hereabout but there was Coldrick, right at the river's edge.

'But I've made good trade and I could make more but I'm leaving on account of the mallard, the bubbling and that scared predator. Been lodging with a widow goodwife who I paid in kind, if you know what I mean. An itinerant has needs like others. Left morning after yesterday . . .'

'You mean this morning?'

'Aye that'll be the one. Well then, this'n morning I woke with a sense of unease. Nothing unusual in that. I often wake knowing I must move on. The goodwife said, "Dodd, get me a fish and I'll rouster up brekkie afore you go . . ." Off I went, upstream to a good lie, and cast out a float and worm, the water being too broiling and bubbling for ledgering. Know what I mean?'

They nodded, as if they did.

'The fish weren't biting; they were jumping like sand hoppers in hot sun. Then there was the pike . . .'

'What about it?'

'It jumped clear of the water, not once but thrice. Dodd says to himself: when a fish like that panics, the rest of us better start doing so too, and I did. I did. Not been back and won't. This place Coldrick got the dumblies on it if you ask me. So I've been sittin' here recovering and considering and now you've come I've decided. I'm going along with you if you'll have me!'

This was not unusual. Lone travellers liked company and in exchange they gave news of ways and means along the route.

'By all means,' said Stort, 'until we turn off.'

'Well you oughter not stay on this route considerin's there's Fyrd about.'

'Fyrd?'

'They were there when I first arrived, looking and waiting.'

'For what?'

Dodd looked at them with a certain cunning and tapped his nose.

'For *you*,' he said, 'if you are who I think you are.'

'Who . . . ?'

'Mister Stort, Jack the Stavemeister and Mistress Katherine, mother of the Shield Maiden. That's the word that's out, though no one's sayin' it. Folk say you've come over from Berkshire way to avoid the Fyrd.'

They set off again.

'Not much more to say,' said Dodd, 'except they were looking for you. Went off yesternoon.'

'Which way?'

Dodd didn't know.

'What I do know, and I say this freely without malice: when they find you they'll have your guts for garters. I know. They had mine once and I've never been the same. Come with you I will. You could use my stave if we meet 'em.'

'How many were there?'

'Six.'

They shook hands, Katherine included.

'You better *had* come with us awhile,' said Jack, 'and tell us what else you've heard.'

It felt like a lucky break for all concerned, as if the sun had been hiding for a time and come back again. They would have liked more of Dodd's company, but after half a mile or so they reached a human fingerpost pointing to the right on which the words *Abbey Mortaine* were painted. In the distance, on lower ground, they saw the arches and walls of a ruined abbey.

They stopped to say goodbye.

'One thing I'm not getting clear in my head,' said Dodd. 'Who's leading your party?'

None of them spoke.

'Mister Stort?' wondered Dodd.

'Not exactly,' said Stort.

'Master Jack, then?'

'I don't think so,' said Jack.

'Then it must be *you*, Mistress Katherine.'

'Must it?'

'Want some pike? Fourth time it jumped it was straight into my lap snapping its teeth and that's what gave me my turn. I mean . . . I *mean* . . . they are carnivorous!'

He heaved off his 'sac and brought out the pike and gutted it and took off head and tail right in front of them.

He cut off three steaks with a sharp knife, wrapped them up and gave them to Jack.

'Can't eat it all,' he said. 'And a fish given is a fish that comes back, as my Ma used to say. So you can safely say we'll meet again and meanwhile Dodd gives you this advice for free: if the mallard are flapping and the river's a-bubbling and the pike's taken to jumping, you better run for your life. Because those omens are not good.'

They turned off the railway track and walked quietly down towards the ruins. It was early evening and getting dark. The last part of the path turned into a steep track that dropped towards the ruins through a stand of pines which made the air resinous and the going slippery with pine needles.

The land flattened out into short grass where the ruins stood. They were extensive, the walls of the long nave standing high in place and the arch of the round west window complete. Other buildings were less so, but there was enough standing to see the cloisters, the undercroft and dorter, and, adjacent to the stream that ran out from a steep hill at one end of the grounds, what had been a hospice, visitors' quarters and much else.

There was a small bridge over the stream, a weir to its left, and other ruins further upstream before the ground steepened to the hill.

All was silent and deserted but for the flap of rooks up in the pines and the distant cooing of doves looking for roosting spots. Though the sun had sunk behind the trees the air was warm and light and the place felt peaceful.

'So, why have we come here, Stort?'

He had said nothing more of that but seemed very excited to be there, poking about the ruins, working out the lie of the land, pointing out the importance of the water supply. Then he sat down and considered how to answer Katherine's question. She was generally more interested in such things and enjoyed Stort's sometimes long and obscure explanations. Jack less so, but he sat down too to hear what Stort had to say.

'For a hundred years or so, in the fourteenth century, Abbey Mortaine had the finest scriptorium of all the abbeys in Englalond. That's where they copied manuscripts and illuminated them. I looked around for its likely location just now but I think it's all gone.

'It's not generally known, and I doubt that humans ever acknowledge the fact, but the best illuminations were done by hydden attached to abbeys like this one. Of course no one ever admitted the fact but hydden have smaller hands and became adept at such work. What is unusual about Mortaine is that what it also made were some of the first notations of music. That was because the choir here was famous and well developed and included both human and hydden choristers, probably the last time the two cooperated.

'The Main Library at Brum has a number of manuscripts, books and a codex, or collection of documents, from this abbey. It is in the codex that accounts exist of a wondrous musical instrument possessed by this abbey and envied by others. It was called a Quinterne.

'No one knows what it looks like but it was probably stringed, like a lute. The legend was that the Quinterne would never leave the Abbey precincts until its music was needed to help save the world. Sound familiar? Like the story of Beornamund's gems, which had that power also?

'My mentor Master Brief thought so. He came to the Abbey when he was young, in an effort to find the truth of the Quinterne, but never did. He said he met with hostility from the remaining monks, who were all hydden, no humans at all. They had left in the sixteenth century but the hydden stayed on – and still produced illuminated books.'

The sun sank lower, twilight descending.

Jack stretched, got up and left Stort talking. He went to the stream to get a drink but, finding it hard to reach the water from the near-side, crossed the bridge to the other side.

He was well within sight of Stort and Katherine so, when he stiffened, turned sharply and suddenly raised a hand as a signal, they got up and went to him at once.

'What is it, Jack?'

'Get your staves and bring mine, *now*!'

They did so at once.

'What *is* it?'

He pointed upstream to where there was a jumble of rocks and stone on the bank and in the water.

'Look!'

It took a moment for them to see the bodies, three of them.

'Are they . . . ?'

'Hydden, not human.'

'Katherine, stay close by Stort, back to back. I'm going to investigate and then we're getting out of here fast, it's too exposed. We can be seen from all sides.'

He knew before he took a step forward that the bodies he had seen were fresh. There was no odour and the blood shone still on the path.

He circled them very cautiously, looking as much at the bushes nearby, and along the bank, as at the bodies themselves. No sign of life, no movement, and yet . . . yet . . . he had a feeling of being watched. Not a bad one, but it was there.

He looked more closely at the bodies. They were certainly all dead, their hands tied behind their backs, their throats slit. A neat, tidy, cruel job.

'Fyrd,' he murmured to himself.

Times certainly had changed so far as humans were concerned. Hydden bodies would never have been left on view a year before, especially by the Fyrd. They would have been burnt.

Their garb was distinctive.

Each wore white fustian robes with woven girdles. Their feet were bare and dirty. Not far off was a pile of sandals. They had been made to take them off before they were killed.

Their hair was ill-cut and short. These were hydden monks who had seen better days.

He retreated back to the others, eyes checking everywhere, near and far. An easy place to hide, especially in fading light. An impossible place to investigate without putting themselves in jeopardy.

'Well, Stort,' he said, 'they were killed very recently. They look like the monks you might have been hoping to talk with . . . but right now we go back up the hill and make camp somewhere safe among the pines, where we are not sitting ducks. I think Fyrd have been here, and recently. We may have disturbed them but I don't think so. Were that the case they probably would have waited to attack us, for to have killed these monks in such a way needed at least as many as us and probably a whole patrol.'

'Shouldn't we get right away?' said Katherine.

Jack shook his head.

'If we've been seen we can be followed. Up there we'll be hard to get at without us hearing them approach. If no one saw us arrive, they'll not know we're here and we can investigate further by the light of day.'

They retraced their steps up the hill and set up camp under a wooded bluff which gave them protection from above and the sides. Jack set up thread alarms   simple stretches of well-placed strong black thread to a cobnut rattle in their tent, easily triggered by intruders into their space – and set their staves and his crossbow ready.

'I'll take first watch,' he said, 'while you two fry up that pike.'

It was going to be another long night and now a cold one.

There was a nip to the air, and mist hung about the trees.

10
RAF Croughton

In the time the military allowed Arthur before they left, he thought hard and fast and collected the few essentials he might need. He included some items from what had once been a workshop and a laboratory in the former stables, among which was some stiff wire and a wire-cutter. He had this for creating structures to hold equipment. He hoped now the cutters would have another use.

He had to be sure that, if he could not find a way to escape to the Hyddenworld before they took him to Croughton, he had what he needed when he got there.

Stressed he might now be, but it was a long time since he had felt so alive.

He went upstairs to pack a small case and returned with it to his study, where he placed it on his desk and removed the item that was inside. It was an ancient leather portersac from the Hyddenworld. Inscribed on the inside of the flap in a Gothic script in black ink was 'Yakob', Jack's German name.

When the White Horse carried the six-year-old Jack to safety in Englalond, and he entered the human world, the 'sac and its few contents was his only possession. It remained his only connection with his childhood and Arthur had decided it was about time he had it back.

For now he took a few small items from his desk, relics of his Hyddenworld explorations: a tiny brass compass of hydden manufacture, a cannikin, the essentials to make fire and a brew the hydden way, a brot holder, a bedroll that looked far too small for him, a flint lighter.

'Oh, and my stave!' he said to himself, taking up what looked like no more than a stumpy stick with brass ferrules at each end, from his walking-stick stand.

He gathered some maps and papers and printed off the attachment which Bohr had sent, which showed the places in the British Isles where there had been recent Earth incidents.

He put the case by the front door. The portersac he kept with him, as if in his haste he had forgotten it was in his hand. If he succeeded in getting to the tree henge he would need the things inside it. 'I'll just make sure the bottom garden gates are secure,' he told the officer waiting, and hurried outside.

'Feel free, Professor. But we need to leave in twenty minutes.'

Arthur left the case but carried the 'sac. If his first plan worked he'd be gone before they knew it with all he needed in his 'sac. If not then he would move on to Plan B when he got to RAF Croughton.

He walked through the conservatory and out across the lawn towards the two trees that marked the entrance to the henge. If he could just get through the trees and turn dexter into the shadows he would be beyond the reach of Bohr.

Five yards, four, two . . .

'I'm sorry, sir, you cannot go any further.'

Arthur stopped abruptly.

A soldier in camouflage appeared from behind one of the conifers. Another rose from the ground thirty yards off. Both were armed.

'But . . .'

There were no buts, none at all.

As Arthur had feared, he was going to RAF Croughton, like it or not. He would have to rely on Plan B. If that failed he had no plans at all.

He went round to check the gates, followed by one of his minders, collected some lemon balm for show and reluctantly turned back to the house.

Back in his library he found his copy of Her Majesty's Stationery Office Royal Commission Report, titled *Archaeological Remains on Ministry of Defence Properties in England, Wales and Scotland*. Professor Arthur Foale was cited with four others as a co-author. His work had focused on MoD properties in the Midlands and South-East of England, of which there were forty-seven. They were listed alphabetically.

RAF Croughton was seventh in the list.

He studied the entry he himself had written, with satisfaction. Then he got up, ran his fingers along his collection of large-scale Ordnance Survey maps and took down the Croughton map. He examined it closely alongside the maps and plans he had drawn for the original report. Then he turned on Google Earth, looking over towards the door as he did so. He scaled up to the largest image of RAF Croughton he could find, closed in on the south-west corner of the airfield and studied it carefully, committing three things to memory: the boundary fence and where two areas he had himself surveyed lay in relation to it: one adjacent to the fence itself, the other a couple of fields away.

A minute later the officer in charge knocked at the door and came straight in.

'Professor Foale? Time to go, sir.'

Less than an hour later Arthur found himself approaching RAF Croughton on the A43.

Even had he not studied the map and Google Earth earlier, he would have known the road. As it was, he knew what to look for, particularly the southern perimeter which they passed before turning into the well-guarded entrance: a high wire fence, checkpoint and white-helmeted military police. Charming.

It all looked very different from the way it had when he had done his archaeological fieldwork around the site three decades before. There were aggressive KEEP OUT signs, legal notices to would-be trespassers, towers, electrical and telephonic structures and satellite dishes beyond.

It looked like a mock-up of a space station and, despite the millions that had probably been spent on the place, even before going through the checkpoint it had an eerie, derelict air. There were squat, pale, ill-painted buildings, concrete barricades, men in the distance in uniform, stopping and staring at passers-by who lingered too long; and, probably, dog patrols, CCTV and listening devices.

Derelict but also unpleasantly futuristic.

But then, he knew, despite its RAF tag, it was a United States Air Force base with a particular speciality, which was why Bohr had chosen it for the location of his ad hoc symposium. RAF Croughton was the most important of the USA's telecommunication centres in Europe. Aeroplanes might be thin on the ground, the runways modest, but the place buzzed with covert electronic activity.

The perimeter fence was certainly higher than he remembered and now had razor wire along the top.

But he knew from experience of other airbases where he had done fieldwork before runways were extended or new buildings put up, that the outer fence was show, the real security lay inside and around the core buildings.

A raggle-taggle group of people with placards stood by the RAF Croughton sign, as near as was legally permissible, shaking placards which read: US RENDITION IS INHUMANE AND ILLEGAL. STOP ALL FLIGHTS HERE.

The driver ignored the protesters, one of whose placards grazed the side of the vehicle as they drove past. The shouts faded away behind them.

Stern-faced, crop-haired, uniformed guards as muscled as bull-terriers stopped the car. The barrier stayed where it was. Other guards, armed, watched coldly from a distance.

Windows whirred down, the vehicle, its driver and the passengers were checked, quiet words exchanged, a salute given and the barrier rose up.

As the car moved forward through the gate, Arthur looked back. The protesters on the road were staring after him, the barrier coming down swiftly, the guards turning back to face a hostile world.

Within seconds, as they drove forward into the base its closed world came down upon him. Unlit, unmarked buildings sped by, anonymous tarmac everywhere, sharp turns to right, to left, the roar of a helicopter engine, silhouettes of men standing, a pause, another guard checking and far glimpses of the same high fence; and sheep grazing on rough grass.

Sheep!?

He might have smiled had not a flock of gulls risen suddenly up from the roof of yet another faceless building and swung, screeching and scattering, over the car.

He already felt restrained, as if his hands and arms were pinned to his side and a fist thrust against his chest. His throat went dry with premonition.

The car stopped.

A blue door opened onto a wide, well-lit, windowless corridor blocked by another officer.

His car door was opened from outside.

'Professor Foale? Good. This way. Your bag will be taken to your room.'

'My papers . . .'

He leaned back into the car, they spilled from his briefcase; he fumbled about and felt a fool.

When he re-emerged, the smile on the face of his greeter was fixed, his welcome not a real welcome at all. He might just as well have been a military asset being shelved. Perhaps he was. One being put into cold storage so the enemy couldn't get at it.

The steps he followed, and those to his side, were military. *Dammit, this is an armed guard*, he told himself.

Arthur's final glimpse of the outdoors was an angled piece of darkening sky through a door.

He was taken to a room whose windows were too high for him to see out of unless he clambered up on a chair. Which, the moment he was alone, he proceeded to do. He had the uncomfortable feeling he was being watched by hidden cameras. The view was not beautiful and he had seen some of it already: nondescript airbase buildings, a sorry-looking baseball field and three structures that looked like giant golf balls, one white, two red.

At least I know where I am, he told himself, *relative to where I need to be.*

The room had a desk and the phone on it rang.

'Twenty-seven minutes, Professor Foale,' someone said.

'Has Dr Bohr . . . ?'

The operator was gone.

He tried the door.

It opened onto a corridor in which two armed men stood.

'Sir?' one said unsmilingly.

Arthur retreated, shaking his head.

He went through his papers, his head clearing. He worked out what his line needed to be about the Hyddenworld. It was to say little and imply less. He wondered now how long he was going to keep them at bay. Not long if circumstances made them think it was imperative to know more, especially if they thought that the hydden might offer a solution to a problem that otherwise seemed beyond the capacity of humans to solve.

But that depended on a lot of things, not least the extent to which Bohr had discussed his brief and foolish revelations concerning Hyddenworld with others. He glanced at his watch: eight minutes to go.

He could play the fool, he could lie, he could try to confuse them, he could plead ignorance. None of it would work, not with some of the sharpest minds he knew, including that of Erich Bohr. His watch showed three minutes before time.

Arthur felt panic and a kind of hopelessness.

He had to get away and fast.

He had to get away before the questions really started, which was going to be tomorrow, early probably.

He . . .

His door opened.

'Professor, please. This way.'

His phone rang again.

The officer took the call.

'He's on the way.'

The briefing room had low windows which gave him a panoramic view to the west and north of the base. The satellite terminals were across the fields to the left, a road to personnel accommodation to the right, while straight ahead, past the baseball field, the tussocky grass stretched for several hundred yards to the south-west corner of the base. The perimeter fence converged from north and east, beyond it rough grass and a public highway behind trees. He could see occasional traffic, but that was a long way off.

The windows were shut tight and locked. He was going to have to use the door.

'Ah, Professor Foale . . .'

He began to shake hands. In different circumstances the greetings on all sides would have been more effusive and taken longer. As already indicated by Bohr, he knew most people there and had collaborated closely with one or two, but the mood was sombre and businesslike and there was no small talk.

Erich Bohr had filled out in the decade since Arthur had last seen him. His face was grey and lined. Responsibility and power had not so much corrupted but worn him down, sucked him dry and removed the last vestiges of humanity from his eyes, his being.

His advisory post was in the gift of the President of the United States, his job was to distribute research funds to the many who needed them. He was therefore both politician and paymaster, a scientist no more. The wonder and excitement of discovery in the brutally ambitious young man Arthur once knew had evaporated in the face of the conflicting realities of the world of men.

Yet not quite all of the Erich Arthur had known, for whom Margaret had had a soft spot, was gone. In the brief moment they half-embraced, Bohr's momentary pleasure at seeing him again was apparently genuine.

But then: 'I'm sorry, Arthur . . . and . . . I hope . . .' and an apologetic smile as he retreated into the shadow land of compromise and impossible decisions, in which he was both king and subject.

He hopes, thought Arthur, interpreting the ambiguity in that whispered 'I'm sorry', *that I'll tell them all about the Hyddenworld but if I don't, he has the power to make me.*

He knew that humans, even when they count themselves as friends, are capable of anything if they believe it to be a matter of survival.

His gaze involuntarily drifted towards the window and the wide expanse beyond, across which lay his only possibility of escape and so keeping from them the knowledge needed to access the Hyddenworld.

'Ladies and gentlemen . . .'

The introductory session began.

They were briefed by Erich and two others about terrestrial events so far and the threat of meteorological ones as well, the wall behind them turning into a firework display of images, graphics and live links. Arthur paid very careful attention. He realized what was happening. By their very presence at that briefing, he and the others became participants in secrets of a kind that it was treasonable to divulge. No wonder Bohr had sent his people to descend on Arthur so fast, and got him somewhere secure. He had been afraid that the few others in the know about the Hyddenworld, particularly Professor Liadov of MIIGAiK, the Moscow State University of Geodesy and Cartography, and Dr Hsueh of the Department of Astronomy, Beijing Normal University, both in the pay of their respective governments, might have triggered those governments' interest in him. Of them all, Liadov was the one he would have trusted most, the only one to whom he might have divulged what he knew.

But neither man was there and Arthur had no intention of asking if they were likely to be. Wrong question to the wrong people. It would have given too much away: that he had something to divulge, that he trusted some more than others.

They were given an agenda for the discussion that was to start after a meal.

'Questions?'

Arthur bided his time, affected to look tired and breathless, which was not difficult.

Eventually he raised his hand.

'I'm not used to being cooped up. Never have been. Do we have access to the great outdoors?'

Erich Bohr smiled his pale and puffy smile.

'I can see no reason why not,' he said slowly, glancing questioningly at one of the military.

It was answered with a reluctant nod before one of the other officers said cautiously, 'For your own safety, ladies and gentlemen, it is better that you are accompanied if you want to go outside. Ask one of the orderlies, and someone will show you where you may go.'

'Tell them to come in trainers,' Arthur called out affably. 'I intend to sprint round the perimeter before supper . . . it'll sharpen my mind.'

He said it with an irony that would have been lost on most of those present had he not smiled with a self-deprecation intended to suggest that the last thing Professor Arthur Foale was capable of was jogging, let alone sprinting around an airbase.

He had created his chance. In the next few days he must find a way to take it.

11

THE QUINTERNE

'Jack! *Jack!*'
       '*Stort!*'
       It was Katherine, shaking them. It was six in the morning, it
was urgent and it was extraordinary.

They each woke from deep sleep, aware enough of the potential
danger their arrival at Abbey Mortaine the night before and the
discovery of the bodies of the hydden monks had put them in, to stay
silent.

Stort slowly sat up rubbing his eyes.

Jack, always instantly alert, rose up and grabbed his stave. '*What is
it?*' he whispered.

It was Katherine's watch and she was doing her job.

'Has one of the threads been triggered?' murmured Stort, struggling
with his trews.

Sensible hydden went to bed with their trews on in such situations
but Stort said he could not sleep without a certain airiness.

The dark hours of night had been trouble-free. Now it was dawn,
and cool air and a lingering mist hung in the trees about them, and
among that part of the ruins they could see through the trees below.
The mist was thickest along the river and it blocked out the disturbing
sight of the murdered hydden.

'*Listen!*' she said.

It was quiet singing, a duet. It came from the steep hillside to their
right but the mist made it impossible see who was singing, or exactly
where they were.

Jack relaxed.

This was not the sound of enemies and it seemed benign.

Stort smiled. What they were hearing more than justified the stops and starts, hesitations and shocks of their journey from White Horse Hill.

'Ancient and old,' he said, 'a music made to an unusual scale which means . . .'

'They can't know we're here,' said Jack. 'They probably saw us arrive yesterday and watched us leave. The sight lines are such that they wouldn't be able to see us from over there, or see us leave higher up. They just assumed it.'

'Ssh!' said Stort. 'Listen! This is a rare privilege indeed. I doubt that hydden have heard such voices or such song for many centuries, but for those who lived here . . .'

First an old, cracked, male voice, as of one who is dying. The voice of a hydden who hasn't got much time left now but needs to pass on what he knows to a new generation. Then, in answer and in counter-point, a much younger voice, a tenor, pure as a lark's flight. It rose above the first, back and forth across the sky, playing and dancing with the deeper notes it had been given, transforming them to something new that sang of life and hope.

Then the old voice again, deeper, broken, warning, encouraging, questioning, challenging, shot through with yearning for an era and youth gone by, shot through with sorrow.

A pause before the reply, which suddenly flew up from the withered undergrowth of the base, beating its wings into the thin air to gain height and find direction, encouraging the older voice in its own turn; the young giving the old a reason to live.

They sang and counter-sang, a duet that was beautiful in its sadness and loss, yearning and discovery. Its thought was all around them, but no more substantial than the mist itself which, as they listened, filled with the light of the rising sun so brightly that they had almost to hold their hands in front of their eyes not to be blinded.

The music that came to them then seemed as if made by the very Earth herself.

The words that were sung were distinct in parts but Katherine and Jack did not recognize the language. They looked to Stort for an explanation. He was standing now in his undershirt, trews round his ankles because he had forgotten to pull them up, head to one side as if to hear the better.

'It's plainchant,' he murmured, 'but of an unusual kind. Its sensuality and feeling of visceral communion borders on the blasphemous. The voices might be mortal lovers, the song an act of procreation.'

Jack ignored him, preferring to concentrate on practicalities because of the danger of Fyrd and his consciousness of the bodies that still lay below.

'Since they don't seem to know we're here,' he said, 'we'll stay just as we are until the mist clears or they show themselves. My guess is that they managed to escape the carnage below and have gone into hiding until they think the coast is clear.'

Stort hauled up his trews.

'This song is a liturgical rite of some kind, a song of celebration for lives led and a farewell to those who can no longer share the future. It will be followed by a funeral.'

Jack quietly packed up the camp while Katherine made breakfast for them all.

'We can't be sure the Fyrd won't return,' said Jack. 'In fact I think they will, and we're going to have to get out of here fast sooner rather than later. Stort, if you've business here, the moment the mist clears you'd better see to it. These choristers may know about the musical instrument.'

'The Quinterne. They almost certainly do; the question is will they tell me what they know? Knowledge of its *musica* may help us in some way in the weeks to come if and when we find the gem of Autumn.'

'Not if, when,' said Jack. 'We have to find it.'

'Why should they tell us?' said Katherine, giving him some mead to fortify him for the day.

'Why indeed?' said Stort. 'If Brief couldn't get it out of them, why should I do any better?'

The sun rose higher and burnt off the mist, revealing the three bodies among the rocks. Already rooks were hopping from rock to rock, eyeing each other, negotiating a pecking order.

'Look!' said Jack, 'There!'

A tall and sturdy young hydden emerged from the mist halfway up the hill. He was leading a much older one, white of hair and hunched, out of a cave and down the slippery slope.

He did so with infinite care, holding the older one's hand and waiting patiently while he summoned up strength and perhaps courage for the next alarming step downwards.

In this way, very slowly, they made it safely back to the riverside, stopping finally a few yards from the corpses.

They stared at them in very evident distress, bewildered and uncertain about what to do. Occasionally they broke into song, but it was in snatches and undirected, as if it was their way of thinking and talking to each other.

'Time for us to join them,' said Jack, 'and make ourselves known. You go ahead, Stort, and greet them; I might scare them off.'

It was a good suggestion.

Stort meandered down the slope, humming as he went, his tall gangly figure and long, thin stave and the way the morning sun caught his unruly red hair making him look the very picture of harmless eccentricity.

He waved a greeting long before he reached them.

They seemed surprised and wary, but after a brief consultation between themselves, after which the younger of the two cautiously picked up a very sturdy-looking stave, they acknowledged him with a wave in return.

Jack and Katherine stayed in the shadows until Stort was closer and had said his piece.

'My dear brethren,' he called out from the other side of the river, 'I, we, saw the cause of your distress yestereve.'

'We saw and watched you,' said the young one, who had a good, strong voice to fit his frame. 'But you'll forgive us, pilgrim . . . we have been witness to vile murder and must mourn good brothers who are now lost friends. Where are the two we saw with you?'

'Hiding,' said Stort frankly, 'for fear of frightening you away.'

'Why are you here? We have no visitors for months on end and then the Fyrd – may the Mirror take them back into its light so they are seen no more – and yourselves arrive. Something's strange with the world. Now . . . now . . .'

He turned away and the two brethren stared at their fallen comrades helplessly.

Stort signalled to Jack and Katherine and they crossed the bridge.

After a while, in which the two brothers chanted in low voices, Stort said, 'I don't know why I was drawn to come. It felt in the wyrd of things to do so. My mentor, Master Brief, came many years ago.'

The old one looked up.

'You knew him, the Master Scrivener of Brum?'

'He was as good as a father to me, brother.'

'He must be white-haired by now.'

'He is no more,' said Stort. 'He was killed by a representative of the Emperor of the Hyddenworld this Summer gone. He . . .'

They stared at each other mutely by the stream which flowed as quietly as their unspoken tears.

'My name is Bedwyn Stort. This is Katherine, mother of the Shield Maiden . . .'

The two brothers looked astonished.

'This is Jack, Stavemeister of Brum and a giant-born. Some who know the legends of Beornamund might fairly say . . .'

'They might fairly say,' said the old hydden, 'that he is *the* giant-born.'

'They might,' said Stort.

'Or they might not,' grinned Jack. 'If you need help . . .'

'We need help to make a pyre, that is what we need.'

Jack and Stort exchanged glances. Ritual and the courtesies of death were all very well but down there in the meadow, surrounded by hills, they were dangerously exposed. The mist had all but cleared, the sun was rising, it was the kind of day that Fyrd, perhaps still seeking something they had not found, would come back.

'Join us,' said the young one, and they did, standing in a circle around the three sorry bodies of the monks.

'Brothers,' said Stort, 'the Fyrd will come back. If they do it will be in numbers, and we are in no position to defend ourselves. Therefore . . .'

They nodded as if they understood and silence fell while they thought.

Finally the old one said, 'The names of our comrades were Compline, Sext and None . . .'

'Named after the liturgical hours of one of the human Christian sects,' murmured Stort.

'You are well informed, Master Stort. It was a usage of those who founded Mortaine many centuries ago. They founded, too, one of the great choirs in Christendom of which we two, old and young, are the remaining survivors and with us the music of the heavens that we sing.'

'So you are the Kapellmeister of this abbey who, if I remember right, is given the title, Meister Laud,' said Stort respectfully, 'and your good, bold friend must be Terce. First and third of the canonical hours.'

'Correct again! Our brothers died defending us – or rather, they sent us up to the caves when the Fyrd came and pretended they were the remaining three. They did not give us away, nor did they give the Fyrd what they wanted.'

'Which was?'

'The same as Master Brief wanted all those decades ago. The same, I am told, that the lutenist ā Faroün wanted when *he* came more than a century and a half ago. The same, I would imagine, you want.'

'The Quinterno,' said Stort softly.

'The same. Now . . . now . . .'

The old one shook his head in sadness and bent to say a prayer over each of the dead brothers, while Terce sang a song so exquisite in its melancholy that the rippling of the stream and the whispering reeds echoed it.

'We'll build a pyre,' said Jack, weakening. Anything less seemed blasphemous. 'Then, brothers, I will insist you come with us so we can get you to safety.'

It was agreed.

It was easy enough to find things to burn from the gorse and undergrowth thereabout. A great, solid pile of it they made of wood and tinder dried by the summer air.

Then Terce and Jack laid the bodies on one by one and Meister Laud suggested Katherine light the fire.

'Our lives have been hard in recent years, devoid of all comfort. Devoted to learning the *musica*. Too hard I think. We could have done with the female touch. Anything less is unnatural. Therefore, Mistress Katherine, I can tell you that our friends would have been content indeed to know that their pyre, which signifies that journey back to the stars, was lit by one as fair as you.'

She lit it as gently as he had spoken, in three places, and they watched together as the flames took.

But already Jack was restless again, eager to leave, aware of the danger of staying too long.

'The smoke will attract the Fyrd and hurry them along if they are already on the way.'

He had no sooner said this than Katherine fancied she heard a shout further down the river valley.

Terce said at once, and urgently, 'Leave this with me for a moment. I know this place . . .'

He retreated upslope a little, but cautiously, keeping to the cover of rocks and shrubs, to gain a vantage point.

Soon he was back.

'Six of them, just as before, coming up the valley. It will take them no more than half an hour to get here.'

Turning to Meister Laud, he said, 'Kapellmeister, we must leave!'

Jack gave a series of orders, putting Katherine and Stort in front, followed by Meister Laud, then Terce and finally himself.

'But . . .' expostulated Stort, concerned about something.

'But *nothing*,' said Jack, who knew Stort's propensity for delay even in the face of extreme danger. 'We go now!'

'But . . .'

'Later,' said Katherine, shoving him on.

'But later will be too late!' he protested.

They heard another shout from down the valley and he protested no more, but muttered instead, frowning and glowering over his shoulder.

Only when they were up through the pines and atop the ridge once more, but well out of sight in the long grass there, did Jack permit them to stop, catch their breath and have a drink.

The pyre was burning fiercely as the dark uniforms of the Fyrd came into view below.

Stort was not happy.

'I did not get a chance . . .'

Meister Laud smiled.

'You did not get a chance to find the Quinterne or learn what it was?'

'Can you tell me?' said Stort hopefully. 'I must assume that that ancient instrument has long since rotted away to dust?'

'Quite the opposite,' said Meister Laud. 'Tell him, Terce: you are now the best part of it.'

'Of what?'

Terce pointed at the distant pyre, at the rising smoke, at the sparks. He pointed at himself and at Meister Laud.

'The Quinterne is dead,' he said. 'Long live the Quinterne.'

Jack looked puzzled, Katherine too.

Stort as well, but only for a moment until his eyes widened in surprised and awed delight.

'That singing we heard this morning, the *musica* you and your ancestors have kept alive for centuries, and keep alive still, is that . . . ?'

Meister Laud smiled but shook his head.

'That singing is the Mirror's voice, or *musica*. We, the singers, are the instrument who keep the holy melodies of time and healing, harmony and peace, chaos and war alive. Ancient these songs, blissful their harmonies. *We* are the Quinterne and you, Master Stort, have found the last two of us.'

Jack stood up.

'Well then, we'd best keep you alive if . . .

'If . . .' said Katherine glancing at her friends.

'If . . .' declared Stort, speaking for them all, because it was now as clear as day to him why their wyrd had led them to Mortaine, 'if we are to fulfil our quest.'

'Which is?' asked Terce.

'To find the gem of Autumn.'

'And we can help you?'

'I think you can!'

12

OVER THE WIRE

In the days following his arrival at RAF Croughton, Arthur made a good show of being old and well below his best. His contributions to the symposium were deliberately vague and circumlocutory. He also insisted on a daily so-called jog, which was a near-comic act put on to delude his captors, as he now thought of them. He was surprised to find that, even after just a few sessions, comic or not, he felt and looked fitter.

An orderly always followed, encouraging him to go to the base's gym rather than the open field, which he refused to do.

'Fresh air's the thing!' he cried heartily, something his father used to say.

He always took his little 'sac, putting into it some deep muscle lotion someone found for him, a knee support and a bottle of water. In this way he habituated the orderlies to his little habits and gradually, not least because he seemed so doddery, their watch over him relaxed.

They did not seem to mind how near the fence he went, nor how he used its structural angle irons to lean on and press against; and, lying on the ground with his feet to the wire as a restraint, aping sit-ups, his hands behind his head. He decided against trying to cut the wire before his attempted escape, though he took the wire-cutter out on one of his keep-fit runs to see if it worked. It did. What he did do was work out which section to cut, choosing an area where the attachment to the ground was rusted and loose.

This was not as near to the area he wanted to get to as he would have wished, but there seemed no better option. The nearer area was fenced in newer, thick wire.

His fall-back was the second area and that, at least, was visible across two fields. This was common ground, along a footpath and over stiles; evidently a right of way. But it ran a hundred yards or more from where he would need to get to.

There were security cameras at various points along the fence, one of which pointed his way. That was a risk he would have to take. It meant he would have to be all the quicker.

The sense of being imprisoned descended nightly and grew ever worse.

Doors were locked, corridors were patrolled, services closed down at ten and most lights went off. Only twice did aircraft come in at night. He was naturally curious to see what was happening but was sufficiently sure he was being watched, or could be, that he played the tired old man, and remained reading or watching TV and going to bed early.

On the afternoon of the third day, after Bohr had put out feelers concerning the Hyddenworld, he finally raised the issues that Arthur least wanted to discuss in an open session, perhaps to draw him out. What he revealed was, to Arthur, a sensational confirmation of what Arthur had only been able to theorize about before.

'In this session,' began Bohr very seriously, 'I want to present some temporal data which has emerged in the field research after several of the major incidents . . .'

He reeled off a list of eight countries where extreme and unusual seismic and or meteorological incidents had occurred in the last week, starting with two European incidents, in Italy and the Czech Republic and ending with two more in China.

'We believe that last episode, which combined the opening of a new fault line across the Yangtze River with perverse rainfall patterns just before, resulted in the drowning of more than eight hundred thousand people. There have been far worse events in Chinese history, but none as bad as that in recent years, or ever in the area affected.

'I will now summarize what we have found and then suggest some lines for further research. This is, of course, the primary area of Professor Foale's interest and expertise and I am sure . . .'

His voice took on the menace of which Bohr was so capable.

'. . . that we will all look forward to his contribution. In essence the facts are these: in every case of those major incidents there has been a dislocation of time. In some cases of a few seconds, in others of minutes, in two cases of three days. Basically, the people within these areas have, in fact, rather than in fancy, experienced a time shift.'

This was the moment which the symposium had been building towards, or rather the revelation it had been led to expect. It was sensational.

'Let me be clear. Our data, which is in the dossier you have just been given, shows that these shifts were real, though localized. Clocks and watches and any other device that measured time moved with the shift. This was no illusion or change imagined in people's minds. Quite the opposite in fact. They were not aware of it until after it had happened and even then could not believe it. It was as if they blinked and on opening their eyes had lost seconds, or hours or days, with no recall of what had happened in that time – *because nothing had.* This was not amnesia, where life went on for three days during which its victim suffered memory loss. It was a real and instantaneous shift. The implications are grave, so grave that you are here to give peer-group scrutiny of our data, methods and conclusions. And then . . . well . . .'

For once Bohr looked less than absolutely confident.

'We can discuss the data and its implications this evening after a break of two hours . . . I will only state the obvious. If it be true that the world is experiencing differential time shifts of even a second, let alone days, then the potential for the absolute disaster of temporal instability is already on us. Time may be relative but what I might call the mortal world functions successfully because it treats it as linear. Time shifts destroy that. Yet there are societies, even whole species, which may well function successfully with such shifts. I might call them other worlds . . .' He looked at Arthur meaningfully before continuing: 'If so, we need to investigate them to prepare ourselves and world governance to cope with that eventuality . . . In that regard we shall welcome Professor Foale's early contribution when we reconvene. Meanwhile, my colleague . . .'

Bohr handed over the presentation to a NASA official who began running through video evidence of the shifts, starting with an interview with a Japanese office worker who blinked and lost two days, and continuing with the bizarre story of an intensive care unit for heart patients in Portugal where the equipment showed conclusively that four days had elided into a period of thirty six hours.

Arthur's concentration waned.

Bohr's reference to 'other worlds' meant nothing less than the Hyddenworld.

'You've been avoiding any discussion about the Hyddenworld, Arthur,' said Bohr, buttonholing him, 'but you must understand that we now need your input. Some folk are flying in from the USA tomorrow and they'll want to talk to you. "No" is not in their vocabulary. It would be better if you talked with us here first, or if you prefer, just to me . . .'

It was the threat Arthur had feared and he knew that the time had come to make his attempt to get away.

His airbase antics had given him a good idea of layout and he used a different route to get to his favourite spot each time. More particularly, it had shown him the spot where he needed to aim for. That afternoon he closed his door, retied his shoes so the laces were tight, though that caused pain to his arthritic right big toe, and packed the 'sac with those extra things he would need, including, once more, the wire-cutters.

His stave he had already been using for his daily routines, aping a television show he had seen where such things were used for a Japanese form of combat. It was ridiculous, he knew, but it allayed suspicion that he had a quite different motive.

As usual an orderly was waiting outside his room, in trainers and a tracksuit.

'Ready, sir?'

Arthur, who was as ready as he ever would be for what he intended, said, 'I've never had a close look at that baseball field.'

The suggestion worked. They exited the building and then turned that way, through a gate and onto the field, most of which was sand and grit.

He let the orderly explain the game until, reaching his arms above his head as if to stretch, he suggested they head off westward across the base.

The base felt wide open on that side. It was windy, the grass rough, the satellite dishes behind them, the nearest part of the fence three hundred yards off to their right. There were security cameras at regular intervals along the top of the fence.

Arthur knew that the greater the distance he could put between him and the orderly, the greater his chances of not being seen cutting the wire.

The grass gave way briefly to tarmac, then a road, then grass again. The perimeter fence got nearer, the guard stayed close.

Arthur made a left, following the line of the fence at a distance. Lights began coming on all round the perimeter and over near the dishes. He saw two men with dogs. His man waved, they waved back and shouted.

'I'll leave you men to chat,' Arthur said, jogging off towards the fence.

He hoped he looked ridiculous.

He did.

The marines chatted, gazing occasionally his way, too polite to say anything about him, more interested in dogs, new postings and sport.

The portion of the fence he needed got nearer, the lights atop them brighter, making what lay beyond impossible to see. But he knew it was there. It had been there for over five thousand years. It was there still on Google Earth. It was a pity it was just beyond the fence. As for the one that was further off, he could not see across the first field for the glare.

He headed for his spot and began his routines, this time punching at the fence as if boxing. Then pressing against it, cutters in hand.

Snip by snip he cut three-quarters of a rough rectangle, first the uprights to two feet high, then the horizontal. He did not bother with the bit along the ground; the bit he had cut would just bend outward and he could crawl over it.

He turned twice to check if he was being watched. He was not.

It felt as if it took a long time and that at any moment he would be seen. The last snip completed, he pushed the wire outward, though with difficulty, for the points snagged each other. But then it was free, lolloping forward, and it was time to go.

He resisted the temptation to look back, went down slowly on his knees, did some silly exercise a couple of times which enabled him to push the 'sac through, and then, clumsily, with difficulty, he pushed his way through the hole.

Cut wire caught at his vest, which tore before he was free. Then he was through and up and looking round to see if they had seen.

Astonishingly they had not, or not quite.

His usual guard turned slowly his way and stared and looked away.

Arthur had the presence of mind to bend down and push the wire back, re-entangling the jagged ends with each other so the hole was not obvious. Then he turned, walked a few paces so sudden movement did not make him obvious, and then made his way quickly across the ground towards the centre of the vestigial Iron Age circle defined by paler grass – a distance of about seventy yards.

As he reached it he heard a shout, then a bark and a whistle. But at first he could see nothing because of the lights in his eyes. As another shout came, his eyes finally made out the pale grass and he turned into the ancient circle it formed.

What now? Dexter or sinister? Feel the circle's power, turn and turn again into its strength, Judith, help me, remind me . . . you did this best of all . . .

As he began running round inside the circle, trying to remember how to work the portal and make the entrance into the Hyddenworld, there was a thump against the wire fence nearby. The dogs had arrived and stood snarling and scrabbling to get at him. They were seventy yards from the hole he had made and began quartering back and forth, trying to pick up his scent.

He circled once, then twice, and one of the guards arrived, also on the far side of the fence.

As Arthur turned sinister in the circle again he felt none of the drag of power he knew he should, or the brief rush of pain through his body. Nothing, nothing at all.

One of the dogs got near to the hole but turned back a yard or two from it, beginning a new quarter again.

The guard began examining the fence, running towards where Arthur normally exercised.

Breathless now, Arthur decided to try the other circle. He set off across the field towards the stile in the distance.

He heard a command behind, the snarling bark of the dogs and ran faster. He reached the stile and heaved himself over it and carried on.

There was a shout behind him: 'Professor, stop! You can't . . . !'

I damn well can!

He reached the far side of the second field, climbed over the next stile. He hoped he might see signs of a circle in the grass but the light was now bad and he saw nothing. But his spatial memory was good and he headed where he knew the second circle must be. He hoped that once he reached it he might feel its power, know its lines, lean his being into the whorl and wend of it, let it take him.

A dog leapt and he kicked at it and it fell back on the far side of the stile as he dropped over the other side.

Another scrabbled at the stile, snarling, whining, and desperate to get at him.

As it forced its way up the first step and through he heard a whistle and shouted command.

Then: 'Professor, you can't get away! Please, stop!'

If they had called off the dogs, fearful of elderly academics suing the base, he had a chance. He took it, stumbling forward once more, the field rough under foot. Another shout. He looked back for orientation, veered left and with his last strength pulled himself forward, leg after heavy leg, knees buckling, head forward.

'Professor Foale!'

He felt the sudden power of the ancient circle, turning dexter at once to gain its power to himself, straining for it. He heaved off his pack and held it tight to his chest to let its hydden power add itself all the more to his weaker energy, closed his eyes before turning sinister just when he should.

The guard, the human, entered the circle too.

Arthur remembered something Stort had told him.

I believe, he had said, *that the last thing you should think of is not the place you want to go, but the thing it is you seek . . .*

The guard lunged towards him as Arthur thought of the gem of Autumn.

Help me . . .

Then he felt the power surge into him, painful and frightening until he began flying into the Hyddenworld. Then he was falling, he was rolling in a whirl and spiralling out of the orbit of the torches' lights away from the circle, to dexter of the man who had almost reached him, all big and murky; and then he was scrambling, the great grass round him; he was running, he was sliding, he was breathing deep, deep gulps of air.

'Pro . . .'

The guard's cry fractured and broke away, flying that way, Arthur this, human no more.

The human world shot away behind him and the Hyddenworld began to welcome him in.

'Sinister,' he heard himself mutter desperately, 'dexter . . . and, and, and . . . what is it that I seek?'

He heard himself say 'gem' but the word was torn from his mouth and stretched away behind him like the white silk scarf his father once let him wear.

Then that was gone and the only thought that came to his retreating mind, over which he found he had less and less control, were two orbs of light dancing in the dark: headlights maybe, torches probably, their beams searching for him, one or other nearer and nearer until suddenly they shone sharp and deep into his eyes, blinding him, taking him, the shadows peripheral now as he was sucked away and out of reach of the puzzled guards who were left alone and bemused in a henge they did not even know was there.

'Professor?' they said weakly.

But Arthur Foale was gone.

13
BACK TO BRUM

'Keep down and stay silent,' ordered Jack, coolly. 'If, as is possible, I come under attack, I will go forward and engage, and Stort will lead you others to safety, with Katherine taking up the rear. Terce, you will stay with Meister Laud and help him along as best you can.'

Terce nodded.

Meister Laud look anxious and confused.

'Jack . . .' began Katherine.

He looked at her sharply and shook his head. This was no time for doubts or indecision. Each must know what they were doing.

'Is that understood?' he said. 'If I am attacked, you flee and hide. I will find you. Yes?'

'Yees . . .' they agreed hesitantly, one by one.

'Stort?'

'Indeed,' he said calmly. Where others' safety was concerned he could be relied on.

'Katherine?'

She nodded, grimmer than all of them. Perhaps she had most to lose.

'So, now . . .'

It was four days since they had left Abbey Mortaine. The Fyrd had not followed them then but they had run into several patrols along the way and the nearer they got to Brum, the more frequent the patrols became.

As did evidence of Fyrd brutality.

They had come upon several corpses of young hydden males who Jack guessed had offended or resisted them.

They had, as well, found the violated corpses of two females, probably a mother and daughter, their spouses or some other male family members nearby, mutilated.

Their journey had ceased to be pleasant in any way. It was now a grim exercise in survival through a landscape that felt increasingly tense as local hydden trusted no one and made themselves scarce, while even the birds, as Katherine observed, fell silent and the vegetation and woods curiously sullen.

It had become the strange and untoward August the village sages predicted when they began their journey three weeks before.

They might have wished that they had returned straight to Brum from White Horse Hill, but had they done so, how much might they have lost? The experience of the Scythe of Time on the Malvern Hills had put a sense of urgency into the quest for the gem; while the strange way they had made their way to Abbey Mortaine, and their rescue of the Quinterne in the form of Meister Laud and Terce gave them all the clear sense that the quest was on the right track. What these things meant they did not yet know, but time shifts and *musica* seemed of the essence, if only they could understand them better.

Now there was a new reason, if a nerve-racking one, for being glad of the diversion. Their route north of Mortaine was by the Gloucestershire–Warwickshire railway line, the same one that Dodd had continued on after they left him. The first twenty miles had proved safe enough, the problem being not the Fyrd but Meister Laud's ailing health.

The climb out from Abbey Mortaine had been hard on him, the trekking since harder still, and grief at the violent loss of his lifelong friends, as the other choristers had been, had taken him over. He was tired, listless and in pain and it was all Terce could do to keep him going.

After twenty miles, the Fyrd's presence was ever greater, especially along the railways lines, and Jack realized that circumstance had put them into the position of being unseen observers of what he had feared might happen since he and Stort had wrested the gems of Spring and

Summer from the Imperial Court in Bochum in July: a punitive invasion of Englalond.

Now, as they reached the main lines into Brum, or branches of them, evidence of the invasion increased. He and Katherine began making notes of how and where the Fyrd were disposed, their numbers, weaponry and supply lines.

He had no doubt that his counterparts in Brum itself – Igor Brunte, Meyor Feld, and the redoubtable civilian leader Lord Festoon – were collecting and collating what data they could.

'That's all very well, Jack,' warned Katherine, 'but data's no good if it dies with you.'

The night before they had reached the little-used railway line between Henley-in-Arden and Turner's Green, in Warwickshire. It was cross-country, but the direct route from Henley was blocked by Fyrd.

It was now a murky early morning and their safe detour had taken them to an embankment, on the other side of which was the London–Birmingham rail track.

They watched as Jack crawled up it to see if the line was clear, it being impossible to see from so far below, and no Fyrd had been seen on top. If it was, then they might pick up a train at one of the stopping points and travel undercroft into the heart of Brum. This was a common form of transport for experienced hydden, where they travelled on narrow boards fixed under trains, lying there for the duration of a journey.

He went very carefully. The bank was made of stones that shifted at the slightest pressure and the sparse vegetation that grew on it was dry, the seed husks of fumitory all too ready to spring open at the slightest touch and reveal his presence to any Fyrd who might be patrolling along the track.

They watched his slow progress up the steep bank, stiffening when they heard him make the slightest sound. There were bushes at the top and they lost sight of him in the foliage, except for his feet and the end of his stave, which trailed behind him. He was there a long time before he came back down, shaking his head.

'Useless,' he said. 'There are Fyrd down there too, near the signals where the train stops and we might have boarded.'

Right on cue, they heard a train approach from the direction of London beyond the embankment Jack had just descended.

'It would be so easy . . .' said Stort, who now wanted to get back to Brum as much as the others.

'Easy to be seen,' said Jack firmly. 'We'll have to find another way.'

The Kapellmeister's condition took a turn for the worse that morning, caused no doubt by the stress of the past days. His chest hurt, the sores on his feet began to weep and bleed, he was unable to keep warm, moaning and whispering, with his fingers fretting at the covers they put on him.

Worse, he stopped being able to sing, his throat being painful and dry, and this caused him great distress.

'He needs the ministrations of a goodwife,' said Stort. 'I do believe I know the best . . .'

He was thinking of his own, Goodwife Cluckett, his stern and forbidding housekeeper, who had nursed him back to health at the beginning of Summer; and later Jack as well.

'She'll know what to do with him,' said Stort, 'if only we can get him to Brum.'

The sojourn under cover confirmed beyond doubt that the line they had now reached had been commandeered by the Fyrd for the purpose of getting troops rapidly into Brum. They saw reinforcements arrive with each train that stopped at the signal above them. The numbers were increasing all the time.

They were heavily armed, more than was needed for ordinary patrols. They were also making themselves more obvious than seemed necessary.

'They want to put off other hydden using the train,' said Katherine.

'And they're succeeding,' said Jack. 'The sooner we get back and warn Brum, the better. The question is, how?'

It was a question answered in an unexpected way.

They decided to leave in the dead of night, having rested up through the day.

All seemed well until they reached that part of the path that was within the light-fall of the M1 motorway, which ran parallel with the railway and the path they were taking to get further north.

They were hurrying along, trying to escape the light above, when they heard a shout from the road's parapet.

Fyrd!

'Move!' said Jack.

But they were plainly visible and there was no obvious way of getting out of sight quickly.

'Stop and wait!' the Fyrd called down.

'Run!' said Jack.

Next moment, a crossbow bolt whizzed past Katherine's head.

'*Faster!*'

A second came hissing down and hit Stort's 'sac.

If they had been able to run under the motorway and out of the Fyrd's line of sight they would have done so, but a hefty boarded fence topped by barbed wire stopped that.

Then a shadow appeared ahead and the bulky form of a hydden.

Jack ran forward with his stave raised, as did Terce, and they might have struck the hydden down had he not said, 'This way, quick!'

He stood his ground, risking being fired upon by the Fyrd above before hurrying them through a gap in the fence into shadows.

When they were all safe, they turned to see who had intervened.

'Greeting, Mister Jack and friends!' he said.

'Who . . . ?'

It was impossible to make out his face in the dark.

'Dodd's the name and it's Dodd again. Been watching and saw you earlier coming off that embankment. Reckoned you'd eventually come back this way . . .'

'But . . .'

'No time for chat, not here. Them up above will come on down, but it'll take them time. Follow me close, it be a windy sort of way, but it's the best out of here now. There are many Fyrd about in these parts.'

He led them away by a route that they could never have found by themselves, under the motorway and back again, on through the night, the Fyrd left behind.

At his first stop Dodd said, 'I suppose you're still wanting to get to Brum? Me too! There's only one way from here that's going to be safe, which I imagine you have already worked out?'

'Well,' said Stort, 'failing the rail, and the road not being easy for hydden unless you know the ropes, which we do not, I fear I am thinking that we're in for a boat trip.'

Katherine and Jack looked at each other. Stort was about to lead them into the unknown. Unfortunately it looked like he had an ally in Dodd, who was nodding vigorously at every word he said.

'Try us,' said Jack.

'All we need is a light watercraft, a large outboard engine and some fuel, and a watercourse between here and Brum. Then . . .'

'No,' said Katherine.

'I don't think so,' said Jack.

'Be bold!' cried Stort, 'and the world is yours.'

He turned cheerfully to Dodd: 'You can't mean a river, there is none direct to Brum. You must mean a canal. The Stratford-upon-Avon perhaps?'

Dodd laughed conspiratorially.

'You know it, Mister Stort? Tell 'em the treat we have in store for 'em is bold!'

'I know it from the towpath only. And what I know is that it's too problematic were we to attempt to take a boat. Too many bends, too many locks. No, if we are to be bold it must be the Grand Union.'

'Which is where from here, exactly?' asked Jack reluctantly.

Stort turned to Dodd and raised a questioning brow.

'Not far, one and all. Less than a mile from here and there's an underpass for cows which will serve our needs should Fyrd be on the track overhead, which they were last time I looked.'

'Why haven't you gone that way already?'

'You can't work the Union without a crew and that's what we're going to be. And with humans about at weekends a weekday is better.'

'And who's to be the skipper?' asked Jack.

'Dodd will step into that breach if Dodd must.'

Two hours and a stolen boat and an outboard engine later, Dodd did.

But just before they embarked on this new stage of their journey Katherine said, looking puzzled, 'Did you say earlier that today's a weekday? I thought it was a Sunday.'

'Dodd did make that observation,' said Dodd, 'because a weekday it is. A Tuesday, in fact.'

'Either I can't count my days,' said Katherine quietly, 'or somewhere since we first arrived at Half Steeple on the Severn, we have lost two days.'

Stort frowned and thought a bit.

'Of *that*,' he finally said enigmatically, 'we must talk more. I would venture to suggest on that evidence alone, that Half Steeple is a place we should be very cautious about ever visiting again.'

'All aboard!' cried Dodd, cutting their talk short. 'After what I heard today from a passing pedlar who dared to do some business with the Fyrd, we have a good reason to hasten back to Brum.'

They fell silent as one and turned to him.

'Good news or ill?' asked Jack.

'Hard to say,' said Dodd. 'It seems that the Hyddenworld has a new Emperor.'

'What happened to Slaeke Sinistral, the old one?'

'Dead. Deposed. Or "Disappeared". Don't ask me! Now, let's be on our way.'

14
THE NEW EMPEROR

As emperors went, Niklas Blut was not an impressive figure, even when dressed in his robes of office and surrounded by the panoply of state and court officials. Sitting upon his throne in the Great Chamber in the Imperial City of Bochum in north-west Germany, his courtiers in attendance, his official champion Witold Slew standing guard, the senior Fyrd present and trumpets and suchlike blowing, he looked like the grey bureaucrat he had so recently been rather than the Imperial leader he now was, having been enthroned, crowned and generally sanctified before the Mirror-of-All and his people on August 2nd of that same year. What a contrast the rough and ready world of Englalond was to the sedate, predictable and orderly life of the Imperial Court. But it was in Englalond he now was, plucked by circumstance, political necessity and his own wyrd from all he knew into the light of day and finding himself where he had no wish to be.

No wonder he was finding being Emperor a lot harder than he could ever have thought possible.

True, the position gave him power, but it was not, he was rapidly discovering, unlimited power. In fact it was remarkably circumscribed – by the civilian wing of his administration on one side, represented by Chief Courtier Vayle, and on the military by the formidable and ruthless General Quatremayne.

Niklas Blut had not sought office.

For the previous twenty years he had been blissfully occupied behind the scenes of Court and Empire as Commander of the Emperor's Private Office.

It was a role that suited him perfectly. He was highly intelligent, highly organized and highly motivated in the practice of the art and science of government and administration.

He was beyond loyal to his remarkable recent employer, the Emperor Slaeke Sinistral I, as he liked to be known. In fact, there was no II or III because Sinistral had been Emperor for more than a century and alive for a good many decades more than that. He was, in Blut's view, and that of many others, nothing less than a genius.

Certainly, the world that the former Emperor Slaeke Sinistral I had created in Bochum was unique. Unlike most hydden cities, which nestle on the surface in the deep secret interstices of their human counterparts, it was largely subterranean. In only seventy years it had become the heart and administrative capital of the Hyddenworld,

It extended from the first to the eighteenth levels of the abandoned coal mines which lie under the human city of the same name in the Ruhr Valley in North Rhine-Westphalia, western Germany, making it nearly half a mile deep.

A very few surface buildings were cleverly concealed from humans in an area of ruined and dangerous mine tips, factories and toxic wasteland to the west of the city. These were used as residences by senior officials, or for occasional respite and vacation by a few lucky hydden workers who otherwise spent their lives below ground.

For the most part, Bochum's life was conducted in the first few levels. Level 1 was a buffer to the human world above, consisting of tunnels used for communication laterally and by shafts vertically to the levels below.

The Imperial Court – its officials, courtiers, officers and the many related institutions that served them – was on Level 2, the airiest and most pleasant part of the city. Bochum's commercial heart was on Level 3, where banks and counting houses and other institutions had been established. The Imperial army or Fyrd occupied Level 4, and from Level 5 downwards much that was covert or required security was carried out. Access there was only by express permission. Here were the city archives, money vaults, penal institutions and the utilities.

These five levels were all serviced by vertical shafts which carried power lines, ventilation, fuel supplies and accommodated various lifts and chutes. The perimeters at each level were clearly defined and it was a serious offence to go, or attempt to go, into the continuation of the tunnels beyond. Below Level 9 little happened until Levels 17 and 18, where the Emperor mainly dwelt.

The many tunnels at all levels beyond the confines of Bochum were degraded, collapsed, flooded, broken and defunct. But everyone in Bochum had a story about the hydden folk who lived there, creatures of the dark and the night, of a lowly uncivilized kind who would kill and eat you if they could.

The only certain thing, because they were seen from time to time, was that whatever the dark history of these 'Remnant tunnels', a peculiar species of bilgesnipe lived there. Which meant that down in the deep levels there must be water, for the chubby, greasy bilgesnipe were a water-folk, skilled in all matters maritime and fluvial. The Remnant bilgesnipe of Bochum were unique for being albino and blind, doubtless caused by inbreeding and living too long without light.

The deepest levels of this great Imperial complex were 17 and 18, which were the Emperor's private domain and the place from which the real work of running the Empire, as opposed to Bochum itself, was done. Access was by way of a lift from the corridors behind the Throne on Level 2, to which only a few senior executives had access

These lower levels, despite the fact that the Emperor lived there, were much less well maintained than the busier ones above. They were ill-lit, unpainted and unswept. The detritus of human mining operations was everywhere – rusting machines, narrow-gauge rail tracks, stacks of wooden pit props, piles of spare parts. Even the skeletons of lost souls, human or hydden, who had found their way into that cold, dripping, eternally dark and draughty place and become disorientated were sometimes found.

The Great Chamber on Level 2 had a strange and mysterious vast counterpart at Level 18, which was why Slaeke Sinistral spent so much of his time down there.

This was the Chamber of Sleep, which was as wide and tall as the greatest human buildings. Its roof was unreachable and unexplored and from it fell endless drips of water, hundreds and thousands of them, carrying dissolved lime. The lime was deposited on whatever lay on the floor beneath, turning wooden sleepers, rails, cog wheels, capstans, coiled hawsers, great metal tools and even a steam engine into sickly pale, swollen versions of themselves, their form only vaguely discernible when light was carried into the terrible dark.

In addition to the endless rain there were constant draughts and contradictory winds from the innumerable fissures, cracks, faults and broken tunnels in the chamber walls and its roofs.

This combination of falling water and draughts, which sometimes whispered and occasionally raged, produced a miracle of sound, which Slaeke Sinistral recognized the moment he heard it as the *musica*. Endless, self-perpetuating patterns of harmonic sound produced in the great Chamber by what he called the four dimensions: falling rain, endless wind, an unfathomable space . . . and time. By *musica* he meant *Musica Universalis*, which ancients called the Music of the Spheres, the harmony of all things, the sound of the Universe. Sinistral had found a place and a new preoccupation for his later life.

The Empire he built from the base of a ruined business, of which the Fyrd were the warriors and enforcers of his power and the civilians in Bochum the executives, became to him no more than a pastime. His real work lay in learning how to meld his spirit and body, his mind and soul, with the *musica* and through that with the Universe.

To sustain himself and his life beyond that normally allotted to mortals – he was born in the mid-nineteenth century in Brum – he had recourse to the power that lay in the gem of Summer which he had secretly possessed for more than a century.

The energy from this gem kept him alive, but cruelly so.

At first its power sustained him for many decades, but gradually he needed more and more of its light and fire – which was nothing less than the Fires of the Universe – because each period of recovery lasted for a shorter time.

Gradually his times of decline and recuperative sleep before another exposure to the gem lengthened.

The last, which was overseen by Blut, who started the period as a young hydden and ended it at the beginning of his middle age, lasted eighteen years.

Throughout these successive and ever-longer periods of sleep, the Emperor lay in the cocoon of a dentist's chair in the Chamber of Sleep, bathed in the *musica*, learning all the time, his body and spirit leaking into the ether as the *musica* fed into him.

His beauty, which was always great – tall, graceful, fair, well made, shot through with the light of intelligence, good humour and a growing compassion – grew greater, yet more fragile as the decades passed.

It had been Blut who dared discover the secret of Sinistral's longevity. Though only a very junior official in Hamburg at the time, aged eighteen, he had minutely studied Sinistral's strange episodes of illness followed by recovery and wondered how he did it. What made Blut so exceptional was that, having asked the question, he found the answer. The clue lay in the stark fact that Sinistral's periods of wellness got steadily shorter, his periods of recovery, which meant retreat and sleep, were getting longer. So much so that he was absent from things more than he was present. Yet he so organized his Court, he appointed representatives with such skill and his charisma was so great that no one ever moved to depose him during his 'sleeps'.

What Blut discovered was that Emperor Slaeke Sinistral's source of strength and startling recoveries to youthfulness and vigour while all around him aged and died like normal hydden was that he possessed the gem of Summer, the second of the 'lost' gems that the Mercian CraftLord Beornamund so fatefully made in the sixth century.

He also discovered that Sinistral came by the gem by dint of removing it from its possessor and mentor, ã Faroün, famed architect, lutenist, philosopher and genius. Whether Sinistral did this through murder or some other means, foul or fair, had been a matter of debate since the nineteenth century.

That Blut had worked this out was remarkable, but it was nearly fatal. He was only rescued from sentence of death by Sinistral himself. He recognized in the eighteen-year-old a talent of a very remarkable kind.

Instead of having him executed, he trained him and later elevated him from miserable Hamburg to glorious Bochum and there put him in charge of his office on Level 18.

It was a stroke of brilliance.

As the power of the gem of Summer had worn off once more,

Sinistral began to age very rapidly and he realized that this sleep might be the longest of all, perhaps terminal. In the event, he slept for eighteen years, during which, having been duly instructed by Sinistral himself, Blut held the reins of power and managed them masterfully.

Through that time he matured, he married, he had two children and he got to know the ins and outs of the Empire better than anyone alive, bar Sinistral himself. As for his loyalty, it never wavered, not for a moment. It even increased as he understood Sinistral's flexibility in imposing the harsh rule of the Fyrd so necessary in founding a great enterprise, and then relaxing it, little by little, as the different parts of the Empire matured.

Sinistral's judgement had been sound. Niklas Blut was the perfect servant: he had a grasp of details, a subtle, clever mind that saw the warp and weft of people and situations, and absolutely no interest in being master.

What Sinistral had gambled on before he retreated to his Chamber of Sleep was that, during his absence, the prophecy concerning Beornamund's lost gems would come true. Simply stated, this was that a group of honest and rather ordinary hydden would somehow find the lost gem of Spring, the first of the four, because it would be needed to save the world.

Sinistral was not sure of that, but he felt certain that if he was to continue his long reign, which he was sure he would wish to do when he woke up, he would need to add to his arsenal of self-recovery the gem of Spring, as well as that of Summer.

What he did not reckon with at all when he awoke was that he himself might have changed fundamentally during his time of sleep, so much so that he might lose all interest in notions of an eternal life, but desire at last to age as mortals do.

In his case, the ageing was rather rapid, for his body had taken youth into itself artificially and, once he eschewed further contact with Beornamund's gems and their power, the years would catch up with him very swiftly indeed.

But that was now of no consequence to him.

He knew the reason for this change of heart, this acceptance of death. His long years of sleep had taken place to the eternal, ever-changing *musica* of the Universe. It had entered his being, his soul, and so sensitized him to life and death, to the Earth and the Universe, that he understood as others could not that his time of rule was over. Like an eastern mystic, or one who has dwelt in the desert and seen the truth, Sinistral had seen the truth of things.

All is illusion.

All is but a reflection which, for the hydden, is made in that infinitesimally thin Mirror-of-All, that fragile shifting plane, on whose near-non-existent surface all things seem to be, yet nothing is at all.

In his remaining months, for he knew that was all the time he had, Sinistral wished to journey into the *musica*, to understand the nature of the gems and the fires that had sustained him, and discover how illusions cease to be and what there is, if anything, once they are no more.

Perfect peace?

Utter chaos?

Endless silence?

No-thing?

Sinistral did not know but he wished to find out.

Which Blut understood, deeply and well.

His master must be master no more if he was to be free to follow where the *musica* led him. To a place, Blut guessed, where illusion ceased to be and all was truth.

To Blut, whose admiration for Sinistral had turned to a nearly filial love, this final decision in the great hydden made him respect him even more.

But he had naturally always feared what might happen after Sinistral's demise. It came as a shock to discover that he wished to abdicate his position, but after they had discussed the reasons why, and Blut fully understood them, he knew what he must do and did it.

He took control and claimed the Emperor's throne for himself, coolly and calmly, without bloodshed or rancour, doing his best to behave, as Sinistral had taught him to, as if he was born for it.

He was clever and assured enough to stake his claim in the presence of the most likely contenders for the office on the military and civilian side and to have them acknowledge his ascendancy over Sinistral.

The primary weapon he therefore had to sustain him in office was legitimate title.

The second was subtler and more powerful by far if only he could act on it decisively. He was greatly feared for what he knew and might do to those who challenged him.

Feared as well for what he knew about every individual in the Imperial Court, the records of whom he had himself compiled.

Feared for the access he had had to Sinistral and all that meant in terms of his knowledge of Imperial governance, law and the strategy of power. Even if Blut was not plotting, it would always be assumed that he was, and that was enough, for the time being, to keep his enemies at bay.

He was feared for the obvious speed of his thought and the eclectic power of his mind. He not only appeared to know more than anyone about the Empire, in detail and depth; he actually did so. He had the power of recall of almost every decision taken over the past twenty years in terms of the pros and cons and the outcomes. It was hard to pull the wool over Blut's eyes.

Though he did not look Imperial close-up, that intelligence shone through and gave him a charisma that he was inclined to underestimate.

Court satirists, when making mock of Blut, had recourse to the same physical characteristic every time to convey the hydden himself: his round gold-rimmed spectacles. These were of flat glass which he kept spotlessly clean. They sent disconcerting oval reflections all about the place as he spoke, which occasionally shone directly into the eyes of those talking to him, leaving the uncomfortable feeling that Blut had glimpsed their soul and laid it bare.

Then, when someone saw past the glass, they found themselves staring into discomfiting pools of a grey, unwavering kind, as unyielding as ice.

This was not to say that Blut himself was hard. Far from it. He had a sentimental side, the wife he loved, the children he cherished, the modest lifestyle that suited him. True, his office had always demanded a discretion that prevented him forming close friendships, but there was no evidence that he had ever abused his position of power and trust, and never had been.

More than that, no one who ever witnessed the robust nature of his conversations with Slaeke Sinistral could doubt for one moment that he had felt for his former Emperor anything but abiding respect and deep love. Nor could anyone think that he had plotted Sinistral's sudden abdication or that the fact of it caused him anything but disappointment and pain.

Blut might well be called the most reluctant Emperor who ever lived.

But that did not make him unmindful of the danger he was in. Feared he might be – for now. He did not underestimate how quickly that fear might turn to simple dislike; dislike to disrespect; and disrespect to that dangerous other place of secret meetings, shadowy conferences and private cabals which, if not nipped in the bud, turned in a few moments to revolt and overthrow.

In short, Blut knew that his new position rested on shaky and fragile foundations which needed attention – and fast.

The question that he immediately began to ponder was to where the people's energies should be directed.

After that, he knew, the next question would be when.

The answer to that was easy: sooner than later and sooner than his enemies expected.

Surprise was of the essence, as Sinistral had also taught him.

But there was a difficulty and it was a grave one.

Blut assumed power towards the end of July, following the departure of Jack and the others from Bochum, where by courage and outrageous good fortune they recovered the gems of Spring and Summer. He knew very well that Sinistral regarded the loss of the gems with relief rather than horror. The bold act by the hydden from Englalond had given him the liberty he needed to give up his dependence on the gems.

But the Court and the Fyrd were a different matter. To them, and especially the intransigent and unpleasant Commander-in-Chief of the Fyrd, Quatremayne, the theft of the gems was an affront to pride and threat to their positions they could not let go unchallenged.

Blut was forced at once to make a difficult and dangerous decision. He knew his history well enough to realize that the first thing he ought to do was to consolidate his power and elevate individuals who would owe their loyalty to him rather than themselves, now that their former Emperor had been taken out of the picture.

The trouble was that before his departure Sinistral had put in place an Imperial visit to Brum, the city of his birth. Was it a purely social call? No one at the Imperial Court now thought so.

Two years before, the city of Brum, under the leadership of Igor Brunte, formerly a Fyrd, and Lord Festoon, the High Ealdor of the City, had renounced its fealty to the Empire. Brunte had gone further and massacred the Empire's representatives for reasons of personal vengeance. The two leaders had then taken up the governance of their city for themselves.

At the time it had taken all Blut's political skills to stop Quatremayne and his colleagues from mounting an invasion to crush Brunte's insolent insurrection.

Now that Sinistral had gone, but a state visit was agreed, it was impossible for Blut to impose his will to stop it without his authority being undermined. He therefore had no choice but to sanction what amounted to an invasion even though he disagreed with it. He knew that if he stayed behind in Bochum he would lose credibility but if he went, he put himself and his security directly in the hands of Quatremayne and his people.

His only ally among the Fyrd was Witold Slew, the Master of Shadows, one of the greatest fighters in the Hyddenworld and loyal to the office of Emperor. But Blut had reservations about him, and about using him. He had another task in mind for Slew.

So Blut's agreement to the invasion of Englalond was reluctant and his decision to journey with Quatremayne more reluctant still.

No wonder that he had crossed the North Sea in the third week of August with great trepidation, knowing that he left his power base behind, was travelling with no allies he could trust and would have no easy way to combat revolt against him if it came.

Which, he knew, it shortly would.

So now he sat, a stylo in hand, a pad upon his desk, his door guarded by two Fyrd, ostensibly for his safely but, as he well knew, really for Quatremayne's satisfaction.

Blut was now doing what he did best: planning a strategy.

He was in a foreign country, without support, in the hands of his enemies.

His list of wants and needs was short – very short.

His spectacles flashed as he wrote down four simple words: *I need a miracle* . . .

Yet he smiled, because he knew that that is exactly what Slaeke Sinistral would have said before adding, as Blut now did, 'Miracles happen.'

15
INTO THE FIRE

Arthur came back to consciousness after his escape from RAF Croughton not knowing what time it was or where he was. One thing he did know, he was hungry. Very.

But first things first.

He needed to know that he was in one piece and that his life was not under threat.

He had not immediately opened his eyes but he did not need to do so to know that he lay on a wet, uncomfortable, slimy surface and that it sloped down towards the water which he could hear lapping at his feet. He wiggled his fingers, which squelched in mud. He half-raised his head and realized that his cheek and ear, and bearded chin, were in rank mud as well. So he was on the edge of a filthy river.

Heaving himself into an upright position, he established two things simultaneously.

The first, which he immediately disregarded, was that he was sitting in a bundle of wet rags.

The second was that he was beneath a very large bridge which soared above him and across the grey waters of the river. There was the sound of water falling behind him which, when he turned, he saw came from a wide pipe set high above in a block of granite, one of many that formed a sheer wall to right and left.

The sound of heavy traffic bounced and echoed all around.

So he was in a city and one that, judging from the buildings on the far shore, the river and the embankment, looked like London.

It took him only seconds to confirm that his passage into the

Hyddenworld was complete. The detritus embedded in the slimy, stony shore contained enough items whose size he knew well. An empty bottle of Merlot wine, a rusted sparking plug and, final proof, a shoe, size ten, his own size. Except it was huge, and the other things were huge, about twice their normal size.

He hesitated to use the word 'shrunk' but that is precisely what had happened to him.

It was one of the mysteries of travelling between the human and the hydden worlds that outcomes were not predictable, let alone logical. He knew that from previous experience.

Clothes, for example, ought not to shrink in tandem with the mortal wearing them. Usually they did, yet occasionally they did not. A matter he once discussed with the late, wise, Master Brief, who could only speak theoretically, since he had never travelled between the two worlds, but felt it might have to do with perception or illusion – 'or both'.

On this occasion, Arthur's clothes had *not* shrunk, and the wet and muddy 'rags' he was covered in, as a tent might cover a child, were his human clothes.

For this Arthur was prepared.

His formerly tiny leather 'sac was now the right size and inside were the trews and jerkin, underclothes, jacket and some shoes that he had brought for just this situation. He changed into them quickly and ate the chocolate he had packed for sustenance, found some plasters and covered a cut on his hand that must have happened during his escape. Then he moved on to immediate practicalities.

If he was right, and this was London, it was not the best of places for a hydden ally of Brum to have fetched up. When the Fyrd originally invaded Englalond, Slaeke Sinistral, the Emperor who had been raised in Brum and wished it to be left just as it was, ordained that the City, as they called London, become the new capital. It had never been more than a garrison town and civilians, especially from Brum, rarely ventured there.

So much, Arthur told himself, *for the theory that a journeyer through the henges arrives where he needs to be. I thought of the gem of Autumn and I end up on the Thames's muddy shore!*

He decided he needed to get out from where he was as soon as possible.

He dug in his 'sac once more and found a digital watch he had put there, not to wear – it now looked giant-sized and the strap was far too big – but to see what time had passed since his escape from RAF Croughton. He had gone through the wire fence on Saturday September 23rd.

'And it is now . . .' he said, examining the watch carefully before making his pronouncement aloud, '. . . it is now Sunday October 1st.'

He was shocked. In his transition from one world to another he had lost a week of his life.

'Humph!' he murmured. 'Can't do that too often or there'll be nothing left!'

He stared about moodily.

'Out of the frying pan into the fire,' he muttered, though, looking at the murky water beyond the narrow stretch of shore, he took comfort from the fact that there was no immediate danger of being burnt thereabout. Drowned, more like.

Arthur looked up at the pipe again and saw in some alarm that there was a weedy tide line not far below it, which meant it was way above his head.

He immediately felt alarm, having read somewhere that the tidal range in London was very great, its pace very rapid.

He stood up, satisfied he could not be easily seen down in the shadows he was in by anyone on the embankment above, nor from the barges which, he now saw, were plying the great river. He peered to right and left, looking for a familiar landmark.

He might have hoped to see something familiar like Tower Bridge, to help him locate himself. As it was, the embankment wall was so sheer and high he could see nothing over it. The opposite bank yielded no easy clues that he recognized, just the lights of modern buildings. But then he had not been to riverside London for years.

He moved along the shore and out from under the bridge into the light and immediately had a clear view upstream to what he recognized as the smooth, modern lines of London Bridge. That meant that the more famous Tower Bridge, with its two crenellated towers, was immediately above him. Sure enough, as he moved further away he could see the towers and chains soaring overhead.

As for the embankment just behind him, he now saw the closed, grim portal of the Traitors' Gate. He had arrived in the very shadow of the Tower of London. What such a location might have to do with finding the gem of Autumn he had no idea, but here he was and he must make the best of it.

He went to the water and saw that it was creeping in over mud, gravel and old cobbles at an alarming rate. He knew that a tide took six hours to go out, six hours to come in and this one looked as if it was already well advanced.

Time was therefore running out.

He looked back again at the embankment wall and realized that it would not be long before the water reached it, and not long after that that it rose in a swirling and lethal way above his head.

Time to leave.

Which was not a course of action he would have chosen just then. From his previous ventures in the Hyddenworld he knew that henge-travel was tiring and disorientating and it was best to lie low at first and take things slowly.

The river splashed eagerly up the filthy shore and a tongue of it ran up towards him. He stumbled back too late. It overtook him and filled his shoes with muddy water.

He dug inside his 'sac for more food and water and untied his stave, which was attached for safekeeping to it. Relatively small before, it was the right size now and ideal for a hydden wayfarer, who might have need of it for many purposes, not least frightening folk off.

His other things were there as well – a hydden compass, a bivvy bag, liquid soap, a flannel which now seemed the size of a small towel, a raggedy hat against wind and rain, writing equipment, a notebook and a good many other items small enough to be useful in the Hyddenworld.

The tide threatened his feet again. It seemed that the river had noticed he was there, sensing that his back was almost literally to the wall. Like a blind, predatory monster it sent tentacles of water after him, trying to grasp his ankles, to pull him down.

As he began wondering with increasing desperation what to do, there was a gurgle high above his head and a great globby spew of watery something came pouring out of a hole he could barely see, in a deluge that nearly flattened him.

'It is the outlet of a drain or sewer!' cried Arthur Foale with relief. 'If something can come out, I can go in!'

He reached up even as the last of the shore was inundated, got hold of the slippery lip of a huge pipe with one hand, and a rusty chain of some kind with the other and, holding himself, for he had not strength enough to raise himself up, he let the swirling, rising water do the rest.

Twice did he suffer a deluge of filth from the pipe, twice did he hold on fast, spitting muck from his mouth but unable to let go a hand to clean his eyes or ears for fear of losing his grip with the other.

The current tried to pull him away but he held on fast until at last his chest got level with the pipe and he was able to pull himself to the darkness within. It was echoing, crawling, foul and without light.

The water continued to rise behind him and he realized that if he did not move on up the sewer it might yet get him and he would be drowned.

But what if it were blocked by a grille? The horrid idea caused him to turn back, though the space was too small to make that easy, but as he did so a wave of water rushed in at him and he knew there was no going back.

If there had been light ahead it would have helped, but at least he was alive and could travel in the darkness in the hope that eventually he must find respite. The water could not follow him forever.

He heard it behind, and the horrible pattering as of a thousand clawed feet ahead, and a sudden deep *drip-drip-drip* before there came a ghastly sound like the clearing of a giant's diseased throat as, gathering his phlegm, he ejected it from his mouth.

Which it might as well have been, for another great gob of whatever it was before deluged Arthur and tried to force him back the way he had come. He clung on, pressed on, closed his eyes and mouth, sensing that the tidal water was not far behind, slipping and sliding his way forward in the hope of finding something not so much better but a little less vile.

He had little doubt that he was now advancing under the vast complex that was the Tower of London. He moved on more easily now, the tunnel larger, grateful for a sudden shaft of light from far, far above, just at a point where the sewer bifurcated to left and right.

Which way?

He turned left, began running again, a panic overtaking him as he thought the tide might come after him even there, even now. Running, floundering, crawling towards the bowels of the Tower, to where no hydden past or present, unless they were insane, would ever wish to visit by the subterranean route.

For a while he drove himself on, impelled by the sense that what lay ahead must surely be better than what lay behind. Then: *Stop!* a little voice told him. *Go no further! Take stock! Consider your options!*

Arthur was in no state to listen to the voice of common sense. In any case, the sounds in the horrible tunnel had changed in nature and pitch. They were high now and seemed like screams right behind him.

Stop, Arthur, journey no more!

He slowed, his reason trying to impose itself upon his panic.

The sewer turned, a sluice gate presented itself as an obstacle, he climbed over it and *whoosh!* . . . he was off and away on a smooth and slippery surface, in total darkness once again, sliding and turning, his hands finding no purchase, his feet unable to gain friction, tumbling down and up and along towards the screams and cries.

Light!

Blinding as if it was a torch to his eyes.

Thump!

A bang as if he had been thumped by a hammer of concrete.

Shouts!

As if they were right in his ears.

Then a grip of iron!

As if an ancient implement of torture had been closed about his leg.

He opened his eyes and peered about as best he could and saw a nightmare come true: he was an actor in some medieval depiction of hell.

There was the rack, the hook and the red-hot brand.

There was a fiery furnace so hot that the filth on him began to steam and dry at once.

'What in Mirror's sacred name, my friends, have we here?' said a voice that had a raspy unpleasantness to it.

He was dragged to his feet, his hands were tied and he was hooked to a metal ring in a wall and hauled aloft before gaining full consciousness again.

Slowly, as he swung helplessly about, two things became certain.

First that he was in a chamber full of Fyrd dressed in black leathery clothing, their heads shorn neat and sleek.

The second was that they were all in a human medieval torture chamber, for in addition to the rack there were chains, iron maidens, fires, spiky things and unspeakable hooks hanging and swinging near his face from the high ceiling from which he himself swung.

To one side was a great hole through which, he surmised, he had just fallen. A chimney perhaps, to allow the smoke of the fires of torture to escape.

'Well, lads,' said the Fyrd who had a leather cannikin of ale in his hand, which he supped deep and cheerfully before saying more, 'we was saying, were we not, that all we was lacking was a victim. Well, now it seems one has been delivered to us. What shall we do with him?'

'The rack!' someone cried.

Arthur stared down as the rough, wooden bed-like structure, with ropes and ratcheted wheels, swam into view.

'The Maiden!' said someone else, forcing his head round so that he stared into the opened metal body, with rough and rusted spikes inside, onto which he must be horribly impaled as the body-shaped door was closed on him . . .

The fact that the torture instruments were of human size and the Fyrd were merely taunting him did not lessen the horror he felt at the sight of them.

But then: 'Let it be the brand,' said a deeper voice, waving something that smelt hot and acrid under his nose, singeing his beard and making him cough with the smell of his own burnt hair. Flames at the end of a stick danced in front of him.

'Yes, the brand, the brand!' they cried ever more loudly as Arthur struggled uselessly to escape from the burning heat near his eyes.

Fire can hurt a hydden as easily as a human. Size was of no consequence now.

'Noooo!' he heard himself cry as they loosed the chain and he began to fall.

16

MANOEUVRES

Tappity-tap, tappity-tap, tappity . . .

Niklas Blut, Emperor of the Hyddenworld, drummed his fingers impatiently on the metal top of the desk in his new, but he hoped temporary, office. He had no intention of staying there for a second longer than he needed to, meanwhile . . .

Tappity-tap, tappity-tap . . .

Such signs of stress were unusual in Niklas Blut and had taken him by surprise. He liked being in control, not for the power of it so much as the pleasant feeling of orderliness it instilled in him. But since he had arrived in Englalond with General Quatremayne's forces, he had lost that feeling entirely. He was now sitting in his quarters in the City, trying to work out a way or ways to get it back.

His discomfort had begun the moment he discovered the extent of the Fyrd's 'pre-invasion' activities in Englalond, at which point he knew he had been cleverly outmanoeuvred by the General.

The invasion, he now understood, was already well under way. True, the assault on Brum was some way off, but the preparations for it were very far advanced and were being planned long before Slaeke Sinistral had even abdicated.

Quatremayne had not lied directly but by default.

Had Blut or Sinistral known his full plans, they could and would have dealt with him. Sinistral would have demoted him, or worse. Blut would not have agreed to cross the North Sea and so put himself in the power of the General, which he now was.

Tappity-tap, tappity-tap . . .

So he sat in silence and the belief that, since miracles do not happen, not really, he was going to have to find a way out of the situation he was in, if he was to regain control over a General who had gone too far – before he went further still and did the inevitable: oust him, probably kill him, and assume power for himself.

If this kind of manoeuvring was what being an Emperor was about – and he knew it was – he did not like it. From the position of a subordinate, which he had been all his life, such games had their charm and intellectual interest. Now he was Emperor, the gloss was fading fast. But . . .

'I think not,' murmured Blut, taking off his spectacles to clean their already spotless lenses. 'I think most definitely we cannot allow Quatremayne the pleasure of success.'

Blut's mentor, Slaeke Sinistral, had said many wise things to him. One of these was in the form of a simple rule: those with ill-intentions always make mistakes and the wise ruler awaits his moment patiently but, when the moment comes, he acts decisively and very speedily indeed.

In fact, the General had already made one mistake in Blut's view, if only a slight one, because he did not know that the new Emperor had a photographic memory.

He had let Blut have sight of his invasion plans long enough for him to memorize them, which in Blut's case was as long as it took to turn the pages and look at each one for fifteen seconds or so. Afterwards, it was as if each page was imprinted on his mind. His recall was total and he was capable of sitting, as he now sat, and turning the pages of almost anything he had ever taken an interest in – and many things he had not – in his visual memory as if they were a book.

The fact he had been shown it at all told Blut something very stark: that Quatremayne already thought he had Blut in a position that made him powerless, so it didn't matter what he knew. Perhaps being careless with the dossier was Quatremayne's way of telling Blut precisely that.

As for the strategy Quatremayne and his staff officers had devised, it was thorough, ruthless and profoundly insubordinate. While still in power, Sinistral had made it crystal clear that Brum was never to be sacked, its citizens massacred, its buildings razed, its ancient sites desecrated. For one thing, Sinistral was born in Brum and had fond memories of it, though he had never returned since leaving it as a boy; for another he understood that the Brummies' love of freedom, their quirky individuality and their sometimes anarchic good humour might be annoying to the Teutonic mind of the die-hard Fyrd, but they were essential to any civilized society.

Therefore, he had often said, Brum was to be handled firmly, and kept in order, but never, ever, crushed.

This, Blut now knew, was what the Fyrd under the General intended to do. The strategy was well conceived, well constructed and, very likely, would be brilliantly executed.

Which was no surprise to Blut. Sinistral had chosen Quatremayne for a reason: he was the best military mind in the Hyddenworld, and the best military leader too. His staff were wholly behind him. He had the Fyrd in the palm of his hand. Opposition to him personally, and now to his strategy in Englalond, seemed doomed to failure.

Tappity-tap, tappity-tap . . .

But, Blut told himself, pondering the details in the dossier now so firmly in his mind, *he has made one mistake; he will make another. When he does, assuming I am still alive, I will use it to crush him.*

That thought too came as a surprise.

Blut had never crushed anyone, or anything, in his life.

But Quatremayne I will, he repeated to himself, *though how I do it remains to be seen.*

From the first day of his arrival in Englalond, Blut had begun to draw the battle lines quite openly, without a word being said.

He had been assigned an apartment and impressive offices in Fyrd Headquarters adjacent to Tower Hill, in abandoned sewers which were as good a base as any for all concerned.

Blut politely refused them, commandeering instead the cramped, damp, undercroft space beneath the nearby Royal Mint. It was an act of deliberate and overt defiance but it was also more than that. His rooms were in the ruins of a church which, though under the building, had been preserved. Its thick, rounded Gothic piers and lanceolate arches added a backdrop to his desk he liked and, though there was no view, the air was fresh.

Such a place, such ruins, irritated the tidy Quatremayne, the more so because he had to make an awkward trip to attend Blut.

Excellent!

The kind of play Slaeke Sinistral had taught him to enjoy.

Better still, the building above was unoccupied. It gave Blut a view of the human London, which also gave him a better perspective on things in general than sewers did.

Tappity-tap, tappity . . .

Footsteps approached along a corridor and Blut's guards stood-to and barked commands. The scrivener in his office looked nervous.

The door opened.

'My Lord . . .'

Blut, who had been looking into the middle distance to his left, turned to the door. The flat ovals of his spectacles flashed.

'Well?'

It was one of his aides-de-camp, as the Fyrd insisted on calling the military personnel tasked with the responsibility of liaising with the civilian sides of government.

Tappity-tap, tappity-tap . . .

'General Quatremayne is here.'

The General did not bother waiting to be summoned. He walked straight in.

He was older than Blut and taller and handsome in a fleshy, humourless sort of way. In his day he had been one of the most ruthless, effective and feared field officers in the Fyrd. For much of his career he had been perceived as a young pretender to high rank. Now he had achieved that, he had adopted the habits and faults that come with seniority: he took himself too seriously, he was impatient with subordinates not as quick or experienced as himself, he inclined to think himself always right and he believed that resistance to the Empire should be quashed fast and, if necessary, brutally.

His file, which Blut himself had compiled and, as with all else, had committed to memory, stated that nearly twenty-five years before, Quatremayne had been directly responsible for some unpleasant military actions in Poland, in Warsaw in particular. The native hydden had been inventive in their resistance to the invaders and showed a spirit similar to the citizens of Brum. When finally defeated they were brutally suppressed.

One long-term consequence of this unnecessarily harsh policy was, strangely enough, the recent insurrection in Brum. Igor Brunte, a former Fyrd himself, who was instigator of the Brum revolt, was motivated by a desire for revenge for the deaths of his extended family in Warsaw at the hands of Fyrd under the direct command of Quatremayne. They had been killed because they had mounted a covert and successful attack on some of Quatremayne's troops. The General had torched them to death himself – Brunte was the sole survivor and had sworn revenge.

Vengefulness was in Blut's view a flaw, whether from hurt pride (Quatremayne) or emotional trauma (Brunte). But there it was.

There were other matters noted in the General's file, certain proclivities in his private life, for example, that left Blut with a feeling of extreme distaste. It was one thing killing people sadistically, another picking up young innocent females from the streets of defeated cities and subjecting them to unpleasant and extreme abuse before passing them on like chattels to subordinates as 'rewards'.

'My Lord . . .' began Quatremayne.

His salute was perfunctory, his expression close to insolent. Things were getting worse.

'Sit,' said Blut.

He was easy in his command of others, having learnt the art from a master of it – Sinistral. Firm, decisive, good-humoured, fair.

The General chose to sit not opposite Blut but at the other table in the room, as if it was his own office. The point was not lost on Blut.

'We are now no more than five weeks from being ready for a full-scale attack on Brum, my Lord.'

'As long as that?' said Blut blandly, to be irritating.

'When we go in, my Lord, we intend to subdue the city very quickly and with a minimum of bloodshed. The natural resistance of the natives is great. Better to be thoroughly prepared and subdue it in one heavy blow. Better to be safe than sorry.'

'Mid-October, then,' said Blut noncommittally.

'By then, all our other positions will be secure. Brum's citizens will have nowhere to hide and their meagre defences will not last more than a day. We have planned for three. We might have gone in sooner but, as you know, my . . . Lord' – how he hated repeating that title – 'humans and their infrastructure were hard hit by the Earth movements in the summer. That has affected our original plan to use the human railway system . . . However, I can confidently inform you that, though the lines from London to Brum were cut for a time, they are now working in a skeleton way. Especially for freight at night, which serves our purpose best.'

'You have alternatives?'

Blut knew well that in any discussion of strategy this was always a question worth asking.

Quatremayne's answer was smoothly evasive.

'I think the risks are low,' he said, 'and we can carry it through, despite what has happened.'

Blut nodded sagely, hoping he looked out of his depth. The more he did, the more likely he was going to be judged harmless. It seemed most likely that Quatremayne would move to get rid of him in the euphoria and triumphalism that would follow a defeat of Brum. Blut had six weeks, then, not much.

Miracles still needed, mistakes by the General would still be very welcome.

'I want daily updates,' said Blut, 'on all the areas we discussed before.'

Quatremayne nodded, making a poor show of masking his indifference. He had, Blut noticed, curiously shiny cheeks, rounded too, as if they were made of fine, pink fat. His black uniform and gold stars of rank were neat and shiny as pins. His schuhe, the laced military kind, were honed like brass door handles.

Blut saw his weakness.

It was his own.

They both disliked disorder.

Both thrived on control.

So, Blut told himself as he stared at the General, *I need to bring a little chaos into your life and I have six weeks or thereabout to find a way to escape your iron hand.*

A clerk poked his head round the door.

'The Master of Shadows is here, my Lord.'

Perfect timing. Blut's one ally. An asset that needed very careful deployment.

'Ah! Yes, good.'

He let his eyes lighten, his body relax, even gain a mite of animation. He wanted Quatremayne to think that something was afoot. He also wanted him puzzled, trying to work something out where there was nothing to work out.

'You have a task in mind for Witold Slew?'

'No . . . not especially . . . not exactly,' said Blut, deliberately evasive. 'But . . . tell me something?'

Quatremayne leaned forward attentively.

'My Lord?'

'What do you know of Claydon? In early October?'

He knew that Quatremayne knew nothing of either because there was nothing to know. He had plucked the place name from a map at random, for the fun of it. Quatremayne would think it significant and waste time finding out what it meant.

'Claydon?' repeated Quatremayne, hoping for a clue. 'Early October . . .'

'Send in the Master of Shadows,' Blut called out cheerfully, adding, 'Good day, General.'

Quatremayne, disconcerted, smiled thinly at Slew as he came in and sat down.

Slew did not return the compliment but sat where he should, which was near.

'I have a task for you, Slew.'

'My Lord?'

Blut eyed him cautiously.

Was he still to be trusted? Had Quatremayne got to him? That cold look suggested not.

His first duty was to the Office of Emperor and no one else.

People thought Slew was the son of Sinistral. Both tall, both sleek, both blond. One beautiful, but this one . . . troubled.

Blut decided to trust him, but then the task was one he would, in his heart of cold hearts, wish to do.

He clicked his fingers and ordered the scrivener to bring him paper, an envelope and sealing wax.

He took his stylo and pulled a bottle of green ink near. The colour itself was a code, one that Sinistral had divined. It simply meant 'read between the lines'.

He wrote three brief lines, blew them dry, folded the missive very precisely and put it in the envelope. The scrivener melted the wax and Blut applied his bloodstone ring to it as his official seal.

'I want you to deliver this.'

He gave the envelope to Slew, who looked at it and looked surprised.

'It is not addressed to anyone, my Lord.'

'Dismissed,' said Blut sharply to the scrivener. 'You guards as well. I wish for privacy.'

He waited until they were gone and turned to Slew again.

'I wish you to take the missive to my Lord Emperor Slaeke Sinistral.'

'My Lord . . . !?' exclaimed Slew surprised. 'He is Emperor no more.'

'Is he not?' said Blut ambiguously. 'Is he not? Take it to him in Bochum. Let him read it. Abide by his instructions before any further duty you feel to me.'

'My Lord . . .'

'That is my command, Slew. You will obey it.'

Blut knew he would. Slew was loyal to the Office of Emperor but he loved Sinistral.

'You will go via Tilbury, where I have arranged for my Lord Sinistral's favourite and most trusted sailor to await you.'

Blut had been able to put that in hand on his arrival, already fearing he was falling into a trap. He was planning ahead.

'You know who I mean?'

'Borkum Riff, Lord.'

'The same. He will take you across the North Sea and on arrival he will await your return. I have instructed him.'

'But . . .'

'You have doubts?'

'You have little protection here, Emperor. Without me you will have none.'

'My Lord Emperor Sinistral taught me many lessons, Slew. One of them is that there comes a point in all our lives when we must trust our instincts and throw caution to the wind. So now, for me. Tell him that as well, he will take pleasure in it. And Slew . . .'

'My Lord?'

'The world is changing very fast. This time of harvest is like no other. Samhain is on the way and Mirror knows what that will bring. Therefore . . .'

He paused, unused to speaking in this way to Slew, whom most folk disliked and all but his closest friends, and Sinistral, distrusted.

'My Lord?'

'Make peace with your mother, the Lady Leetha. Make peace. In the time coming we will all have need of those who love us and no time for divisions. In any case, it distressed my Lord Sinistral that you and she do not see eye to eye.'

Slew flushed with anger but Blut ignored it.

'Make peace,' he said again, adding, 'we are all of us flawed, we have all made mistakes. Trust me in this.'

Leetha was Sinistral's adoptive daughter, remarkable and beautiful. People thought Slew was their son, but he was not. She had two sons, of whom Slew was the elder. He believed she favoured the younger, who was Jack, a fact Jack himself had only recently discovered.

Witold Slew stood staring at him for a long time. Shadows hung about his form, menacing and strange. His great stave shone with danger; his being was as powerful as any hydden Blut knew. Yet through it all there came the ancient hurt, the sense of being wronged which Leetha's seeming dislike of him had caused.

Yet Blut's words had entered into him and taken his mind off this old wound. He looked at him with respect.

'Lord, Emperor, I shall do as you command.'

His dark eyes lightened.

'What is it, Slew?'

'I am glad it is Borkum Riff you chose. He . . . is . . . like me, Lord.'

'Difficult?' smiled Blut, 'I believe he is!'

A rare look of genuine concern crossed Slew's face.

'Will you be safe until I return, Lord?'

Blut smiled again.

'Miracles happen.'

Finally: 'My Lord, I think it wise that I take two others with me, the Norseners Harald and Bjarne. The former Emperor will be weak, he may be threatened and I need ones I trust with him at my side.'

'Take who you think best fitted to the task, Slew. The Nordic lands have produced some of the finest fighters, I am told.'

'Thank you, Lord.'

Slew left and the Emperor's clerks appeared, papers and dossiers in hand.

17

ARRIVAL

It took Jack, Stort and the others eleven days from the time they left Turner's Green to reach Brum along the canal. They had travelled by night, hiding up by day, and bodily hauling their frail craft round those locks that were chained. It had been laborious and hard but they had learnt one thing: the Fyrd steered clear of canals, which perhaps they were not used to, so that the main danger was from human beings.

'But now we're on the outskirts of the city it's not the Fyrd we need worry about so much,' said Jack, 'but our own kind. The slums of the Hay Mills have many rough and dangerous elements, but from all I've heard Sparkbrook will be much worse.' Dodd nodded his head in agreement.

The built-up areas they were now travelling through made portering their craft increasingly difficult, yet not so much so that the alternatives were better.

'Another day, one more night, and we'll make it,' said Jack. 'If we can get into striking distance of Digbeth, where we have many friends among the bilgesnipe who are the experts on these waters, I believe I'll be able to get us all safely back in no time at all.'

But, as Jack feared, when they got to the bleak and barren depths of Sparkbrook, where the canal ran through deep caverns of ruined factory buildings occupied by low types and criminals, disaster struck.

They were passing under one of the many arched bridges as discreetly as they could, from one factory area to another, when a boulder was thrown at them from above, which crashed straight through the bilges.

As they began to sink they heard laughter above and the running of feet and moments later they were floundering in the water.

They pulled themselves up onto a derelict factory frontage on the canal which seemed a place of relative safety. Jack decided it would be safer and quicker to leave the rest of the group where they were while he set off into the night to get help.

They slept well enough and without disturbance. But through the day that followed Meister Laud became confused and difficult. To make matters worse their food was running out.

As the second night fell and still Jack had not returned, they all began to worry. Dodd knew Sparkbrook by reputation and understood that it was one of the most dangerous districts in Old Brum. True, they were safe where they were, protected by the canal on one side and deserted outhouses and wasteland on the other.

'We best be prepared against attack,' he said. 'A boulder from a bridge might be no more than a thoughtless jape by a passing youngster brought up to distrust strangers but if a group of 'em forms we're in trouble.'

'What do you suggest beyond vigilance and making sure our staves are handy?' said Katherine.

'That'll have to do for now,' said Dodd.

The hours passed towards midnight and creaking and footfalls in nearby buildings made them ever more fearful that they were being watched. The great city hummed quietly about them, the glow of its lights making the low clouds above livid and threatening. It was unlike Jack not to come back when he had said he would and though they were confident he would return, Meister Laud was now shivering and fretful, and they were all growing very tired and cold.

'If only we could light a fire,' said Terce.

Dodd and Stort shook their heads. A fire would only attract attention.

'He's getting worse,' said Terce later, by now trying to keep Meister Laud warm by wrapping him in his own coat and holding him in his arms. 'We need to warm him somehow.'

Katherine made a warming brew, using a buried fire, which sufficed to heat water in a slow and smoky way. They fed it to Meister Laud but he had barely strength to sup it, his limbs shivering now quite violently.

When Katherine fancied she heard someone or something again in one of the buildings beyond the flames, Stort got up to investigate. He was gone longer than she liked.

When he returned, he said, 'There's folk about all right and I don't like the feel of 'em. Which being so we might as well light a fire as not. Better to die warm than die cold and if anyone comes we can see 'em if they get too close.'

'And not at all if they stay out of the orbit of the light,' said Katherine. 'But I suppose it won't make things worse and will help Meister Laud.'

Stort and Dodd set to building the fire near the canal with Meister Laud between it and the water, the rest guarding on either side. A stretch of wooden fence provided a measure of protection along the canal side.

At first they smothered the flames with vegetation dampened with canal water. Then, when that provided insufficient heat they lit another, then a third. Finally, with the canal behind them, and the lights of the city glowing high above the canyon of old buildings that rose on the far bank side, they let go all pretence and allowed the fires to join forces and burn free, facing the rustling darkness of derelict Sparkbrook with their staves in their hands.

Meister Laud soon perked up, reached his hands to the warmth, his white hair and cheeks red with the fiery warmth, a slight smile on his face.

'Better,' he said, 'better . . .'

Occasionally the flames grew too bright, breaking through the barrier of moist vegetation Stort cleverly placed on the far side of the fires, and he went to shore it up again. Then, to Katherine's alarm, he disappeared again towards the concrete buildings they had explored when they first arrived. She heard movement, clattering and dragging sounds. He came back, busied himself round the far side of the fire again and eventually returned to the light and safety of their little sanctuary bounded by water and fire.

His eyes were streaming and he smelt of oil but he had a satisfied look on his face.

'What have you being *doing*?' hissed Katherine.

'Things,' he said coolly. 'Defensive measures, in case. Unless Jack gets here very shortly I have a feeling we'll soon have some most unwelcome visitors. I have constructed a last-resort measure . . . I'll give 'em sparks in Sparkbrook!'

'What do you mean?'

He shrugged and said nothing, preferring to hunker down and keep an eye on the water behind as well as the shadowy buildings all about, whose broken windows now danced with firelight.

The fires served their purpose well and all of them felt better. Dodd made a fortifying hot brew of his own, which burnt their throats with something more than heat.

'Jack'll come soon,' Katherine said, to encourage them. 'Jack's never failed me yet. Maybe it's a longer way than we thought, or there is some difficulty . . .'

'I expect that may be so,' replied Stort, doing his best to hide the anxiety from his voice that she obviously felt as well. The truth was they were now sitting ducks. They could not see a thing beyond the darkness and . . .

Thwump!

The first stone came sailing out of the darkness and hit the ground next to Stort's stave.

Thwump, thwump!

The next two came hard and fast, accompanied by unpleasant laughter and running shadows in and out of the buildings.

Clatter! Bang!

Some tin cans and a bottle arced over towards them.

Smash!

The bottle caught a stone and broke, sending shards of glass over them. As the figures got nearer and grew more distinct, the laughter grew louder and deteriorated into jeers.

Stort said quietly, 'They look to me no older than children, Katherine . . .'

To her horror, he rose from their shelter as if to go and talk to them.

Thwump!

Something shot past and lodged in the wooden upright next to him. Katherine hauled him back down and they looked at the bolt juddering in the wood of the fence by the canal.

'Youngsters with crossbows, it seems,' said Katherine grimly.

Thwump! Thwump!

Two more bolts hit the wood.

Terce shifted his bulk in front of Meister Laud to protect him. Dodd looked furious, Stort's eyes narrowed.

'This is getting dangerous,' said Katherine, who had gathered their things together ready for a quick escape by water. They knew already that the canal was not too deep and quite narrow. It would be worth a try to get away by crossing to the other side, but not something to do lightly. It might be a step too far for Meister Laud.

'Where's Jack?' asked Katherine. For the first time desperation had crept into her voice. The dancing, jeering shadows became suddenly clear. They were a mob of rough-tough-looking hydden youths, attracted by the smoke, now seeing beyond the flames and beginning to realize that their advantage in numbers was overwhelming.

Most of the mob were throwing missiles, many had clubs, some nasty-looking knives, and they finally saw the one with the crossbow, who was more adult than child.

'What we need,' said Stort, 'is a broom or some other such long implement. Our staves are a mite too short for what I have in mind.'

'A broom!' cried Katherine, the flames turning her fair hair golden.

'Or something like it,' said Stort calmly.

The mob advanced nearer, the missiles slowing, as if getting their hands on what they obviously saw as intruders on their turf would be more fun. Knives glinted in the night, eyes narrowed with pack-like blood lust.

'Or,' said Stort, 'we could tear one of the boards from this fence.' But they were impossible to move.

'For Mirror's sake, Stort, talk sense, or we'll have to take to the water any minute now, but . . .'

Terce had now stood up to face the crowd, the flames of the fires seeming insufficient defence against the ire of the mob.

Katherine saw the one with the crossbow raise it and take aim. She grabbed Terce's robe and hauled him sideways.

A bolt just missed him and Meister Laud, disappearing into the canal behind.

'Charge the buggers!' someone shouted from the crowd and a great roar went up as their assailants gathered up like some great wave before surging forward towards them.

'Whoa there, me hearties!' a new voice cried out from the water. 'Who'm be aiming bolties at my good old craft!'

As the crowd before them began their charge, an extraordinary figure leapt onto the canal bank between Katherine and Stort. Meister Laud's eyes widened into surprise, then terror. It was as if a demon was attacking them. The figure who had leapt into their side of the fray looked like a pirate from an arabesque nightmare.

Thin, turbaned, bare-armed, with golden rings in his ears and dark, shiny hair that caught the light of the fires like streams of crimson ribbon. He wore a loincloth, had powerful bare legs and bejewelled sandals on his feet.

'A troubly eve it seems, Mistress Katherine, a gangrious night, Mister Stort . . . !'

'Ah, Arnold!' cried Stort. 'You have got just what I need. Pray give me that pole!'

Arnold Mallarkhi was the best boatyboy in Brum, and a friend to them all.

'You and no other, Mister Stort, may have it,' said Arnold. 'Here it be!'

The bilgesnipe swung it over their heads and placed the handle end in Stort's stave hand.

'Stand clear or stand low, me mateys,' said Arnold, guessing at once Stort's intent, 'for that pole's longer and harder than it looks!'

As they all fell to the ground, Stort raised the pole lengthways, turned a circle to get momentum, such that the pole swung whirring over their heads, and as it came back he directed it through the three fires, one by one.

The fiery debris was scattered towards the charging mob, some shooting up as sparks into the air, the heavier material falling on the ground at their feet.

Then . . . *whoosh!* and *whoomp!* and great fireballs shot towards their attackers, driving them back.

'Fuel, diesel, old paint,' said Stort, who had collected it in the dark from cans discarded in the outhouses. It was why he smelt of oil. A great mass of flame shot up, forming a protective arc right round them, and turning the charging mob into screaming retreat, stones dropping, clubs falling in the flames, the crossbow thrown aside.

'Bugger off, me Sparkyboys!' cried Arnold with delight, before, turning back to the canal, he put his hand over his eyes to shield them from the sudden light and added, 'Master Stort, my pole, if you please! And where be my Grandpa!? He be old as time but 'ee can still pole a boat if he has to!'

They saw the second craft coming then, Jack at the prow, rope in hand and ready to disembark. He was flushed and powerful in the light of the flickering flames, watching the rout, working out, as Arnold now was, how best to embark the passengers and get out fast, before the flames died back and the attack was resumed more ferociously than before.

Behind him in the stern, pole in hand, tottered the ancient, ragged figure of one of Brum's best-known citizens, Old Mallarkhi, proprietor of the notorious but much-loved hostelry, the Muggy Duck. He had been on his sick-bed for years but, when circumstances demanded it, he could still show something of his old mettle. But his steering was shot.

His craft banged into the bank, first prow, then stern, which Jack escaped by stepping nimbly off in time. But Mallarkhi was not so lucky. He fell ashore.

'Nary worry yer nettle-nottles, lads,' he cried, winded though he was. 'Ol' Mallarkhi's got the pole and Jack the lad the boat. Pile aboard mine and me Arnold's sharpish and let's get outerway!'

They needed no second telling.

Meister Laud was helped aboard and then half the group went in one craft, half in the other.

'Grandpa, you'm to lead the way 'n I'll afollow shinderkin!'

'Boy, you'm the best I ever knew,' cried Old Mallarkhi. 'The Sparkyboys were allers fools, 'tis gnats' piss their beer, it daggles their heads and droops their dongs! Let's make our way home 'n get these our goodly guests a bath, a beverage, a bake and a bed!'

18

CITY FATHERS

The city of Brum, whose southern suburbs Jack and his friends had now reached with such difficulty, was one of the most famous in the Hyddenworld. It was very ancient, its beginnings dating back to the sixth century when Beornamund, the most famous of the great Mercian CraftLords, first found work in those parts as an apprentice blacksmith.

At first his living came from such ordinary fare as shoes for horses, nails, hoops for barrels and the like. But the lords of the Court of the Mercian King had need of finer things. They sought buckles and brooches to adorn their robes, decorated bosses for their war shields, and bracelets and pendants for their ladies. Beornamund found he had a rare talent for such fine work.

Soon he founded his own forge as metal smith up on the slopes of Waseley Hill. He liked the fresh air and the wide open sky, where the sun and moon, stars and Earth's plenty were his inspiration. The special qualities of what he made were recognized by one royal courtier after another, who said that he could make even the simplest ring or diadem 'sing' with life.

Soon folk said something more and they did so with awe, respect and finally love: Beornamund's work seemed touched by the Fires of the Universe itself.

His workshop was not far below the source of the little River Rea, which bubbled up and flowed as sweetly then as it does now.

It was along the banks of the Rea that he met Imbolc, his one true love. But he soon lost her, a tragedy that informed his life and work thereafter, to his sadness but Brum's subsequent gain.

For from that time on, there ran through his work something more. It was a thread of loving sadness, as of one who knows that all things perish, all things end, all must finally return to the Mirror-of-All, in whose reflection we live our lives.

This deep sense of the impermanence of life, having entered the CraftLord's spirit, passed through his hands into the things he made. They held a fragile beauty and gave to those who possessed them a sense that they were guardians, not owners, not just of those artefacts but of the Earth itself. From this he came to understand, as they did, that the life of mortals being short, they had best take care to cherish what they had or else they might destroy it.

But as time passed and his wisdom deepened, Beornamund came to see that it is in the nature of mortals, and of humans in particular, to destroy beauty as if they fear it, to covet even those things they have no need of, to seek to control the natural liberty of life itself, to enshadow even the light of life. He therefore came to fear that the end of the days might come when Mother Earth grew tired of the children she had made who so squandered her abundance and, growing tired, she might grow angry; and from that anger might be sown the seeds of the extinction of all things, even the Universe itself.

Then, remembering the perfection of the sphere of crystal and metal he had made in his youth and that the gems that remained held the Fires of the Universe, he declared that if ever the lost gem of Spring was found and reunited with the other gems of the seasons, perhaps, if it was done with a true heart and honest purpose, a threatened Universe might be saved from extinction and find recovery.

Such was the legend that Beornamund created in his lifetime.

His renown became such that by the end of his long life many crafts-folk had journeyed to Mercia to set up shop near him. After his death, the process continued and soon the banks of the River Rea, which ran for only twelve miles south and east from Waseley Hill before it lost itself in the bigger River Trent, became renowned for the quality of the goods made there.

In early times it was named Brummagem in his honour, that name being an affectionate corruption of his own. In the following centuries it grew into one of the great manufacturing cities of the human world and as time and language changed so did its name. Today the human city is called Birmingham.

Brum remained its hydden counterpart, within its medieval heart. Its many different crafts and trades benefit from the wastefulness of human commercial enterprise all around it. It was said that the hydden Brummies knew how to turn dust into diamonds, spoil into scent and dirty water into the finest brews.

They knew too how to exploit the structures humans made, built over or abandoned, living in the deep interstices between, their existence unknown to their human benefactors. Like all over great human cities, as time passed, the ground level rose, the footings of one building being built on another. As for the River Rea, along whose banks their city was first built, the humans eventually found it a nuisance. They built over it, or diverted it through culverts, or simply walled it out of sight. As they forgot that it even existed, except when it flooded, the hydden moved in. Old Brum, as the first hydden city became known, was centred around the low parishes of Deritend and Digbeth, within whose noisome shadows the Brummies and their economy thrived.

With the coming of canals and rail in the eighteenth and nineteenth centuries, old parts of Birmingham were knocked down to make way for the new. The hydden exploited these developments too and so, on higher ground, north of old Brum, in the arched cellars, basements and waterways beneath the rail tracks, New Brum was born.

With that birth came an influx of many different kinds of hydden, the most distinctive and also most useful to the city being the bilge-snipe, a cheerful, tubby, water-folk whose wyfkin wore coloured silks and ribbons and bedecked their heads and bosoms with jewellery and whose males were renowned for their navigation skills.

The bilgesnipe moved into Old Brum, traded their willingness and ability to maintain the city's complex and dilapidated waterways for tolerance and acceptance, which the native Brummies gave them. In time the bilgesnipe became essential to Brum's economic health, their boatmen plying trade of freight and ferry, post and policing, to make the city one of the most efficient and least rule-bound in the Hyddenworld.

By then the city and Waseley Hill were places of pilgrimage, drawing folk who wished to pay homage to where Beornamund had lived his life, from all parts of Europe across the North Sea. No doubt they hoped too that they might find the gem of Spring, which he himself never found.

For many centuries Brum was the capital of Englalond, its High Ealdors recognized as first among equals of the ealdors of other cities, small and large.

Its demise as capital began with the birth of a male child to one of its great trading families, the Sinistrals, in the mid-nineteenth century. His tutor was ā Faroün, architect of New Brum, composer and lutenist. Slaeke Sinistral was a born trader, a business genius who saw his opportunity across the North Sea and took it. When his business was destroyed with the human bombing of Hamburg in 1940, it was Sinistral's genius to turn loss into gain. He moved his headquarters into the tunnels of the coal mines abandoned by humans beneath Bochum in the Ruhr. He turned his surviving employees into the army of the Fyrd, using them brilliantly to invade the surrounding countries of the hydden, from Spain to Siberia, from the hot Africk Lands to misty Englalond, where the cold and rain and stolid intransigence of its sturdy northern inhabitants finally brought Imperial expansion to a halt.

No matter.

Sinistral had no interest in the sterile Pennines and wild Cumbria, or the sea-swept littoral of Northumbria. As for the bleak vastnesses beyond Hadrian's Wall and the midge-ridden lochs and forests of Scotland – there was nothing for the Empire there.

Sinistral was equivocal even about the lowlands of southern Englalond, and Brum itself, city of his birth and place of his first training in matters administrative and commercial. Whether out of sentiment or guile – for all great rulers know their people need a little latitude – he let Brum stay relatively free, certainly liberal. Its governors were Fyrd, but retired from active military duty and wanting only a quiet life in a city fabled for its ancient history, its quirky freedoms and its rough and ready individual worship of the Mirror.

Famous, too, for being a focus of pilgrimages from all parts of Europe, though as time went by even Sinistral's patronage could not stop stricter elements of the Fyrd from making it difficult for all but the most persistent pilgrims to reach Brum.

But its liberties remained intact, as did the rule of the High Ealdor who, in the last fifteen years or more, had been the remarkable Lord Festoon, formerly corpulent scion from another of the great families of Brum, the Avons.

Fabulously rich, a collector of gold and silver artefacts, a historian, a *bon viveur*, a seemingly self-indulgent fool in the Fyrd's thrall, Festoon was very much loved by a citizenry who benefited from his wealth and patronage. His obesity was legendary, fed by the genius of his close friend and personal chef, Parlance. So large did Festoon become that he had to be ministered to – that is woken, raised, washed, fed, clothed, supported – by the Sisters of Charity, an order whose lives might be wedded to the Mirror itself but whose adoration was focused on Festoon alone.

Chief of these was Sister Supreme, a severe, tart, female who terrified all who knew her and chilled their hearts. Some early damage had been done to her, in childhood perhaps, and she served others in the name of Charity from a cold distance, never letting her emotions show.

It was fortunate for Festoon, and for Brum's subsequent history, that the cheerful Parlance had come into his life as his cook and helpmeet, helping him fight free of the Sisters to whom his parents had abandoned him.

Yet even so all might have stayed as it was, Festoon growing fatter and older, the Sisters ever more adoring, the Fyrd governors more lazy and unthinking, and the citizens even freer to trade, to manufacture, to acquire wealth, to complain, to do not very much more than live – had not a belligerent newcomer arrived in the city and changed everything.

His name was Igor Brunte, whose lifelong mission was to harm the Fyrd who had destroyed his family in an attack in Poland led by General Quatremayne personally.

Brunte swore vengeance and, at first in small ways, took it. He joined the Fyrd, learnt their ways, murdering and harming his peers and superiors in any way he could. He was clever and cold-hearted where his enemies were concerned, but he looked benign and trustworthy: a stocky build, trusty with stave and dirk, a ready joviality, eyes that wrinkled with a mirth that always hid a darker intent, Brunte gained promotion to the very heart of the Fyrd.

His chance to cause lasting damage came when he was tasked to accompany one of the Emperor's relatives to Brum. He killed Lavin Sinistral en route, along with his aide-de-camp, and arrived alone in Brum, where he waited and watched.

When he finally struck, he struck hard.

Most of the resident Fyrd were killed, and some collaborating Brummie citizens, but Festoon escaped, with the help of Jack, Katherine and Stort. Whether a coincidence or not – certainly it was in the natural wyrd of things – this marked the beginning of the present quest for the gems of the seasons.

Brum was truly free; Festoon returned, he and Brunte made up their differences, recognizing that, together and representing the civilian and military impulses of the city, they had its citizens' fullest cooperation and support. Brunte retreated into the background to organize defences against the day, surely inevitable, when the Fyrd fought back and tried to retake the city.

Festoon lost weight, massively so, and took up his office of High Ealdor once more, finally revealing that his collaboration with the Fyrd had been a sham, a way of making sure, through his own wealth, that Brum's people and their trade stayed unharassed and healthy.

Mister Pike, the Chief Staverman or law enforcer, returned to the city too, so that Brum held its destiny in its own hands, so far as wyrd and Fyrd allowed it to be so.

It was to this triumvirate of city elders that Jack and the others were now returning with news of the Fyrd's advances to south and east of the city.

19
MIRACLES

In the days following Slew's departure, and to keep his mind off the machinations of Quatremayne and his colleagues, Blut had to find a way to keep busy.

It was not difficult.

In the absence of the normal procedures of Bochum – routine daily reports, matters of Court organization, budget statements and the like – Blut was occupying himself with matters in the City. His clerks were finding it hard to cope. No one ever asked for, let alone looked at, the kind of information the new Emperor did.

'Put them there,' said Blut as more dossiers arrived.

'My Lord Emperor, there is a lot here that is really not . . .'

'Everything,' said Blut, 'I like the detail.'

He felt his interviews with Quatremayne and Slew had gone well and he needed a walk, which he took upstairs to his eyrie over London. A small unseen figure viewing a vast urban landscape, wondering.

Later he slept.

Later still he returned to his office and attended to his paperwork, piles of it.

A clerk and a scrivener stood by, impressed. The Emperor consumed paperwork as a raptor might strip carrion off red meat.

They waited; an orderly replaced the candles; the candles burnt down again.

Then suddenly he stopped and sat back, peeling his spectacles from round his ears, wiping them, putting them on.

He was frowning and thinking.

Tappity-tap, tappity-tap.

'Something,' he said very softly.

'My Lord?'

He waved his hand for silence. No one moved. In the distance, high up, the sounds of London hovered, moved in waves, night or day, he didn't know.

Something.

. . . an emotion?

. . . something he had seen but not understood in those papers?

. . . a connection he had failed to make?

'*Something . . .*' he said again. He had seen an opportunity. But where in all those papers? What had almost passed him by?

What would Sinistral have done?

He would have listened to the *musica* and let his mind drift.

Lacking the former, Blut stood up and did the latter.

He had missed something. A name? A place mentioned?

The connection was . . . with . . . with . . . *with* . . .

The pathways of his mind trembled as they sought a connection not quite made.

Uffington?

Where he understand the White Horse was.

Uffington!?

He smiled, relaxed, sat down once more and reached out for the right-hand pile.

It was the tenth or eleventh thing he had dealt with – or rather scanned, and found, as he thought, that there was nothing to deal with.

He riffled through the papers, pulled one out, placed it in front of him.

'Water!' he commanded.

The water came.

He sipped and read.

It was a report filed that morning on occupations and occupants in Building 24. Which, in hydden garrison parlance, was the Tower of London.

'Which is, I presume, the building opposite?'

'That is so, my Lord. On the far side of Tower Hill. But it is large.'

Blut pointed to a name on a list in the report. One of one hundred and twelve.

'Bring that one to me. Now.'

'*Here*, my Lord? Into your actual presence? *Now?*'

The surprise was real and reasonable. Emperors do not meet common criminals.

'It's as good a time and place as any for interrogation.'

'But . . .'

'Do it. Now. Without further reference to anyone. Understood?'

'Yes, my Lord.'

The orderly left and Blut stood up. The long days and nights had taken a slight turn for the better. His instincts were feeling good.

'*And hurry!*'

Arthur Foale was woken from a drifting kind of sleep by a kick to his shins and a clanking of chains.

'Yer wanted!'

'Ah,' he said with grim resignation. So the moment had come. Torture was about to be his.

'Who by?' he asked pointlessly.

'Shut up, get up and wise up.'

His chains were undone and he was pushed from the cell he shared with twenty others.

So far he had got off lightly, considering the nature and place of his very unfortunate arrival. Had he not smelt so badly, they might easily have applied the torch and the rack as well. As it was, they sent him to be cleaned up, forgot about him, and he ended up in a cell in which most of the inmates had been prisoners for many years.

Well, torture and death were perhaps a better prospect than such a life.

The only question he was asked through all of this was, 'What's yer name?'

His only pleasure was in making up the answer, which amused him.

'Mister Silas Uffington,' he had replied. Not a bad alias in the circumstances. No point giving his real name: someone might know it. The Fyrd kept records and his time in Brum had not gone unnoticed.

Days of nothing followed.

Now ... well ... torture is torture whatever time of day it is inflicted.

'Perhaps,' said Arthur, in a thin voice to the guard, 'I should explain that ...'

'Shut it.'

'... that I still have much to offer, old though I may look ...'

'Now.'

'... because, you see ...'

The corridor was low, dark and narrow, the cells on either side redolent of pain and misery; distant laughter seemed to mock him; his big toe hurt.

They reached some spiral stone steps, worn by the feet of the lost. He turned one way but was roughly pushed another.

'Up, not down.'

He had always thought that torture in the Tower was done in the basement. But, no, it seemed not.

'Sir,' he said, 'I would prefer ...'

If he was to have his nails drawn and his thumb screwed, he would prefer it to happen without a view. The grand vista of London might add to his pain.

'Shut it. I said it once, I say it again. I will not say it a third time.'

Arthur shut it, his mind beginning to blank as he thought of better things, better days, happier times.

He was pushed along one corridor after another, down some stone steps, along an echoing walkway ...

'This is the prisoner, sir,' said his guard.

Someone else took over.

Black leather, sleeked hair, a Fyrd.

'Straight on.'

'Er, yes,' he said.

When, finally, he reached the room they had been taking him to, the light was too bright for his eyes. He stood in his prickly clothes, the candles were like suns. As his eyes adjusted he found himself standing before a grey metal desk. Behind it a hydden sat, staring at him.

Arthur was sure he had seen him before. Dozens of times when he was a youth. In black and white. Yes, he was an actor who appeared in wartime movies, a would-be Nazi officer. Same spectacles. Arthur was utterly lost for words.

He would begin with a smile and offered cigarettes but the next thing . . .

'Mr Uffington?'

'Um, I think . . . er, yes, yes indeed. Silas Uffington of, of . . . Wantage.'

Where did the rubbish he spoke come from? He had no idea.

'I think not,' came the reply at once.

'Yes . . . er, no . . . um . . .'

Should he lie?

Who was this hydden in spectacles?

Arthur's head swam.

Darkness threatened him and he reached for support, he swayed a little and then resumed full consciousness.

'You are not Mister Uffington.'

'Am I not?'

'I don't think so. It's a place name, not a surname. So, why would you fabricate a name like that?'

Arthur had always imagined he would hold out longer, but if he was to be tortured or executed he would prefer it to be under his real name.

'My name is Arthur Foale,' he cried, standing up boldly, 'do with me what you will!'

His interrogator looked taken aback and stared at him intently.

'Foale as in F – O – A – L – E?' he finally said.

'The same. Not many can spell it correctly. They forget the E.'

'Arthur Foale?' said Blut faintly. '*Professor* Arthur Foale.'

'You have the advantage of me, sir!' said Arthur, very surprised his name would be known in such a place by such a person, who looked to him like no more than a jumped-up office clerk.

But whatever he may have looked like to others, Blut knew all about the Professor's excursions to the Hyddenworld in recent years and his visits to Brum. It had been his job to monitor such intelligence on Sinistral's behalf. Naturally he recalled Foale's extraordinary expertise in matters cosmological. But what was he doing here? On whose side was he? Brum's? Quatremayne's? His own?

Arthur found Blut's continuing stare very unsettling.

He decided to go on the offensive.

'I don't know who you people think you are,' he said, 'but I'd be grateful if you would charge me, try me, and punish me or, even better since I have done no wrong of which I am aware, let me go. Forthwith.'

Blut continued to stare, amazed.

Sinistral had always said that opportunities come to those who wait and here, beyond doubt, was an opportunity.

Arthur Foale! No one was better placed than he to make sense of the Earth's destructive behaviour in the past year or so.

'We are not going to charge or punish you,' said Blut, standing up and reaching out a hand, 'we welcome you!'

'That's all very well, my friend,' replied Arthur, ignoring the hand now proffered in friendship and respect, 'but I have been ill-treated and abused by the . . . by your . . . who *are* you, by the way?'

'Niklas Blut,' said Blut.

'And your role here is?' said Arthur dismissively. He felt this was a battle of wills and that he was winning it. Welcome, indeed! He felt he now had the upper hand and what he now wanted, and intended to press for, was an apology and his freedom.

'Mr Blut,' he continued, 'take me to your superior at once.'

'That will not be possible, Professor.'

'And why not?'

'Because I am . . . as it were . . . the superior. There is no authority higher than myself.'

Arthur gaped at him. Obviously he had landed up in a world of madness peopled by deluded bureaucrats like the one before him.

'Really!' cried Arthur dubiously.

'Yes, really,' said Blut, 'I am the Emperor of the Hyddenworld.'

'Really?' said Arthur after a long silence.

'*Really*,' repeated Blut.

Arthur gasped and it took a long time for him to be persuaded that it was so. When he finally was, all he could do was shake his head in wonderment. The last thing he had thought of when using the henge portal into the Hyddenworld was about finding the gem of Autumn and clearly this strange and unexpected meeting was part of what the hydden called his wyrd, which was in its turn a part of the wyrd of everything.

'You,' said Blut impulsively, 'are the first human I have ever met.'

'And you, sir, are the first Emperor *I* have ever met.'

They stood facing each other like explorers whose paths cross in a vast desert and who wish to preserve the proprieties.

Then they shook hands and first Blut and then Arthur began to laugh.

'It seems,' said Blut, 'that miracles do happen.'

'It seems,' replied Arthur, 'that they do.'

20

SUNDAY

It was a Sunday, which the hydden always observed as a day of rest, following the pattern set by humans. But this was the day of the Brum harvest festival, the second Sunday of September, midway through the season.

The work of the early harvests was done and the last and greatest festival, that of Samhain, was but six weeks off. It was the time when folk let their hair down, celebrated a good deal and got a second wind for the hard work yet to come in field and city, from where so much produce came.

It was therefore as well that the boats carrying Stort and the others did not finally arrive at the Muggy Duck until the early hours of that day. Had Arnold Mallarkhi, the best boatyboy that Brum had ever known, been alone, he could have done the trip in half the time. But the craft was laden with passengers, Old Mallarkhi steered awry here and there and the condition of Meister Laud was so weak that they had to stop three times to tend to him.

But Ma'Shuqa, the redoubtable landlady of the Duck, mother of Arnold, daughter-in-law of his grandfather, was ready and waiting just as Jack had asked her to be.

Jack's own journey in to get help had been troublesome, hence his delay, but he had been able to report the condition of the party, its size and his concerns about its oldest member.

'We need the best goodwife Brum has,' he said.

'There's none better than my friend Cluckett, Mister Stort's housekeeper. What she don't know about keeping old dodderers alive ain't worth the knowing! She'll be ready and waiting.'

'Tell no one else,' warned Jack, without much hope of the secret being kept. 'Now – we need two craft.'

'I've sent for my boy and Pa's risen from his bed o' pain to lend a hand, Mirror help you all. There'll be no stopping 'im and he knows them nasty Sparky waterways and filthy folk better than he should.'

She raised an eyebrow and smoothed her silk dress over her ample hips and tossed her ribboned hair in a disapproving way.

'He were young once, was Pa, and he were errant. That's why he knows them waterways of wickedness!'

So it was that when the exhausted party hove into view hours later in the early morning, some strong lads were ready to hoist Meister Laud out and get him inside the Duck for Cluckett's fierce attention.

'Steady!' she cried. 'He'll die on the spot if you shake him like that. Easy! And I'll have his habit and drawers off in a trice.'

Whatever nightmare Meister Laud now thought he was in could not have been worse than what was actually to come – as Stort and Jack both knew, themselves having fallen prey to Cluckett's stern attentions.

'Who's his next of kin?' she called out.

'I am,' said Terce.

'Well, he's not well and there's no quick cure and I need your help and Mister Jack's. The rest of you can stay outside.'

What she required of them neither afterwards said, but as Ma'Shuqa plied the others with wholesome food, heady brews and questions aplenty, they heard falsetto cries from beyond the sickroom door, terrible pleas from one they thought was as good as dead, and finally shouts of near-geriatric rage before there was a whimpering bleat of resignation.

Then silence most terrible, and they all held their cannikins in mid-quaff out of respect, for they were sure the old chorister had passed on.

Not so.

Jack and Terce emerged, sleeves rolled up, sweating from some extreme exertion, but able to say Meister Laud lived.

Then Cluckett came out, adding that he slept.

'Be that old gent cured or driven insane, Goodwife Cluckett?' asked Arnold, winking at Stort.

'We've halted the dying in him,' she replied, 'and tomorrow we'll attempt to start up the living.'

'That'll kill 'im,' said Old Mallarkhi, winking at Ma'Shuqa.

'Drink up and eat up and leave Cluckett to her trade, eh Mister Stort?' she replied tartly.

'None better,' said he, turning to his housekeeper, whom he had not seen for six weeks or more, saying, 'Madam, I am glad to see you!'

'Mister Stort,' she cried, for she admired and loved him more than any hydden alive and with him she was uncharacteristically soft and gentle, 'if these folk were not about I'd . . . I'd . . .'

She impulsively embraced him, which raised a cheer and brought colour to her cheeks.

As the day ahead looked likely to be a busy one, and the arrivals probably in much demand, they retired early.

Cluckett stayed with Meister Laud, Katherine offering her company for the night. Stort, Jack and Terce bedded down in a room adjacent to the sick room.

As so often with Stort, he lay restless for a time before rising for fresh air, to let the day's events settle in his mind. He went out onto the wharf and reached a hand towards the stars, dull though they were, and stood up as if to be a little closer to the moon, sad though it seemed.

His thoughts and his unspoken words were of love unrequited for Judith the Shield Maiden, who was so often on his mind. She was a source of such exquisite yearning that he would rather suffer than not know love at all. He murmured a few words and sentences of romance which, in better circumstances he might have said for real. He took comfort from the fact that if, now they were in Brum, their quest for the gem of Autumn could find more solid form and direction then, surely, he would likely see her again.

'It is I who must place the gem in its rightful setting in the golden pendant that she wears!' he murmured. 'Then, if only for a moment, I will see her close enough to almost touch!'

It was a sweet hope and put in him new determination to pursue the search more vigorously.

He might have continued in this vein and spoken his thoughts yet louder but that a discreet cough from the shadows and the flare of a lucifer at a clay pipe drew his attention. It was Dodd, also insomniac.

'Well then, Mister Stort, we made it in one piece!'

'We did, and I would have thanked you before now had you not made yourself scarce.'

'Never worry about that. Dodd does his own thing and is glad to. Any road, Mister Jack and that good wyf of his the lady Katherine have already done so and she pecked my cheek into the bargain. So, what now Master Scrivener? Your quest for the gem of Autumn can resume I suppose?'

'It can. I will start in the Library with certain items stored in the archive of ā Faroūin's books, papers and effects.' he replied.

He was thinking of the Embroidery of the Seasons but preferred not to be too specific as yet.

'And yourself, Dodd?'

'Heading south and westward with the sun. Dodd does not like Fyrd and it's certain they're coming this way.'

Again, the tremble and flicker of light, a sense of the shift of time.

Stort glanced at his chronometer. It was not much later than when he had first come out onto the wharf, but who could say what minutes a hydden loses without realizing it? What was there in Dodd's words to provoke such a thing? Stort tussled with the thought for a few moments before giving it up. He was too tired.

'Goodnight, Dodd,' he said.

'Fare thee well,' came the reply. 'I hope we meet again.'

Stort stared at him: strong but ageing, good-hearted, trustworthy, estimable.

'I believe we might,' he said.

No, he told himself as he turned to go in, *I believe we will*.

News of the arrival of the city's favourite heroes, Bedwyn Stort and Stavemeister Jack, in the company of Katherine, mother of the Shield Maiden, had spread rapidly. The normal crush of people eager for a glimpse of the proceedings in the Main Square, where the festival was formally started, was increased by the expectation that they would make an appearance.

The Parlement Building, the High Ealdor's Official Residence and all the other public buildings that offered vantage points were full, with folk hanging off rails or climbing up lamp posts to get a better look.

As usual there was much to see: hawkers, tricksters, evangelicals, beggars, buskers and sellers of savouries and sweetmeats.

One memorable sight was that of Terce, who, in no way put out by the grandness of the place or urgency of the situation, headed a strange procession, singing as he went. It had been decided that Meister Laud should be taken to the Hospice on a litter and Terce wanted to sing a healing song for him on their way. It was most beautiful and brought a silence in the Square as Meister Laud and his litter-bearers passed through and up the stairs of the Hospice.

Most Brum citizens had never heard such strange eastern cadences and lines of melody as Terce sang, and their hearts were filled with the wonder and majesty of it.

A few bilgesnipe labourers, sweepers of the street, clearers of the gutters, porters of heavy goods, stopped to stare in surprise. Some shook their heads in amazement, others dropped their tools and fell to their knees, and all began to hum the melody, deep and beautiful, as the song they heard touched some deep vestigial memory of songs their kind knew. Together, these voices summoned up, for a brief time, more exotic worlds, other dangerous times, the sorrow of parting, the long burden of exile.

There were the usual drunks and troublemakers, but the city's stavermen kept order with fierce word and occasional rough justice. Folk quietened into respectful silence when they spied the toughest and most respected of the bold stavermen of Brum, Mister Pike, pass by. He was grizzle-haired now, yet still a fit-looking fighter who wielded his stave better than anyone in Brum, barring Jack himself.

The crowd buzzed with excitement when Bedwyn Stort and Jack took a place up on the Library steps opposite the High Ealdor's Residence.

Jack raised a hand to quieten the crowd once more and invited Stort to speak, which he did, briefly and cheerfully to the delight of all. He then invited Jack to do the same.

'Our full report must be made to Parlement itself,' said Jack, 'and some of it is good news, other parts less so. We all know these times are dangerous and will be difficult. But here comes Lord Festoon himself and it is for him to speak, not me, nor even Scrivener Stort, beyond what he's already said!'

The excited crowd was now once more diverted, their attention drawn to the steps of Festoon's Official Residence. Its great doors had opened, a few functionaries appeared and stood talking among themselves for a few minutes before silence fell.

These days Lord Festoon cut a fine figure – tall and well-made, his cheeks shiny and pink, his eyes twinkling with good humour, his hair prematurely silvered at the sides, his demeanour at once magisterial and benign.

On this occasion he came out smiling broadly, his chain of office splendid on his chest, with its thick links of gold and pendant crest that showed the CraftLord Beornamund with his anvil and hammer on one side and his beloved Imbolc in a flowing dress on the other, flowers in her hair and a palette and brushes in her hand as emblems of creation.

He had a strong and pleasing voice and no difficulty in being heard right across the Square.

'My fellow citizens, my friends.'

How loud the cheer at that beginning!

'Welcome to you all this Harvest Sunday . . .'

He spoke briefly on this and that before giving alms from his own purse to poor widows, bachelors and mothers in straitened circumstances.

This duty done, he gave light sentences to various individuals hauled before him, not least those who had attacked Stort, Katherine and the others at Sparkbrook.

Lord Festoon next raised a hand towards where Stort and Jack stood on the far side of the Square.

'You have already welcomed Mister Stort and our Stavemeister back to Brum . . .'

Another great cheer went up.

'. . . and let us also welcome too Jack's wyf Katherine who is, at this moment, helping in the Hospice . . .'

A further cheer and a few ribald shouts, for Brummie folk, especially the males, like a fine well-made fair-haired wyf, which Katherine was.

Festoon forbore to mention the Shield Maiden which, for some, was a matter of private belief and debate as well as being a subject, resonant as it was, with a wyrd and mystery that must affect them all. A subject best left off the agenda in a public forum.

'Citizens of Brum,' he continued, 'it has been my custom to keep to the happy spirit of this festival and avoid matters more suited to our Parlement and the Council of War, of which there is a joint meeting later this week. However . . . *however* . . .'

A hush fell, for it was too clear that the High Ealdor had something on his mind he felt he needed to share with the wider public.

'However, there may not be another opportunity in the near future to address you all as I am able to now. I had thought to say nothing more of the dangerous incident concerning Mister Stort yestereve but now I must, to allay your fears. Some have suggested that the person accused of wielding a crossbow in our peaceful streets was not a citizen of Brum but one of a group of Fyrd, sent by the Empire to cause trouble and dissent. In fact the individual is well-known to Mister Pike's stavermen as a dangerous troublemaker and has been dealt with accordingly. Our community is close-knit and strangers quickly spotted and I am satisfied there are no Fyrd in Brum.'

A murmur of relief ran through the crowd.

'But you are all aware of the threat of Imperial invasion. It is something we have lived with for more than two years. But now the crisis is deepening. The new Emperor Blut is already upon our shores and has taken residence in the City, where he and his entourage, military and civilian, are making their plans against Brum in secrecy.

'The recent tremblings and devastations of the Earth, which mercifully have not disturbed Brum itself in recent weeks, have, I think, slowed the Fyrd's progress. Maybe there is no intention to invade.

'These matters will be discussed by Parlement, as will other matters over the next few days, as I have said, concerning the gems of Spring and Summer, wrested by Messrs Stort and Stavemeister from the grasp of the Empire.

'We are entering troubled and dangerous times with both Earth and Empire knocking at our gates.

'Some of you already have your orders. Others should be ready to receive theirs. All should watch out for Fyrd spies and suspicious strangers, always remembering that no one is guilty until proven so. The stavermen will come down hard on those who seek to impose justice with their own hands, as will I if any such are brought before me.

'Therefore, know that matters are in hand, plans being discussed and made daily by our Council of War and preparations made against the day – which I hope may never come – when we must defend ourselves against our enemies, who are the enemies of freedom!'

The claps and cheers were sombre but heartfelt.

'Meanwhile,' Festoon concluded, 'this is a festival and you would do Brum less than justice if you did not celebrate in good heart as you always have!'

This last raised final and more cheerful shouts of approval, but the mood remained anxious, the celebrations muted.

As for Stort and Jack, they briefly visited Katherine in the Hospice, where the condition of Meister Laud, having been stabilized by Cluckett, was not yet improving.

They walked then to Stort's humble, where they found refreshments left ready for them in the kitchen by Cluckett, who thought of everything. Shortly after, Katherine joined them.

'A last bite and a final drink before rest! That's what we all need. It's been a long hard journey.'

But they did not go to bed at once. The evening was warm and they took chairs out into the street. Stort's neighbours had done the same. They kept their voices low and respected each other's privacy, as was the way with Brummie folk.

'A lovely evening,' said Katherine, as the stars began to show between the high buildings and moon-caught clouds drifted slowly by.

'Calm before storm,' said Jack.

'Cluckett,' said Stort, when she brought out a spiced bread and joined them, 'what day is it?'

'It be a Wednesday, Mister Stort, and going on the twelfth day of the month. Calm it may be, gennelmen two and lady one, but I be frettered with worry and concern.'

'Of the Fyrd?' asked Katherine.

'Fyrd be blowed. It be a relative, sick. Wanting a visit just when you come along and I'm not going!'

'But you must,' said Stort.

'I mustn't, sir, not when you'm back and Mister Jack and his good wyf here.'

Katherine smiled. It was as good a description as any for her relationship with Jack.

'Toppermost is quiet,' said Jack, referring to the human world of Birmingham, in which Brum sat low and secret.

'Toppermost is ailing,' said Cluckett. 'Bain't just hydden who are leaving town. Humans have been for weeks past. Not just hereabout neither as I've heard. All about Englalond they're flighting the cities.'

They fell silent, each to his thoughts, and let the sounds of Brum take over.

21

ALLIES

The extraordinary world into which Arthur Foale had tumbled from the filth of a London sewer was all the stranger for the apparent normality of its inhabitants, particularly its most powerful one, the Emperor.

If he is *the Emperor!* Arthur told himself several times before he was convinced that Niklas Blut was real.

It was not the first time that Arthur's journeys into the Hyddenworld had taken him to the very top, very quickly. Perhaps it was in his wyrd that it was so.

His earlier experiments in the lost art of using henges as portals had soon taken him into the presence of Lord Festoon, High Ealdor of Brum, as adviser and friend. It was the kind of role Arthur found he occupied very easily, providing him as it did with good company, good food and a comfortable base from which to explore the world which he had gatecrashed for the purpose of his research.

Now it had happened again, but this was survival, not research, and the food and accommodation were rather more austere.

He might have expected an Emperor to live more lavishly than a High Ealdor, but he soon found it was not so. Blut was a very different character to Festoon and much less demanding of physical comfort or the grandeur of office.

But he was expansive in other ways: his mind and intellect, his eye for detail and his nearly obsessive pursuit of order based on 'rightness', whatever that might mean.

He was also astonishingly welcoming to Arthur, greeting his arrival with relief rather than suspicion and insisting that he stay in his company, or near it, and positively laughing at the notion that the professor might be sent back to his prison cell.

'I was not aware there was such a place, Professor,' he said. 'Please describe it.'

When Arthur did, stressing the cruelty and discomfort of the cells, Blut ordered immediate reform. Meanwhile, Arthur himself was given a spacious though not very airy suite of rooms, regular meals and all the comforts. In return all he had to do was to keep the Emperor company and answer a stream of questions, first about the human world, later about Brum.

The only grumble Arthur had was the garb he was given to wear, which was that of a Fyrd officer.

'Professor Foale,' said Blut, three days after he had first arrived, 'you are pensive. What is on your mind?'

'Well, my Lord,' said Arthur, who since he was dubbed 'Professor' was content to call Blut 'Lord', though he would have preferred something less grand, 'I confess that this garb that has been found for me is very uncomfortable and I would wish to be allowed to wear something else.'

Blut's clear grey eyes did not blink behind the spotless shine of his spectacles.

'It seems fine to me.'

'You're not wearing it, my Lord.'

'Mine is not dissimilar and it feels comfortable.'

Arthur was finding that Niklas Blut had the irritating qualities of an intelligent doctoral student – he came back swiftly with answers that were slightly challenging.

'Anyway, Professor, you make an impressive figure in the uniform of a Fyrd officer, if not a very senior one,' replied Blut.

Arthur stood up.

He felt like an elderly biker who had lost his Harley-Davidson. A paunch is bad enough, he told himself, but one clad in black shiny leather is ridiculous. Then there was his leather jerkin, of which the sleeves were tight and pinched his armpits.

Also there was the high collar which made his beard prickle.

The boot-things – Blut called them schuhe after the German – were callumphy.

'The only thing I *would* say, Professor, is that as the Fyrd generally go, you are a little overweight. So much so that in normal circumstances you would be put on a regimen which, if you did not follow it, would result in your being dismissed from the service.'

'I'll settle for that,' said Arthur. 'Dismiss me and let me wear civvies.'

Arthur noticed that the Emperor's aides-de-camp permitted themselves thinly disguised smiles.

'Meaning,' said Blut, 'not civvies, as you put it so agreeably, but a death sentence.'

'Ah!' cried Arthur, taken aback. 'Well then . . . where did you find this uniform?'

'It was worn by an elderly quartermaster who used to work in this garrison some years ago.'

'What happened to him?'

'He was executed, I believe.'

He turned to his aides-de-camp for confirmation.

'Two bolts from a crossbow, my Lord.'

They're serious, Arthur told himself uneasily.

'Professor . . .' began Blut once more, but stopping when a thoughtful expression crossed Arthur's face.

'I would be happier if you simply called me Arthur. I am content to call you my Lord in deference to your office.'

'Agreed,' said Blut. 'Now, to more difficult matters . . .'

Arthur was rapidly finding that Blut's mind moved on to other things fast once matters were settled and decisions made. He was capable, Arthur soon realized, of conveying something of the menace that comes with supreme power if he needed to. Obviously he now felt he needed to press Arthur on other and more urgent issues.

'I think, *Arthur*, that there is something more on your mind than the uniform it pleases me that you wear.'

'There is.'

What Blut missed most of all was the cut and thrust of his discussions with Slaeke Sinistral. No one he had ever met had quite his subtlety in verbal play, nor the ironic incisiveness of that great hydden. The Lady Leetha was playful and mischievous and that was a delight, and emotionally intelligent too, a challenge, but her mind was not as broad as Sinistral's.

Arthur Foale was different from either of them. Blut saw at once that he had not yet got anywhere near plumbing the depths of his knowledge, his intellect and perhaps his good nature.

'So,' persisted Blut, 'what else is on your mind?'

He glanced at his chronometer.

'We have a few more minutes before the General and his Staff arrive for what may be the meeting that decides our schedule for the invasion of Brum. Well, er, Arthur?'

Blut got up, stretched, as he liked to do, sipped his glass of water, nibbled at a piece of toast powdered with fennel, and sat with Arthur.

Once again the eyebrows were raised inquisitorially above the spectacles.

Blut, Arthur had decided, was a hydden it was impossible to dislike. He might look and behave coolly but there seemed no harm in him, no mal-intent. He exuded a calm intelligence.

'Well, then . . .' began Arthur, 'I suppose that . . . it seems a little . . . I cannot quite understand why . . .'

Blut turned and signalled his clerk and all but one guard to vacate the room.

'You cannot understand why *what*?' he said in a low voice.

'Why you trust me not to spy on you, try to kill you, or do anything that might help Brum, to which, if you were able to identify me from the nom-de-plume "Uffington", you must already know I am committed. Are you using me in some way, I ask myself. Am I to be liquidated by the Fyrd? Is this the cruel game of a power-crazed, um, Emperor?'

Blut took another sip of water, turned to the solitary Fyrd remaining in the room and summoned him over, and asked, 'What would you do if Professor Arthur Foale attempted to kill me?'

'Kill him, Lord.'

'Of if he tried to escape?'

'Kill him, Lord.'

'Or if he attempted to pass information on to a third party?'

'The same, my Lord, but the penalty for spying by a Fyrd officer . . .'

'I am not a Fyrd officer, dammit. My Lord.'

'. . . or by one *impersonating* an officer, as this gentleman appears to be doing considering the uniform he is wearing, is rather more severe than mere death, my Lord.'

Blut nodded and said, 'Quite so. Succinctly put.'

'My Lord?'

'Yes?'

'If that gentleman so much as touches a hair of your head there's plenty hereabouts will have his guts for garters and pay for the privilege, if you don't mind my saying so, my Lord.'

This unexpected vote of confidence took both by surprise. Perhaps Blut had won some allies among the General's staff and that was why he could not move against him here in the City: there were more than a few Fyrd such as this, loyal to the Empire and its supreme head before all else.

'Thank you for that,' said Blut politely, 'I appreciate it.'

He turned back to Arthur and said wryly, 'So you see, I am not in much danger from your good self and nor is the Empire. But let me answer your question about trust as succinctly as I can.'

He glanced at his chronometer again.

'I have a few minutes. As a young hydden, living and working in Hamburg in obscurity, I took it upon myself to investigate the mystery of the then Emperor Slaeke Sinistral's enormous longevity. I found that it lay in his possession and use of the precious stone which is generally known as the gem of Summer. Revealing this truth was deemed treachery and I was arraigned, tried and sentenced to death. The Emperor heard of it, stayed the execution and summoned me to Bochum . . .'

'The Imperial headquarters?'

'Just so. He talked to me for only a few minutes before deciding that I might, if trained, be able to run his Office. The rest you can work out for yourself. His view at first was that I was a potential threat who was best neutralized by keeping me close to him. That is my view of you, Arthur. His only instruction was that I should always tell the truth. If I did not, he said, he would kill me. The truth is what I expect of you and it is all I ask.'

'But you are not, I hope, expecting me to run your Office? I am not even able to keep my own desk tidy.'

Blut smiled slightly and shook his head.

'No, that is taken care of. What I lack is a sounding board, a companion, a similar *intelligence*. Your reputation precedes you, and in the short time you have been here I have seen nothing that makes me doubt it or you. You know a very great deal about the Hyddenworld from a perspective that no other hydden, except possibly the famous Mister Bedwyn Stort, and Jack if you count him a hydden . . .'

'He's a giant-born.'

'. . . ah yes, quite. You have a perspective other hydden do not have.'

'Which is?'

'The human one. We are in troubled times. The Earth is angry and she tells us so. I rather think she is more angry with humans for *their* abuse of her than she is with us. Yet we hydden will suffer all the same, perhaps terminally so. We are already beginning to. You know that she has expressed herself worldwide? Destruction looms for all of us.'

Arthur nodded. The briefing he had at RAF Croughton had made that graphically clear.

Blut lowered his voice.

'I have no wish for Brum to be invaded. Rather, I would like to debate these issues and what to do about them with our friends in Brum. At the moment, as you may already have guessed, it is difficult for me to escape Quatremayne's control.'

'Yes,' said Arthur, who had disliked the General on sight, 'I had worked that out.'

'To be frank,' said Blut, 'I am not so sure that I want escape from Quatremayne's control. This way at least I can keep an eye on him and perhaps dissuade him from a policy over which the former Emperor fell out with him.'

Arthur waited.

Blut's face registered displeasure and concern.

'You see, he believes that Brum might be hard to defeat by conventional means. He advocates the use of arms. I mean guns . . . the kind of weaponry that humans use.'

He looked appalled.

'That has never been the hydden way, nor should it ever be. We leave that madness to humans.'

'Crossbows are not much different from guns,' said Arthur reasonably.

'They are different in nature and range. And they are discriminate.

Guns and suchlike are not. But I fear that, given half a chance, Quatremayne would use them, stealing them from humans and then having our own made. It would be a catastrophe if such a hydden ever became Emperor. Imagine how different the human history you have told me about would have been if your kind had confined themselves to staves and crossbows!'

Arthur agreed.

'Now, to a happier subject. I believe, as I think those in Brum do, that our future health lies in reuniting Beornamund's gems. But that needs courage as well as caution. The former Emperor used a gem for his health and it finally caused him much trouble and pain as most drugs do. It badly affected Witold Slew, our Master of Shadows. We mortals should not ever think that we can use such things as if they were . . .'

He took another sip of water. '. . . like drinking water.

'I had wished to go to Brum to say such things, to negotiate but . . . well, matters are out of my hands at the moment. I am working on that. And now you may be able to help. Incidentally, I believe that though Mister Stort and his friends had no right to take the gems of Spring and Summer, it is in all our interests that they have done so. And, too, that they find the gem of Autumn which, I would imagine, they are in pursuit of even now. But that quest may be harder than anyone yet understands.'

'Why, Lord?' said Arthur.

Blut hesitated, looking for the right words.

'When I researched the matter of my Lord's longevity, I naturally had reason to ask myself what each of the gems represents.'

'Did you reach any conclusions?'

'Clearly Spring is about renewal, Summer about abundance.'

'And Autumn, the season we are now in?'

'It is the time of harvests, when we gain the benefits of past actions – or otherwise, as the case may be. The Earth seems to be against us just now.'

Arthur nodded his agreement and said, 'My own research has shown that about every fifteen hundred years or so the Earth experiences a period of seismic disturbance and climatic change. Usually on a relatively minor scale, meaning that there is no danger to Earth's very adaptable human and hydden inhabitants. Occasionally such episodes are more extreme and cause widespread destruction and millions die. Very occasionally the record shows something far worse in which wholesale extinctions of life, or sections of life, occur. I believe we have just entered one of those . . .'

Blut was fascinated but an orderly appeared, came over and whispered in his ear.

He nodded and murmured, 'I must attend a meeting with General Quatremayne. You will tell me more about all that a little later?'

'I will, my Lord.'

And later Arthur did.

22

REMNANTS

The White Horse stood restless, pale against the steep black coal tips of the mines scattered along the Ruhr of Nord-Westphalia, Germany.

Its tail flicked uneasily among white wisps of mist. It was a cold, wet September day which already heralded deep Autumn. The Horse's hoofs clattered and glittered through the coal dust and discarded shale; its great thick mane caught the sullen breeze, shifting to and fro like moonlit wheat at the approach of a storm.

Massive was the White Horse – as great as the heavens, and like the heavens it was troubled.

That morning its mistress the Shield Maiden had dismounted and not returned and now it searched the ruins of the mined-out Ruhr by way of Schalke and Horst, Bottrop and Rotthausen, Gelsenkirchen and Herne, old Essen and Wattenscheid.

It stamped over the hard ground through the old places, seeking, sensing, snorting, rearing, its form as awesome as a glimpse of a great mountain between shifting clouds.

Bochum, headquarters of the Hyddenworld, lay underneath the surface of the Earth, as secret and rotten as fallen fruit overgrown by fresh green grass. Down there beneath the surface, where the White Horse's hoofbeats echoed, beyond the boundaries of the Imperial Court to where the Remnants made their lost and lonely lives, was where the echoes went. Beneath the wastelands of Westenfeld and Gunnigfeld, Höntrop and Weitmar.

Judith, its Rider, she who was Shield Maiden, had not returned and the White Horse was bereft, its neighing the wind in the rusting sails of old water pumps, its wheezy whickers and moans the rub and batter of old fence posts among the oaks of the Weitmar-mark.

So the White Horse wandered, distressed, its mistress searching the subterranean darkness while the Earth got ever angrier, eager to harvest mortal life to satisfy her hungry rage.

Maybe Mother Earth will gobble Bochum?

Maybe she'll suck into her maw the Remnant tunnels west and south, like coal-black spaghetti?

Maybe she'll eat up the sad, wasted ground on which the White Horse stands, fretful and alone.

The Horse rose up again, mist corporeal, snorting in fury, and brought its front hoofs thunderously down upon the ruined land.

Judith the Shield Maiden heard it.

A whole miserable, frustrating week she had been down there seeking Sinistral, feeling tired, the air cold, her body feeling the pain of ageing moment by moment, health and joy leaking from its poor pores in the dark. That was a week in human terms, not her own.

'Where are you, Slaeke Sinistral?' she whispered, 'I've been down here for years. Where are you when you're most needed?'

She knew – though how she knew she knew not, knowledge and wisdom came to her like great flakes of blizzard snow out of the dark – that the gem of Autumn would not be found without him. Without any of them. Bedwyn Stort was essential, but Sinistral's help was needed too.

At least she was not alone down there in the labyrinthine tunnels, which was a mercy. The Reivers, her followers and servants, were with her, more or less, riding their filthy hounds and mastiffs, chasing rats, sniffing at the phosphorescent marvels of that place, slavering at stuff, baleful and scared.

Morten, her own dog, was there too; his coat might have been beautiful in the dark had she been able to see it clearly, or him, which she could not. The Reivers raced here and there through the tunnels, chasing things they could scent but not see, harrying the poor and miserable Remnants that lived down there, beings cast out by history and time to this edge of things: hydden, bilgesnipe, and all the forms between and beyond and to the side. Life marginal, miserable and lost.

'Where are you, Emperor, my Lord, Majesty . . . where *are* you?' she screamed, her cries making thunderous, ear-splitting echoes in the dark.

Then, hearing the White Horse's frenzied hoofs stamping its distress above, she bellowed upwards, 'I'm not coming up without him, I'm not!'

Judith turned and turned again, sniffing the air, animal-like, her bare arms filthy, her white garb black with coal dust, the dogs whining at her legs, sniffing at her stink, the Reivers chattering to themselves, saying she had a new scent and soon, Mirror be praised, they'd have him and the whole lot of them could get up to the light and warmth again and real food and not the crap down here.

While they ate she stood in total darkness, removed her clothes and stood beneath a waterfall of icy-cold water, washing the grit from her hair, her armpits, her legs, between her legs, drinking at one end, peeing the other and muttering in her pain and seeming madness.

Bastards!

She was ageing fast, each day and each minute.

Her breasts were no longer as firm as they had been.

Bastards!

When she got back out she would be perceptibly older than when she went in. Hair beginning to grey? Eyes bagged? Stomach sagging?

She was ageing but nothing was actually killing her, not even the hunger and cold and the wet as she showered and the dogs ate.

Time was her enemy, not disease.

They crunched at the albino worms, the translucent freshwater shrimps, the rats, the body of a fox. They licked fungi of the stinking sort and they tore at slimy weed, tongues dripping with filth.

Please, Mistress, can we leave? whined the Reivers.

Sometimes the phosphorescence wove about the walls and showed their ugly faces, malevolent, protective of her but hating her, eyes shining green with jealousy for what to them was her raw beauty.

Judith turned to answer them, snarling.

'Not till I find him, only then. You've had the good times. Now live with the bad.'

The language of others in her far-off youth of four months before it rushed into her and spewed back out: 'Where are you, Sinistral, you . . . ?' Her four-letter words were filth.

Here . . . his taunting whisper carried to her on the draught, as she dried herself in its flow, *here my dear. You think you've been here years? You have been here only seconds of* my *life.*

'Well *that's* debatable,' the Shield Maiden said to the Reivers, cheered that he had spoken to her. 'Now let's start to get clever about this because otherwise, at this rate, he'll continue evading us until we're dead and then, what will the years or minutes mean, or time itself?'

Time, that was the thing.

It was always running out.

It was September or October more or less, she knew that. She needed the Autumn gem by Samhain, which began on November Eve, not for herself but for the hungry Earth. She felt the pendant at her breast, the gems of Spring and Summer, and she stilled, thinking of love, thinking of Stort, touching what he had touched, her forbidden mortal counterpart.

What would you do, my love?

How would you find Slaeke Sinistral?

You'd find a way, always find a way, that's why I love . . .

She stilled and listened and thought.

She did not dare add the final word that was everything: *you.*

But it was so, she loved Stort.

Sinistral had spoken to her a day or two before, his voice carried to her then, as now, by the draughts and breezes of those tunnels, but from different directions. Always teasingly, no more than whispers. There was, despite his reputation for past deeds, no cruelty in Slaeke Sinistral's voice, though plenty of pain. She should be able to recognize *that* in another. She was an expert.

'He wants my company,' she said.

'. . . and our dogs want his flesh,' replied the Reivers. 'Then we want out of here.'

'And Morten, my dog?' she said softly, reaching a hand to find him and finding nothing but a wet and slimy tunnel wall. 'Where is he? *Find him.*'

One of the Reivers spat, looked disgusted, pulled the rein on her mastiff, whispered in his much-scarred ear, and gave an instruction. They reared, turned in the dark, pushed others out of the way, and went in search of Morten.

Judith laughed. She guessed he had been up to the surface to take live meat, chomp at flies and slaver in the blood of rabbits and a hare, before returning fortified. The only sensible one among them.

Maybe he went and said hello to the White Horse, which was why there had been no stomping of hoofs of late.

Her thoughts returned to Sinistral and finding him.

'I think he's along there in front of me. His voice sound is comfortable, rich with the sound around him, richer than he's ever been before. We're near.'

She leaned forward and down to speak into the ear of the great bilgesnipe Remnant they had captured and said, 'Tell me where he is or I'll rip your eyes out.'

'I'm blind already,' replied the bilgesnipe gently.

'Fat thing,' she whispered more softly still, 'it'll still hurt, blind or no. Your white orbs sense light and therefore will feel pain.'

He blubbered and heaved himself forward on the lead they had put round his neck.

'Quietly,' she ordered everyone, 'very, very quietly.'

Then she called in a sing-song way: 'Where are you, Sinistral?'

Where you wouldn't think to look, the former Emperor of the Hyddenworld replied, *and as for that mutt you call your dog . . .*

'Morten,' she said.

. . . he's on his way back to you so you have no need for that Reiver and her dog to go searching, they might get hurt.

Judith breathed more easily. She had known that before Sinistral had. She was catching him up.

Then a distant scream, which fell away from them, spiralling down into darkness level by level, unable to fly up against the downdraught, or orientate in such pitch-black darkness, down and down into water so cold it froze the other Reivers' minds and those of their dogs.

The fallen Reiver's hands and legs reached out for guidance, to get a sense of direction in the black water they were in, where no light was or ever would be. The dog's great mouth opened, snapping, its claws seeking anything to hang on to the half-life that is the lot of such dogs and their mistresses.

The Reiver screamed weakly down in those depths, a bubbling thing, as did her dog which, lacking any other contact, caught her, clamped a thigh between his teeth, scrabbled his paws down her face and chest, tasted her half-blood, little more than water but warmer than what he was in, trying that way to stay alive.

Her screams were his extra seconds.

Then, in the pitch of their watery night, on which no sun would ever rise, nor any moon set, they juddered, stilled and died.

'Bastard,' shouted Judith at Sinistral.

She could almost feel his shrug of indifference.

He said: *Theirs was the rush, theirs the slip, theirs the long fall, I and you are but its witnesses. We should not blame ourselves for others' lives; our own are hard enough to bear while we negotiate the currents and the storms of the ocean sea of time before we find the calm where we are free of our troubled selves. And anyway, don't Reivers come back to life again?*

Words which travelled the levels and the tunnels, the adits and the elevator shafts, while Judith whispered to her followers to scatter in all directions, making noise, confusing the tunnel sound.

'But, mistress, that will leave you alone and unprotected, of which the White Horse would not approve.'

'Do it,' she commanded, 'and watch out for the unmarked shafts, they end in a watery grave which is unpleasant and necessitates a painful return.'

But they needed no such warning. They could hear the screams of the drowned Reiver and her dog as they crawled out of the shaft of death into life again.

So now Judith went alone with her bilgesnipe captive, his fat body squelching with the cold sweat of fear against her, making her shiver with disgust. Yet his nature was warm, that was the thing about bilgesnipe, they had good hearts. It was, she knew, her constant pain that made her so uncharitable.

Mirror, was she cold!

'I'm sorry,' she said.

'I understand,' he replied, which nearly brought her to tears.

'How far?'

'Ssh, Shield Maiden, we are close.'

'If you make a sound to warn him I will . . .'

'I know what you will do, but even if he heard us it wouldn't matter. He wants to be found now, can't you feel it?'

She shook her head.

'Can't you *hear* it, Shield Maiden?'

'No.'

'You have very much to learn. But learn you will as life is leached out of you and age brings knowledge. Now, let me free for I too have pride and would not have him see me like this, bound round the neck like a slave.'

She felt a sudden shame and let him free.

Sometimes she could not bear the dying of the life she lived, each day a season of time, four days a year of ageing, her life mortal in its consciousness but not its timescale. She had less than a year to live a mortal's three score years and ten.

'Why was I made?' she sometimes cried in her loneliness. 'Why must I be?'

At such moments, down here as up there, now as just a little while before, on the back of the Horse and off it, by Earth's vast beauties and mortal kind's urban ugliness, by coal tip and waste and by the running waters of the clear streams of fell and hidden vale, she would feel the pendant which Stort had put round her neck, feel the gems of Spring and Summer he had found and put in place, feel his knowing of her through and through, his love which could never be, her love which must never be spoken, and find a solace from her lot.

The bilgesnipe stopped.

'Mistress,' he whispered, feeling her face with his chumpy hand and touching his fingertips to her lips so she didn't speak, 'he is very near and thinks he hears you, but isn't sure. It was wise to send your Reivers off and about to make confusing sound. Clever, that. I will go forward alone, you will stay. I will set the beeswax lamps aflame about the Chamber we are about to enter. Do you know what that Chamber is?'

She shook her head, her lips brushing his fingers.

His touch was comforting as he made her understand that she was on the edge of the Universe. She began to hear its *musica*.

You are – a shard of a future memory came – *you are my only love.*

And her reply: 'I knew you'd find a way to come to me.'

Was it Stort, whispering in a dream he would never know he was going to have, whispering her on? Was it her imagining of his voice that made its sound? Was it love that gave her the courage to still her rage enough to hear and forget her pain?

'Listen!' said the blind old bilgesnipe in the dark. 'Watch! Feel! Only when you're ready and you see the light should you venture in. He's there, waiting. Anxious too.'

He went on forward and she did as he asked: listened, opened her eyes to see, opened her heart to feel, her fingers to the pendant and the gems that were love-gift from Bedwyn Stort, touching them as the bilgesnipe had touched her lips, her life raft through the rough seas of her great journey.

The first light the bilgesnipe made looked watery, seen through subterranean rain that swirled about in the draughts.

The second brought sound, filling the rain, made by the rain, a whorl of exquisite sound that drew her in.

The third was higher, the fourth lower and by the fifth, the Chamber taking shape beyond the entrance he had brought her to, she finally saw Sinistral and sighed.

He was most beautiful, his form slanted into fragments by the endless draught-driven dripping from the ceiling high above and out of sight, drips which fell at an angle, mist whose droplets turned like flocks of starling in the light.

He stood by . . . what?

She could not quite see what it was his hand rested on, so she moved forward, through the great arched entrance her guide had brought her to, into the Chamber in which, when he had needed succour, Sinistral had been kept alive for eighteen years.

His garb was white, his hair sleeked back, his presence powerfully benign.

'Shield Maiden,' he said softly, 'I have felt your pain since the moment of your conception. Where *was* that?'

'In Englalond.'

He sighed and whispered, 'Englalond'.

It too was the country of his birth.

'I long to return,' he said.

'That is why I have come. To take you home. You are needed, Slaeke Sinistral.'

He smiled, his teeth white, his eyes glittering black.

'Come closer.'

As she did so, the mist between them thinned, the rain moving away, and he aged, his skin ravaged by the long decades of his life, but not so much wrinkled as crazed, as if he was made of porcelain, the rain shiny on his cheeks, like varnished tears.

'You are very beautiful,' she said wistfully, touching her own prematurely ageing face.

'You are too, my dear,' he replied, 'more than I think you know or can believe. But ageing is hard and painful, is it not? I should know: I've spent a long time doing it, probably too long. But that is why I hear you and truly see you. We sing the same song, Shield Maiden. Can you hear the *musica* yet?'

She listened to the rain, the echoes, the melding of the dripping sound, his voice, the soft beeswax light, she heard that too.

'I hear something,' she said hesitantly.

'In time, I daresay, you will hear it all. Now listen, Shield Maiden, I cannot yet come with you.'

'You must. I can make you.'

'Not yet, you can't. I am the stronger of us two for now.'

She eyed him and shook her head.

'They need you, Sinistral.'

'My Lord – I prefer you to call me that.'

'My Lord,' she said softly, with the sudden love that all who had known Slaeke Sinistral down the decades of his long life had come to feel, sooner or later.

He closed his eyes, holding tighter to the strange thing on which his hand rested.

'Have you seen her?'

'Leetha?'

She did not know, even now, how she knew these things. They came to her mind when needed: names, places, people. She came to them when she had to. The wyrd of those memories was hers.

She shook her head.

'I have not.'

'Go to her before you come back for me. Whisper my love to her, learn its language, see her beauty before you see mine again. Find yours in all of ours. For, Judith, Shield Maiden, you too are beautiful.'

She backed away, the anger returning.

She had no beauty that she knew of. Age was her trial, ageing her doom. Like their mother the Earth, ageing all the time, growing cold and sterile, turning in the end in darkness and in space, into the ice time of all the long millennia.

She too would be ice and Stort would cease to love her because he too would be ice. Two static, frozen forms, reaching endlessly for the other, made of ice.

'Go to her,' he said. 'I have not finished here.'

'The gem of Autumn . . .'

He nodded.

'I shall help them find it,' he said softly, 'but I shall not touch it. Never for me, never again. *Never.*'

Did he stumble then, or weaken? The curious chair-thing he leaned on moved. She went closer to look. His face shone with tears lit by a beeswax light. The bilgesnipe moaned in sympathy, coming a little nearer than before.

The *musica* swelled, the rain drove down, the mists swirled in the new wind and the Reivers' dogs' barks and snarls were carried in, spiralling about, jagged in the dark air, threatening their peace.

'My Lord,' she said, as if Leetha herself said it, 'rest and sleep . . . you will be safe here until you are ready. Then will you come?'

She and the bilgesnipe turned the dentist's chair together. It was his haven, to sit and rest in the cocoon it made.

'Tend to him,' she commanded.

'You know what she is,' he called out, 'to you?'

'Leetha is my father's mother,' replied the Shield Maiden.

'She is your grandmother, Judith, and she has need of you, as you of her. She too . . .'

He let that thought drift into the *musica* about them, taking up another instead.

'I will come. Blut will know what is needed to get me out of here. He probably already has it in hand!'

'I can do it,' she said.

'No, no, you have better things to do than that. Your time is short. Delegate. Blut will know whom to send.'

'I think he's on his way already,' she heard herself say, which was another thing she did not know she knew.

'Who?'

'Slew. Is that a name that means something to you, my Lord?'

He laughed.

'Did you know that ã Faroün made an embroidery? In it is woven the wyrd of all our lives. Slew is your father's brother, Leetha's other son. People used to say that I was the father. Not so.'

'Who was?'

'Ask Leetha, my dear. That is her business, not mine. Now . . . let me sleep. You have done all you can with me for now. Like the warp and the weft of the seasons, our lives will criss-cross, criss-cross, again and then again and then . . .'

'Sleep, Lord,' said the bilgesnipe, tending him, 'sleep . . .'

She turned from truth into the darkness back through the arch, strong again, his tears her own as one by one the lights went out and the *musica* caressed his mind and being.

'I know where Leetha is,' she said. That too had come to her.

The White Horse stood in the darkness of the night, still as the stars above, readying itself for the arc of the moon, at peace again.

She was coming back.

She was nearly there.

The dogs and the Reivers rushed on by, turning in the night, their job well done, hers too, no doubt.

The Horse knelt, for she was tired.

Judith the Shield Maiden clasped its mane and pulled herself onto its great back.

'You know where to go,' she said. 'You always do,' she cried.

The fingers of one hand clutching his strong neck, her thighs to his

great flanks, her neck and head along his warm neck, her other hand
and its fingers, for comfort, holding the pendant about her neck.

'You always do,' she wept.

The mist flew over the slag heaps of the Ruhr, the wind rose, and
the rain fled as together they crossed the night sky. While Lord Sinistral
turned and tossed in his chair in the darkness and finally slept.

23

IN THE BUNKER

Arthur Foale was now in a bubble of Imperial comfort and safety, cut off entirely from the world he knew. He was finding it very hard to hang on to the idea that a hydden so civilized, welcoming and polite as Blut was, in fact, the enemy, for Brum had always been against the Empire. Yet nor could he pretend that the unexpected situation of being at the very centre of things, permitting him to see nearly all of what was going on, was anything less than fascinating.

But he knew that each moment that passed in the alluring presence of the Emperor, his clerks and orderlies sapped the resolve he needed if he was to escape.

Naturally, the threat of death which Blut had so blandly warned him of if he tried to do so, hung heavily on him. Arthur Foale was a portly seventy-year-old academic who felt aches and pains in the morning and sometimes forgot what he was meant to be doing, hardly a serious threat.

He could take comfort from the fact that he had got away unscathed from RAF Croughton but he could see that escaping the Imperial quarters, guarded as they were by Fyrd, was going to be a lot harder and that death, probably an unpleasant one, was a distinct possibility. He sighed and faced the truth that all those who find themselves in the hands of an accommodating enemy with every freedom but that of actual liberty must face: that it is morally wrong not to try to escape, especially when one's friends' and allies' lives are endangered by the very people holding you, but there is little incentive.

It was sometime in the evening of another day with Blut, at the end of another very pleasant supper discussing the Theory of Gaia and the issue of the Earth as a possibly vindictive organism, that he realized his position was untenable.

The Emperor, with his usual perspicacity, eyed Arthur quizzically and said matter-of-factly, 'Something is on your mind.'

'It is, but I cannot say what it is.'

The Emperor gave leave for the guard who was normally with them at that time of the evening to retire to his quarters, leaving them alone.

When he was gone Blut said confidentially, 'Because you don't know exactly what it is, or that I might disapprove?'

'The latter.'

'But I explained before that you are no use as a companion if you do not tell me the truth.'

'I do not wish to be your companion,' Arthur replied testily. 'I wish to be free!'

With his usual equanimity Blut considered this without apparent offence. Then he said: 'Well, we all wish to be free. So what do you propose doing about it?'

'I . . .'

Blut was a master of using few words to say a lot. Suddenly there was something in his face that suggested conspiracy. Arthur's heart raced. If he suggested escape, might the Emperor wish to join him? Or might it be a trap?

He said a curt goodnight, went to his room, and paced about, restless with thoughts of escape, of punishment, of an absurd plot to escape with Blut and much more.

Perhaps he might have concocted such a plan in the following days had not his door opened in the middle of the night and a hand grasped his shoulder and shaken him awake. It was an orderly.

'We're moving, sir, right away.'

'Who's moving?'

'The Emperor's Court is being moved to a place of greater safety.'

'From what?'

'Danger,' said the orderly vaguely, who Arthur noticed was armed with a crossbow, which he was not before.

'Where are we moving to?' grumbled Arthur, rubbing his eyes and straightening his hair and beard.

'Not at liberty to say, sir.'

A short while later Arthur found himself being herded with others onto a narrow-gauge train which started underground but eventually emerged into the night outside. Of the journey that followed Arthur afterwards remembered little: he was tired, it was night and he was disorientated.

When they finally stopped and were told to get out he saw they were in a deep cutting with trees looming above. They were led away down a wide concourse towards a massive concrete wall lit by a single bulb. A small steel door was set into it, with a wheel for a handle, which made it look like the entrance to a safe. Inscribed in faded black lettering to one side was an alphanumeric descriptor of some kind: M.O.D. A/W/263.

Arthur just had time to register that this was a Ministry of Defence building before they were taken inside and the door clanged shut behind them.

The outside had looked neat and clean enough but the interior, which was a foyer area with three corridors leading from it, was a mess of fallen plaster from the ceilings above.

This had been brushed to one side to give easier access to the main corridor, the only one, it seemed, with working lights, but its ceiling had also collapsed. Hanging from a barred broken window were fronds of ivy and other vegetation, beyond that the shift and squeak of branches and the sound of wind.

No wonder the air smelt damp and woody. Wherever it was they had come to, they were buried beneath a wood and, more than likely, well hidden from human eyes.

But it was late and they were all tired, the Fyrd as well, and Arthur was glad to be shown to new quarters to turn in for what remained of the night. He slept deeply and well.

In the morning any hope that he had of freedom and escape evaporated. He was directed to an old-fashioned canteen of stainless steel and plastic and saw at once that he was back to square one, but in a more depressing place.

'Ah! Arthur!' cried Blut cheerfully, 'Good morning! You slept well? Help yourself to breakfast.'

The Court was depleted: fewer orderlies, fewer clerks, fewer Fyrd to keep an eye on them. No special treatment any more.

'Things don't look good,' said Arthur.

'No, they don't,' agreed Blut. 'We need to get out of here . . . The escape to freedom you hinted at last night is now an imperative. If you had stayed long enough I would have said so.'

'I thought it dangerous to mention it more directly.'

'It *is* dangerous. Quatremayne will keep me alive only as long as I am less useful dead.'

'And I?'

'He is keeping you as companion to me, to keep me amused, I suppose. Now we need a strategy.'

'Ah! Yes. A strategy.'

Arthur had never had one of those in his life. He had jogged along and things had happened and then he had jogged along some more and more things had happened. Then Margaret had died and now he was in this mess.

Blut studied him and understood.

'Let me worry about strategy, it's what I do. You find the means of escape – that's what *you* do. There are fewer Fyrd guards than before and they'll focus on me. You can probably slip away unnoticed. It's a warren of a place. They'll think you're in your quarters.'

'It would be a good start if we knew where we are.'

'That I can answer,' said Blut. He half closed his eyes, consulting the dossier he had been able to read and memorize.

'We are in the Ministry of Defence building A/W/263. It is what humans call a Cold War Bunker, whatever that means. You know, I expect.'

Arthur did and he explained.

'There are dozens dotted about all over the place in Englalond and many across the Channel too. All but a few have long-since been decommissioned. Some destroyed, some put to other uses, and some, built in secret, now all but forgotten. This may be one of those.'

His eye was caught by a tatty old map half-taped, half-pinned, to a noticeboard. It had been left behind by the former human occupants of the bunker and he needed to stand on a chair to look closely at it. It was an old inch-to-a-mile Ordnance Survey map with all the symbols, gridlines and many different typefaces he knew so well. Someone had used a red crayon to put a circle around their location on the map.

Arthur studied it for a long time, breathing easier to know where he was and to read names so familiar to him: Northampton, Rugby, Market Harborough and Kettering, where he and Margaret once spent a night in a horrible hotel. How far off that time, that human life, now seemed.

He soon discovered that Blut was right, it was not difficult to disappear for a few hours. Whoever had done the original reconnaissance of the bunker had not done it thoroughly. The wide concourse down which they had come when they first arrived was well lit by electric lights. The many side-corridors off it less so. The main nexus of activity was a crossroad of corridors not far from the Emperor's quarters. In that area the corridors were covered in grey linoleum which had once been stuck fast to the concrete beneath. Time had caused it to become brittle, chronic damp had lifted off the substrate. But there was enough left to give an illusion of smartness, helped by the fact that the walls thereabout were white, the doors grey. They were numbered twice – once by humans, with letters and numbers, and more recently by the Fyrd, with numbers from 1, the Emperor's Quarters, to 20, which were latrines.

The command centre was Number 5, a big room with a table on which maps of South Englalond had been laid and a viewing platform on two sides from which they could be studied. Off this operations room there was an old radio station at which two young Fyrd worked with earphones and Morse keys, transmitting messages.

Good old Morse code, thought Arthur.

Radio hamming and its associated activities had been a hobby when he was a boy, and the operators were happy enough to show him how the system worked in the bunker.

'The condition of the wiring is nearly perfect, Professor,' one of them explained, 'and all we had to do was establish a frequency with

Bochum, reset our codes to match theirs and avoid unwanted contact with humans and we were away.'

'Unwanted contact?'

'Who knows who would tap into the old settings? Probably all defunct now and it would probably be impossible to trace us. But our own settings in Bochum are definitely secure. The new Emperor made sure of that when he was a Commandant. It interested him.'

It was a point that interested Arthur too and a new topic for conversation and reminiscing with Blut.

'Morse? Yes, any communication method interested me as Commandant of the Emperor's Office. It was illegal for non-Fyrd to communicate that way, or most ways involving equipment of that kind. But . . . people did.'

'So you executed them?' said Arthur heavily.

'We warned them. Only one was sentenced but the sentence was never carried out.'

Arthur looked surprised, then remembered that Blut himself lived because of an Imperial pardon.

'No, he was not pardoned. We couldn't find him even when we got to the little place he lived on the Dutch coast. But no one, not even his family, knew where he was. After that he became an irritant but harmless. The Emperor finally decided to let him be.'

'Not even a name?'

'We worked that out but when the Fyrd got there . . . His name was Arald. Of course, Brum had some Morse coders too, but then it would have, Arthur. They were untouchable. I think you know one of them rather well.'

Arthur thought for a moment and laughed.

'Mister Bedwyn Stort! Sort of thing he would do. I visited his laboratory once but I cannot say I remember a Morse key or a wireless but, well . . . it was untidy.'

'Tell me about this Stort.'

Arthur did so.

While these conversations continued Arthur took an occasional break from them by exploring the largest of the unlit tunnels he noticed when he arrived. Lacking any map of the bunker he began making one of his own, realizing very quickly that the system was far bigger than he had imagined and its layout more complex.

The secondary tunnel had lights with no working bulbs, until Arthur found hundreds of them in a storeroom. Most of the light fittings were corroded but not all. He soon fixed up enough lights to make exploration possible, though he left dark places to discourage anyone from following him.

The air was cold and draughty, which implied some kind of exit to the world above. The floors were wet, in some cases sludgy. The walls were mildewed, the plaster ceilings all gone, exposing a network of pipes, many rusted. There were chairs, desks, rotten bedding, unopened supplies of everything needed for human survival underground, from towels to bandages, tins of food to unused brooms and hardware such as sinks, pipework and what looked like a rusted industrial heater.

Here, too, he found rooms for administration and planning and some empty ammunition boxes. Several times the lights flickered; once they went out.

Arthur proceeded cautiously, aware of the dangers of methane gas, tunnel collapse or rusting and jagged obstacles. Once some pipework he brushed against collapsed a little while later; another time a door swung to, sheered a hinge and nearly fell on him. At such times the torch he had brought with him, which no one had thought to confiscate, was crucial. But mostly he used it very sparingly.

Desolate and cold though the bunker was, it forcibly reminded him of the strange and extreme nature of the journey he had made. Humans seemed a long way away, their paraphernalia odd, eccentric even, and the business of secrecy and war an unpleasant and alien one.

Soon after, in another corridor, he found a secondary communications room. There was a Morse key and typewriter pad on a half-collapsed table and a fuse board on the wall, all corroded. But underneath a counter, inside a drawer, in boxes, he found supplies wrapped in brown, greaseproof paper. There was cable, fuse wire of various thicknesses, clips and crimpers, screwdrivers, pliers, all kinds of things that offered communication potential: radio parts, valves . . . and three Morse keys. These were oiled, wrapped and sealed. They were in perfect condition, laid ready against the day, surely long gone, when they might be needed. Arthur decided to try to get them working.

Blut was fascinated.

'If you succeed, you could communicate and send for help. But that carries risks. I will think about it.'

It took Arthur another day to find a transmitter and receiver, again in near-perfect condition. He got them working easily and by moving them about was able to pick up high-frequency signals.

He felt a moment of connection with the world and his youth. The feel of them, the touch, the smell of the coils, brought back Arthur's boyhood when his father showed him such things, first how to care for them, then how to make them.

How long he sat there he did not know, working by the light of a single bulb, sometimes just his torch only, his stiff fingers trying to do what once he did so swiftly and well.

The Fyrd operators had said the cables were good and they were right. He eventually traced a live supply, activated no doubt by the Fyrd elsewhere in the bunker. He cut out the corroded Morse key attached to it and hooked up one of the good ones.

With the box came a cheat sheet for the Morse letters and abbreviations, which was just as well since his memory of Morse was limited.

Later, Blut, being Blut, said he remembered his Morse instantly.

He shrugged and said, 'I cannot help it. I remember the most useless of things. Sometimes . . .'

He frowned and scratched his chin.

He cleaned his spectacles.

Then he scrivened a short string of letters and numbers on a piece of paper. 'For example,' he said, thrusting the paper towards Arthur, 'I remember this as the call sign of our elusive friend Arald in Holland.'

Later still, back in the communications room he had discovered, Arthur pulled out his notebook, in which he had secreted the piece of paper.

He was ready to begin and he did. He knew the Fyrd operators were deliberately avoiding the frequencies humans used, which suited him perfectly. He did not want them picking up on what he was going to transmit, which was a call for help, giving some very precise information about their location to anyone who knew how to read it. It was an S.O.S. and incorporated the call sign Blut had given him as well.

Someone, somewhere, might respond. Maybe Arald himself. That particular hydden would have good reason: simple curiosity.

If and when anyone does respond, thought Arthur, *I might dare to think we have some hope of getting out of here.*

24

LEETHA

'She's not here,' cried Judith the Shield Maiden angrily, her voice the rattling of pine cones across the forested slopes of the Harzgebirge in Germany, in whose eastern lee the giant-born Jack was made.

'Nor here,' she rasped, twisting on the back of the White Horse to survey the bleak fissure of the Sonnenberg, where no sun shone that day.

The Horse turned and galloped on.

Judith was looking for the Modor, or Wise Woman, who had lived from time immemorial with her consort, the Wita, in those parts. She wanted advice, comfort, help. She needed something to assuage her loneliness.

'Not even *here*,' she snarled, whipping the wind to make a frenzy of patterns over the blue surface of the Oderteich before she dived in, stayed under for a time in the cold below and emerged to remount and gallop on.

'Let alone *there!*' she snapped, pointing at the disfigurement of the place that was the Brocken, covered now in human towers and antennae, its *musica* all but gone.

'The truth is, you don't know where she is!' she said.

She was speaking to the White Horse which picked its way among the great rocks of the high passes, silently looking here and looking there, seeing everything but what Judith wanted.

'Where is she, the Modor? I have a question for her.'

The Horse reared, its hind legs all muscle, its flanks all shine, its neighing the beginning of torrential rain.

How desperately Judith wanted to meet her, talk with her, the Wise Woman, the elusive one.

She wanted to say, 'I am the Shield Maiden and I need guidance for my angry ride across the Earth. The Earth? *She* doesn't talk to me and you're nowhere to be found so you're no use either. There's no one. *No one.*'

The White Horse lowered its head and turned from the rocks in among the conifers, which were stiff and dripping without but dry and dark within, giving Judith a place to be.

She dismounted, her pale robes almost as white as the Horse among the trees, the pendant disc about her neck shining in the dark where she waited out the rain, the Horse turning up to the slopes above, up into the vast sky and the overwhelming storm of rain. A raven flew up as if to attack the mist which the Horse had become. It turned upside down and flew backwards and cawed wildly, as black as the shadows where Judith sat below as she waited for the Modor she could not find and who did not come, despite her calls.

The Horse had been warm to her thighs and inner arms, its mane soft to her desolate cheek, its eyes patient and deep before her rage. Now she felt cold, but with her feet on the prickly ground she was calm.

Movement.

Human?

No, hydden, breathed the Shield Maiden, glad to find company. But it was not who she expected.

Like a dancer Leetha came, her streaming ribbons a rainbow, laughing and bedraggled, indifferent to the rain and thinking she knew who it was she heard call.

'Modor, where are you? Did you find him, the Wita? *Modor!?*'

It seemed she sought the same person as Judith did, perhaps for the same reason.

It was months since Leetha had visited the Modor. Ageless and wizened because she had lived herself free of time. Then the Modor had been missing her consort, the Wita, who was as wise as she, though in different ways. Inclined to wander off by himself for weeks and months at a time, he had been gone longer than usual.

Leetha knew someone was there. She saw the shift of white cloud that was the Horse, she heard the cones rattle and the clip-clop of hoofs over rocks. She saw the heavy, fractured shadows where Judith stood invisible. Then, over there, where she waited, watching, Leetha saw her more clearly.

'*You're* not the Modor,' said Leetha, shaking her head, for there was much anger and sadness in those shadows, and the Modor, though often sad, was primarily about compassion. Leetha did not feel that among the trees.

'Have you seen her?' Judith said. She stood taller than Leetha, stronger, still younger.

'I haven't,' whispered Leetha, mother of Slew, mother of Jack, beloved of Sinistral; she had danced all her life among the trees of the Harzgebirge in search of wisdom and peace and often found it. Not least because she knew the Modor loved her.

'Are you the Shield Maiden?' asked Leetha. 'Did I hear you in the pine cones and see your eyes glittering angrily on the surface of the Oderteich?'

She came closer, her natural impulse to reach up and cup Judith's cheek in her hand.

'Better not,' said Judith, pulling back a little, 'I am more than mortal. A dangerous thing to touch me.'

Tears came to Leetha's eyes but she said nothing of them, flicked them away. They fell like dew on her bright ribbons, making jewels.

'The Oderteich is where Jack learnt the arts he had to forget he knew when he went to Englalond on the White Horse. Jack, your father.'

Judith nodded.

'I swam beneath it,' she replied. 'Exploring, for weeks. The Earth does not like such manmade scars. I dwelt once beneath Kielder, where Arthur was my only friend.'

'Arthur,' said Leetha vaguely, suddenly tired, 'who nurtured Katherine, Jack's wyf?'

'He nurtured us all and suffered Kielder with me, as I nurtured the water-filled scar you saw me in. You are . . . ?'

Judith wanted to touch, but knew she must not.

Judith was as alone as anyone, human or hydden, in all the wide world.

'I am your grandmother,' smiled Leetha, twining her greying hair in her fingers, 'and so I suppose there are things I should tell you, but don't ask me what they are, no one ever told me.'

'My grandmother,' said Judith, eyeing her with indifference. Jack, her father, never mentioned her.

'Your father didn't really know,' said Leetha, her granddaughter's thoughts dancing along with her own.

Judith laughed, free of pain at a sudden sense of joy, indifferent for the moment to the storm that was mounting where the White Horse had gone.

Father? *Dad* . . .

He was gone before she was old enough to call him that in the way she would have liked.

'Didn't he? Know?'

'I had to let him go, Judith, let the White Horse take him. Folk hereabout would have killed him and without him the gems would be harder to find. Without him, the world would have been a different place.'

Judith shook her head, shivering.

'He was always there,' she said softly, 'that is what wyrd is, always. Just *musica*, endlessly changing, sometimes forming into us, sometimes mountains, sometimes the fear you feel, that is *musica*, all things, there all the time, so beautiful. I knew Dad was there.'

Leetha laughed and shouted, 'Oh, yes! Ask my Lord Sinistral about *musica*!'

'I have,' replied Judith. 'I think he is turning back into the *musica* from which we all came. He will be more beautiful the frailer and less substantial he becomes.'

She didn't know where that came from but it did. The Earth told her all sorts of things without ever speaking a single word.

'Have you heard the Chimes?' she asked Leetha.

'Tell me, my dear.'

'Have you even *seen* them?'

Leetha shook her head.

Judith told her then about the Chimes and the mystery of their coming and going and never being quite the same.

She told her about the sharp scent of Arthur's tomatoes, which grew nearby. And how she picked one for Stort and another for herself and the sweet bright taste of them broke in their mouths like shared kisses of life. For each of them, unforgettable.

'*Stort?*' asked Leetha.

'Tall, red-haired, and sort of gangly, eyes bright and smiling like yours. He felt my movement when I was in my mother's womb; he was there by the Chimes when I was young; he watched me age and grow and understood my pain; he . . .'

'You love him!?'

It was as much statement as question. It was as obvious as the raven flapping and cawing in the trees above their heads.

It was as plain as the coming storm.

It was not to be denied.

'No!' said Judith.

Then: 'Maybe!' she cried,

Until, 'Yes!' she laughed.

But later, sitting down as well, nibbling the titbits Leetha offered her, which she had prepared for the Modor, she said, 'But it can never be. Mortal and immortal can know no love, though Mirror knows I don't feel like an immortal, or even half of one.'

'You ride the White Horse.'

'So did my father!'

'Only briefly. He was – he is – half hydden and half human and a giant-born. There is the immortal in him too.'

'Who was *his* father?'

Leetha smiled and shook her head.

'Not Sinistral?'

'People thought that, but in time they did not. Sinistral is like father, like brother, and knows me better than most. But never lover.'

Leetha paled, her smile gone.

'You say you saw him. Is he all right?'

'I think he's dying.'

'We all are, Shield Maiden, you too.'

'Especially me! Not having seen him before I didn't know what he was meant to look like. He is beautiful, isn't he?'

Leetha smiled again and nodded. 'Do you mind ageing?' she asked.

'It makes me angry. Every day I lose what I might have had.'

'Do you know what he said to me once, my love?'

Leetha felt her granddaughter's pain and wanted to take it from her. But she could not, it would be taking her life away.

Judith shook her head.

Leetha explained, 'He said that every day you gain something you didn't have before.'

She laughed before adding, 'And then he said he envied me because I found that out before he did. Where did you find him!?'

There was yearning in her voice.

Judith answered, 'He was in the Chamber of Sleep by a dentist's chair. He stood tall, but had to hold on to the chair for support. The rain and mist swirled about him. A bilgesnipe lit floaty lights. Sinistral's eyes glittered black, like coal and I liked him. He loves you as if he were your father, not lover.'

'How do you know?' said Leetha, sighing.

'He told me to come and see you. Maybe he thought I would comfort you, but it's the other way around.'

'That's what grandmothers are meant to do. I'm learning; I haven't been one before. Might never be again. You're a strange grandchild to have, Judith.'

'Am I? Maybe he also thought you were lonely without him. He's clever, things with him mean several things.'

'That's why I love him,' said Leetha, 'he deepens things to the point where you hear the *musica*. Can *you* hear it yet?'

Judith the Shield Maiden frowned.

'Too well or not at all, like days of sun and rain, wind and calm, hot and cold.'

Leetha looked over Judith's shoulder. The storm was mounting. A black anvil cloud was nearly half the sky, wisps of white cloud in front of it, like froth driven before a wave.

'I came looking for the Modor,' said Leetha, 'I have a question to ask her.'

'Me too, but I think she sent you instead. Let's ask each other the questions we have.'

Judith's voice was almost light, almost happy. The only time she had really talked to her mother Katherine, she felt like this: light, free, making a dance of things together, things understood.

'My question was about Jack,' said Leetha, 'Should I go and see him?'

Judith stared at her, thinking. Maybe, maybe not.

'He needs you to,' she replied.

The branches of the stiff trees began to sway, the air freshened fretfully, the light dimmed.

'*My* question,' she continued, 'is about Bedwyn Stort. Should I love him?'

Leetha laughed, her laughter snatched away by the wind and she as well as her ribbons streamed again, her flounces flew and the grey in her blonde hair began to shine with rain.

'There's no *should* about love,' she called back to her granddaughter, 'it just is. So ride its wonderful storm, my love, don't hold back! I never did.'

Judith was left alone among the trees, rain teeming, wind driving, lightning chasing Leetha's laughter all the way down the mountain, all the way home to where her son, Judith's father, was born.

Some storms are stronger even than Shield Maidens. This one was. The trees bent, loose rocks were torn from the ground, the roar was *musica* and death and Judith screamed into the wind, raged at the Earth trying to kill her. As the White Horse galloped by, eyes wide, nostrils flaring, she grabbed its mane, swung up on its back, gripped it with her thighs, put her arms and hands about its neck, and rode time and the sky.

Or tried to.

Shards of reflected life shot about her up there in the heavens, lightning caught in crystals of ice, thousands of fragments of thousands of lives.

'Oh . . . there . . . mine . . .'

She reached too far and fell one way while the Horse tore another, tumbling down and down, rolling over, turning, hands and feet unable to touch a single solid thing, trying to catch that shard in her hand. They raced around her, tinkling, Chimes in motion, hers and his, theirs and ours, swirling around Judith as she fell, down and down through the storm of ages, down into the Autumn, into harvest-time, down to a raggedy place where she was alone, so alone, with just one shard in her hand.

All she had was that one Chime-like-a-Chime, which, when she looked, was a fragment of him, her beloved, Bedwyn Stort, surrounded by . . . but it melted before she could see; saying to her . . . the words gone before she could make them out.

'Are you there?' she cried out from the darkness of the world. 'Because I cannot see you.'

'Yes,' he whispered, 'yes.'

Down there on Earth where she was lost, Judith thought what she should not.

Are you there, my love?

'I am.'

Even the White Horse had deserted her and she had lost the shard that was something of Stort.

Judith the Shield Maiden screamed out of the darkness she was in and saw at last the far distant light in which the Modor stood waiting.

She was answering Judith's lonely cry, but Judith could not hear.

'He will always love you,' the Modor said, 'and one day he will find his way back to you.'

25
EMBROIDERY CLASS

Bedwyn Stort's researches in the Library were delayed because Lord Festoon insisted that he attended the Parlement he had summoned. But meetings never had been Stort's thing and halfway through the third he left the Chamber for some fresh air and knew at once he was unlikely to go back.

He stood outside the Chamber for a little, heard the talk continuing, and then looked out into the Main Square through the open doors. The Main Library's own doors were open and welcoming, and he knew at once what it was he missed and needed: books, the dust of books, fellow Readers, the echo of his own steps down into the stacks, the friendly face of Scrivener Thwart, Master Brief's successor, and above all sitting in his old place with books open, others closed, and his mind exquisitely adrift upon a sea of ideas, of facts and most of all of random associations.

'Yes, that's what I need!' he said to the nearest passer-by, a clerk. 'Space to be myself. But not in these formal clothes!'

He hurried back to his humble, dressed in his old, familiar garb, had a hasty brunch courtesy of Cluckett and was off to the Library, as so often in the old days.

His arrival caused a mild sensation. The Readers looked up briefly, a librarian whispered, 'Good afternoon, Mister Stort!', a cleaner nudged another and pointed him out and Stort, suddenly happier than he had been for weeks, sought out Thwart in the basement.

They were old friends and understood each other well.

They shared a few thoughts about the passing of Brief; Thwart said

something of how the Library had been since; and finally they got to
the purpose of Stort's visit.

'Need to think without interruption,' he said simply.

'Well, Mister Stort, this is the place for that. As you see, your old
place is as you left it. We have not moved a thing and apart from . . .
no matter . . . nobody has even sat there.'

'Apart from who?'

'I regret to say that Witold Slew sat in your chair before . . .
before . . .'

He could not continue. Slew had nearly killed him before killing
Master Brief and stealing the gem of Spring which Stort had, perhaps
foolishly, hidden in the stacks.

'I shouldn't have mentioned it.'

'But I'm glad you did,' said Stort, and he was.

Thwart had done more to get his mind working on the gem problem
in a few minutes than a committee might achieve in several years.

Or rather, to *begin* working on it as he sat down in his comfortable
chair and Thwart left him to it.

An hour passed and Stort ordered up some books on medieval
harvest traditions, which, when they came, he leafed through half-
heartedly because his focus had switched to the odd image of the
corvids he had seen flying backwards, in the hours after he and the
others escaped the Scythe of Time. He could not get them out of his
head.

'This is no good,' he muttered, though not unhappily. He knew what
his mind was doing. It was a predator stalking prey. 'Take a turn about
the Square for some fresh air,' suggested Thwart, 'and I shall make a
brew for us in my office upstairs when you are ready.'

Stort did just that and stood on the spot in the centre of the Square,
as he sometimes did. It was the place which Brum tradition claimed
was the centre of the Universe: a star of cobbles, laid by the famed
lutenist and architect ā Faroün who designed the Square a century and
a half before and had been Slaeke Sinistral's tutor. Polished by time
and pilgrims' feet, the stones were pleasing to stand on and the 'star'
more in the way of a compass of cardinal points, indicating how far
various places in Englalond and beyond were from that spot.

He stood there pondering this little history, not even guessing that the very sight of him, just there, was to some who knew Brum well and were walking by, a sight that gave them pleasure to see. It meant that Stort was back, things would happen, all was well.

'Afternoon, Mister Stort!'

'Ah! Yes! Of course . . . it *is* a good afternoon.'

He went back inside, supped tea with Thwart and in the peace of the moment, made comfortable with things familiar, he felt his mind centring at last and said impulsively, 'Ā Faroün's Embroidery, that's what I need to see. I had forgotten the fact though I knew it before.'

They went back to the stacks in the basement, fetched the Embroidery down from its dark shelf and draped it over an empty desk. It fell down on all sides.

'It must be three or more yards long,' said Stort, 'and four feet wide. It's much larger than I remember.'

'Indeed it is large. A very remarkable artefact whose meaning, I confess, I can never quite unravel.'

'Then let me explicate,' said Stort, who knew that in so doing he might find a way of getting closer to what it was he sought.

They talked about the Embroidery for an hour, Thwart fetching the monograph that Brief had scrivened on the subject as well as his biography of ā Faroün, who had had a hand in making the Embroidery and most certainly used it in his designs for the creation of the Chamber of Seasons in the High Ealdor's residence.

'Interesting as this is,' said Thwart eventually, 'time has passed and I must close the Library.'

Stort felt a sudden pang. He was connecting with the Embroidery and did not want it to go back to its dark and lonely place in the stacks. It felt like betrayal. It felt wrong.

'My dear fellow,' said Stort, 'it would be irregular, of course, but I would be obliged if I might take the Embroidery to my humble, along with Brief's monograph and text. I feel a need . . .'

'I seem to remember hearing that Master Brief used to let you take texts home to work on.'

'He did.'

'Well then, take it and return it when your work is done.'

Thwart left him, but Stort himself did not immediately leave. As he went to roll the Embroidery up, he found himself entering once more into the world of seasons it depicted.

To the left was Spring, to the right was Winter, and all the passage of the seasons between. But just then it was not the overriding image that drew him but a solitary character who appeared, as did others, again and again, in and out of the shadows and the light of all the seasons.

She started as a child, caught in the light of Spring. She ended as a crone withered by the icy cold of winter.

'Judith,' he whispered, 'the Shield Maiden, always alone as she journeys through the seasons, no one knowing how to help her, not even me, who . . . who . . . who . . .'

Was it for this that Stort had come down to the stacks: to get as near as he knew how to what his heart felt?

This world of a feeling to which he, until so recently, had been a stranger.

This chaos through time in which a hydden is whirled along helpless, not able to make sense of the feelings he felt, nor why something so glorious should hurt so much.

This thing whose word he found so hard to say.

This mountain so vast he could never climb it, never see beyond.

Bedwyn Stort reached out and touched what, in real life he could not, which was her, from birth to old age as he felt he knew her. From life to a living death.

He stayed like that until Thwart called his name.

Sadly, he rolled up the Embroidery and put it under his arm with the other things. Perhaps in a different time and place, when his mind was clearer, he would be able to make more sense of it all.

Thwart let him out, the last Reader of the day, and Stort crossed the Square again, turning on impulse towards the centre of the Universe and standing there, as he had earlier.

What then?

The stirring of a wind through his head, the Embroidery opening out and him inside it, an Autumn landscape in which he could never catch her up as leaves fell across her body and her face and she grew old, the child he knew in Spring; older than him now.

Out of darkness came her scream and he, speaking her name, knew he could not be heard, not there, not then.

His feet rooted to cobbles, the compass on which he stood showing him the way, and as someone called out, 'Morning, Mister Stort!' he heard the hiss and hish and the uprooting of buildings, cut down by the Scythe of Time.

Then he was running because it was after him, running all the way home and banging for Cluckett to open up.

'Mister Stort, sir, wherever have you been? We've been worried sick for you. Where have you *been*!?'

He put the Embroidery on the table in his laboratory, Brief's texts too. He took food and drink and noticed that the clock seemed wrong.

'Cluckett?'

Somehow, somewhere, between leaving the Library and getting home, Stort had lost more hours than he knew and no one, not a soul, had seen him do it and he did not know where they had gone.

26

OUT OF THE ETHER

A week had passed since Arthur had found the secondary communications room and set things up so he could send and receive messages. That was the good news.

The bad was that he had no way of knowing if his message signals were being picked up. He had received nothing back and had no real hope that the ticker tape-style machine he had rigged up was capable of receiving and stamping out a message from the outside world.

'It keeps me occupied and it gives us hope,' was the best he could say to Blut.

Like a fisherman who casts out his bait in water that never yet produced a fish, he held onto the hope that he might yet receive a bite.

Certainly the routine needed to send another message and check for anything received gave him a daily occupation.

His lighting system was a success but he was careful to leave the first part of the tunnel unlit so his activities beyond that point remained unsuspected. Soon he knew the tunnel and its hazards so well that he had no need to use up his torch's battery.

This habit of walking in the darkness also helped him make a discovery he might otherwise have missed. It was while he was retracing his steps one day that he noticed a dull glimmer of light under a door which he had thought led nowhere. In fact it went via another into a subsidiary tunnel and the light, dim though it was, filtered in from a low tunnel off that. Crawling down it to find the source, he discovered a vertical shaft upward with a grille that gave him a view of greenery. It was an air shaft which led up into the wood under which the bunker was buried.

The floor beneath the shaft was no more than decayed earth and cement, in which a forest of ferns grew up towards the filtering light. The grille itself was square, made of thin metal bars, held in place by rusted bolts. Vegetation grew thickly in and around it. On his second visit, rain dripped down. He had never tasted water so sweet.

He saw at once that it might be a useful escape route, though not one he was yet willing to test by opening the grille. Blut had established that the Fyrd routinely patrolled the wood above the bunker and he had heard them walking on that small part of it which actually projected above the forest floor. He and Blut decided that he should build up supplies under the grille all ready to grab and take with them if the opportunity came to make a run for it.

But as the days went by that possibility began to seem less likely as Arthur began to receive the unpleasant attentions of a new and stricter orderly.

It had already puzzled him that he was given such freedom to roam, but two things were in his favour. First, the Emperor's support for and liking of him; second, more subtly, the Fyrd under General Quatremayne were a force so well disciplined and fit that they saw Arthur as old and so out of shape and useless that he could not possibly be a threat or source of danger. But one orderly, a junior Domo, was actively hostile, perhaps feeling that since he could not be seen to bully the Emperor, he could safely project his feelings onto his friend. Domo Krill was pig-eyed and belligerent, slow on the uptake but physically very strong.

So much so that his seniors used him as a workhorse, lifting boxes others couldn't, heaving open doors that were corroded and stuck, shifting the heavy wood and metal tables that many of the rooms had as standard issue.

The rest of the time he cooked bad food for the Emperor's small entourage, whom he treated more like undeserving prisoners than guests. If he thought his authority and honour were being slighted, he reacted rudely and with subtle violence: a hard step on a toe, a deliberate bump of his shoulder, a too-tight grasp of an arm. He was a dam waiting to burst.

Increasingly, as the days went by and it felt as if Blut's position was weakening, Krill's aggression became more overt.

He would bring his bloodshot eyes near Arthur's and hiss, 'I know your game, Prof, I know it. Give me my chance and I'll show I do. Okay?'

He would finger his stave as he said these unpleasant things, as if about to use it.

'Prof, you didn't eat yer food today. Tryin' to tell me something? Eh? Yer saying I made it bad?'

'Er, no . . .' replied Arthur, disliking such confrontation and not sure what to do about it. He did not want to trouble the Emperor and he doubted that Krill's seniors would be sympathetic if he complained.

Sometimes Krill would turn away, muttering oaths about upstarts and uppity ones, pulling out his stave and smashing it into the walls hard enough for lumps of plaster to fall, always when no one else was around.

Then, from a safe distance, he would turn and look back directly at Arthur and shout, 'Friggin' bastard – meanin' no one particular of course, yeh!?'

Then some coarse laughter as he left and a muttered, 'One foot wrong, Prof, and I'll get yer!'

Was he serious or mad?

Arthur decided he was both.

This personal unpleasantness only added to the general and growing tension Arthur felt in the bunker. From being allowed into all meetings, he was suddenly barred from some. At times Blut was more irritable than he had been initially. At others General Quatremayne looked aloof and cold, his liking and respect for Blut appearing to falter, his inclination to huddle with his staff to the exclusion of others – including the Emperor – increasing.

'My Lord,' Arthur essayed more than once, 'is anything the matter?'

'Meaning?'

'Er, well . . . You appear distracted.'

'Nothing is the matter.'

'I . . .'

'All is well, Arthur, all is in hand.'

Blut said the right words, looked the right looks, but something was not right. A day or two later, Arthur noticed more than once the lenses of his spotless spectacles were less than spotless. They were smeared for the first time ever.

Something felt very wrong indeed.

'You should take a stroll outside, my Lord,' said Arthur. 'Fresh air, exercise . . . it will do you good. Surely that's permissible for you if not for me.'

Blut shook his head.

'They say they do not wish me to risk my life,' he said, referring to the Fyrd Command, 'and insist I stay down here.'

Blut, normally so much in control, seemed suddenly a little out of it and he began to look ill. The battle for power and authority with Quatremayne was beginning to be lost.

Then: 'I think Krill is poisoning me,' said Blut, 'though I am eating only food that I believe cannot be contaminated. But he is sly. Arthur, we need to leave, our time is running out.'

Arthur took his own advice, for the bunker was oppressive, the endless dark lit only by wan electric lights, depressing the spirit. He took to standing beneath the grille onto the outside world and breathing in the cool air of the wood, letting any rain that came in fall on his face. The routine of visiting his Morse station several times a day to tap out his messages, the general one and the particular call sign, and checking if the ticker tape had moved to show he had a reply, and the walking about, kept him alert.

He and Blut had discovered a great deal of the Fyrd's routine outside and in. The patrols outside were regular, the changeover four times daily, at midnight, six, twelve and six in the evening. It was the evening one he had his eye on because the individuals concerned were slacker than the others, slower to get going, inclined to chat, their boots too clean on their return for them to have walked their full round. That time of day, too, would give them the cover of darkness if they were able to get away after supper.

Blut confirmed that he had committed the General's invasion plan for Brum to memory and knew exactly how the Fyrd intended to carry it through. It was now a few short weeks away at most. From the talk of the Fyrd they heard, it seemed that troops were coming in daily from the Continent and billeting in the City. Supplies were being

brought forward and placed at strategic points along the London–
Birmingham railway line and some others they intended to use for
rapid night runs into the heart of Brum.

Arthur knew that this intelligence would be useful to his friends in
Brum, if only he could get it to them.

It was plain enough from conversations both witnessed and over-
heard that there was a division of opinion between some of General
Quatremayne's junior officers and his more senior – and more cautious
– staff, including himself. The former began urging immediate action
before Brum could get its defences in place, but Blut and the General
were more cautious.

The supplies for the longer-term occupation were taking time to
gather, so too the troops required. Two transport craft carrying
troops and supplies were lost in a violent North Sea storm; the
rail lines into Brum were disrupted by minor Earth movements; the
earlier good weather had now given way to floods, one of which caused
water to seep into the bunker and put the main corridor, and the one
Arthur used, under three more inches of mucky, muddy sludge and
water.

This worsened morale, as did the hold-ups caused by bad weather.
Everybody was getting irritable and, while the tunnel Arthur had made
his own was his diversion and life-saver, he realized that it was a matter
of time before he was found out.

Arthur made a point of never letting Krill see him enter the tunnel
but was concerned that the *slosh-slosh-slosh* echo of his feet in water
would be heard when he walked back and forth.

Darkness and the whine and howl of the wind became his friends.

As for the grille to the surface, he finally overcame his reluctance to
risk opening it one evening, when the 'lazy' patrol was on duty. He put
a crate beneath it to give him better height and cautiously eased the
rusted bolts he had found, for fear of being heard.

It creaked and it was heavy but the biggest problem was lowering it
back on itself to the forest floor. But he did it, and there it was,
freedom, up above him through brambles and nettles, up towards the
darkling sky and trees he could see straight above.

He heaved himself up sufficiently to look around without getting
out.

The wood was an old one, its floor littered with fallen branches and thick layers of the rotting leaves of deciduous trees.

The air was fresh, the wind clear, freedom was his for the taking.

Not yet, not quite yet. He felt he owed a duty to Blut.

He lowered the grille back down, checked the ticker tape, sent his messages out again *tappity-tap* and returned to grim normality. Later, he lay on his bed reliving that moment of smelling the wood, feeling the wind.

Next morning, Krill swore to his face and deliberately spilt a scalding flagon of brew close enough to burn his leg.

'Sorry, Prof, Sir, really I am,' he said muttering curses under his breath.

Time to leave, Arthur told himself.

The day was an odd one, the tension and differences in the bunker turning to arguments on all sides, crackling around corners and from under doors.

Arthur kept a very low profile, sensing a decision or decisions had been made. Equipment was collected and placed near the entrance, the train loaded and set ready.

In the late morning, Arthur escaped into his secret world and to the grille and a breath of fresh air. He heard movement above, and conversation.

The patrols were different, maybe more thorough.

Things were changing fast.

Definitely time to leave.

He heard the word 'tonight' and hurried back inside, a new nervousness making him stumble more than once. By a door marked 'Kitchen' he slipped in water, fell on a pile of rusting cutlery, broken china, a frying pan.

He righted himself, thought for a moment and impulsively picked up one of the kitchen knives and thrust it in the sheath that hung from his belt, empty until now.

Then back to the main corridor where officers and orderlies were hurrying about.

'What's happening?'

Not even Emperor Blut would say, his skin taut and white, his eyes wary, his smile extinct.

'Nothing,' he said.

'Tonight?' murmured Arthur.

'Perhaps,' said Blut, 'perhaps.'

Things had worsened for them both.

Orderlies who had been friendly before no longer looked Blut in the eye.

It felt like a death sentence had been passed but the hour of execution not yet set.

If he and Blut could have fled there and then, Arthur would have insisted on the attempt, however great the risk. The bunker air had the thick odour of death about it.

'You!' a voice murmured in his ear.

It was Krill in passing, sneering, confident, turning as he often did to stare. This time he ran a finger across his throat, his big teeth showing in a grimace.

For the first time in his life Arthur was glad he was carrying a knife.

The Emperor detained him after lunch and engaged in a strained conversation about nothing, as if he did not want him to go. His voice was thinner than usual; it was as if he wanted to say something but could not. Was someone listening?

'Sinistral?' said Blut suddenly, quite loudly, out of the blue. 'Did I tell you that he taught me to survive?'

'Er, no, you didn't,' said Arthur, puzzled.

'He used to say, "When the moment comes and you'll know it, Blut, leave. Waste no time in making the decision. Leave." Now . . . you had better go to your room . . .'

It was said as a command.

As Arthur rose to go, he understood all in a rush. Blut was saying he could not get away but if Arthur could, he should. Now.

Perhaps if he went and got away to Brum he could find a way to send help back for Blut. It was no more than an empty promise made by someone who was in the act of leaving someone else behind.

Leave . . .

In a moment, as he walked towards his quarters, Arthur decided to do so and he headed straight for the tunnel.

Then he was there, heading into darkness, *slosh-slosh-slosh*.

He had almost reached the point in the tunnel where it turned and he felt safer when he heard *slosh-slosh-slosh* behind him, noisier than his own sounds, and that voice he had grown to hate: 'Hey! You, Prof. Come here, you friggin' . . .'

A crossbow bolt purred by and slammed into the tiled wall, sending sharp shards into his face.

Oh dear God, his voice screamed inside his head. *Oh God.*

'*Prof, come back here!*' roared Krill, beginning to run *sloshety-slosh, sloshety-slosh.*

Arthur ran on, as best he could, the normally silent tunnel now echoing with the noises of pursuit and flight. Another bolt shot by, bouncing from wall to wall before it splashed in the water.

He reached the turn into his tunnel, but the grille was just too far off for it to be possible for him to run there and climb out before Krill could reach him.

He froze, Krill's steps getting nearer.

His breathing became difficult, his throat dry, his heart hammering.

'Where are you, Prof?'

He had not yet turned on the light and so could see Krill's torch, dancing here and there as his feet sloshed nearer.

Arthur could see his own hands shaking, caught in the dim sidelight from the grille down the tunnel.

He backed away into darkness.

'Hey Prof, I want a word.'

Arthur saw Krill then, his light, his teeth caught in the flash of the torch, getting nearer and nearer as Arthur backed away, his mouth dry, his heart thumping painfully.

Then Krill turned off his torch and, but for the faint glimmer of the grille tunnel out into the corridor, there was nothing but pitch dark.

'I'll play it your way,' said Krill, his voice happy and cruel. 'I'll smell you out in this murk!'

Arthur knew that if he moved he would be heard. If he stayed still he would be killed.

His options had run out.

His mind stilled, his heart slowed and his hand reached for the knife in his belt and he knew what he must do.

As Krill came nearer, almost into the glimmer of light from the tunnel but not quite, Arthur stepped sideways and he reached up to turn the lights on, closing his own eyes tight as he did so.

One, two, three.

'What the . . . ?' shouted Krill, momentarily blinded.

It was that moment of brightness in Krill's eyes Arthur needed.

He turned the lights back off, waited a moment, opened his eyes, watched as Krill floundered into the dim light, struggling to get his lost vision back and turn on his torch.

It was time.

Arthur Foale moved forward fast and aimed at the one place he knew a Fyrd was vulnerable when in uniform: his throat. He thrust the knife hard into it, and pulled it straight out, then as Krill let out a gurgling scream, he thrust forward again, Krill's rising arm pushing the thrust up.

Arthur let it go, stepped back to be clear of Krill's flailing arms and turned on the lights again, closing his eyes as he did so. He took a step back and turned off the lights once more. Then he opened his eyes.

Arthur was shocked by what the need for survival had forced him to do and he continued now almost as an automaton, distancing himself from what was happening.

Blinded for real in one eye, temporarily in the good one, blood spouting from his neck, Krill fell to one side, hit the wall and fell to the flooded floor with a splash. Then, lit by dim light, not dead but immobile, the knife a rusty alien thing he had to pull from his eye but could not, he whimpered like a child and began to die.

Time to leave.

This time Arthur did run, past the terrible turning, reaching, filthy water-bubbling thing Krill had become, into the tunnel with the grille, down to the crate, grabbing his 'sac, onto the crate, and reaching up to heave himself up, to listen, listen . . .

Be sensible, listen!

God and the Mirror only knew what was out there in the woods.

No going back.

So, breathing heavily, every instinct telling him to get out and run, Arthur listened.

Wind in trees, gurgles out of the tunnel below, the sloshing softer now, dying, and somewhere, high, high above, a human sound: an aeroplane, white light flashing through the tree tops.

Normality.

Leave . . . !

It was then, even as he began to heave himself up, that he heard it, clear and urgent, coming from the tunnel below him: *clickety-click . . .*

It was the ticker tape!

Click, clickety-click . . .

A message was coming through. Someone, somewhere out there had received his message.

Arthur's entire being screamed to get away but someone might be offering immediate help. Trying to escape might mean immediate death.

. . . click, click, clickety

Going back might save Blut's life.

Oh dear God, Arthur whispered, his hands and arms shaking, his whole being afraid. *But . . . I . . . must . . .*

He pulled back the grille, lowered himself down onto the crate and back into the bunker of death. Then he turned into the darkness of the tunnel, back past Krill's, through bloody water, sloshing his way into the communications room to see what message he had received.

27

VISITATION

The days were shortening, the nights drawing in and in the last days of September the weather suddenly worsened into grey clouds and rain storms. Brum grew depressing and folk went down with coughs and flu.

The staff in the Hospice noticed it soon enough for old ones weakened, some died and the dark impassive faces of the morticians and undertakers pulling the death cart became a regular sight in the back alleys on the north side of the Square.

The Kapellmeister had rallied when he first arrived in Brum but he too was affected by the cold, grim days and began to decline once more.

Stort found lodgings for Terce next to his own humble but the chorister spent most days and many nights at Meister Laud's bedside. He held his Meister's hand and when Laud was well enough he gave instruction. Once in a while Terce would sing, but for the Meister that part of his life was over. His once beautiful voice was a cracked vessel, no use now for anything much at all.

Katherine and Cluckett took their turn to give Terce respite, but there was little they could do.

'If an old body like him don't want to talk, Mistress Katherine, and he don't, there's not a lot we can offer. Just stay by, meet his needs, and hope he suffers no pain.'

'I wish he'd tell us something about himself,' said Katherine, 'his proper name even. Terce says he had a twin sister but she's dead and there's no other family.'

It was a familiar story among the older patients. No family, few friends, a forgotten history.

One night Terce knocked on Stort's door in distress.

'He's been fretful, crying out in his sleep, saying things.'

'What things?'

'That he needs his sister. That if he can't teach me, she can. But she's dead.'

Cluckett shook her head sadly.

'They talk like that and feel real distress. It's the past catching up with them. Things unspoken for years, things never said. He's beginning his journey back to the Mirror and for him – and mayhap for us too, things being as they are in Brum – that'll be the best place.'

'But I'm not ready,' said Terce simply, 'I have not learnt all the music.'

There was desperation in his eyes.

Katherine went to the Hospice with him to see if she could help the Meister settle. But he was as restless and unhappy as Terce said and insisted his sister wasn't bothering to see him and Terce needed her.

'But she's dead, isn't she, Meister?'

'She dead to me, but she could sing . . .'

His eyes lit up at this memory, his face relaxed and he fell into a deeper sleep than before, his breathing now slower, ever slower. The window was open despite the night chill because his austere life had made him used to cold and fresh air. The candles flickered, mist drifted in and out of the window, the night grew quiet.

Goodwife Cluckett, more used to the passage of old age perhaps and sensing a crisis, came to keep Katherine company.

She took his pulse, listened to his rough irregular breathing and looked at his pale, waxy skin. She shook her head but said nothing. She had no need to. The Meister was dying.

Stort called by, his progress down the hushed street slow because the mist had thickened and a strange wind got up, swirling it around, making shapes against the street gas lights and the candles in people's windows.

'It's more than mist is making Brum seem silent this night,' he observed, 'there's a feeling of moment in the air.'

'Moment?' queried Katherine.

'Historic moment, I would say. Like a whole city holding its breath.'

'That's nerves,' opined Cluckett, 'folk worrying about the Fyrd coming. Waiting saps confidence and breeds tension.'

There was a companionship in sitting around the Meister's bed: Stort, Katherine, Terce and Cluckett, holding his hand, murmuring words, closing their eyes for a little and once in a while Terce singing a song of the night all low and gentle, singing an old soul home.

The mist was another presence, mostly held off at the open window by the warmer air within, but spiralling up sometimes in the candle flames and reaching in towards the bed.

They heard a rumble outside.

'What was that?' said Stort suddenly, starting up as if woken by a sudden sound. 'Thunder on a night like this!?'

If it was thunder it was distant and fragmented, a thin thudding across the sky.

Then *whoosh! Bang! Bang! Bang!* And like a raptor swooping, now almost unnoticed and unheard, then right there with claws outstretched, beak open and eyes aflame *bang!* It was on them, more than thunderous, demanding and imposing, stilling the strongest heart with fear.

They stood up in alarm and peered at the window as if expecting thunder personified to start climbing in.

Bang! Bang!

Plaster and dust fell from the ceiling and Cluckett reached up to get the stuff from her hair, when they heard the mighty clatter of hoofs in the courtyard outside and then it was there, a horse's leg rising into mist, the whisk of a vast slow tail which guttered a candle, and the slow, heavy clip-clop as it settled to restive rest.

It was the White Horse, right there, at the window. Or its hoof and leg.

Then a curse, a command, someone furious, and from the front of the building the sounds of noisy arrival.

They opened the door, heard the noise, saw the Horse, but no one else in the Hospice did.

Then she came like a cloud's shadow racing across an open field, maybe even faster, and pushed them aside and loomed into the room.

'Where is he?' the Shield Maiden demanded. 'Take me to him.'

She spoke as if he was miles away.

All of them gaped but could not move. She seemed bigger than the room, bigger than Brum, fiercer than a thousand Fyrd, and she did not look amused.

Her hair was greying and she was already so much more aged than Katherine remembered that she did not at first recognize her own daughter.

Only Stort stood up to her, staring into her dark, angry eyes. He was astonished to see her and astounded at his reaction. Back in the Summer he had dreamed about her like a youthful lover, whispering words of love to the sky, but now he faced Judith as the Shield Maiden, instinct took over and an unaccustomed masterfulness. Her strength and purpose made him the same. They mirrored each other.

He guessed her coming had to do with Meister Laud, or Terce. Or, more simply, the Quinterne. If so, it affirmed he was on the right track in his search for the gem.

'You're looking for the Kapellmeister, aren't you?'

'Of course I damn well am,' she said.

He pointed to the bed.

'If he's dead I'll kill you,' she snarled, her robes like whips as they slashed past their legs and caught at their hands as she went to the Meister's bedside.

'And who are *you*?' she demanded of Cluckett, who was on the far side of the bed.

'C . . . Cl . . . luckett,' the goodwife stammered, backing away at the apparition before her.

The Horse shifted outside, its flank an exquisite sheen in the gaslight.

'Don't hurt the old gennelman,' Cluckett whispered.

'*Hurt* him? Are you insane? He has not done what his wyrd demands he do and now he is dying and all you all do is sit and hold his hand and wait on his end without doing what he has asked you to do. Isn't it obvious to *any* of you what he needs?'

The Meister's eyes had opened and he too looked astonished.

'But . . .' began Katherine, who could scarcely believe the terrifying presence her daughter had become, or even that she was 'Judith' at all.

'You!' snarled Judith, cutting her short. 'You're the only one round here can do it, so go and do it.'

'What?!' asked Katherine faintly.

'Get to his sister, of course. She's the only one who knows what to say and how to say it.'

'She's dead,' whispered the Meister, speaking for the first time in hours.

'Dead, my arse,' said Judith, 'she's pathetic, not dead. And so have you been. I should knock your heads together.'

'She . . .' Laud muttered, angry now, still smarting from some old hurt.

'Not interested,' said the Shield Maiden brutally.

Katherine could not help noticing that the Meister looked better already. There was a point of colour in his cheeks. Maybe it was anger but it looked good.

Judith turned back to Katherine and said, 'The White Horse will show you where she is.'

'But . . .'

'It's there. The window's the quickest way out. Go on!'

Katherine went to the window and before she knew it Judith had grabbed her arm and heaved her outside.

'Go on!'

She looked up at the towering, living thing that stood there, rising into the mist and out of sight, its hoofs big enough to crush her.

'It doesn't bite,' said Judith coldly, 'and meanwhile I'll try to keep Meister Laud alive.'

She turned, swearing, back to the bed.

'All of you,' she said, 'out, *now*. Except for Mister Stort.'

They filed out; Stort moved to the other side of the bed and looked at her. There was no fear in his eyes. They were as open, as innocent, as accepting and as honest as only real love can be. But they were firm.

Her breathing slowed, her dark robes subsided into nothing very much, her fierce eyes and strong mouth softened to a sudden smile. She looked young again.

'Am I terrible?' she said.

'Terri-*fying*,' he replied.

'I have to be. It's what I have to do, it's . . .'

'You look tired.'

'I look old.'

'I said tired.'

He wanted to reach across the bed and touch her but he knew he could not, not then, not ever.

Firmness fled him. He wanted to tell her he loved her.

He could not do that either except through thought and action and the way he was with her.

'Why is the Meister so important?' he asked.

'He'll tell you better than I can when he's healed a little. Should have done already. It's his job to do so, not mine. You can drag a horse to water but you can't make it drink, and that includes the White Horse, incidentally. I can do nothing for mortal kind but show the way.'

'By kicking them?'

'Yes, if need be. But I can tell you this. The more gems you find the more the *musica* is needed to control them. The Quinterne's history stretches back centuries, Stort, and its song may hold the secret of all harmony.'

'*May* hold,' queried Stort, 'not *does* hold?'

'Just so. Laud here holds the secret; he must live long enough for Terce to learn it.'

Stort watched as she reached to the Meister and held his hand as soft now as the evening sun. Yes, she did look old, or at least older. Her face was beginning to line, her hair turn grey. Of the rest – her hips, her breasts, her shape – Stort hardly dared look, or acknowledge that he wanted to. She was the Shield Maiden, that was all. Beyond that he could not think.

You are Judith who I loved from the first and will love to the last. Judith who needs one person in the world to know who you are, deep down, where no one else dares go. That's where my love for you takes me.

These words were stumbling things in his mind, uttered uncertainly because he had never thought them before. Perhaps she heard the words he thought, perhaps she felt the stirrings too. They were reflections of each other in different form. She bent close to the Meister and said, 'Your sister is coming and she'll know what to say.'

'No one ever spoke my name as she did,' he said suddenly and unexpectedly, 'and I . . . I . . .'

'Tell us,' said the Shield Maiden.

He spoke of love lost and the hope of love found again. It seemed he had so missed his sister since the day of their parting decades before he found it easier to pretend she was dead than believe she was alive. Now hope had returned.

Katherine found the flank of the White Horse was smooth and welcoming and when it knelt down and let her use its mane to mount it, it felt like she had come home.

It rose up, the humbles falling away beneath her out of sight, and she was riding the waves of the mist, the night sky clear above her. Riding the great creature she had loved all her life in imagination, from her home opposite White Horse Hill. Letting it take her where it must.

Later, the lights of Brum and the human city of Birmingham far behind, it came down to Earth again. No mist, just a wind over wet grass and a hydden village whose name she did not know. It clip-clopped to a humble at whose window a candle burnt.

She dismounted and knocked at the little door, which opened as if she was expected.

Katherine gasped in surprise. She found herself staring into the eyes of someone she herself had briefly known and who had frightened her. Someone once proud but fine-looking. Who, when she knew her, appeared so forbidding that it would have seemed almost insolent to think she had another life than that which her position gave her, something real of flesh and bone.

But there she stood, a shadow of her former self.

'Has he passed on to the Mirror?' she asked. 'Is my brother dead?'

Katherine was looking at the one who had once been Sister Supreme, the most important of the Sisters of Charity who, before all the recent changes in Brum, had been maidens in the service of Lord Festoon, High Ealdor of Brum. Briefly, Katherine had been a Sister herself and remembered the chill command of Supreme with displeasure.

It had never occurred to Katherine to think what might have happened to the Sisters after their Order was closed by Festoon and Igor Brunte following the latter's successful ousting of the Fyrd. Nor had she for a moment thought of Sister Supreme as ordinary flesh and blood, whose forbidding exterior was a consequence of inner grief caused by some cruel and terrible event in her secret past.

Sister Supreme's little home was forlorn, as if she lacked heart and purpose to make it a home at all. As if she had lost the will to live. Katherine saw at a glance that this impression was correct, and the Sister saw she did.

'I had no purpose in life, you see,' she said, even as they stood by the door. 'My brother was taken from me when I was only eight and I put into the Order, me powerless to help him or myself. My life seemed to end that day and since then . . . since . . . I have permitted myself to feel nothing that hurts my heart. Just pride in rising through the Order to the rank of Supreme, but pride is a lonely comfort. I long ago . . . concluded . . . he was dead.'

Katherine was suddenly angry.

'"Concluded he was dead" – but you just more or less admitted you knew he was alive, but gravely ill!'

'It's difficult . . .'

'*Difficult!*' thundered Katherine, as if she was the Shield Maiden herself. 'He needs you and *we* need him. So come with me!'

The Horse stamped its hoofs on the road beyond the gate.

Sister Supreme began talking again but Katherine had no patience for any of it.

'Come now or I shall drag you there.'

The Sister hesitated, looked at Katherine and for some reason, for the first time in a very long time, she smiled.

'He needs me?'

'Yes,' said Katherine loudly, as if talking to an obstinate child. 'He needs you and *now!*'

She got her coat, took up her key, closed the door behind her and locked it.

'What must I do?' she asked.

'Ride the Horse with me,' replied Katherine.

The White Horse's return to the Hospice was swift and the two of them were set on the ground by the window.

'Climb in!' said Katherine brutally, heaving her in just as Judith had heaved Katherine herself out.

'About time!' cried Judith. 'Here he is, hanging on by the skin of his cracked old teeth. You know what to say to him.'

Sister Supreme said that she did not think she did.

'Then work it out!' said Judith unsympathetically. 'Get on with it!'

Stort backed away from the bed, as did Judith. They discreetly stood in the shadows of the threshold of the room.

'I don't know how . . .' Sister Supreme whispered, staring down at her brother, whose face was grey, whose hands were still, whose consciousness and life were on a knife edge.

'Tell him what he most needs to hear,' Judith called out with sudden compassion. 'Only you can save him now.'

Sister Supreme stood stiffly, trying to find a way to let go of the armour that a lifetime of self-control had put around her, terrified of releasing it. She wanted to reach down to him but didn't know how; she wanted to speak but didn't know what words to say.

'I . . . you . . . I . . .'

He looked so old, so frail, and in his face, beyond the line of his nose and mouth, the set of his closed eyes, she saw again the little boy she had so loved and so missed when he was gone.

'You . . . you . . . broke my heart,' Sister Supreme whispered, bending down to him, 'I didn't know . . . what . . . to . . .'

Tell him what he needs to hear, the Shield Maiden had told her, and finally, reaching towards him, she knew exactly what that was. It was what she had spoken every day in her prayers for seventy years.

She stroked his cheek as Judith had, but nervously, not having touched him for so long.

'I missed you after you were taken to Abbey Mortaine . . .' she began, hesitating to speak the one word that she realized only then might bring him back to her. 'And I was so angry. I've missed you so much . . .' she said.

Then Sister Supreme, her stiff back bending, her old fingers finding his, whispered what he needed to hear, spoke it with her touch, kissed it with her lips, cried it out with her cheek to his cheek: his special thing, which their parents gave but which was taken from him the day he was taken from her, the thing that was his own. His first and last thing.

Sister Supreme spoke her brother's name.

But miracles are rarely one way, the gift is as much to the giver as the receiver.

His eyes opened, he stared into hers, he reached his hand to her cheek and his eyes wrinkled to a tiny smile as he spoke hers too.

His and hers, their identities, their very being, the essence of themselves which they had lost so long ago: harvesting now the love they never lost but did not know how to find again.

Whispers in the night, no more solid than mist, the impatient clatter of hoofs in a narrow lane, the snort of a Horse, the Shield Maiden's work done, almost.

Outside, standing in the mist all together, Stort coughed and said, 'I . . . would be much obliged . . . if . . . you could give us some kind of indication as to . . .'

'As to what?' Judith said.

She reached a hand to the mane of the White Horse, the pendant around her neck all shining gold, the gems of Spring and Summer bright in their settings, that for Autumn empty and the one for Winter a bleak, chill void.

'Where's the gem of Autumn?' said Stort, knowing at once that it was not a question even worth asking. She didn't know herself. 'Perhaps you can give us some help?'

The Shield Maiden laughed and said, 'I just have!'

Then the White Horse and its lonely Rider, laughing still, faded into the swirling mist and were gone into the night.

28

BACK TO LIFE

From the moment Stort brought the Embroidery back from the Library, things in his laboratory began to go wrong.

Or rather, they began to do things they never had before.

Or, if not that, they did things they had not done in very many years, in some cases decades, in one case for a hundred years.

Stort's interest in things scientific had started young and continued all his life, moving rapidly from one enthusiasm to another. Lately he was most interested in chemistry. When he was young it was mechanical things, like model steam engines. He moved from that to telegraphy and wireless, which opened his ears to the world beyond and, ultimately, to questions great and small about the Cosmos.

He knew, of course, that such interest in things human, especially those concerning communication and warfare, was seen as unhealthy and dangerous by city elders. But in having Brief as mentor he was lucky. To him knowledge was truth and the pursuit of it should be unfettered, provided of course it was not harmful.

Stort was too much an innocent to be capable of lying about his interest in telegraphy. Brief knew him too well to think it was an interest that would last long or be used dangerously, so he let it be.

Only when Stort once expressed the opinion that human weaponry might be a subject worthy of research did Brief get truly angry. Stort never ventured that view again and stuck with his promise to leave that subject well alone.

These varying interests, marking as they did the different periods of his intellectual life and development, were easily traceable throughout his home and laboratory, since once a new enthusiasm took hold he simply abandoned the paraphernalia relating to the old and left it where it stood.

His telegraphic period occurred when he was twelve when he had been in Brum, under the tutelage of Master Brief, for only a year or two. He made a crystal radio set; he fiddled with telephones and tapped into the human system; he became, for a time, a radio ham, which had the attraction of bringing him into contact with humans anonymously and, as he discovered in time, some hydden enthusiasts as well. This was by Morse signal, not voice. In fact, listening in to human radio was not of interest, since human voices are generally too low and fractured for hydden ears.

But through Morse code he did make contact with some hydden, though none from Brum. Usually they were based in Europe, in which Stort's facility with languages, particularly ones of a Teutonic origin, helped him make friends. But the communications were technical and rarely flowed or touched on subjects that interested Stort. For him, once the initial buzz of making contact had waned, communication was a means, not an end. Still, he kept the equipment live, and once in a rare while an old contact was in touch and for a few moments Stort relived those excitements of his youth.

The equipment he used was mainly human-made. It was easy enough to find in the basements of certain buildings around Brum because the moment such equipment becomes outdated, it is forgotten and often left in boxes from which it is never even unwrapped.

The young Stort built up an impressive collection of equipment, ancient, recent and relatively modern. His favourite devices were Morse keys, made of brass and wood, beautifully crafted and in many different patterns and styles. His favourite find was a late nineteenth-century ticker-tape machine which looked good but didn't seem to work.

That phase passed when astronomy caught his attention and as suddenly as his interest in telegraphy had started, it one day came to an end. But there the equipment still was, in a far corner of his laboratory, some of it connected to power or telephone lines by rotting cables, buzzing and clicking and whirring occasionally through some random electronic impulse or radio signal. Electronic storms could wake that part of his laboratory up and make the equipment start even though the only thing it was connected to was the old iron pipework around his walls, which itself was not connected to much except, perhaps, earth wires near and far.

The moment Stort cleared one of his many benches of rubbish and laid the Embroidery out so he could get a better view of it, his old equipment began to wake up. The first he knew of it was not by sound or sight but odour, a very particular one. Dust settles on old radio valves. When they are activated and heat up, the dust burns and that special scent is one immediately recognized by anyone who has dreamed a night away listening to high-pitched whistles, rapid-fire Morse signalling and wavy, indistinct voices from round the globe.

Soon after Stort spread out his Embroidery, he smelt that familiar smell and was surprised to find that one of his old pre-war radios had come to life.

The following day, a crystal radio spoke to him and two of his Morse keys began operating themselves.

Impossible, he told himself.

But then it happened again, so it seemed it *was* possible and that intrigued him very much. The Embroidery had powers beyond its status as a piece of fabric into which colourful designs and depictions had been cleverly woven.

Perhaps, Stort mused, *it is in some way, or shape, or form unknown to me just as much a machine, or at least a piece of equipment, as these old artefacts it activates. If so, then some proper scientific inquiry might get to the root of the problem, if problem it be. My hypothesis must be that this 'equipment' which ā Faroün collected, or made, but certainly preserved for good reason, will show me the way to the gem of Autumn which, thus far, I have been struggling to find!*

'Mister Stort,' cried Cluckett from the threshold of his laboratory, 'you have been working all night! It is time to stop. I have made coffee and coddled eggs and insist that you come and enjoy them.'

Bedwyn sighed with pleasure.

The world might be falling apart, Brum on the eve of death and destruction, but in his small world all was well and comfortable.

Not so thirty miles away, where the situation of Arthur Foale and Emperor Niklas Blut had become desperate. They had woken to find that General Quatremayne and his staff had abandoned the bunker utterly. The familiar faces they knew had been replaced by a unit of eight Fyrd whose role seemed to be to keep them in minimum comfort with as little contact as possible until . . .

'Until what? That's the question!' said Arthur many times.

Blut knew only too well but did not say it more than once.

They would be dispensable once Brum had fallen and Quatremayne could claim a popular victory of his own making and, as well, the Imperial throne for himself.

Astonishingly, Arthur's killing of Krill had gone unnoticed, coinciding as it had with the day the changeover took place. Perhaps each group of guards thought the other accounted in some way for Krill and he was not missed.

Arthur had realized almost at once that his body had to be moved as far from everyone as possible. The water in the tunnels helped, because it gave slight flotation and made for less friction. Even so, it was one of the most unpleasant experiences of his life to have to drag the foul thing through the dark, noisome, back tunnels of the bunker, heave its stiffly flopping form over the threshold of a storeroom, lie him on a wet floor among rusting and stinking cans of bully beef, pile them over him and close the door, lock it tight and slosh his way back to his communications room.

The message he had bravely returned to the bunker to read had been initially hopeful. It said, 'What do you want? Be specific.'

Arthur, still afraid that it was Fyrd operators who were picking it up, sent back a message that was very specific indeed, to anyone who already knew what it meant. He asked that it be passed on and added it was urgent.

There was a very brief reply in Morse which translated as WILLDO, followed by a call sign.

After that, nothing at all, nor any response to further messages.

Two days later, the ventilation system in the bunker began to emit a faint but foul odour which got worse with each day that passed. It was Krill, decomposing.

'The guards won't like *that*!' said Blut. 'It's surely just a matter of time before they start trying to find what's causing it.'

. . . And it was.

Arthur managed to get two more messages out before the inevitable happened. A team of guards sloshed down the tunnel he had made his own, worked out that the smell came from an old food store. Arthur had had the sense to go back and tumble more tins of human food over Krill's body so that when the store was opened and lights flashed inside the stench was so unbearable that no one felt inclined to investigate further. That section of the tunnel was sealed up.

'My communications room is now inaccessible but the shaft out into the wood can be reached. The trouble is they've been outside and put something over the grille.'

Blut pulled off his spectacles and wiped them. Another miracle was needed.

In Brum, Stort's researches were not going well.

That Embroidery was hard to focus on, its imagery curiously elusive, its colours too, which changed with the angle from which he looked at it and the lights he had on.

The now continuous clacking and buzzing, glowing and flashing of his old telegraphic equipment, so interesting at first, now disturbed his concentration.

But he could not let the matter rest.

'There's something in this Embroidery which is staring me in the face which I cannot see,' he told Jack.

Then Barklice.

Then Terce.

Then Katherine.

In fact anyone who would listen.

'He's a dog with a bone,' Cluckett told them one after another, 'and all he does is eat, sleep and look at that Embroidery, which, if I've told him once I've told him a dozen times, has got its perspective all wrong. What's the point of a picture if things aren't as they're meant to be?'

Whatever the truth of that, Cluckett was right about one thing: Stort needed fresh air and a daily walk. In fact she insisted on it, colluding with his friends to come at the required times and drag him off.

He went reluctantly, talked unwillingly and ended up in the same place every time: the Library and standing on ā Faroün's star of worn cobbles in the Main Square.

'It brings me closer to him,' he said, 'as do his books and other artefacts in the Library. But the closer I get, and the more I read the texts he is known to have written and ponder the meaning of his great work, the more I feel I am missing the point! But at least I know as I stand here on something he made with his own hands, I get a sense of . . . of . . . something. It is driving me mad!'

It was after such a walk with Jack, back at his humble, a brew in hand as they yet again stood staring at the Embroidery, that the telegraphic corner sprang to life once more.

'It is irritating,' said Stort.

'Fascinating,' said Jack, wandering over and peering at the complex jumble of equipment.

He reached forward to try a switch.

'Don't touch!' cried Stort. 'The wiring is dangerously . . .'

Too late.

But the shock Jack got was not an electric one. The ticker tape machine suddenly sprang into frenzied life, as if it had been storing up its thoughts and impulses for years in the hope that someone might actually switch it on.

It began clacketing furiously and yellow-white paper tape began spewing forth, tumbling all over Jack's legs and feet.

He picked some up and examined it. The punched holes meant nothing to him, but they did to Stort.

It was, yard after yard, the same brief message: Stort's old call sign followed by a question mark. Then yards of blank. Then a message.

'What's it say?'

Stort consulted his code book, dictating it letter by letter to Jack who scrivened it down: IMNOTABLOODYMESSENGERBOY-HEREITIS.

'What's it say?'

Stort took it and read it aloud, 'I'm not a messenger boy, here it is.'

'Very helpful,' said Jack. 'Obviously a human.'

'I wouldn't be certain of that,' said Stort. 'When I played around with telegraphy for a while you'd be surprised how rude some of the hydden operators could be, especially to someone new. It was one of the things that made me stop. This reply is typical of that mentality, be it hydden or human.'

They had managed to stop the tape but there was plenty more left of that which had already come out, which they pulled along through their fingers.

'Nothing,' said Stort.

'Something here, at the very end.'

It read STORTHELPSW453268AFURG.

'Stort helps who or what?' said Jack.

Cluckett made lunch while they pondered the brief alphanumeric message and its meaning.

It was Jack who worked out where the spaces ought to be.

'Stort help SW453268 AF URG'

They each got a different bit of it simultaneously.

'AF is Arthur Foale!' cried Stort.

'SW453268 is a grid reference,' Said Jack excitedly.

'. . . and URG,' they said together, 'is urgent!'

They were right. The reference was the one Arthur worked out from the Ordnance Survey map he had examined so carefully in the canteen in the bunker. The Embroidery was forgotten and they set off at once to Marshal Brunte's headquarters because it was there, Jack knew, that Ordnance Survey maps might be found that would allow them to use the grid reference to plot Arthur's location very precisely indeed. To within one hundred yards, in fact.

29

LEAVING

The former Emperor Slaeke Sinistral had found new peace. He had finally learnt the lesson that eternal beauty is not found by clinging to a false eternal mortal life, but in the graceful acceptance of inevitable death, without fear and in a spirit of compassion for self and all others.

Sinistral had grown wise.

His abdication in favour of Blut so that he could retreat into the Remnant tunnels to think and to ponder the *musica* was the best decision he ever made. More and more he was able to rest again in his chair to reach out with his mind and search through threads of sound for that same thing which Bedwyn Stort now sought and which the Shield Maiden needed soon: the gem of Autumn.

Each, in their own way, was seeking the same thing.

'Finding *this* gem,' he told himself pragmatically, 'cannot be done without these others. What we have to combine to do is make sure that those of selfish intent do not lay hands on it. Meaning . . .'

Meaning he did not know what, but he found as his mind explored the melodic threads of sound to places far beyond Bochum that there were certain inconsistencies, which were disharmonies, and these formed shards of imagery which added up to . . .

To . . .

It took him days to work that out.

'Just now,' he finally cried out. 'It adds up to General Quatremayne.' He levered himself out of the chair and waited for the bilgesnipe to come and clean him, tend him, feed him and ready him to leave.

'Where's Slew?' he called out into the wet, teeming musical dark. 'Where is he when he's needed?'

'Lord,' murmured the flabby blind bilgesnipe, 'you ordered the Master of Shadows to serve your successor.'

'Well, well,' said Sinistral, 'perhaps it seemed that way to you but it will not have done to Blut. He knows my needs better than I myself. He will send Slew back and Slew will come because . . . he knew the gem of Summer, he stared with me into the starry night holding it in his hand and a yearning woke in him. He will come.'

'When, my Lord?'

The bilgesnipe heard movement, felt it, reached chubby fingers into the strands of the *musica* that flowed about them both. It was like the caress of a lover's tresses.

Three hours later Sinistral replied.

'He is on his way,' he said. 'I can smell the salt sea spray.'

'Me too,' said his bilgesnipe aide, 'sharp as that fresh air I've heard about but never tasted.'

'You mean smelt,' said Sinistral.

'To us it is the same thing, my Lord.'

They were right, Slew was on his way. He was halfway across the wild North Sea, tossed and turned in Borkum Riff's famous black-hulled cutter.

'Tell me nothing of your mission, Master,' rasped Riff, eyes like the darkest seas, 'but this: is the Emperor's hand in it?'

'Which Emperor?'

'There's only one.'

Slew laughed.

'Yes, that hand is in this work,' he said. 'He'll want you for the return journey.'

Borkum Riff stood his great strong bulk to the wheel, leaning this way and that with the craft and the seas, fingers like iron pinions on the varnished oak.

'Be your mates trustworthy, Master?'

'They are. One wasn't; killed him.'

'That's what I would do.'

They disembarked at Emden, north Germany, but Riff said he'd do the pickup at Helledore.

'Why? Easier? Wind? Currents?'

Borkum Riff shook his head.

'The Emperor will know why and that Riff remembers. It's harvest-time across the sea, Master of Shadows, not just across the land. Time my Lord sees for himself what he sowed.

'Master, you weren't sick last time and nor this, but your mates were. They can clear it up before they leave my cutter.'

'We already have,' replied the two Slew had brought from Englalond for the mission, Harald and Bjarne shakily. 'We have.'

Two days later they were in Bochum, readying themselves for the Emperor's emergence.

Days after that, on Level 18, Sinistral uttered a cry and up on Level 2 Slew heard it as he glowered at Court life while the two Norseners made free with the ladies.

He gathered other Brethren to him, as he called his followers, commanding them to be armed and packed for travel.

'Now,' he said, 'when the Emperor appears he may be weak, he may be strong; he may talk sense, he may talk gibberish. Whatever he is or does I shall kill any among you who show the slightest disrespect towards him.'

He took only Harald down to 18, even then leaving him by the lift.

Then he advanced into the Chamber and eyed his Lord Emperor Slaeke Sinistral, tall and blond, thin and shaky.

'My Lord . . .' began Slew.

'Yes, yes, it is I. Let us begin. I have nothing to take but what's in my heart and head. Is it day or night toppermost?'

'Dusk and the first day of October, and Samhain but four weeks off – a good time for travel. Better not to be seen or the word will get out and you'll be mobbed. You are much loved. We have all your needs: garb and such. Take my arm, Lord.'

Which Sinistral did.

In the lift going up Slew said, 'Borkum Riff brought me over the sea.'

'Ah.'

'I presume we are sailing to Englalond.'

'Yes.'

'Riff awaits us in Helledore.'

'Aah . . . yes. Reason? The winds I presume.'

'No, Lord, he mentioned harvest-time.'

'Did he now? Well, well, Slew, Riff is as subtle as the currents in the sea and as unstoppable. Harvest, eh?'

They emerged at Level 2, behind the Chamber, and took the way out which Stort and the others had but weeks before when they escaped with the gems.

'Has my beloved Leetha come?'

'No, my Lord Sinistral, she has not.'

'Did you summon her?'

'Blut told me to, so I did.'

'She'll find me when she needs to. She always has. But you and Blut had no need to ask her; I told the Shield Maiden I needed her.'

The Brethren joined them, nodding respectfully. Sinistral, taller than all but Slew, ignored them.

The feral dogs that lived on the surface above Bochum came ranging and snarling among the vast and stinking rubbish tips, circling them. Sinistral was not afraid, nor Slew, but the others were.

'Leave them to me,' said Sinistral, detaching himself from Slew's arm and advancing straight at the largest of the red-eyed dogs, a bitch. He stared at her and she shivered, the others whined and they all soon backed away.

That was Sinistral's guard of honour as they left the confines of Bochum; panting dogs, tails low under their bodies in obeisance, eyes downcast, flanks shaking with fear.

My Lord Slaeke Sinistral was nothing less than the Angel of Death to them, and Witold Slew his shadow.

'To Englalond,' he said.

'To Englalond,' the Brethren all repeated dutifully.

One of them, Stuber, winked at one of the others disrespectfully when Sinistral stumbled on old tin cans.

'Stuber,' purred Slew, pulling him back as the others went on and the dogs caught up, 'come here. You're not on this mission any more.'

The dogs, sensing blood, nipped at Stuber's legs.

'But, Master . . .'

The Master of Shadows turned and sent the stubby end of his stave into Stuber's stomach and winded him so badly he fell to his knees, clutching at air.

'Goodbye, Stuber,' said Slew and followed after the others.

One dog caught Stuber's right hand, another his left and before they had pulled him down the others were ripping at his guts.

Goodbye Bochum . . .

Sinistral did not look back at what had been his home for more decades than most ordinary mortals live. His exit was through piles of rubbish, to the stink of foul and poisonous waste and the sound of scrabbling hounds ripping a hydden apart. He was finally leaving his past behind.

Soon they were clear of the tip, into fresh air and a gathering night.

'I'm going home to Englalond,' said Sinistral again, 'and not before time.'

They helped him along, step by step, on through the night as he stared at the stars, talked of this and that, laughing sometimes, and they began to understand why, tyrant though he had been, he never lacked for people who loved him.

'How's Blut?' asked Sinistral in the dead of night as they rested for a time.

'He is well, Lord, well. But under siege by Quatremayne, without a friend.'

Sinistral laughed again, ready to lie down but not to sleep. He had had enough of that.

'I doubt that Blut is without a friend,' said Sinistral. 'I think, Slew, you mean yourself.'

'Yes, my Lord.'

'Remember when we looked at the stars, that gem of Summer in our hands?'

'I do.'

'Look at the stars again now. You don't need a gem any more to know you have a friend. You've grown.'

'Yes, my Lord,' said Slew. 'What did Riff mean about harvest-time?'

Sinistral laughed gently in the dark and moved shoulder to shoulder with Slew.

'You'll soon find out. We sow, we tend, we reap, we die. It is the time for reaping now. That's what Riff meant, as you'll see.'

30

BEHIND ENEMY LINES

Jack took the news of Arthur's call for help to next morning's War Council to seek support to mount an immediate rescue bid. It seemed to him the perfect use of his particular skills and abilities and the kind of way Brunte had said he was best deployed.

He delayed raising the idea until he had Festoon and Brunte alone, with Barklice and Pike to back him up. He wanted both to come on the mission with him.

'Arthur Foale is certainly well known to many of us,' said Festoon cautiously, 'and better informed about matters cosmological than anyone I've ever met. Stort thinks that may be of importance. To have him at our side in the present crises posed by an angry Earth and threatening Fyrd can only be advantageous. But if your mission is a failure, Jack, and we lose you and whoever goes with you, then it be the very opposite of a boost to us all!'

Brunte eyed Jack shrewdly.

'I take it you need some additional support?'

'Your aide Lieutenant Backhaus helped logistically with our mission to Bochum on which, of course, Meyor Feld came and proved he was indispensable. I'd like to think . . .'

Brunte shook his head.

'I cannot spare Feld. He has created our defences and knows them better than anyone. Nor would I like to see Mister Pike here leave Brum just now. The stavermen respond to his leadership better than to mine . . .'

'But . . .'

Brunte raised a hand.

'Before you protest, what I was going to add was that Backhaus has been behind a desk too long for his own liking. He is hungry for a mission. So he needs an outing and this mission may be ideally suited to his skills . . . we can agree from the maps that Professor Foale is in some kind of bunker?'

'Seems so.'

'So it's a quick in—out hostage situation?'

'I suppose it is,' replied Jack.

Backhaus was summoned.

It was several months since Jack had seen him. He looked as though his hair had been shorn for duty five minutes before. He was all neat and tidy with shiny buttons, a clipboard and a pencil at the ready.

'Marshal?' he said.

'Sit. Stavemeister, please explain the situation.'

As Jack did so he appraised Backhaus. He looked very fit, carried himself with confidence and had a sharp and calculating seriousness which instilled both liking and respect. He was quick to grasp the nature of the mission.

When he asked a couple of questions he retained the formalities and addressed Jack as 'Sir'. Jack liked that. Backhaus looked the kind of hydden who liked to keep his distance and stay professional.

'So, how can *I* help, sir?'

'I've suggested you join the party, Backhaus,' said Brunte.

Backhaus look surprised but pleased.

'Your logistical expertise may be needed and I'm sure the Stavemeister could do with your rather special combat skills.'

Backhaus nodded and fell briefly silent.

'Any questions?'

'Who'll make up our unit, sir?' he asked Jack after a pause.

'Myself and Mister Barklice here. He is our best route-finder and a master of all modes of transport. I had thought of Mister Pike but Marshal Brunte prefers he stay in Brum.'

Backhaus nodded.

'He'll be needed if the Fyrd launch a surprise attack. How much do we know about where Professor Foale is being held?'

Jack told him what they knew.

'If it's a bunker made by humans we will need specialist help. May I suggest someone?'

They nodded.

'Bombardier Hans Recker is a munitions and explosives expert . . .'

'Bring him,' said Jack.

'One other thing, sir. How did you get the intelligence concerning the Professor's whereabouts. Is the source reliable?'

Jack explained about how Stort had received the message and investigated it.

'May I . . . ?'

'Ask anything.'

'Have you been able to verify the message is genuine and originates from the Professor himself? The Fyrd are good at playing tricks. They use Morse all the time. We pretend we don't understand it, but we do.'

'And this helper,' asked Brunte, 'the one who relayed the message. Who is he?'

'We don't really know. Stort only has a code name for him so far. Whoever it is sounds human and must have thought the message was also from a human.'

'That's probably good,' said Backhaus, 'but we'll check for the reassurance we need. I suggest that if it is affirmative the mission should proceed.'

'In any case,' said Brunte, 'such a mission will gain intelligence from behind the Fyrd line and on that basis alone may be worthwhile.'

'When do you want to leave?' asked Festoon.

'Before dark today,' came Jack's reply.

They left at dusk, their point of departure being a container depot known to Barklice, who had used it before.

'The Fyrd now control the railways, which rules them out,' he explained. 'Trucks have their virtues if you know what you're doing, and I do. Empty ones travel to and from all points east from this depot, including other depots. There is one east of Coventry, which is where the bunker is located, so it's just a question of finding the right truck. Follow me . . .'

They dodged under massive vehicles, hid in the shadows of wheels, hurried between great corridors of stacked containers and arrived eventually at a truck rather smaller than the rest.

'We hide under tarpaulins in the back, entrance through the side panels. Come!'

They followed him, used the back wheel to clamber up, and hid under a tarpaulin until the truck departed.

Then, safe in the knowledge that they would not be disturbed again until the vehicle stopped, they came out into the rattling, shaking darkness into which the lights of street lamps above, headlights behind and vehicles passing on the other side came as a kaleidoscope of yellow, white and red.

Jack and Barklice were dressed in shadowed green, their portersacs empty of all but absolute essentials. Backhaus and Recker were in black fatigues and might have been mistaken for off-duty Fyrd.

'Deliberate,' said Backhaus. 'Might be useful.'

Recker was wiry thin, with wrinkly eyes that shone and smiled in the dark. His portersac seemed disproportionately large but he had no difficulty toting it.

'Gear,' he said ambiguously. 'For all eventualities.'

They spent most of the journey with their backs to the rear wall of the truck, 'sacs between their feet, staves beneath to stop them rattling, weapons on their belts, except for Barklice, who had none. Escape and hyddening was his defence.

'. . . and not getting caught in the first place . . . now, sleep.'

Darkness fell, the journey became monotonous; they dozed, trusting Barklice would wake to tell them when to disembark.

The truck stopped twice.

The first time Barklice just listened and muttered; the second he got up to check, peering outside.

'Next stop, be ready, it'll be a short one. Follow me. The Lieutenant first, the Bombardier second and Jack last. Fasten your 'sacs tight, don't want no loose noise. Watch the staves and watch the stop: it's sudden. Then out you go, one at a time, nice and neat. Ten minutes to go.'

They stood up, heaved on their 'sacs and stood one behind the other behind Barklice, using their staves to keep their balance, and fell silent.

The lorry turned off the road right on cue and, despite the warning, its sudden stop sent them lurching forward.

Barklice was out at once and down to the ground, using his stave to hold the tarpaulin open for Backhaus.

They dropped down easily enough, Backhaus steadying Recker, who carried the heaviest 'sac, as he landed. As Jack followed after them, Barklice set off into the shadows beyond the lay-by in which they had stopped and they were away and out of sight before the lorry driver had even opened his door to get out.

A few yards on they found themselves on the edge of a vast ploughed field, the noise of the busy road muted by the trees and shrubs through which they had come.

It was dark where they stood but the horizon right around was lit with ambient light from roads, factories and human settlements. They had all been in such situations before and know the drill: pause plenty long enough for the eyes to get used to the dark, set off single file, keep a close formation, no talking once they started until Barklice stopped or one of them signalled with a touch for all to stop.

'Right,' said Barklice while their eyes adjusted to the dark, 'the great big glow in the sky behind us is Coventry. Straight ahead, across this busy road, is Binley Wood. We'll head one o'clock because that'll stop us floundering into the wood and giving warning of our approach. There's no way we'll find the bunker at night without a little help. That'll come in the form of the narrow-gauge railway line that leads straight to it, probably in a slight cutting. That's our way in. Jack takes over from there because somewhere along it we'll likely meet Fyrd . . . Ready?'

It was the first time that Backhaus and Recker had followed Barklice in the dark. They soon found out why he was so renowned for his route-finding skills: he moved fast, confidently, was not afraid to stop and consider, appraised everything from wind direction and the stars to vegetation under foot to the hooting of owls as he went. He moved silently, so much so that Backhaus had to use sight, not sound, to make sure he kept the right distance behind.

He diverted from his bearing regularly, usually because a wheel-track offered easier passage through the tilled earth, or to avoid scrunchy vegetation. It was quick, professional and unremitting.

The night was warm, the cloud cover seventy or eighty per cent, but the sliver of the moon gave just enough light to add a silver edge to their silhouettes against the horizon.

On the far side of the field they came to a stile, though how Barklice found it so precisely the two military had no idea. He was up and over and on through a plantation of small trees at once, the ground sloping down, the route less straight, the dark around them deeper.

Barklice slowed, stopped, reached a hand behind him to Backhaus. The others clustered round.

'We're near the cutting,' he said. 'Likely there'll be wire, possibly a short steep drop, maybe the going will get loose, stony and therefore noisy. I'll get you to the track and you can take it from there, Jack.'

He set off again, more slowly now, reaching behind frequently to check Backhaus was close.

The ground steepened and he stopped.

Below was a void, out of which silver rails snaked away to their right.

'Listen!' he whispered.

At first they heard nothing but gradually they could make out a murmured hushing, a deep whisper, coming and going.

'Binley Wood,' he said, reading the landscape they were about to enter by sound and common sense. 'The cutting falls away and the ground flattens, so we must hope the cloud cover stays as it is . . . Now . . . be cautious: cuttings have a way of tripping folk up and causing noise.'

But they made it to the track without incident and squatted a little way off it for a break and to listen to Jack's orders.

'Right, I lead, Barklice to the rear, Backhaus and Recker in the middle. If we come across Fyrd, leave me to make a move with Backhaus in support. You other two watch our backs. There should be guards but they'll not be expecting us. Four maybe six. Arthur's seventy and not that agile but he's strong. I'm assuming he's alone, maybe he's been forgotten, alone and trapped, his single message didn't say. By now he might have got out or . . .'

The last alternative he did not explore.

The notion of Arthur not being alive did not bear thinking about.

'Come on,' he urged them, 'let's get him out safely and back to Brum.'

The arrival point Barklice had found was well judged. It took no more than half an hour of careful trekking along the track before they reached the wood. Its trees rose on either side of them, whispering in the slight breeze, hiding the moon and most of the stars.

Ten minutes later the track began to sink and the cutting to rise high on either side.

Jack stopped at once.

'This feels like the drop down to the main entrance. It'll be guarded. We'll circle round through the wood and lie low from a good vantage point until first light ... Take refreshments here and if necessary relieve yourselves too because once we're in position, watching, we'll need to be silent.'

They were wise precautions.

They found a spot that looked down on the entrance, though it was too dark to make anything out. There was no light, no movement, no sign of life at all, but they stayed still and silent all the same.

A hedgehog bustled past them at midnight; a fox barked soon after. The clouds grew thicker, their drift across the sky slower, so that there were long periods of no stars or moon at all.

At two in the morning there was the pull of bolts below them, a heavy door opened and dim light spilled out.

A single hydden appeared, walked a few paces, breathed the air deeply and relieved himself noisily. Then he went back inside.

'Could have had him with a bolt in moments,' said Backhaus, 'but . . .'

There was no need for an explanation.

They needed to find out how many others there were and what the layout of the bunker was and whether there were other entrances in the wood.

'It gives me hope that Arthur's still alive in there,' said Jack, 'otherwise, what are they guarding?'

31

QUATREMAYNE

That same night General Quatremayne was enjoying himself.
During the previous evening and into the small hours he
had had some 'business' to attend to of a personal nature.

Now he was wide awake and had very deliberately decided to hold
some hearings in the small hours concerning members of his staff and
units who had infringed rules in some way. It pleased him to have
them hauled from their iron bunks and brought before two fellow
officers and himself.

His command headquarters for the invasion of Brum were located
in a small area of scrubland beneath the Warwick Road Bridge in
Coventry.

The spot had been carefully chosen for its advantages in directing a
railway-based campaign. It was adjacent to the London–Birmingham
railway line, with the north–south Tamworth line joining from the
north to form a junction a few yards in one direction, while a fourth
main line, coming up from Warwick to the south, formed another
junction not far the other way.

In addition, sitting very conveniently between these major junctions
to the east was Coventry's mainline railway station.

It would be very hard to find anywhere in Englalond which offered
such a complex of lines, junctions and routine stopping points as the
Warwick Road Bridge. It was not overlooked, and security fences above
and to the sides to stop vandalism also prevented interference with the
Fyrd operation from humans.

Little wonder that on moving forward from the bunker in Binley

Wood, Quatremayne felt a growing sense of relief. His new quarters were noisy with trains back and forth and road traffic above but he could see what was going on and breathe fresh air.

There was something else.

Quatremayne's whole life had been a professional service to the Empire founded by Slaeke Sinistral. He had regretted Sinistral's abdication, though there were few in Bochum who had not found the Emperor's long-term 'sleeps' ultimately unacceptable, but he was used to him. He also respected him.

Blut was a different matter.

There was something about the way he looked, his spectacles, his austere neatness and the complete impossibility of unsettling him from his calm, logical approach to things that got under Quatremayne's skin. He had no apparent leadership skills and at a time of war the Empire needed an Emperor who had experience of battle, which Blut did not have.

'The nearest that damn little runt has ever got to killing anything is kicking a filing cabinet and I doubt very much he's done that!' Quatremayne had said very recently to his coterie of senior officers.

Naturally they laughed, whatever else they might have privately thought. It was unwise not to laugh at the General's little jokes.

Now that he had left Blut in Binley Wood under guard of one of his best units, Quatremayne was beginning to think of a future without him, which meant of his own future as Emperor. It was going to be much easier to give the discreet order to have Blut disposed of when Brum was taken.

Quatremayne had done that kind of thing before, though never at the ultimate level.

So the move was a welcome one marked by his change into a new uniform, a shade more regal than his previous one: it was black and grey with the usual flashes of red but with additional gold here and there which, he fancied, looked impressive.

He was of spare build, but tall and patrician with silver hair. He was disinclined to friendliness, only smiling with his closest and most trusted colleagues who smirked with glee as they shared some moment of mirth, almost always at the expense of their inferiors. There was a strain of self-serving and immature cruelty in them all and its fountainhead was Quatremayne. Some joke that excluded others, some 'uproarious' quip, some idiocy committed by a junior: these were the things that made Quatremayne smile.

Then, too, the matter of wyfkin. One might think that the General, being so cold, did not have feelings of what his circle called a 'base' kind. It was not true. But his feelings found vile and brutal expression which his minions could neither quite ignore nor quite acknowledge. Females were found for him. They left at dawn bruised, battered and frightened, feeling that the money paid them was no recompense for the secret humiliations they had suffered.

The trouble was that Quatremayne's power in his own domain was absolute. If he said, with that little snort of an awkward laugh, 'I . . . appreciate . . . *that* one . . .', then whether she be wyf, sister, daughter or even a bilgesnipe girl, his need better be satisfied, or else.

His smirks and nasty laughter were of the victor over the vanquished. He felt the same contempt for life that he did for Blut. There was no compassion.

Such perversity had been his evening's important 'business'.

Now, washed and changed, the military machine under his command in hand and in control, he found time and mood for less important matters: courts martial and hearings in which the unfortunates beneath him who had offended the Imperial or military code were tried, sentenced and summarily punished.

That night there were two court martials of ranking officers and the trials of various civilians who had been unlucky or foolish enough to displease the Fyrd since their arrival in Englalond. In addition there were one or two personal scores to settle.

Quatremayne used such occasions to instil fear and respect and did not hesitate to impose and carry through the harshest sentences. Punishments, from beatings to executions, were under the direction and personal hand of the head of his security, the unpleasant and diminutive Gritt Grolte, who was also the individual who most often found the General his females.

The General occasionally carried out executions himself; and sometimes, quite unpredictably, he enjoyed granting a pardon. It made him seem merciful. It made him feel powerful. It ensured that he had people about the place who owed their lives directly to him.

The hearings took place in a small compound near the Warwick Road Bridge consisting of tables and chairs and a place for the accused. This time, as so often in the past, at night. His victims' fears were greater then.

As the first of the accused – a senior officer charged with weak command because intoxicated – was brought before him through the cold night, Quatremayne continued with other minor business, in particular hearing verbal reports. This had always been his habit. So it could easily be that a Fyrd private or officer might be having his fate decided by a commanding officer who simultaneously was listening to a verbal report about latrines. Worse: if the report pleased or irritated him, that spilled over into Quatremayne's attitude to the accused, for better or for worse.

That particular night the General was in a bad mood, made angry by a slight division in his own ranks concerning transports that were not yet fully ready. These were in Walsall to the north of the city and Kidderminster to the south, where a combination of minor Earth movements, of the kind that had bedevilled Englalond in recent months, and irritating human unpredictability meant that nobody could be sure when the transports would arrive. It was, he knew, the kind of upset that could seriously undermine matters when it came to the invasion of Brum.

He waved away this latest report and gave his full attention to the hearing. His former comrade in arms and quartermaster, Stoll, was the one charged with inebriation. Not for the first time.

A token trial for a token offence, demanding a token punishment.

The overweight Stoll certainly seemed to think so as he stood before Quatremayne, who listened to charge and counter-charge with furrowed brow that did not appreciate Stoll's evident complacency.

'Guilty,' said Quatremayne looking either side to the other two officer-judges, 'I think we can agree on that.'

Naturally they agreed. The court waited idly for the sentence, all in good humour, Stoll included. This was just a warm-up, that was why he was first.

But Quatremayne pursed his thin lips.

The issue of the inefficient transports had worried him. Such things should not be happening so close to the coming major advances. Time for an example to be set.

'Garrotte,' he said quietly, 'now.'

Gritt Grolte rose, two hefty Fyrd at his side. His eyes were black holes, his face pallid, his hair greasy and dark.

'But . . .' began Stoll, the realization slow to dawn, *'but . . .'*

But he was stood up, turned, marched away barely able to struggle against Grolte's painful grip.

'Do it where we can see,' commanded Quatremayne. 'Next?'

Nothing subdues a crowd more than harsh sentences instantly carried out there and then. One after another.

'Garrotte.'

Again, 'Garrotte.'

Short-drop hanging.

Fire.

Bolts.

All in quick succession, the accused were hauled away and they saw and heard the slow and terrible squeezing out of a sequence of lives by Grolte. As the verdicts came one after another, the court had to listen to guttural hisses of terror and pain against the background of the noisy shunting of trains and carriages.

32

POLITICAL ASYLUM

For Jack and the others in Binley Wood, the last hour of their vigil outside the bunker felt the longest.

Only when the dark turned to grey-black and then to grey dawn, and the nearby trees became visible, did they begin to stretch, warm themselves, sip water, prepare.

'Barklice, I want you to make a circuit of the area . . . see if there are any other entrances or guards.'

Backhaus offered to go with him but Jack shook his head.

'Mister Barklice works best alone on these occasions. You will hardly know he's gone and you'll certainly not hear him return.'

It was true. Barklice had already melted away into the lightening dark, from tree to bush, from bush to fallen branch, and on around, silent as the dead.

He was gone half an hour and he reappeared as silently as he had gone, up some steps from the cutting below.

'There is no other entrance like the one below,' he reported. 'There are air vents above, but heavily cowled and overgrown. There are also vents in the forest floor, covered in steel doors. I found three, there's probably a fourth. The doors have been weighted down with stones, recently. One shows signs of having been forced from beneath, before the stones were put on it. That's one to watch.

'Not sure how many guards, but I'd guess six. Their patrol routes are easy enough to find, they're trampled and obvious. They're not expecting visitors. The patrol uses four stopping points, all at the edge of the wood . . .'

'And the routes all start from the entrance down there?' queried Jack.

'I can't see any other way in or out.'

'How near are the roof air vents from where we are now?' asked Recker.

'Thirty yards. Through those shrubs.'

'Can you draw me a plan of the structure?' asked Recker.

Barklice took a twig from the wood floor, cleared the humus, and quickly did so on the bare earth beneath, marking in the roof vents and the doors in the forest floor.

'What are you thinking?' Jack asked Recker.

'Diversion,' he replied. 'A small charge in the cowlings will serve to open them up and it'll be heard throughout the structure. Unless there's someone directly below, no one will get hurt. It might draw out the guards . . .'

Jack stiffened and whispered, 'No need for that right now!'

The great doors at the entrance were opening.

Two Fyrd came out, both armed, two more stood at the entrance covering them. They looked about, saw the coast was clear, nodded at the ones inside and the doors closed.

The two talked briefly and set off round the bunker in different directions, one away from where they watched, the other up the steps Barklice had used a short time before.

Jack smiled grimly.

'I'll take him down,' he said.

'I'll cuff him,' said Backhaus.

The Fyrd came up slowly, breathing heavily. Not very fit, it seemed. Jack took a place behind a tree, stave in hand.

Backhaus behind another.

The other two retreated out of sight.

'Good morning,' said Backhaus, stepping from behind his tree.

The Fyrd froze, not sure if he was facing friend or enemy since Backhaus looked like a Fyrd himself. Jack stepped up behind and felled him with his stave.

'Cuff and gag him,' he said, 'while I go and meet the other one before he realizes that his friend has not come to meet him. Barklice, show me the way.'

They met Number Two ten minutes later, this time adopting the guise of hydden who had lost their way and were surprised to see a Fyrd in the wood. He too was easily overpowered and gagged. Jack slipped Barklice's stave through the crooks of his arms and marched him back to the others, where he was laid on the ground next to his colleague.

A change had come over Jack.

He was taken over by a new purpose and energy. He seemed bulkier, more resolute and dangerous. There was no doubt he was the leader, and that he meant business, whatever that business might be.

'Barklice, guide the Bombardier to the cowled vents to set charges ready. We need to flush the others out before dawn advances too far and our friends are missed.'

'For what time?' asked Recker coolly, eyes glinting. He liked his work.

'They should go off five minutes after you get back here. Speed is of the essence.'

They nodded and were gone.

Jack pulled out his dirk and eyed the two prisoners.

He knelt down by the younger-looking of the two.

'We have little time,' he said, 'certainly no time to argue. I am going to ask questions, you will answer them.'

They stared at him, the younger one with insolence, and the older nervously.

'How many of you are guarding the bunker? Nod your head when I get to the right figure. One . . . two . . . three . . .'

They stared but did not nod their heads.

When he got to ten he continued, 'More . . . ?'

Still no response.

Jack glanced at his chronometer.

He placed the dirk just above the kneecap of the younger one and pushed the point in not quite enough to break the skin.

'I'll try again, pushing in a little way with each number. One . . .'

The Fyrd writhed but showed no sign of weakening. The other looked desperate at the prospect that awaited him as well.

'Two . . .'

The dirk broke skin, entered flesh.

'Hold him,' said Jack.

Backhaus did so.

'Three . . .' and blood spurted.

The Fyrd writhed desperately, but it was the other who broke and tried to speak.

'That's better,' said Jack, turning to him but keeping the knife where it was in the first.

'Four . . . five . . .'

Only when he got to eight did the Fyrd nod.

'Eight!?'

Again he nodded.

'Guarding how many?'

Jack took off the gag of the one who was cooperating but shoved his dirk into his throat.

'How many?'

'Two.'

'Two, *sir*,' said Jack to maintain dominance.

'Two, sir.'

'Eight guarding two seems disproportionate . . .'

Recker and Barklice returned.

'Five minutes,' said Recker.

Backhaus took up the questioning.

'Who are they?'

The response was surprising.

Total defiance on the face of one, real fear on the other.

'Can't say, sir. Mustn't say.'

'Professor Foale?'

'Ye . . . yes.'

'The other?'

'Mustn't say.'

'Four and a half minutes,' murmured Recker.

Jack thought fast.

'Where are your six friends?'

'Two are sleeping, four by the entrance. They'll do internal rounds when we return.'

'Where are their quarters? Near the entrance or not?'

'Near. I didn't want . . .'

'Four minutes,' said Recker.

'Where are the prisoners?'

'Inside the bunker.'

It took a moment for them to appreciate what this meant.

'You mean,' said Backhaus, 'that the guards are *outside* it?'

The Fyrd nodded.

'There's an antechamber, but I never . . .'

'Shut up,' said Jack, 'just answer the question.'

'We're all outside. The bunker has inner as well as outer doors. The prisoners are locked inside and we have no quick access.'

'Three minutes,' said Recker.

Jack thought fast, the others let him.

The sky was lightening and soon the sun would show. Whichever way they played it, time was running out.

'Can they see you when you come back? How do you signal you're outside?'

'We knock, they can't see us.'

'A particular knock?'

The Fyrd nodded.

'Two minutes, sir.'

'Right,' said Jack, 'here's how it's going to be . . .'

He told them briefly and they all got up.

Barklice retreated back into the wood in case anyone found a way to use the trapdoors on the forest floor. The younger of the Fyrd was tied tightly to the nearest tree. The cooperative one was hauled to his feet, the point of Jack's dirk firmly in his back.

They guided him down the steps towards the entrance.

'Don't make a sound until I tell you.'

Jack pushed the dirk in a little to make him understand what would happen.

'Sixty seconds . . .'

'Count me down,' ordered Jack, before whispering in the Fyrd's ear, 'On my signal I want you to give your normal knock but make it sound urgent. Backhaus, you'll follow me; Recker, find Barklice and watch our backs. This is going to be swift and brutal.'

'Thirty seconds, twenty-nine, twenty-eight . . .'

The seconds shot by.

'Twenty . . .'

'*Now!*' said Jack urgently.

The Fyrd began knocking.

Rat-tat-tat-tat-rat-rat-rat-tat

Then a pause and again: *rat-tat-tat-tat-rat-rat-rat-tat*

A sliver of sunlight hit the door as he and the others moved to one side to be out of sight when it opened.

'Three, two . . .' murmured Recker to the sound of bolts being thrown.

As the door swung open there was a loud *bang! Bang!* above their heads.

'By the Mirror, what was *that!*' said the guard inside, opening the door still more.

Recker stepped in and heaved the door wider still, Backhaus felled the Fyrd they had caught and pulled him aside and went straight at the one who opened the door and sent him tumbling backwards.

As he grunted with surprise, Jack went hard in, leaving the others to deal with the two now on the ground, his stave raised ready to deal with what he found.

Three down altogether, five to go.

Two of the five stood right in front of him, one with a cannikin of water in his hand, the other just standing there, shaving.

He drove his stave straight in, one to a temple, the other to the neck; they fell straight down, and the only sound was the rattle of the cannikin skittering across concrete.

Recker and Barklice moved inside to cuff and gag the four who had now been downed; Jack and Backhaus moved straight across the court to where the steps came up from the level below, flattening themselves against the wall either side.

Five down, three to go.

Silence, an interrogative shout which Jack answered with a grunt. They heard someone mounting the steps.

Jack stepped round from his hiding place, grasped the Fyrd by the neck, heaved him up and shoved him to the ground and left him for Backhaus to deal with.

Six down, two to go.

Jack listened once more; the sound of Backhaus neutralizing the

Fyrd behind him and sleepy voices below. Signalling Backhaus to follow, he headed straight down the steps, eyes alert, stave ready.

Ten seconds later he might have been killed. He arrived as one of the remaining two Fyrd, deciding that the sounds from above were unusual, but still in his nightshirt, was trying to arm his crossbow. The bow went flying one way, the bolt another, the Fyrd a third.

That left one, also half-dressed.

'Deal with him,' commanded Jack, ducking through a door to see if there was access into the bunker at the lower level that would offer a quicker way than through the great doors above.

There was none.

'Up the steps!' ordered Jack, heaving the conscious Fyrd to his feet. '*Now!*'

Backhaus brought up the other and moments later all seven of the Fyrd were lying in the court in a nice neat row, the last of the eight still up in the wood tied to a tree.

'Right . . .' said Jack, '*right . . .*'

He eyed the Fyrd grimly as he caught his breath.

The first phase of the operation was over but now came the second: how to get Arthur out of the bunker and then get away as quickly as possible. The day had lightened still more and Jack was worried that another Fyrd unit, perhaps stationed nearby, might soon appear.

'We need to get into the bunker,' said Jack quietly, pulling out his dirk again. '*Now!* Does one of you want to tell me?'

In truth they were in various stages of grogginess, and two were still out cold. The others looked defiant, as had the one they had left in the wood.

As he approached them, one or two flinched as he considered which one to work on first. The biggest? The most defiant? The weakest-looking?

He was still making up his mind when they heard the sound of metal banging on metal from the woods above. Looking up to the high edge of the bunker's roof, the head of Barklice appeared.

'I've found Arthur Foale,' he called down, 'but we need Bombardier Recker's help to get him out . . . He's below one of the blocked trapdoors.'

Jack considered this.

Three of them in charge of the seven on the ground were easy enough. If he let Recker go up to help Barklice that would leave two, and the danger of something going wrong increased dramatically. Cuffs did not always hold. Get too near and one of these Fyrd could easily have them down.

Barklice could read his thoughts.

'It'll take no more than a moment to get the cover off,' he called down, 'but it needs more strength than I have.'

Backhaus said, 'It's good, Jack. I can handle this lot. Go.'

'If any of them move while we're gone, kill them. Understood?'

Backhaus unbuckled his crossbow from his belt. It was a hefty triple bolt. He loaded it fully and played it slowly over each of the Fyrd.

'Understand,' he said coldly

They understood as well.

Jack and Recker went back out of the gates and up to join Barklice. They checked the other Fyrd on the way. He was as they had left him and looking both furious and apprehensive.

'Won't be long,' said Jack cheerfully.

Barklice led them through the trees for fifty yards to a clump of brambles and nettles. Even close to, the vent was not easy to see but the verderer had always had a knack for such things.

He parted the brambles and there it was, a heavy rusty metal cover aslant another flimsier, corroded grille, flat to the ground, its hinges rusted.

'I told them to stay silent until I returned in case someone else appeared who shouldn't,' said Barklice.

He coughed politely but loudly.

Kneeling down and putting his mouth to the small gap between cover and grille he said loudly, 'Er, Professor, the Stavemeister is here.'

'Jack!?' a muffled voice shouted.

Jack laughed and banged the metal.

'Arthur?' he called out, delighted.

'For Mirror's sake, get us out of here!'

'How many of you are there?'

'Two,' replied Arthur irritably, 'now, *please* . . .'

'Stand well clear,' said Jack.

He and Recker heaved off the slab the Fyrd had put there.

The rusting grille underneath, which Arthur had managed to lift off a few days before, was easily lifted from above.

They peered in and the upturned face of Arthur appeared, his face grimy.

'A moment!' he cried, standing on the crate beneath and pushing his head and shoulders through the rectangular hole.

'Ah! Barklice, Jack and . . . ?' he cried, pausing when he saw Recker.

'Introductions can wait,' said Jack. 'I want to get you out and away from here.' They leaned down and hauled Arthur up.

He beamed at Jack and said, 'I had not *quite* given up!'

He immediately knelt down himself and reached a hand back into the shaft. Blut grasped it and emerged blinking.

'My friend Blut,' said Arthur, who had decided that for the new Emperor's safety it might be wise to be economical with the truth until they were certain they were in safe hands.

Jack eyed him, sure he had seen him before but unable to remember where.

'Have we met?' he said.

'Possibly,' said Blut ambiguously.

Jack would have pursued the matter had not they heard the sudden *thut! thut!* of two bolts being shot from a crossbow.

They ran back to the spot to which Barklice had gone earlier, above the courtyard where Backhaus had the Fyrd under his guard.

Two lay a little way from the others, blood pooling around their heads on the concrete. The others lay deathly still.

Backhaus looked up at Jack and shrugged without saying a word. Jack had given his orders, two of the Fyrd had tried it on, he had killed them.

Jack's expression did not change but the war against the Fyrd felt suddenly very real for him, and perhaps for them all.

'We need to get out of here,' he repeated, 'and fast. But we must deal with these Fyrd.'

They got the one up by the tree and took him back down the steps.

'I want one of you to open these damn inner gates,' said Jack. '*Now.*'

He waited only a few seconds before looking at the Fyrd Backhaus had killed and adding warningly, 'Lieutenant Backhaus . . .'

One of the Fyrd mumbled through his gag that he had keys.

The doors were opened in moments and Jack ordered the Fyrd inside the bunker, making them drag the bodies of their colleagues in as well.

'I presume,' he said to Arthur, 'that getting back out is only possible through the shafts into the wood.'

Arthur nodded.

'We'll lock these doors and block that shaft up again so they'll need help from outside to get out, like you did.'

'What about the cowling we blew off the vents?'

Recker shook his head.

'There are still grilles there which are impassable even if they were in reach.'

'Any light?'

'We had this one candle left . . .' said Arthur, pulling a candle from his pocket.

'Give it them.'

Arthur quickly did so.

'Communication?'

'There were Morse keys connected to Bochum. I have destroyed them.'

'Good,' said Jack.

'Food?'

'Plenty.'

'Gentlemen,' said Jack, 'we must leave you. I suggest you stand well clear of these doors . . . !'

With that they exited the bunker and pushed the doors to. The last thing they saw as the doors closed with a heavy *thwunk* was the Fyrd with the candle desperately trying to light it with a lucifer.

'What was that about standing well clear?' said Barklice.

Jack glanced at Recker and Backhaus, eyes glinting.

'We didn't have time to search them. They probably have a spare set of keys between them. However, the Bombardier here knows what to do.'

For the third time Recker set to work, swiftly and expertly. He set four charges in the walls adjacent to the doors, fused them and ordered everyone beyond the outer doors, only one of which he left ajar.

'Right!'

The four explosions were louder than before and bits of concrete drummed against the doors near them.

When they looked they were astonished to see that he had somehow managed to bring part of the walls adjacent to the inner doors down against the doors themselves which remained in situ.

'Opening them from inside is impossible,' he said. 'It'll take any rescuers a long while to clear away that mess. Even then, I expect they have been sufficiently disturbed now not to open at all . . . Now, I'll reseal that trapdoor in the wood . . .'

Half an hour later, the time now nearly eight-thirty in the morning, they were clear of the wood and ready to head back to Brum. They were about to set off back down the line and round to the road where they had started when Jack stopped. Something worried him: Arthur's friend.

'Who is he exactly?'

'Ask him yourself, Jack,' said Arthur, eyes twinkling.

'So, who are you?' asked Jack.

Blut eyed him, took off his spectacles, cleaned them and put them back on. He did this unhurriedly as if thinking through his options. He had, they could all see, unexpected natural authority in one who at first seemed so . . . bland.

Blut eyed Jack and said, 'My name is Niklas Blut. I am the Emperor of the Hyddenworld. Under the Eighteenth Article of the Imperial Protocol, I claim political asylum of the City of Brum.'

They stared at him dumbfounded, then at Arthur, for confirmation. He smiled and nodded but didn't say a word.

'May I make a suggestion?' said Blut calmly.

Jack continued to stare, stuck for words.

'It is simply that we should get to Brum sooner rather than later. I have intelligence concerning General Quatremayne's strategy that will be more effective if acted on swiftly.

Everything, Jack realized, had suddenly changed.

'You're serious!?' he said.

'I'm afraid he is,' said Arthur.

'I thought Slaeke Sinistral . . .' said Jack.

'He has abdicated. I am his successor.'

Blut! It all came back to Jack. He had been there when they had wrested the gems of Spring and Summer from under the noses of Sinistral and his Court.

'Are you telling me . . . ?' began Jack, trying to get his head round the situation.

'I am saying, Stavemeister, that the survival of law and order in the Empire depends now not upon the armies of the Fyrd, which have been temporarily taken over by one of my generals, but upon . . .'

He looked from Jack to Backhaus, from him to Recker and Barklice and then to Arthur.

'. . . upon us six until we get to Brum. Then we can spread out responsibility a little.'

'But . . .'

Blut's face grew more serious.

'I wish you to take me at once to Brum and that is . . .'

He blinked, thought a moment, and continued, '. . . that is technically a command from your Emperor. But let's just call it a polite request.'

'Understood,' said Jack, who understood in that moment something more.

Arthur Foale was a considerable prize, but the Emperor was something entirely different. If he could get him safely back to Brum and his intelligence was good, a mighty blow would have been inflicted on the Fyrd before their invasion of the city had even begun.

33
DEN HELDER

B y October 2nd, when Slaeke Sinistral and his party reached the north flatlands of Holland after a slow seven-day trek from Bochum, the inclement weather of late September had worsened into driving rain and wind.

The prospect of their proposed crossing of the North Sea was a grim one; even on land, the going was already very hard. Unpleasant north-westerlies blew in across the bleak landscape and their route now took them headfirst into them.

All they could do was hunch forward and keep going. Two of them always walked protectively in front of Sinistral to reduce wind and chill, plus one behind with a hand solicitously at his back to try to stop him falling, which he did several times.

They wore what Fyrd infantry called 'binnies' – a loose outer garment made of green refuse bags used by humans – which provided camouflage and kept out all rain.

Sinistral walked erect and proud and preferred to wear no hat or head covering. His thin blond-grey hair sleeked and darkened in the rain. His face colour, initially so pale from being underground, had improved. Even close up, his smooth, taut skin belied his age, as did his eyes, being clear and alert.

But closer still, this impression changed. His face with its myriad tiny cracks and the papery thin skin looked ready to tear at any moment. The bright whites of his eyes were patterned with tiny red veins. When he grew tired, which he frequently did, his humour deserted him and he got sharp and cranky.

Strangely, it was this which distressed him most, as if he was discovering in himself something he did not like. Later, if he had been rude or discourteous, he would apologize with a shake of the head and a charming smile.

The hydden under Slew's command soon came to both respect and like him.

Den Helder was two miles east of its human namesake, a large, thriving port whose ambient light they had seen across the flatlands for two nights past.

They arrived at dusk and had a final rest between the human and hydden settlements, sheltering behind a concrete sea wall from the cold, moist wind.

Sinistral was as well and vigorous as he had so far been, and now talkative.

'In former times it was known as Hell's Door or Helledore because of these fortifications you see all about. Hardy sea folk are born and raised in this place, Borkum Riff among them.'

'You've been here before, my Lord?' one of them asked, handing him a warming drink.

'Once. Seventy years ago. I have reason to remember it but . . .'

Seventy years.

They shook their heads in wonderment. That must mean . . . but no one dared ask his age, though they knew the rumours. One hundred and fifty years! He was already old when he came here last, and very old when they were born.

He said no more. Instead, turning round and raising himself up to look over the wall towards the driven, spumey waves and grey sea, he said, 'Let us move on.'

Riff's place was on the far side of Den Helder, among sand dunes, on the neck of a spit of land with shores and jetties on either side, allowing craft to land in all conditions of wind and tide. If, that is, their skipper had the skill to do so.

A cutter bobbed against a granite jetty on the south-east shore. Steel hawsers rattled in the wind. Waves roared over sand and shingle. Sturdy, salt-bleached grass stuttered at their feet. Riff's humble was half underground, the smell of woodsmoke coming from some cleverly hidden outlet, its odour driven into their noses then whipped away again.

He stood alone, apart from his humble, on the wild, dark shore, in oilskins from head to toe, his sou'wester black, his beard thick but short. He stood and stared, waiting.

'I will go to him alone,' said Sinistral and then, blown sideways for a moment, he got his footing right, leaned into the wind, and went down to where Riff stood.

'My Lord,' said Borkum Riff, reaching out a hand.

Sinistral took it and said, 'Where is he?'

'He clings on to life.'

'He knows I am here?'

'He allers swore he'd stand erect the day you came back but . . . my Lord . . . he has a pride as hard and sharp as flint.'

'Your father is ill?'

'Old, infirm, unable . . .'

'Where is he?'

'Abed, but he'll not see you lying down.'

'Take me to him.'

'No, my Lord, that I cannot . . .'

But he paused and, glancing over Sinistral's shoulder, looked surprised.

Slaeke Sinistral turned and looked where Riff did, and Slew and the Brethren too.

The door of the humble had opened and a tall thin hydden, very old, thin as a beanstalk, his white nightshirt flapping in the violent wind, a young wyf trying to haul him back inside, stood on the threshold.

Sinistral went to him at once.

'My Lord,' said the old one stepping out into the wind which caught him and began to blow him over, 'I allers said to 'em that you'd come back and . . . and . . .'

Sinistral suddenly lost years. He stepped forward, as if out of his own weakness into a stronger body and took the old one in his arms and embraced him for all to see.

Who or what they were to each other none there knew.

'I *said* you'd come!'

They laughed like young things, the foul night resonant with memories the others could not share.

'You know why I've come?'

'Aye, it's time. He's ready to skipper your boat to the furthest shore. Now he be ready, Lord. And I too. But . . . do you want to see 'em afore you go? It is your right. You do?'

He turned to his son.

'Whistle 'em up, Borkum, let my Lord see and appraise 'em, every one!'

The wyf who had tried to drag the old one in reappeared with a long, warm coat which she draped around him, and a scarf which she wrapped around his neck and head, standing on tiptoe.

Then Borkum Riff pulled a ship's silver whistle from around his neck and raised it to his mouth and blew, playing the note up and down three times.

At first nothing happened, the wind just blew and the dark continued to hang about the dunes and the waves to pile up palely on the shore.

But then the light of a humble, unnoticed till then, went on, followed by another, then a third.

Out of the doors of these buried dwellings, hydden began to come, males and females, one or two Riff's age, more a little younger: wyfkin, spouses, kinder nearly grown, dressed in the rough, tough garb of the polder folk and mariners of those wild sea-roads.

They came and stood in awe, staring at the old hydden, then at Borkum Riff, and finally at Sinistral, who stood so tall.

'These be my kin, my Lord,' said the old hydden. 'These be the true harvest of that night you saved my life! These be my progeny your great courage made. Touch 'em, Lord, so they know you did.'

They saw the pride in the Lord Emperor's face.

'All these are yours?'

'That night you gave me life, that same night you made 'em be. These be your kinder too, my Lord. Touch 'em now!'

Then Sinistral went from one to another of Riff's father's descendants, Borkum at his side. He introduced each by name and Sinistral shook their hands.

'This be Lord Slaeke Sinistral, Emperor of the Hyddenworld, who saved my life and Borkum's there, that was a babe, where none other dared to go that night long past, out on a sea-road that was hell. Then, though she be gone to the Mirror now, he went out again alone and saved she I loved who was Borkum's Ma and thine. Honour him!

Remember him. He is your Lord and mine, who comes this night to take his due.'

Sinistral shook his head and pulled back, looking round at Slew as if for escape.

'I cannot do it!' he said.

'You can and will. I promised Borkum'd skipper you when you crossed the sea again to that furthest shore. These be my harvest, he be my tithe. His wyrd will bring him back or no!'

'So be it,' said Sinistral, 'Borkum Riff shall skipper me over the sea and beyond.'

'I will, My Lord,' Riff replied.

They supped in a boathouse and took good brew.

They talked and heard that tale of seventy years before from Riff's Pa, from Riff himself and from one of the wyfs, who heard it from Ma.

All different in detail and degree, all like the ocean, never the same on the surface but always the ocean still.

They listened to songs from the young and the old, they each found their way to say thank you and goodbye.

Until the wind howled and spray spattered along the boathouse wall and Borkum Riff growled, 'Tis time!'

He rose, his crew with him, and they went to rig and to range his black-hulled craft, ready for the fray.

Sinistral stood tall and said his farewell, Old Riff the same.

They went outside and Borkum Riff came back up the sandy shore, the waves thundering after him. He stopped short by the shell and shingle bank where his kin stood to watch him leave. Like his Lord before, he went to each and every one to say his last farewell.

It was only then that Slew and his friends understood that Riff did not expect ever to come back.

'You know,' said Sinistral, 'I thought my Lady Leetha would come. I thought she'd journey on with us.'

Old Riff laughed.

'In a boat, with males like you, my Lord, and Borkum and Slew? Too confined for her, she couldn't dance . . . *Does* she still dance, my Lord? My Lady Leetha?'

'She always will.'

'A boat would be too confined for your beloved, Lord.'

His face, so dark, so caught up with tides and seas, lightened. He flashed white teeth at a memory.

'I came; she will,' said Sinistral. 'But you can't pin her down to time and place; never could.'

'No, never could,' agreed Borkum Riff, 'but we must, Lord, if we're to catch the tide. That never waits, not even for her.'

Then, 'Time!' he called out again, embracing his Pa at the very last, turning his heel in the gritty wet sand, climbing aboard, checking all was well and the crew well stationed and his passengers safe, before raising his hand to the land-based helpers, which was his family, down to the babe who squealed like a juvenile gull on the wind to see him go.

'Now my lads!' he cried and the craft was pushed out into the waves towards the spit. 'Pull good!' as it reefed and turned and gibed into the wind and waves. 'Pull hard!'

He didn't look back, not then nor later, until that place some call Helledore was not even a light, nor a shadow in the night they left behind.

'Whither bound, my Lord?' he sang out.

'Unto Samhain,' replied Slaeke Sinistral, naming a time not a place.

'Aye, aye, sir, Samhain!' cried Borkum Riff, who understood, and set his craft to its course.

Having got up that night, Old Riff stayed up, knowing he might never again.

He had seen his Lord one last time, now he wanted to see the end of it and greet my Lady.

His wyfkin kept him warm, plied him with brew, pressed close to his thin shanks, wrapped his coat and his scarf tighter, lingering. They wanted to see her too.

'Be gone,' he growled like he used to do when he was younger, but he didn't say it harshly nor enforce his will. They had a right to see as well.

At dawn she came on the White Horse, along the strand, picking their way through shadows and the casts of lug and razor shells, staring at the shine of the rising sun on wet stones.

Oh, she was beautiful, that lady was, so much so it brought tears to his eyes.

'Am I too late?' she said, as the White Horse knelt down by him and she embraced him so tight her wild hair blew right round his old head and tickled his ears.

'Course you are, Leetha, but we'm known that'd be for all of twenty years and more.'

'Was he angry?'

Old Riff shook his head.

'No.'

'Does he love me still?'

'My Lord Sinistral does.'

'Shall I dance?'

'No. But you can say a warm morning to my progeny and Borkum's too, made by my Lord all those years ago.'

'He never forgot.'

'Nor I.'

They came out with the sun, shy but not afraid, and of course Leetha danced for them and made them dance as well.

The tide had gone out, now it came in, and they had seen things they would never forget.

But there was one more thing.

'Where's he gone, that White Horse?' asked Old Riff. 'You wouldn't think that a beast that big would make no sound when it left.'

'Don't need it,' said Leetha. 'I borrowed it from my granddaughter the Shield Maiden.'

'Well, you're not ending your days on this foreign shore, though Mirror knows . . .'

He didn't say more but sat right down, his hand to his chest, sweating, breathing heavily, in pain.

'Borkum's not here to hold your hand,' she said, 'and that's why I've stayed. Don't talk . . .'

'Don't dance, for Mirror's sake . . .' he gasped, 'don't even laugh . . .'

But she did, she did, as they talked the day through and his breathing grew slow.

'What'll you do, Leetha, when I'm gone, which I will be soon.'

'Follow after them across the sea. I'll surprise them.'

'And who of our brood will have courage enough to skipper your craft to Samhain?'

'I think you know.'

'That wasn't . . .'

'You know Old Riff . . .'

'You mustn't . . .'

'But I will . . .'

'Just don't bloody dance . . .'

But she did, and her skipper, who was barely a man but had Riff all over his face and in the strength of his arms, watched in silence as she did and Old Riff died with an old cracked laugh.

'Don't dance . . .'

But she did.

That night, his pyre burning, Leetha said, 'You know who I am?'

He did.

'Have you sailed the North Sea?'

'Sailed, not skippered.'

'With your father?'

He nodded.

'Time for skippering now.'

'Where to, my Lady?'

'Don't call me that . . .'

'What then, my . . .'

'Just be,' she said softly, 'and the right word will come.'

He rigged and ranged his own new craft, made by his own hand. A dozen would have crewed for him but he chose just three.

They launched into a gentler sea, the pyre a glow on shore, and he said as his father had, 'Whither bound?'

'Didn't he tell you?'

He shook his head.

'Take me to Samhain.'

'But that's a time, not a place!'

'Just so,' said Leetha. 'Just so.'

34

LESSONS

The hope that the return of Jack's unit to Brum with their two rescued hostages would be as straightforward and Fyrd-free as their outward journey had been was soon dashed. They made their way back to their starting point, the depot in the industrial estate, undetected, but when they got there it was closed, its gate padlocked, the site under the watchful eye of two security men.

'And dogs,' reported Barklice, after a short reconnaissance. 'They scented me and would have *had* me but . . .'

He waved a rueful hand over trews, boots and hair wiped in engine oil to put them off his scent.

'Needs must,' he murmured. 'Now, the alternatives. If speed's the thing then the quickest way is undercroft a train on the London–Birmingham line which, gentlemen, is no distance at all.'

'General Quatremayne has his forward HQ on that line, in Coventry itself,' warned Blut.

'The alternatives are to go round north or south, the first by rail to Tamworth, also undercroft, of course; or south by green road, which is a long and probably difficult haul if Fyrd are thick on the ground.'

'Which they are,' said Jack.

They debated it more and decided there were too many imponderables for the different risks to be properly assessed.

'I am tempted to suggest,' said Blut who, like Arthur, was recovering fast in the fresh air and with good food supplied by the others, 'that we take the risk and go on the main line. If we can go straight through . . .'

Barklice shook his head.

'Not on this line: all trains stop at Coventry except freight trains in the night. Do you know where Quatremayne's HQ actually is?'

Blut recalled the layout of the maps in the dossier and said, 'I think there are two junctions near each other which join the mainline to Brum . . .'

Barklice nodded. He knew them well.

'His HQ is between them,' said Blut.

'Must be under the bridge after the station,' said Barklice confidently. 'It's a well-known place. Any train we take will definitely stop in Coventry but the chances of it choosing to do so right where the General's sitting having his brew are remote.'

'In case something like that happens,' said Jack, turning to Backhaus, 'we'd better plan now for it.'

They decided that the only ones in their party likely to be recognized were Blut and Arthur. The former hid his spectacles while Arthur hoped that a woolly hat with ear flaps that Recker carried against the cold might serve as a partial disguise and hide his give-away silvery hair.

They were to masquerade as a team of inventory clerks who 'someone' up the line had decided would be needed in the immediate aftermath of the invasion of Brum. The story was that Backhaus and Recker were their minders, tasked with getting them to Brum in the vanguard of the invasion. The routeing had gone wrong and now the imperative was to get them forward as fast as possible.

It was a dull and tedious kind of cover story, likely to be passed quickly over in the dash and rush of the moment, not least because most Fyrd would have little idea of what 'inventory' meant except that it sounded vaguely official and possibly important.

The ruse very soon came in handy.

They took the first chance that came and under-boarded a train heading into Coventry in the hope they could get off it before arriving in the midst of Fyrd activity.

No such luck.

The train pulled into a siding before the city and they glimpsed Fyrd watching closely from the shadows, and stayed right where they were, waiting on Jack's lead. He had planned for this, guessing that it was likely that the Fyrd were actually expecting arrivals with that train. It creaked to a stop, the carriage they were under shifted back and forth and fell still.

While the others stayed put, Jack lowered himself towards the track, pressed against a hot, oily wheel for cover and craned round to look one way along the train and then the other. He spotted another group of hydden, all civilian, disembarking further along the train before trying to scurry off with their 'sacs and crofting boards before they were seen.

The watching Fyrd were ready for them along the verge and challenged them aggressively before herding them out of sight between a pile of rusting axles and wheels and piles of sleepers.

'Backhaus,' he whispered, 'you know what to do.'

He dropped to the ground, emerged in full view of the Fyrd, gave them a quick, uninterested glance and rapped out an order for his group to disembark.

They did so with an air of confusion added to by Recker, who followed officiously behind, hurrying them straight towards the Fyrd.

'And where the Mirror do you think you're going?' barked one of the Fyrd.

Backhaus did not need to pull rank; he simply looked the part and behaved as if the Fyrd were there to serve him.

'Wrongly routed, behind schedule, need to make up time,' he said sharply once he had identified himself. 'These volunteers do not wish to be seen by locals. We need a train going forward.'

'We all need that, sir!' said one of the Fyrd insolently.

Backhaus smiled unpleasantly.

'Name? Rank? *Attachment?*'

This last was said threateningly, as if Backhaus, having learnt which group the hapless Fyrd was with, would go at once and report him to his commanding officer.

The Fyrd muttered a few reluctant and indistinct words by way of answer before giving what information they could about other transports.

'Two goods trains are imminent, sir,' one of them said, whether to curry favour or get rid of them they were not sure.

As another train raced past without stopping and the civilians who had tried to get away grew restive, Backhaus led his group off.

'Look lively!' cried Recker, shoving Barklice onward. 'And you too, you layabout!'

This to Jack, who allowed himself to be harried along. Soon they were by themselves once more.

A short while later the tracks crossed a conduit, through which a stream ran from scrubland adjacent to human houses and then on past the line towards factories. The odour was malign and when they leaned over to look down they saw why. A hydden corpse projected into the water, his head shot through.

Jack dropped down the bank to have a closer look, putting his hand to his mouth and retching at what he saw. The others joined him, Blut alone unable to see clearly, though he too recoiled from the stench of death.

'Blut,' commanded Jack, with no respect for the Emperor's rank, 'put on your spectacles and look. The Fyrd of which you are meant to be Supreme Commander did this.'

Blut pulled on his spectacles and peered into the conduit under the tracks. There were fifteen bodies there, both sexes, all ages. Some had been shot with a crossbow bolt to the back of the head. Many had been garrotted.

They turned on Blut, even Jack, as if he had done the deed himself. Blut looked not at them but at the corpses and without a word went among them, not retreating from sight or smell at all. Rather the opposite.

He moved from one to another, pausing at each, shaking his head with unexpected compassion. Recker wanted to respond angrily too, but Backhaus stopped him. Blut was saying more to them through his silence and what he did than any words could, and they could see he was much moved.

'My Lord Sinistral,' he said suddenly, 'would not have sanctioned this and nor have I. My Lord would . . . would . . .'

A wisp of smoke rose from something at the far end of the conduit, where light came in again.

Backhaus came to his side.

'Here's something even worse . . .'

They stood by the charred body of a Fyrd officer.

'He has been torched alive.'

His whole garb had burnt and melded with his contorted body, his curled outstretched hand seeming like an echo of the silent scream on his open mouth, his eyes half open, grey-white.

'This is the work of Quatremayne's units,' said Backhaus.

'My Lord Sinistral,' said Blut with terrible purpose, 'would have decreed that whoever did this should die like this. So now do I make that decree.'

'There will be more like this,' said Jack.

Blut wheeled round.

'And why do you think I resisted my own Chief of Staff? Why do you think he incarcerated me? What do you imagine I think when I see this? I feel shame, I think punishment. I think as my Lord thinks . . .'

'He is dead,' said Jack, matter-of-factly.

Blut hesitated and then said, 'The Emperor is never dead, Jack. Long live the Emperor.'

Then: 'Come, gentlemen, let us get ourselves to Brum, let us make sure we live to fight this kind of savagery. Let us do what My Lord Sinistral would have done.'

He was not impressive of stature, nor of appearance. Yet just then the glass orbs of his spectacles caught daylight and shone it around that place of death like sun and stars and moon, and with it his spirit shone too, his words as well.

'They will not be forgotten and they will be avenged. That is the simple wyrd of it. We will avenge them. That is our wyrd now.'

Simple words spoken powerfully.

It was extraordinary.

He was the Emperor.

'Don't underestimate Niklas Blut, Jack,' murmured Arthur as they retraced their steps and continued on their way.

'But wasn't the hydden he served so long a tyrant?'

'Sinistral? Was he?' said Arthur ambiguously, as if he knew more than he was able to say just then. 'I am not so sure what that word means any more. One thing is certain. If Quatremayne succeeds in taking Brum and consolidates his power, he most certainly will be a tyrant in the worst sense of the word. The cruelty we have just seen is, I am sure, but a small sample of what he has done already and a signal of what he might do in the future.'

It was two more hours and early in the afternoon before another train arrived and they were able to under-board. But Barklice's nightmare came true and it stopped yards from Coventry's main station. They had reached the area of junctions and the bridge near where Quatremayne had his HQ. To the casual eye it looked deserted and not at all the scene of the busy activity which a military rendezvous is normally subject to. But there were humans doing repairs on the line and a large signal box set in the midst of the tracks and the Fyrd were lying low.

Backhaus had removed insignia from one of the bodies and given himself a more senior rank, though not so senior that he ought to be known to any other officers they met. The main Fyrd activity was in an area of former coal yards on the west side of the tracks and it was here that the trains were stopping before signals ahead. Quatremayne's bridge was down the line and in sight but only just.

Various parties of Fyrd and civilians went back and forth, some near, some far. Jack's party kept themselves to one side, sitting in a neat and orderly way with an air of expectation, as if they thought something was going to happen soon that would mean they would move on.

A couple of Fyrd nodded in their direction, and an officer ambled over to pass the time of day, but Backhaus and Recker gave them all short shrift, looking impatient, as if others had let them down. Once only did they catch sight of anyone who seemed important and that was further down the track, on the same side, when a tall well-uniformed officer surrounded by aides briefly showed himself.

'Quatremayne?' asked Jack urgently.

Arthur wasn't sure.

Blut momentarily pulled on his spectacles, had a look, and put them away again.

'Not Quatremayne,' he said.

The officers moved away.

'We're running out of time,' said Barklice, 'but there's not much we can do except wait and hope.'

What they were doing was waiting for a train that looked bound for Brum whose stop position, combined with an absence of anyone nearby, might offer them a chance of going undercroft. They had found a cache of crofting boards and had placed them nearby. Two trains arrived that might have been suitable and they saw no one entrain or disembark. Both were examined underneath by a Fyrd whose job, it seemed, was to check for anything untoward, but he did his work cursorily as if he thought it impossible that anyone would try so foolish a thing.

But for Jack, it was getting Arthur under the train quickly that presented the greater problem, for that was the moment they were most likely to be stopped and checked.

'When we go, we go fast,' he said, 'so I'll pair up with Arthur myself and make sure he does what he has to . . . As for you, Blut . . .'

'As for me,' said Blut, 'I am fitter and more agile than you might think. It will help if, just for the time of boarding, I put my spectacles on, otherwise things will be blurry and difficult in the shadows beneath.'

A suitable train rolled in slowly an hour later. It was old rolling stock, a powerful diesel pulling a combination of freight trucks and empty passenger compartments.

'Perfect,' pronounced Barklice as it eased to a creaking stop. 'When we board follow me. We'll take the filthiest, the one Fyrd won't want to travel under.'

The nearest Fyrd glanced at it, the one doing the checking came forward briefly onto the track and then was either distracted or grew bored and retreated once more, and the engine began rumbling again.

They broke cover in pairs, Barklice with Blut at the rear, Jack and Arthur next, and Backhaus and Recker last, ambling to the train side at their ease, with the intention of keeping others away if need be.

The Fyrd emerged again and stared in their direction.

Backhaus gave no more than an unfriendly nod and slight movement of the hand which said no more than *you're doing your job, I'm doing mine* . . .

The train began to move and he and Recker ducked between the wheels, positioned their boards as it began accelerating and pulled themselves aboard.

But the acceleration was misleading, suggesting as it did that the train was going to run right on through the complex of points in Coventry and out the other side on a clear and direct run Brumwards.

Not so.

It began to slow; it finally stopped. Jack dropped down to check where they were and saw a red signal changing back to green and hopped aboard again.

Whatever the cause, it was the beginning of a start–stop progress through miles of sidings and detours, some of the stops so sudden that they were sometimes nearly thrown off their perches.

Yet every time they were able to disembark briefly and check progress, they were further down line and nearer to getting clear of the Coventry conurbation. Better still, they ran into no more Fyrd at all.

But time ticked on, they were tired and aching, a late afternoon gloom was setting in.

'If there was an obvious better alternative,' said Barklice at one stop where they were able to gather briefly to stretch and drink some water, 'I would suggest it. Sometimes all we can do is stick with what we have and hope . . .'

The train began creaking and they were up and off once more, this time accelerating to a decent speed, the changing points and jolts diminishing as the train returned to better lines.

Then the familiar screech of brakes, the jolting and the now-too-familiar halt.

But this time something new and ominous.

The light was bad, the stench of diesel thick, the sound of voices near.

Jack lowered himself cautiously and looked about.

They were in a deep cutting, its walls made of brick stained black and inset with support arches. Some of them extended back into tunnels. The train juddered forward and then back then forward again. Jack saw lights in the tunnels, figures moving, activity – Fyrd.

Fyrd crunched along the line towards them, Jack heaved himself back up, heart beating.

The Fyrd on the track reached the point where Blut lay in the undercarriage, pausing while others hurried to catch them up.

Someone said, 'Not that one, looks too damn dirty, try this one!'
Thank the Mirror for Barklice, thought Jack.

The Fyrd grouped and then continued on down line and they heard
the clatter of boards as they too took their positions undercroft.

Silence but for the hum of the train.

A group of Fyrd emerged from through the arch where the activity
was.

A voice, commanding.

Others, laughing in obsequious union.

'*That's* Quatremayne,' Blut murmured.

Jack risked lowering himself a mite to catch a glimpse and reposition
his stave lest it was needed. At the very least, if a fight ensued he could
attack and perhaps kill the one who mattered most.

Blut had described the General earlier and his depiction had been
good.

The Chief of Staff was tall, silver-haired, commanding, and a flash
of light in his face from a lantern showed cold eyes, a thin mouth and
austere cheeks.

'Keep that light out of my eyes, fool!' he said, striking someone to
his side.

Jack, who had closed his eyes as the beam travelled round, still had
his night vision.

Quatremayne had briefly lost his and stared in Jack's direction but
did not see him.

It was enough.

Jack felt he had finally engaged the enemy.

The train eased forward, someone ran out with a leather messenger
pouch.

'Where are they? Which carriage?' he said.

Maybe someone gave him the wrong direction, maybe an unclear
one, but he ran forward between the now slowly turning wheels to give
the pouch to one of the Fyrd under the train and found himself staring
straight into the eyes of Blut, his spectacles still on.

Barklice, too far to reach, said, 'Here!'

The confused Fyrd turned, moving along the track with the train,
uncertain what to do with the pouch. Jack, further along, saw it, but
the train was gathering speed and he could only issue a command.

'Hold him. Hold him fast!'

'Here!' shouted Barklice again.

'I . . .' began the bewildered Fyrd as he tried the dangerous business of keeping up with a moving train. 'You . . .'

If they had doubted Blut's resolution or fitness they did not doubt it more.

He grabbed the Fyrd from behind, turned and tumbled him backwards and . . . held on.

The Fyrd slipped between the wheels and under the train, tried to free himself but his legs were pulled from under him.

'Help!'

'Let him go,' shouted Jack.

Blut did so.

The Fyrd dropped to the track, bounced and was caught by the train and rolled along before it carried on and he bounced away behind them, screaming.

A thud, silence, and the body, or bits of it, bounced horribly away in the dark, under the next carriage.

Then another scream, as the body hit one of the Fyrd undercroft who, dislodged, reached up for the helping hand of another and dislodged him too.

A melee of bodies turning, twisting, shouting, clinging hopelessly on under the moving train, wheels running over arms and legs, bodies fragmented; three Fyrd gone.

The train stopped once more, this time in near-darkness.

Jack's group knew to stay silent.

The remaining Fyrd dropped down to the track, in shock at what had happened. Jack followed in the darkness, not ready to risk his group being discovered then or later, and Backhaus followed him.

There were four other Fyrd there, sitting ducks to Jack's stave one way and Backhaus's another. *Thud, thud, thud* . . .

A grunt from Jack as he made the final hit.

'Bastards,' said Recker pulling them unconscious under the train and laying them on the line.

The train moved forward and the wheels destroyed the Fyrd.

It was ugly, horrible.

But it was war and the lessons they were learning were bitter ones.

35

ENTWINED

Bedwyn Stort returned to the problem of the Embroidery the moment Jack set off on his rescue mission.

He had begun to feel that the inanimate and strangely elusive artefact was a being in its own right, as alive as himself or Cluckett, and that it wanted to tell him how to find the gem of Autumn but didn't know how.

He paced about his laboratory, muttering and glowering at the Embroidery, holding it up, putting it down, squinting and peering at it and even creeping up on it in the dark and turning on a flashlight as if hoping thereby to catch it out and make it reveal its secret.

None of it worked.

He felt himself sliding towards desperation. Samhain was but three weeks away, when he had to deliver up to the Shield Maiden the gem he felt he was as yet nowhere near finding. Failure would bring disaster.

All that was certain about the Embroidery was its uncertainty: its imagery of location and character never stayed the same.

'No good, no good . . . I am on the wrong tack . . .'

Cluckett attempted again and again to bring him food and drink.

'Go away, Goodwife Cluckett! I want no food. Leave me undisturbed.'

'It is,' she observed from the sanctuary of her kitchen, pursing her lips with Katherine on one side of her table and Ma'Shuqa on the other, 'as if he is going mad before my very eyes! He paces up and down, he does not eat the food I make, nor sleep in his bed, nor even any more look at his books! He vexes me, he really does and I am tired of it *and* there is a family visit I must undertake; not one I wish to, mind you. But I feel I cannot go because who knows what will happen to Mister Stort if left alone and unattended?'

Stort felt as if he was trying to grapple with a reflection of himself seen from the corner of his eye in an angled mirror which, when he turned to try to see it full on, slid away out of sight.

The gem of Spring he had found where it might have been expected to be, upon Waseley Hill.

That of Summer had been in Slaeke Sinistral's possession in Bochum and it was simply a matter of travelling there and finding a way, and the courage, to grasp it.

But from the first, the gem of Autumn had been more elusive, requiring him to find not so much the place it was but, rather, the place he needed to be within himself if he was to understand what he must do to win it.

It seemed to Stort that the difficulty of his challenge had been made infinitely harder by his discovery at the end of July, when he delivered up Beornamund's gold pendant and the first two gems to Judith the Shield Maiden, that he loved her and she him.

It was a yearning that could never be satisfied and it created a cloud of confusion that addled his brain and confused his spirit as he tried to grasp this ungraspable thing which was the search for a gem whose nature he could not understand.

Meanwhile, he did not doubt for a single moment that ã Faroüin's marvellous yet disturbing Embroidery contained all he needed to find the gem, if only he could . . . could . . . what? That was the thing! *What* was he meant to do?

Well, there was one thing another could do.

He rushed back to the kitchen.

'Cluckett,' he cried, 'I need perfect peace for a few days and you have talked of responsibilities too long unattended. Do not take offence if I suggest you go and attend to them forthwith, today, perhaps within the hour. I need to be alone! I am losing sleep, my sense of time, all sense of place and, to be frank, all sense of purpose because you persist in hanging about, getting in the . . .'

'Mister Stort,' rejoined Cluckett, furious yet compassionate, 'you are finally impossible! But I will pack my bag and leave.'

Half an hour later she was packed and ready to go.

'Mister Stort,' she said, 'it would not be my choice to leave you in these critical days. But I can see that the dusty old tablecloth thing from the Library and now in your laboratory is having a delicious effect on you.'

'Deleterious,' murmured Stort, who still made the occasional effort to correct Cluckett's misappropriation of words.

'Be that as it may, I would prefer to stay. But since you insist I should leave for a little while, and I have an ill relative, duty calls and needs must.'

'Be off, Madam! It will not matter to me if you linger in your return.'

'I take no offence, Mister Stort!' she cried and was off and away down the street long before he had closed and bolted his door upon the world.

With Jack and Cluckett now absent, and Katherine and Terce away helping Laud and his sister, Stort was able to focus his mind upon the Embroidery to the exclusion of all else. He abandoned all rules of domestic order from the hour of the goodwife's departure. Dishes began piling up in the sink, a burnt bean stew was left smoking on the hob, clothes were left where he had taken them off, his bed was unmade, the floor was unswept and such books as he looked at were opened willy-nilly and then left wherever his need and interest in them flagged.

Some people lead simple, uncomplicated lives, moving along as shadows do, leaving no visible trace behind. Others cause disturbance. Some create a chronic mess which grows exponentially with each hour that passes.

Stort was one such and within two days the neat and tidy humble Cluckett left was a chaotic tip. But Bedwyn Stort did not care; it was only his work that mattered now.

He broke down the Problem of the Embroidery, as he conceived it, into two parts.

First, what was the true subject of its beautiful imagery?

Second, why and how did it keep altering in small ways to create a sense of more significant changes in the world at large?

Cluckett herself had once made the point that the perspectives in the Embroidery were fickle and inconsistent. To her this was 'wrong'. To him, he now saw, it was a clue to something that might be right.

He soon decided the Embroidery might be easier to see if he hung it vertically, like a wall hanging, rather than draping it horizontally, like a tablecloth. The easiest place to do this was on the wall of his main corridor, where it turned at right angles after the kitchen, towards his laboratory. He tacked it to the wall and was able to see all but a small portion of the right-hand side if he stood with his back to his front door, his parlour on the right.

Alternatively, if he retreated into the scullery, which was through his kitchen, he could see all but a sliver of the left-hand side of the Embroidery. Imperfect though they were, these two vantage points enabled him to see the brilliance of the Embroidery's overall design more clearly and how it echoed the remarkable panels in the famous Chamber of Seasons in Lord Festoon's residence. Which was created first he had no idea, but each had the same dynamic quality of changeableness.

The Embroidery was divided into four vertical parts, each depicting one of the seasons, starting with Spring, ending in Winter. The base fabric was damask and the Embroidery appeared to be a combination of silks, fine wools, and appliquéd materials of cotton, silk and other fabrics.

The colours were at once vivid and subtle and he now confirmed that they did change with the light, the angle at which they were viewed and – and this was the first of many discoveries Stort began to make as this strange journey began – with his mood.

The basic story of each section was the same.

At the top were mountains and tumbling rivers, at the bottom were the shore and estuaries; in the middle verdant valleys, meandering water courses, woods, vales and vistas above to the uplands and below to the lowlands.

There was no doubt, he now also confirmed, that these vistas changed from one moment to the next. It was just that he could never quite catch them doing it.

Each section was dominated by the appropriate colours of its season, exemplified by trees in leaf or not, flowers in bloom or not and all the other variations in the annual life of flora. But broadly, as might be expected, the first section, Spring, was green; the next, Summer, was yellow; the third, Autumn, was rust-brown; the last, Winter, began with shades of grey and, towards the end, harsh black and white.

These different seasonal landscapes were peopled by mortals, though it was unclear whether they were hydden or human. Their garb was generally medieval and the same characters appeared in each seasonal scenario, a fact not immediately obvious until Stort understood that with each passing season the characters aged more than the three months of each season. They were not ideal figures in a landscape, but ordinary flesh and blood on the path of normal life.

He saw again what he had seen before, that these characters were similar to, yet not the same as, people he knew well.

There were two characters in the Spring section, a boy and girl aged about six who by the Summer section were about eighteen or nineteen. Stort liked to think of these as Jack and Katherine, for that was the kind of period over which he had known them, one way and another.

These two did not age much more in their subsequent depictions, though the Embroidery was vague and indistinct where these two were concerned through Autumn and Winter, as if they were a work in progress.

Then there was a 'Master Brief' – a character very like him and certainly a scrivener, who was already grey-bearded when he appeared in Spring, and a mite older in Summer; he disappeared altogether in Autumn, just as he had died in the Summer at the hands of Witold Slew.

But if all this was coincidence, the treatment of another character confirmed that the Embroidery, though seemingly old, had the power to reveal recent history and perhaps the immediate future – and therefore, as he hoped, offer clues to the present whereabouts of the gem of Autumn and perhaps Winter too.

This was a large corpulent figure who appeared in Spring with a diminutive sidekick serving him food: surely Festoon and his one-time chef, Parlance. By the end of Summer, Festoon had lost weight and Parlance had gone, just as happened in real life.

These and other revelations came to Stort through the nights and days following Cluckett's departure. He visited and revisited the Embroidery, looking at it from all angles, making connections, yet only slowly coming to those that might affect him most. These were whether he himself was depicted and if so, how; and how Judith the Shield Maiden was treated.

It was as these more personal inquiries began to occupy him, first deep in the night, later at the end of an uneasy day, that Stort began to experience what he thought must be hallucinations. The figures in the Embroidery appeared to move, even to talk quietly among themselves. The seasons of Autumn and Winter went out of focus however much he stared at the images, drank a wakening chicory brew or slapped his face.

Someone knocked at his door – but was that just now or yesterday? Was it perhaps tomorrow? Whenever it was, he ignored it.

As a new night came, Stort lay on the floor of his corridor in a state of restive unease, feeling that his humble was stretching away from him in all directions, unsure if the darkness was dark, or the new dawn was light. Seeing both reflected in the Embroidery, trying to reach towards the bright, cheerful elongated figure he saw in the middle ground of Spring, whose hair was ginger and whose 'sac was overfull, he found himself whispering, 'Are *you* me? If so, why are you there and not here? Why cannot I remember where I am or bear to look at where I might go?'

Day came, time passed, nothing seemed to change, though moments were hours.

Then, aching, he rolled sideways and upright, his back and head squashed against the jamb of the kitchen door, and saw himself again in the Summer just passed, not so happy as before, aged a little, his hair wilder, holding a little girl's hand.

'Myself? Judith? The Shield Maiden?'

No sooner had he said those words than she grew older, older than him, and smaller, as if seen at a distance, and unhappy, unhappier than him.

'Judith?' he murmured again with feeling, reaching the few short feet towards the Embroidery before getting up and going right up to it, only to find that she had receded still further and his hand touched the material as he tried to reach across the ever-widening gap between them.

'*Judith!*' he cried, tottering into the kitchen, eating what food came to hand, scattering dishes, not knowing what the day was or which part of night he might be in, forgetting the layout of his humble because it too was moving, shifting, changing. It too was an Embroidery, or part of the one that had hung on the wall, wherever that now was.

When he woke he did so with a conviction that he had found a way of fixing in place the moving images and notions that were the Embroidery.

Perspective: that was the thing. It shifted all the time so he would fix it there and then.

'Twine!' he cried. 'A cold chisel and a hammer and some nails! Now! It's just a matter of lines.'

Stort went into a frenzy of activity, banging meat skewers and nails through the Embroidery into the wall behind to mark certain parts of it so they did not move again. Then he attached twine to the skewers and pulled it taut this way and that, extending certain sightlines right to where he stood.

But the twine needed fixing at its other end.

So he knocked holes through the laboratory wall and stretched twine from some place inside it back through the hole and right through the Embroidery and thence on into the kitchen.

Not once, or from one place, but many times, from many different points until his rooms and corridors were a cat's cradle of twine lines, some of which turned corners on fixings he made, returning through different walls and then back to the Embroidery through which, with due care, and using a crocheting needle of Cluckett's, he threaded them onwards, through a different part of the wall to a new fixing.

Until every corridor, every room, up to the ceilings, down to the floor, through each wall and hundreds of times, out of cupboards, under the beds, up and round and between and over and then across to the far, far corner of the room and up and down again, straight as an arrow, the twine lines came and went; and still he made more. Stooping, crawling, and reaching with twine in hand to make real and fixed the shifting beauties of the Embroidery of ã Faroün.

It was madness, yet throughout it he ate, he slept, he washed, he moved furniture, he emptied drawers, he piled clothes, he even had a bath and sang.

'Oh yes!' he cried, drying himself and dancing about in his naked state, the sharp corners of the Chime round his neck, which Judith gave him, drawing blood on his white chest as he created more twine lines before he got too cold to make more and dressed. 'Oh *yeeees!*'

He glimpsed a future which made sense of the images in the Embroidery.

A great beach with thundering surf, a fort and a fight to the death, a mound ten times as high as a hydden, the sun rising over a nearby hill, its rays like fire and the White Horse coming.

A song he heard, exquisite, filled with the harmonies of planets and stars, part of which he had heard before, all of which was yet to be.

An angry Earth and a sight no mortal should ever see: a whirl of death, a horror too far.

Stort saw so much, and glimpsed far more, swirling about him in the form of shards of light and time, moments transfixed to shards that moved.

The end of it came quite suddenly when he believed he had made sense of things and he stopped, panting, slumping to the floor, the huge effort to master the Embroidery and understand it suddenly over. He had found some of what he needed and saw at least the direction to take to find the gem. But he had not found all.

It felt as if the lines came through the back of his head and out of his mouth and eyes, straight into the image on the corridor wall.

He stared and saw a figure come unfixed from where he had trapped it down to lines and perspective and, standing on the ocean shore towards the end of Autumn, it turned and looked at him.

The figure was tall, red-headed, and portered a 'sac too large and too untidy for any sensible pilgrim to be carrying if he was to get to the truth of things.

The figure stood still, seeming to think, seeming to understand.

'You are me,' said the figure with words that journeyed along the twine from a mouth that spoke into Stort's mind.

'And I am you.'

He straightened up, turned and looked at the sea, then back at the mountains, all over the world he had travelled and, standing still at last, listening to the world about, he looked out down the corridor from the Embroidery and Stort looked back at him and saw himself.

In seeing that, he saw the Shield Maiden too, up on her Horse, across the sky, reflected in the wet sand, mists in the mountains and foam in the sea, nothing permanent as she raged at the passage of time, her grey hair, her aching body, the lines and the sags and the beginning of age and her loss of him.

'Where are you, Stort?' he heard her scream.

'Here,' he replied, 'just here.'

Only then, reaching into the three dimensions of the Embroidery he had created, whose skeleton was twine which to him was clothed with all the sights and sounds of the seasons and the people therein, of whom he was one, did he see where the gem of Autumn might be.

'Autumn we might find for you, my love,' he murmured, 'but Winter is surely beyond us all.'

October winds ruffled his hair and juddered the twine lines in Stort's humble. The winds were cold and very strong, catching at his tired body, pushing and pulling and dragging it into the future that he saw, from which he knew he could not return without help.

'Help me home,' he called out, 'because I'm tangled up in the future and cannot find my way back, help me now . . .'

Someone knocked at his door again but now he was too weak to answer.

Help, he silently cried as they knocked again and went away not knowing that Bedwyn Stort was lying just inside, betwixt his parlour and kitchen, his humble in chaos and a tangle of twine reaching through and round and back and into the Embroidery, a tangle of silk and wool, a tangle of colours and different versions of the same people tangled through time, in the midst of which he, unable to move, felt the twine tighten round his neck so he could no longer breathe, causing him to begin to die.

36
COMING HOME

I t was Katherine who had knocked on Stort's door, on her way back with Terce from taking Meister Laud to his sister's cottage. He had rallied with his sister's arrival but they all sensed it would not be for long. He wanted to see his sister's humble, which was near where they had been raised, and to die in a place he remembered with affection.

His farewell to Terce was a touching one and they knew it would be the last. It was the Meister's wish they should part. Terce feared he had not learnt enough, with which, until then, his Meister had always agreed. But when his sister came and he saw his days were drawing in he wisely said, 'I can teach no more, nor sing any more. When Winter comes, you'll remember the music and the words. But you may be needed before that too.'

'But you never taught them to me!'

'Those last words, that *musica*, you learn for yourself. You reap what others sow, as others will harvest something of your life and take it to themselves.'

'But . . .'

'Now go with Katherine, lead your life as I have taught you, the *musica* is now almost yours, Terce.'

Such was their simple farewell and he, like Katherine, said little on the way back. But he relaxed as the journey through the Autumn landscape took them on, breathing deeper, letting go at last the responsibility for Laud and the others he had always felt. *He* now was the Quinterne, he himself.

'Travel on with us for a time,' Katherine said, 'for the one thing that's certain for us all is that we're going to have to journey on soon to find the gem, before Samhain and after that into the dark dark days of Winter, before light comes again. Your presence will be welcome and much needed.'

When her knocking on Stort's door got no reply, she and Terce hurried on into the centre of Brum, where they soon learnt Stort had not been seen for days and was nowhere to be found.

When Bratfire, Barklice's son, appeared to tell her Jack had returned in safety with Arthur Foale her joy was overlain with this new concern for Stort. She sent Bratfire to summon Jack to Stort's humble as she and Terce set off back there themselves.

'Something's wrong,' she said. 'I should have knocked harder, waited longer or beaten the door down!'

In his dying moments as the twine strangled him Bedwyn Stort found himself in the peculiar position of being in two places at once.

In the first he was on the floor of his humble, his head near the front door, his feet reaching towards his parlour, his mind now in a state of deepening unconsciousness as his body let go of his spirit. His eyes were half closed so that just the whites showed, very horribly. His face was a dreadful blue-grey, his freckles now mauve, his breathing difficult and his arms and legs were angled and bent in all directions, as if he was falling through space and time uncontrollably and at speed.

In the second place in which he simultaneously existed, his mind was clear as crystal but quite free of those many doubts and questionings with which his essentially enquiring nature (he now saw) had plagued his mortal life, moment by moment. Latterly on the subject of the gem of Autumn.

Rather, he found himself floating very pleasantly in a bright, white light some feet above his prone other self; a comfortable, ruminative, warm kind of place above which, through the ceiling, the roof space and beyond that, the Earth's atmosphere and then the whole Universe itself, was a tempting destination where all questions would be answered, not because they had answers so much as there was no need for the questions in the first place.

Floating thus in his own humble he looked down upon himself in full knowledge that he was near death, without regret, but with enormous compassion.

So much so that he wanted to reach down and touch his own cheek in a loving kind of way and say, 'It's all right, Bedwyn, old fellow . . . really, it's all right . . .'

Yet he did not do so.

Why?

Because he knew that way down there on the floor, inside his body – not his head, or heart, but in his very being – it was *not* quite all right. There was something he had not finished.

Something he now saw in all its terrible clarity that he had not done.

Something that whatever else he had achieved would remain a kind of niggle, a little weenie worm of doubt, as he journeyed on into the hereafter where all things were meant to be resolved, all doubts assuaged, all things settled for all time.

That thing still undone was – and now the deep pool of his white-light calm *was* finally disturbed by uncomfortable ripples – something his good friends had done without seeming difficulty, as if it was the most natural thing in the mortal world.

His beloved mentor, the late Master Brief, had done it.

Their much-respected mutual friend Mister Pike had done it.

His great friend and travel companion Barklice had done it, though it took him some years to realize that he had.

And, of course, Jack and Katherine had done it, and done it well.

Even Lord Festoon, once one of the most self-centred of hydden, as it had seemed, had done it and done it better than well – why, he had shown his mastery of it by his treatment of the citizens of Brum as he had in all his dealings with those who knew him personally, not least his chef Parlance.

Why! the floating Stort upbraided himself, *Parlance has done it and no one could be more narcissistic than he!*

What had they done that he had not?

'They have known how to love truly and deeply,' Stort uttered into the ethereal light around him, 'and I never did! How then can I leave my mortal self until I have learnt that? How can I let myself die if I have never let myself truly live?'

Irritation had moved to self-anger; that had now moved on to existential discomfort, as if he might soon be in what some called heaven but with a painful splinter in his thumb.

The breathing of his other self grew weaker, more shallow, as the ethereal Stort told himself that it was not so much that he had not loved but more that he had not known how to do it well. 'Therefore I must stay alive until I've done it better!' His weak, wretched fingers tried to free himself a final time.

As he strove to do so it seemed to him that a figure appeared out of the Embroidery and advanced upon him.

'Judith!?' the two Storts said simultaneously.

She shook her old, worn head, smiling slightly, coming to him where he lay.

'No, my dear, but you know who I am,' she said as the door behind them both reverberated with renewed knocking.

You are the Modor, the Wise Woman, said Stort triumphantly in the silence of his dying mortal mind.

She reached her withered hand to the tight tangle about his neck and said, 'The knot is not as cunning as it seems but I cannot help you, you must help yourself or your friends must. Still, I can put your hand where it should be.'

She took his flaccid hand and curled its fingers round the impossible knot.

'Judith?' he said again, for she touched him with the same love he imagined she would, were she ever to touch him.

'No, my dear, not yet. I am the Modor and I cannot let you go, there is so much for you to do . . . Hold on, your friends are nearly here, they are knocking at your door.'

'My love?' he whispered, still confused.

'I am not her, Bedwyn Stort, but you summoned me because I too am in the Embroidery and I have come. Now your hand is in place and I must leave . . .'

The knocking on the door grew louder.

'Undo the cunning knot and you will breathe again,' she said, retreating into the Embroidery.

As she did so the door fell down on top of him, smashed into his face, forcing it sideways and a melee of feet thundered over it, accompanied by voices, all of which he knew very well indeed.

'Stort!' cried Jack, 'Stort!'

'What the . . .' shouted Pike, floundering into tangles of string and falling forward onto Jack, who himself began falling.

'Jack, I think he's . . .' exclaimed Katherine, 'he's . . .'

But she was knocked over by Barklice and then Bratfire, all tumbling in across the broken threshold and the fallen door.

Death, which had stalked so close not much earlier, now returned in more palpable form to Bedwyn Stort, whose thin and weakened frame found itself spreadeagled beneath his own front door.

'Help!' he cried.

'Where are you, Stort?' cried Jack, upright once more.

'Dammit,' cried Stort in a crushed and muffled way, thinking it was as well his door was solid enough to spread their combined weight so evenly or else he would have been pulverized in parts, 'I'm *here*!'

'Where is he?' asked Katherine. 'I can hear him.'

'Underneath!' he called out weakly.

'He's here somewhere,' said Barklice.

'Look!' gasped Stort, doing the one thing that might attract their attention.

It was Bratfire, who was still standing on the door, who worked it out.

'There, Dad!' he said, pointing. 'Those feet are wiggling!'

Which indeed Stort's were, poking out from under the door and moving back and forth in mute semaphore to signal his distress.

'He's under the door!' cried Jack. 'Careful! Don't stand on it! Bratfire, what are you *doing*!'

Bratfire backed out of the house, a staverman who had had the sense to stay outside picked up one end of the door, Jack picked up the other and eased his end past Stort's gasping form as they took the door out of harm's way into the street outside.

'It's all right,' whispered the Modor gently, as she too moved past him, caressing his cheek, nearly unseen by the others, the twine falling from her in the light of day and the street outside.

Stort reached after her, not wanting her to go, if she had been there at all, which he was not quite sure, as Katherine knelt by him on one side and Jack squeezed down on the other.

'Are you all right?'

No I am not. I'm choking to death.

'He's choking,' said Jack, trying to pull Stort's hand away and undo the tangle of twine that was tight around his neck.

Neither hand nor twine budged.

'He's nearly strangled himself with string.'

'If we hadn't got here when we did . . .'

Do something!

'Wait, he's trying to speak.'

Blessed silence fell as Stort tried in vain to hold on to the Modor's visit and what went before, as to a dream which on waking flies away to the corners of mind and memory.

'She . . .' he said.

'Who?'

'The Modor, I think . . .'

'There *was* someone, did anybody see that person? Where . . . ?'

'She was the Modor. She . . . she . . . said . . . *musica*.'

It was his last gasp and the hand that Jack had tried to wrest free now began to loosen its desperate hold as Stort began to give up.

'*Musica*.'

It was Katherine who understood and she raised a hand slowly and with such authority that all fell utterly silent.

'Terce? Where's Terce?'

He came near and knelt down.

She took his hand and placed it on Stort's.

'He needs help. He needs to hear the *musica*. He needs it now if he is to come back to us.'

Terce looked afraid and shook his head.

'I cannot; no one can. I have not learnt everything, I cannot.'

'You can because Meister Laud taught you to. The last thing needed he could not teach. Have confidence in the gift you have . . .'

'But Meister Laud . . .'

'Is dead,' she said, the twine about her thrumming on her legs, showing what truly was, letting her hear a little of what Stort knew.

'Now you sing for his memory, sing down the centuries of the song you learnt, sing from the beginning of time.'

She took his other hand and placed it on Stort's chest, which fluttered with no more strength than a dying moth.

'Sing! That is what he taught you, for now, for later, for the *musica*.'

And then Terce could.

His voice trembling at first, the sound of the beginning of all things; then stronger, the sound of life born; then soaring, as life takes wing and is stronger still, a sound ethereal. It filled Stort's humble, it stilled their restless minds, it brought bright light to all their shadows and was so beautiful it seemed their eyes closed before it and they sailed into the sky.

Stort's fingers moved, they bent, they clutched the twine, they tried to pull and then they caressed it and it slipped away, insubstantial, a ligature no more.

Still Terce sang and still they heard but did not look, lost in the beauty of his song.

Katherine opened her eyes and saw that as the twine fell away Stort's chest heaved. Air rushed into his mouth, his lungs, and his body came back to life.

He reached for her, confused, thinking Katherine was Judith, or maybe the Modor.

But the Modor was gone, already gone, except for her touch and her words and what he had seen before she came. They lingered still.

Terce's voice faded and Stort spoke.

'I . . . I know . . . I have discovered . . .' he said feebly.

'What's this string *for*?' said Jack.

Stort tried to sit up, normal colour returning to his face.

'It's twine not string,' he said matter-of-factly. 'All in the nature of research and discovery.'

'Which nearly killed you,' said Katherine.

It was as if none of them wanted to acknowledge what they had heard. Or perhaps it was too much for mortal hearts to long remember and be at peace thereafter.

Even Stort, whose life Terce's singing had surely saved, seemed concerned with simpler things.

'I have found . . . or discovered . . . or worked out . . .'

'What?' said Katherine softly, shushing the others, including Jack, pushing them back. 'What have you discovered?'

'I know where the gem of Autumn is,' he said, finally able to sit up unaided, 'Yes, and I know . . . or I think I know . . .'

A look of alarm came to his face as Katherine pulled the rest of the twine off him and set him finally free.

'I am sure . . .'

The memory of what he had discovered was fading too and he did not want it to.

'I know where the gem is but . . . but . . .'

'Where?' said Jack urgently. '*Where* is it?'

'Well, I know more or less.'

'Yes?' demanded Katherine, unaccountably fierce.

'If you know, tell us!' cried Barklice, annoyed.

'I . . . it . . . er . . . um . . . I can't remember *exactly*,' said Stort. 'It's kind of slipped away, as a dream does. But that's all right.'

'All right?' said Jack frowning. 'It is definitely not all right.'

'But, you see, she came . . .' Stort tried to explain, 'she came and I saw and understood. I know how to find it now.'

'How?' they asked.

'I'm tired,' replied Stort. 'She came and touched me and I . . . am most definitely in need of sleep. I'm sure it was her!'

'Don't talk any more,' said Katherine finally, heaving him to his feet with the help of Jack and guiding him towards his bedroom.

'In fact, do you know what she helped me understand?'

'Try to calm down, Stort . . .'

'She let me see that even I can love with my whole heart!'

It was as joyous a moment of discovery for Stort as any in all his life.

'Yes, but what about the gem?' said Jack, ever practical. '*Did* you discover where it is?'

Stort looked at him very seriously, shook his head and sighed.

'You're missing the point,' he replied. 'She showed me how to get there, not where it is. It's the "how" that's important.'

'You saw Judith?'

'Maybe,' said Stort happily, 'and maybe not. I thought it was her. But at least now I know . . . I know . . .'

He was falling asleep.

They tucked him in.

Katherine bent down and kissed him.

'Judith? Modor?' whispered Stort.

'And me,' said Katherine softly, 'all three.'

'I know how to love,' he said.

37
PANIC ATTACK

Jack finally returned to Brum with Blut and Arthur nearly a week after they had left. They entered Brum even more discreetly than they first left it. They knew that there were real dangers in revealing that they had the new Emperor of the Hyddenworld with them and decided to lie low in Deritend for a few days.

It was as well that Blut did not look the part, or adopt regal graces, because that would have attracted attention in the Muggy Duck, their first 'official' port of call. They knew that the moment they showed their faces, word of their arrival would get out. They introduced Blut as someone who had been a fellow prisoner with Arthur, which was true. More they did not say.

If Ma'Shuqa guessed something she kept quiet about it. Jack noticed she treated Blut with great respect and gave him a better room, along with Arthur, than he himself normally had, with 'some extra vittels thrown in for the gentleman in case he gets peckish in the night'.

In the short time he had known him, Jack, like Arthur, had become rapidly impressed by Niklas Blut. He liked his seriousness, his occasional flashes of self-deprecating humour, his obvious compassion for those hurt by the Fyrd and the rapid, dispassionate but effective way he dealt with any issue that arose.

There was also no doubt that he had courage and a strong nerve. Brunte and Feld liked to talk of military assets. In Jack's view, Blut was an 'asset' beyond value. He delayed alerting Festoon that the mission had been successful until he was sure he could keep Blut safe. Certainly he intended to say nothing via missive or messenger except to say they were back in Brum.

When it came, the response surprised and disappointed him. It came in the form of a hastily scrivened note which said no more than that Festoon was pleased at the result and 'maybe' in a day or two there might be time to see Jack and Arthur.

'There's a real panic on at the High Ealdor's Residence about the Fyrd coming,' the messenger explained, 'and you won't get much more from that quarter for a while, if ever until the invasion is over. Then it'll be too late! Me? I may get out of Brum sooner than later. The place is falling apart and folk are ignoring the procedures laid down for orderly departure.'

Blut heard this too and was appalled.

The likely truth of it was supported by the dour mood in the Muggy Duck. Numbers were down, the talk was edgy and folks' nerves were shot to pieces.

'Ere, we haven't seen you in these parts before. Where are you from?'

It came out of the blue, a challenge to Blut as he sat harmlessly supping ale.

'I am just . . .'

'And yer accent, and yer business?'

Another burly client rose, and more surrounded Blut threateningly.

'Get up and face us yer little . . .'

'He's with me,' growled Jack, looming near.

'And *me*,' said Backhaus.

They backed off but it was a sign of things awry. It would not have happened in the Duck even weeks before.

Blut's response later was a surprise.

'Before I meet Festoon and your other leaders I would like to walk a little through Brum, to get a tenor of the people here and see if that incident is typical. It bodes ill, very ill, for a city on the brink of attack. You don't defeat the Fyrd by turning on each other.'

'You won't find out much by walking about anonymously,' said Jack.

A glint came to Blut's eye.

'Anonymity is just the point,' he replied. 'Anyway, I need to do it. The needs of the city of Brum and the citizens of the Empire, whatever and whoever they may be, take precedence over a mere Emperor. What is my office without its subjects? What am I worth if I cannot hear their voices? Show me your city, Jack, let me listen and learn. Take me to where its heart beats loudest. Then take me to the Lord Festoon and Igor Brunte and we shall see what we shall see!'

Of that night's tour of Brum's greatest parts and its underbelly, and of Blut's tireless questioning in the company of Jack and Backhaus, no record was kept. But by morning, Blut was the only one still going, the others exhausted by his energy.

'Now,' he declared, after a hearty breakfast of fried eel and shattered spuddikin in a rough eatery off the Bullring, where Arthur and Barklice joined them and folk began to think there was more to their party than met the eye, 'I am ready for the fray. Take me to the High Ealdor of Brum!'

When they arrived at Lord Festoon's Residence in the Main Square of Brum, everyone but Blut was surprised to see an angry crowd gathering outside.

'What do you expect?' he said grimly.

The normally relaxed citizens of Brum, already in a state of growing panic about the likely invasion of the city, were not getting the reassurances and action they felt they needed from their High Ealdor.

No doubt that explained why, in addition to what they had learnt in the course of Blut's private tour, they had seen some families already packed up and leaving the city in precisely the disorderly way which Jack had heard about and which Festoon and Brunte had been hoping to avoid.

They gave Blut a false name and hurried him past the stavermen guarding the door. They were now even more fearful that if someone realized who he really was he might be attacked. The crowd was looking for someone to blame and who better than the Emperor of the Hyddenworld himself?

It was as well no one yet knew what he looked like.

Nor did they reveal the truth when they got inside and stood about waiting for an audience with Festoon. His officials were usually the model of courtesy and calm, as he was himself. But the collective panic inside the building was as bad as that outside.

Officials and clerks ran hither and thither without any clear purpose; there were untidy piles of paper where none would have been seen before. They heard raised voices behind closed doors and huddles of angry department heads surrounded by unhappy clerks at the far ends of corridors. People ran upstairs and down as if their life depended on it, stopping halfway and turning about because they had forgotten what mission they were on.

As for Lord Festoon, when he finally appeared, he was perspiring, pale and breathless.

'My dear Jack . . . Arthur! . . . my friends . . . of course it is good to see you all safe and sound, but . . . this is no time for niceties . . . which will have to wait . . . I am expecting Marshal Brunte any moment and we have much to discuss and organize, so if you don't mind . . .'

It was in vain that Jack and then Arthur hinted at the importance and potential value of the nondescript stranger they had with them.

'Of course,' said Festoon, pausing for a moment to shake Blut's hand as he was introduced under his assumed name, in an attempt to be civil but brushing their attempt at a proper introduction aside, 'it is always good to make new acquaintances but just now is not the right moment. Eh? You can see that, can't you?'

He might have dashed off then and there had not, to Jack's astonishment, Blut himself taken the initiative.

They were standing in the central foyer of the Residence, the front door on one side, a grand staircase opposite and various doors to various rooms and corridors to either side and behind.

'My Lord Festoon,' said Blut in a sharp and commanding way, 'I would suggest . . .'

The voice alone stopped Festoon in his tracks, as it did several officials nearby who heard it.

'. . . that it might be a good idea to . . .'

Blut took Festoon's arm with ease and confidence and led the startled High Ealdor towards the stairs.

'. . . stem the tide of this unhelpful disorder in your Residence, which I understand is the very heart of the city's administration and therefore . . .'

He mounted three or four steps and turned Festoon round to face the foyer, continuing in quieter voice, '. . . is a place that should be an exemplar of how things should be seen to be done. Disorder breeds panic. Order, calm. *Therefore* . . .'

Festoon began to realize that the stranger had brought him to a situation and place where he had no particular wish to be and began to look at once irritated and puzzled.

Jack and Arthur had followed them up the stairs and the sight of this little knot of notables, perhaps particularly Jack, who was carrying the Stavemeister's stave of office, had the effect of stilling and quietening the whole area.

'. . . therefore,' continued Blut with a curiously persuasive persistence, his spectacles flashing about the place, 'I suggest that you tell your people to stay calm, that there is no immediate danger and that in a short while, after a further meeting, you will have an important new plan to announce.'

Blut stepped back, raised his hands and clapped to indicate that Festoon was about to speak and then looked expectantly towards him.

'I . . . um . . . gentlemen and ladies . . .' began the nonplussed Festoon.

Blut's calm resolution had spread to those nearby and to his credit Festoon was always, on public occasions, measured and impressive. This quality kicked in now and, faced by his own executive officers and clerks, he spoke just those calming words which Blut had suggested he should, and a few more too by way of welcoming Jack's return with Arthur and of course . . . of course . . .

He eyed the inscrutable Blut, hoping in some way to be told his name which, naturally, he did not yet know nor even guess.

'And of course . . . that welcome extends to their friend who . . . I believe . . .'

Festoon searched for something to say and finding the right sentiment and turn of phrase, now that Blut had calmed him down, said, '. . . accompanied our Stavemeister and Professor Foale, in a manner of speaking, er . . . back again, with, I am sure, that same fortitude and courage which any citizen of Brum would show – and will show – when faced by challenges near and far!'

It verged on the nonsensical but was very well said and the mood began to change.

'Therefore, my dear friends,' concluded Festoon, gaining strength from the sudden calm about him, 'pray go about your business as our citizens expect you to! When the hour of action comes, which it will, I know you will each play your part and be a credit to yourselves, your families, this Office and this great city!'

The cheering was loud and prolonged, the mood now better still.

'Now,' said Blut, who had assumed a position at Festoon's right hand, as he often had before so expertly with Slaeke Sinistral, 'I would advise my Lord to go and stand on the steps down to the Square, and address the anxious crowd in a similarly suitable way . . . and then . . .'

'Then?' murmured Festoon as if in a hypnotic trance.

'Then we shall talk in private and see what we may do about the grim situation this great city faces.'

'We shall indeed,' cried Festoon, and his friends and colleagues could not but agree.

38

IN HIS ELEMENT

Half an hour later Jack and some others, including Blut, convened in a private conference chamber with Lord Festoon.

A fuller meeting of the War Council had been scheduled for the afternoon but he had exercised his authority and sent out notices that he wanted it to start earlier.

Festoon now looked considerably happier than he had for several days, colour having returned to his cheeks and the breathlessness all gone. Officials waited on him as calmly as they had always done until recent days, setting out water, tumblers, pads and stylos, and certain papers, dossiers and city plans. Jack had been privy to earlier meetings and now suggested these be ready for perusal.

The table was oval and Festoon sat at one end of it. He had accepted Blut without question as a friend of Jack's, such was the ability of the Emperor to instil confidence, even without being recognized. Now Blut took a seat in the centre of one side of the table, Jack and Arthur on the other. Backhaus had appeared with Meyor Feld as well as Barklice, who had a gift for being in the right place at the right time.

Jack had sent Bratfire off to fetch Stort.

Of the others who had been summoned, the main one still missing was Igor Brunte. Jack particularly wished him to be there before the truth about Blut was revealed.

After a reasonable wait, Festoon felt he should begin.

'Well then, gentlemen,' said Festoon turning amiably to Blut, 'I think it's time . . .'

No doubt he was going to say it was time that someone explained who the stranger was and what he was doing there and, come to think of it, why he should assume with such confidence the role of adviser to the High Ealdor, if that was the role he had taken. Of which Festoon was not quite sure.

But he had not even begun to say any of that before Blut cut across him in the compelling way he had and said, 'It's time we brought order to this chaos. Time we made sure our right hand knows what the left is doing. Time to . . .'

It was at this moment that Blut himself was cut short by the arrival of Igor Brunte.

He looked at his most formidable: head thrust forward, stance determined, black eyes ranging round the room from the door he had unceremoniously pushed open, the smile lines round his eyes and mouth re-forming into a belligerent scowl.

He had several other aides in uniform at his side, and Feld and Backhaus, who were seated at the table, stood up. In addition were some senior civilians and the city's Sub-Quentor or law enforcement officer.

Brunte had heard before his arrival and now saw with his own eyes that an unknown hydden appeared to be hijacking the meeting. He eyed Blut unpleasantly and moved at once to freeze him out.

'And who the hell are you?' he said, advancing to the far end of the table from Festoon and signalling to those with him to take their places.

Before Blut could reply, Brunte sat down, scowling all the more, and ignoring him, addressing his next remark to the High Ealdor.

'There'd better be a good reason for calling this meeting early, Festoon!'

'There is,' said Blut, cutting in quietly, his face impassive, his grey eyes shining, 'a *very* good reason, er, Marshal Brunte.'

An uneasy silence fell, which Brunte let hang among them for a moment or two.

'I'll ask my question again,' he said and still speaking to Lord Festoon. 'Who the hell is this?'

Only Arthur made to speak, rising slightly, his mouth opening to protest and perhaps explain, but Blut stilled him with a firm hand on his arm.

'I . . . I . . .' began Festoon, the odd befuddlement into which Blut had put him still having its hold, even as he realized for the first time the absurdity of the fact that he had no idea who this stranger was.

Brunte laughed briefly, but his eyes stayed cold and were now menacing. He glanced fleetingly to his side, nodding to one of the two guards who had stationed themselves behind him, both armed and formidable.

The meeting had taken a dangerous and potentially violent turn.

Jack too was on his guard, reaching down discreetly to take up his stave of office, alert and ready to stop anything extreme. Yet even then he sensed Blut's extraordinary control and fearlessness.

Brunte stared at him.

'Get out,' he said, 'now.'

He nodded to his guards who, as one, began moving round the table towards Blut.

He simply smiled and shook his head slightly.

'Who am I?' he asked rhetorically, eyeing the guards with such composure that they hesitated, uneasy before his calm assurance and looking back at Brunte for clearer instruction.

'Who *am* I?' repeated Blut, the emphasis filled with seeming surprise that Brunte did not know, implying that the others did, which was not yet true.

'I will tell you who I am, Marshal,' he said, pausing for emphasis before adding quietly: 'I am the best ally that you have in your hour of crisis and need. The only ally probably. Certainly the only hydden who can get you out of the potential mess and chaos into which you all seem to have got yourselves.'

He paused, the guards did not move, they all stared transfixed. Festoon and Brunte certainly had a charisma of their own, and the power to lead, but this was something none of them had ever experienced or been witness to.

It was quiet, it felt benign, and it was utterly masterful.

Only then as Blut spoke again did one of them, apart from those who already knew his identity, realize who he might be. That was Feld, who had been at Jack's side during their brief and violent visit to the Imperial Headquarters in Bochum in the summer to wrest back the gems of Spring and Summer. Blut had been there too, at Sinistral's side.

But before Feld could alert Brunte, Blut turned to the two guards whose looming presence so near him added greatly to the unease in the chamber.

'Before you move to arrest and eject me,' he said coolly, 'I must formally warn you against laying hands upon my person or in any way threatening me. It is against Article Fifty-three, Clause Seventeen, of the Imperial Code. I should know. I drafted it. The penalty is death.'

They fell back in alarm. There was something increasingly formidable about the stranger.

'That, gentlemen, was when I was Commander of Emperor Slaeke Sinistral's Private Office.'

There was stunned silence, but Brunte persisted.

'And what office might you hold now?' he growled.

'Following my Lord Slaeke Sinistral's abdication and retreat due to declining health, I am . . .'

He finally stood up, stared around at them all, and such was his command he actually took off his spectacles, wiped them clean as he often did at moments when a pause for emphasis was needed, so that they sparkled with light and sent their oval reflections all over the place, including into Brunte's eyes, put them on again, adjusted them around his ears, one after another, and finally said in a clear and commanding voice, 'My name is Blut, Niklas Blut. I am the Emperor of the Hyddenworld.'

The shock, surprise, consternation, bewilderment and alarm that rocked the chamber was total. It was at once heady and scary. Even Arthur and Jack, who had the least cause to feel surprise, felt the power of that moment for the history of the Hyddenworld's most fabled city.

'And before,' said Blut, raising his hand in a gesture that combined peaceful orderliness with continuing command, 'one or other of you – or perhaps all of you – condemn me out of hand as the arch-enemy of this great city, let me say this . . .'

He sat down again, and he and his flashing spectacles and grey eyes were now the absolute centre of attention.

'The imminent invasion of Brum by the Fyrd is an illegal act which is against my express wishes. More than that, it was most certainly against the wishes of the former Emperor, my Lord Slaeke Sinistral. I know that because he told me so. Indeed he signed a document to that very effect which, as it happens, I have here . . .'

To everyone's surprise, including Arthur's, who thought he knew all about Blut by then, he dug his hand into his inside pocket and produced a piece of neatly folded paper which he passed to Festoon. The High Ealdor glanced at it, nodded his head, and passed it at once to Brunte, who examined it minutely and grunted. It looked official enough.

'Let us now be blunt,' said Blut. 'This city is under immediate threat of invasion by a force that, however brave its citizens and well organized the forces at their command, will inevitably defeat it. The Fyrd are too powerful, too well organized and led too well by General Quatremayne for a single city to be able to resist them. Recent history shows that to be true. If the doughty Poles of Warsaw were defeated by the General . . .'

Brunte started in surprise, not guessing that Blut had chosen his example deliberately. He knew it was in Warsaw that Brunte had lost his family to the Fyrd forces commanded by Quatremayne.

'. . . and subsequently put down in a cowardly and vile way, you can take it from me that the same story may soon be told of Brum, unless certain measures and safeguards are put in place at once.

'Nor will courage help you, even if your citizenry fights to the last hydden, male, female and child. If you attempt to fight the Fyrd on their own terms you will lose.'

He paused again, frowned and considered things for a few moments.

'Forgive me for adding this comment, based only on what intelligence I have gathered from Jack here, on our journey through enemy lines to Brum, and what, very briefly, I have seen with my own eyes since my arrival.

'You are ill-prepared and the panic in the population concerning your leadership is, I'm afraid, justified.'

Brunte was looking furious and yet he remained silent.

Blut turned to him.

'We have never met, Marshal Brunte, but I know a very great deal about you. I know what Quatremayne did personally to your family in Warsaw. Apologies are pointless in the face of such horror but I make mine to you on behalf of the former Emperor and the Empire. If you now help lead Brum on the right course, I believe you will have your revenge upon a hydden who is our common enemy.'

There was real anger and compassion in Blut's voice.

'However,' he continued, 'I also know that, though you will have done your best with the resources you have to ready this city's defences, without real intelligence . . .'

A look of hope came to Feld's eyes.

Brunte simply leaned forward, his scowl retreating, his doubt weakening, his interest rising.

'. . . you cannot get very far.'

'We have a good deal of intelligence,' responded Brunte. 'Meyor Feld, explain.'

'It is circumstantial rather than actual,' said Feld, pulling a blue dossier nearer to him but not opening it, 'and we are having to interpret field reports as best we can and from those surmise the vital facts we need to know if . . .'

'For you to have a proper counter-strategy in place?' said Blut.

'Precisely.'

'Do you know the date set for the coming invasion?'

'We can guess it.'

'Do you know where it might start?'

'No.'

'Do you know the strength of the Fyrd forces and assets?'

'To some degree, but . . .'

'Would it be helpful to know at what times and exactly where their troops might arrive?'

'Of course, but . . .'

'And what their strategy for the containment of Brum and its subsequent governance might be?'

'Yes, but this is . . .'

Blut permitted himself a slight smile.

'If I were in your situation, gentlemen, faced by me I would first want to see my credentials for sitting at this table and then I would want to gain, as fast as hyddenly possible, whatever intelligence I have that bears on these issues.'

The others looked around the table at each other. It was impossible not to agree with him.

'Let us kill two birds with one stone and then, as rapidly as possible, put a strong strategy, based on the intelligence I am about to give you, in place and operational.'

Lord Festoon, who was taking his sudden displacement in good heart, and even feeling relieved about it, said, 'What do you suggest?'

'Time is of the essence. The intelligence I have needs to go to as few people as possible. On that I insist. I therefore suggest that the only people who remain in this room, before I reveal what I must if you are to trust me and we can move forward, are . . .'

He looked round the table.

'Lord Festoon, General Brunte, Meyor Feld, Jack here and Mister Pike. Do we have a scrivener to hand?'

'Well, it wouldn't be difficult to find . . .'

'Who we can trust *absolutely*?'

'There are two,' said Jack. 'One is Bedwyn Stort, but he may be hard to find given his present preoccupation with the gem of Autumn.'

Blut nodded. Jack had told him about that.

'Which is, in my view, a matter of the utmost importance. We may lose a battle in Brum because our forces are limited, but finding the gem may very well win us the war.'

This statement seemed to galvanize feeling in the room even more, but Blut ignored that and turned back to Jack.

'Yes . . . the best scrivener might be Thwart the Librarian, whom we all know to be trustworthy beyond all meaning of that word.'

It took only a few minutes for those not needed to vacate the room and for Thwart to be hurried over from his office in the Library across the Main Square.

'I wish the doors to be closed and guarded on the outside,' said Blut, sipping some water.

'The intelligence you have . . .' began Feld. 'Is it somewhere nearby, in a scrivened form?'

'It soon will be,' said Blut, '*very* nearby. At present it is in my head.'

There was a look of disappointment between Brunte and his colleagues. Memory is an unreliable thing.

Jack grinned; Arthur had told him about Blut's extraordinary memory.

Blut looked at Thwart and said, 'Ready? This may take some time Gentlemen, I suggest you listen carefully. What I am about to reveal to you is a testament of my sincerity and my position. It will also form the basis of all future discussion of this Council of War, as you will see. So . . . now: Librarian, let us start.'

Then Blut began one of the most remarkable exercises in memory any of them had ever been witness to.

'TOP SECRET. FINAL STRATEGY OF . . .'

It came out, minute after minute, the summary, the clauses, the detail, the footnotes, the four appendices – everything relevant to the impending Fyrd attack on Brum ·

Nothing could have demonstrated Blut's credentials better, nor could anyone afterwards deny the obvious thing: that he was indeed Emperor, he was a leader and that he had the interests of Brum, and all it stood for, in mind before all else.

Nor did he let up when the dictation was over.

'I do not intend that further copies of the dossier you have just heard in its entirety be made. One is enough. It is absolutely essential that none of you talks about what you have heard. I cannot expect my arrival in Brum to remain a secret for long, but it would be good if Quatremayne does not hear of it until his campaign has begun. What I will require, for reasons that are obvious, is that he has not even the slightest suspicion that his plans are known in such detail. We wish him to proceed exactly to the plan and strategy he has already set. On that will depend a great many lives and, apart from the issue of the gem I have mentioned, the final outcome of this treacherous attack on Brum and Englalond.'

He reached out his hand to Thwart, who gave him all he had just scrivened.

'Thank you, Librarian Thwart, I shall make quite sure that when this little matter is over to our satisfaction you receive this dossier back into your safekeeping for the Library's archive.'

He leaned back and breathed deeply, now obviously very tired. He had been awake for more than twenty-four hours. But he was not yet finished.

'I have chaired many committees in my time, though never in a war situation. I will retire and leave you to decide what is to be done with me. I suggest you invite me back to take overall charge of Brum's strategy in the face of the illegal invasion led by Quatremayne. You see, gentlemen, this kind of thing is what I am trained to do and I do it very well, very well!'

He got up to leave the room and had opened the door to do so when Festoon spoke, after an exchange of glances with Brunte.

'I think . . .' he began.

'. . . that we can agree . . .' continued Brunte.

'. . . here and now . . .'

'. . . that it is in all our interests, er, My Lord Emperor Blut . . .'

'Plain Emperor will do,' said Blut.

'. . . that you take over . . .'

'. . . take overall charge,' concluded Brunte.

'It will be for the best for all of us and our great city,' said Festoon finally.

There was a murmur of approval and relief and Blut sat down again.

He said at once in a purposeful way, 'I propose that we reconvene in three hours. By then our military arm, having reviewed the facts as Marshal Brunte will reveal them, can make their new proposals for Brum's defence, while our civilian arm can reconsider the best strategy for an orderly evacuation.

'As for myself, I need to rest. When I have, with the help of yourselves, I shall create my own skeleton staff to aid me in administering such matters as are essential to my role. Agreed?'

Again, a warm murmur of assent.

Yet there was one thing outstanding and it was Igor Brunte who raised it.

'There was one thing missing in that strategy document.'

'Yes?' said Blut, eyes narrowing.

'The date,' said Brunte.

'Aah . . .' sighed Blut, 'the date. I felt it wisest to miss it out. Best that you all assume it is tomorrow . . .'

A ripple of alarm spread round the table.

'. . . or perhaps the next day . . .'

Blut smiled.

'Do not worry. I know the date. It is not far off. When the right moment comes I shall reveal it.'

Soon after, as if by some general telepathic communication, the officials and clerks and some members of the general public in the building who seemed to have sensed that a moment of history in the affairs of their city was taking place gathered in the foyer outside.

Someone reappeared at the door Blut himself had left ajar as he had ventured to leave. It was a double door, and someone else opened it and the other as well. A crowd very quickly gathered, some even coming into the room as others came behind.

Blut saw it and smiled in a welcoming way. He did what Sinistral would have done. He spoke to them in a way that embraced them all.

'Let me say one last thing,' he concluded a little later. 'In all our deliberations from now, whether here as a committee who will lead this great fight or those of you who work in this building or beyond it, it will help if we try to see our endeavours as something more than the saving of a city.

'I think few if any of you ever met the recent Emperor, my Lord Sinistral. I believe it may be true that his reputation in this great city, in which he was born and which he loved and which he never ever intended should be destroyed in any way by Fyrd, is less than it should be.'

There were nods and grumbles of assent which Blut ignored.

'But I know the former Emperor Sinistral, and have done for very many years, and I can tell you . . .'

He had let his voice swell and rise, though he spoke no faster, but in the same measured way.

'. . . I can tell you all that he loved the city in which he grew up and always held the belief that Brum contained within the heart of its citizens the very essence of what it is to be a true citizen of the Hyddenworld: freedom of the individual, liberty of thought and a profound sense of the need for equal justice for one and all.'

He paused again to let his words sink in.

The only sound was from outside the room, as yet more people came to see what was happening and whispered 'Shush!' to those who did not yet understand the full import of it all.

'Marshal Brunte, Lord Festoon, my friend Professor Foale, and my new friends one and all,' continued Blut gravely, 'our enemy the Fyrd is at our gates. It has fallen to our lot to be our generation's champions of those ideals that true citizenship represents – champions not just for ourselves or this city but for every individual in the Hyddenworld.

'The task is great, the struggle to win it will be a hard one, but that is what we must and we will now do! Let us now begin!'

This was met by a great cheer and clapping and the crowd retreated as Blut instructed those around the table as to what they must next do.

Blut finally stood up to go and rest, but before he could do so, there was a commotion at the great doors from the foyer, the crowd parted, and in stumbled Bedwyn Stort, in a state of breathless haste.

'Have I missed anything?' he cried.

'Ah, Mister Bedwyn Stort, I presume?' said Blut.

'I am he. But . . . ?'

'You have missed nothing too serious,' said Blut amiably, 'when it is set against the work you do! In fact your timing is perfect. I have a question for you.'

'Lots of people have, but I am busy and have news to impart, so if you don't mind I shall leave again.'

This provoked good-natured laughter from Stort's many old friends and Blut's very new ones.

'My question is simple,' said Blut, 'and requires a single word answer: yes or no.'

Blut applied to Stort that same steady gaze that had already quelled and calmed so many that morning.

Stort wrinkled his face, contorted his eyes, sought to find a way to drag himself from the gimlet stare he would have preferred to avoid.

'A question?' he said vaguely.

'Indeed,' said Blut.

'Well, I really, I mean I would prefer, if, well if you *must* . . . but who *are* you? I have never seen you in my life and I only came here because someone said there was another meeting of some kind which I was meant to attend, but quite frankly . . .'

'Mister Stort,' said Blut firmly, 'far be it for me to drag you from your work but what you have to say may affect greatly the plans we are about to put in place. Please answer with a plain yes or no.'

'If I must,' said Stort.

'Do you know where the gem of Autumn is? Yes or no?'

It was no easy thing for Stort to answer anything simply. In his world there were no simple answers until there were simple questions, and on the matter of the gem such simplicity had been hard to find.

'Yes or no?' repeated Jack very unexpectedly.

'Who is this personage?' cried Stort.

'I think, Stort, old chap,' said Barklice in the understanding way he had, 'that you should give an answer. It'll make things easier.'

'What was the question again?' said Stort, in evident distress and difficulty to be so pinned down.

Blut repeated it. The room stayed hushed.

Stort stretched himself upwards, as if reaching for the answer, then he gyrated sideways, as if he had lost it. Finally he grabbed a chair and sat down opposite Blut.

'Do I know . . . ?'

'We all know what the question is, Stort,' said Igor Brunte sharply. 'It's the answer we're waiting for.'

Stort sighed, shook his head wearily and finally said, 'As a matter of fact . . .'

'Just one word,' said Blut.

'I don't,' said Bedwyn Stort, 'but . . .'

'But what?' snapped Brunte.

'I am getting closer,' said Stort apologetically.

There was a brief silence which Blut himself broke.

'Good,' said Blut cheerfully, 'that is excellent! Gentlemen, ladies, citizens of Brum, we have a city's reputation to save while Mister Bedwyn Stort, with the help of his good friends, has a gem to find! I have every confidence that we will find success in both these endeavours! To work!'

39

ON THE WILD SHORE

Ten days into the journey to Samhain, the weather worsening, Sinistral wanted firm land under his feet and a fire on a wild shore. A more sheltered resting place might have seemed more suitable just then but he had been cooped up below ground for so many years, and now on the small craft, that real weather and land underfoot would be a joy to him.

Borkum Riff had been unsettled from the moment they had set off. Not by the sea, that was his natural element, but by the talk of the past with his father before they left, mention of things he didn't want mentioned, and shadows that blew about him in the high winds and had him glowering as he hefted his body into the wheel, eyed the strong sails and took the food his crew made without a word.

'Brot!'

They brought him more.

'And hot brew.'

They brought him more.

It was made of forest fruits, garnered by the wyfkin, rendered into cubes powdered with cinnamon and mace.

He had no alcohol aboard, never had, and damn his passengers. But that brew they had in stormy weather was better than intoxication. It grabbed a hydden's innards and made 'em fierce against the weather.

But five days out he became unhappy and now it was ten he was unhappier still.

'We're being shadowed,' he declared suddenly one night, 'closer than a babby to the breast. Keep watch for 'in.'

They did, slowing and gibing, turning and cursing, pausing at dawn to let the follower catch up, then setting more sail to shake him off.

'Bastard,' said Riff, 'that'n comes close in the dark and watches our light but come the dawn 'in's off and about beyond our sight.'

'Who could it be that follows?' asked Sinistral, amused that Riff was perturbed by something so simple, peering into the dark where the follower lurked, standing tall at dawn to catch sight of a sail.

'Nobody,' they said, spitting into the waves.

'Don't do that aboard my craft!' Borkum Riff roared. 'Yer don't gob into your mother's face so don't into my sea. Use the spittoon.'

'Stupid,' muttered Bjarne, a sailor himself, 'because we clean out the spittoon in the sea anyway . . . What's the difference?'

'Respect,' said Borkum Riff.

They made landfall for fresh water and a stretch on the east side of Sark, in a wide cove Borkum knew. Next door was a much smaller inlet, where they hauled in the craft. Cut off at high tide, not visible over the great overhanging cliffs above, it was a place that screamed with gulls, roared with waves and sent shudders through a sailor's bones.

But the bigger cove was where they camped, up on dunes above high tide. Slaeke Sinistral was well enough now and better still for being ashore and stretching his legs.

There were steep, steep concrete steps up the cliffs, winding in and out of the rotten ground to the top where there was a road.

'Nice view,' said Sinistral after his first climb up.

''In's gone,' said Riff, with evident relief. He meant their followers. 'I don't like shadows out at sea. But weather's bad and we needed respite.'

He said no more.

He could be gentle at times but there was no need to show that to the crew.

'Fourteen days to Samhain,' said Sinistral one evening. 'How many days can we stop here more and still be sure of getting to Samhain in good time?'

'Three or four. Better to get where we're headed early and heave to in a cove as we're doing here.'

'Make it three.'

That night there was a cliff-fall in the smaller cove and they found the watch on the boat knocked clean out with a smile on his face.

The crew laughed themselves silly but Borkum Riff wasn't amused.

'It's the follower's shadow,' he said, 'making mock of us, sending shards down upon our heads.'

Sinistral shrugged, slept all day, ate good fish in the evening and climbed his concrete steps to the heights above as if he was young. He stayed up on top a long, long time and Riff swore he heard him laugh on the wind.

Slew said, 'That's just gulls.'

It was Riff who was right. Sinistral was still grinning when he came down.

'You should go on up, Borkum,' he said, 'there's a view and a half up there.'

'What's the view of?' asked Slew.

'And the half, what's that?' Riff wanted to know.

They went up as the sun set, so on their side it was nearly dark. But as they reached the top, its pink rays came into their eyes and the wind caught them hard.

'For Mirror's sake!' cursed Slew. 'He could have warned us.'

It wasn't the wind he needed warning about, or the setting sun, nor even the view. It was the fact that the top was no more than three feet wide before it dropped away sheer down to another cove, smaller than their big one, bigger than their small one, both flooded with sun that made the sea bright.

'Bastard!' roared Slew, but Borkum laughed to see what they saw far below.

It was the follower's craft, set well and fair, bobbing and bright.

On the shore was a fire, better than theirs, and on the sand was their follower, dancing with a lad. Well, he was trying to. He had a sailor's gait and strength and was not made for the ballroom floor. But she held his hands and they swung about and the crew made music with a tuble and girdhe.

'Might have known it would be her,' grumbled Borkum, 'might have known! My Lady Leetha likes her little surprises, always did. She's the one was following.'

He looked neither quite angry nor quite relieved but a good bit of both that she was there and alive.

Slew, he noticed, looked as sick as a pig.

'Who's the lad she's dancing with?' he said through gritted teeth.

By the Mirror, you look like Sinistral, Riff told himself, but he knew for a fact that the rumours weren't true. Sinistral was never Slew's father.

'That lad is one of my sons,' said Riff, 'which is why he can follow me so close to the wind. Might have known Leetha would take him on to skipper. Best there is next to me. Maybe better these days.'

Slew was still scowling and looked so angry that if he could have ripped a few big rocks off the cliff he might have thrown them down at her.

'Why?' asked Riff. 'What you narked about? What's she to you?'

'The Lady Leetha,' said Slew, 'is my mother.'

Riff nearly fell off the cliff in surprise.

'Your *mother*!' he said. 'I don't believe it.'

'Well you better, Borkum Riff, because it's true. And there she is doing what she never did with me: dancing with your son!'

Riff stood dumbstruck a while before a smile came to his dark face and crinkles to his eyes.

'Leetha's your mother, Slew! Well, that explains a lot!'

His face closed up again.

'Explains what?'

Borkum backed off but he was laughing too. My Lord Sinistral had steered them both into dangerous waters.

'*What?!*'

'Don't matter.'

'You know who my father is?'

Borkum was never one to tell lies. He steered true because he was true.

'I do,' he said.

'Tell me.'

He shook his head and said, 'That's for her to explain, or Sinistral, not me.'

They looked at Leetha far down in the cove, the dancing stopped, the crew making food, Borkum's boy and she staring out to sea.

'There's something else you should know, and that I can tell you.'

'What.'

'That lad, my boy, old enough to be skippering now.'

'What about him.'

'He's her boy too. He's your half-brother.'

This time it was Slew's turn to nearly fall off the ridge. He swore into the wind, he shouted, he screamed like the gulls. Maybe he wept, maybe he did break up a few rocks, but he never hurled anything down.

'You mean you and her . . . ?'

'Yes,' said Borkum staring him straight in the eye.

Slew swore more, then he shook his head, then he cursed and kicked the rocks.

'You're laughing,' said Slew.

'Yes, I am. Your mother Leetha is the best you'll ever get, and you can swear and curse if you like, but if you take my advice, and I've had time to think about it, you'll laugh and be content.'

Slew didn't laugh.

'Why should I?' he said eventually.

'Because you reap what you sow and a harvest of tears don't make for friends.'

Slew frowned and stayed silent a time.

'What's your boy's name?' he asked grudgingly.

'Herde Deap,' said Riff, 'after the sound.'

'Which sound?'

Riff pointed across the water, way out west towards Englalond.

'The great water out there, Herde Deap, we named him after that.'

Slew stood silent a very long time.

Borkum, as true and warm a hydden underneath as ever was, put a strong hand to his shoulder and said, 'Learn to laugh, lad, and she'll give you joy all your life as a mother, like she gave me as a lover. Don't rail against a natural phenomenon like Leetha; you'll never win. You go with the tides, and the wind and the moon and sun and you go with Lady Leetha. If she's your mother, be proud. That's what I told Herde the day he was born and ever since.'

'But he's got to see her from time to time . . .'

Riff shook his head.

'See them down there? This voyage is the first they've ever had. Dancing's the first time. Standing staring at the sea's the first time. Make it happen, Witold Slew. Let yourself laugh.'

And Sinistral too was laughing when they got back down.

'Have a nice time, gentlemen?' he asked innocently.

'My Lord,' said Borkum Riff, 'for the first and only time in my life I'm going to give you advice. Give us our food and then some more and say not a word – not a single word – until the sun comes up again.'

Sinistral heeded the advice.

But later, walking the shore, youth in his stride, they heard him laugh with the sea and the wind and the rising tide.

He opened his mouth to speak when he got back but Riff shook his head, put a finger to his mouth and then called out, 'Not a word, my Lord, if you want to live!'

40

THE HEART OF A CITY

News of the fact that the new Emperor of the Hyddenworld had switched sides and was now in Brum electrified its citizens.

His rescue from imprisonment with Arthur Foale from under the noses of the Fyrd made a great story, but it was his words after the War Council that really impressed. An edited version of these taken down verbatim by one of Festoon's clerks was published as a broadsheet and disseminated throughout the city: *The task is great, the struggle to win it will be a hard one, but that is what we must and we will do! Let us now begin!*

This helped shift the mood of anxiety and panic in the citizenry to one of purpose and determination.

But Blut deliberately kept himself out of the public eye, working through Lord Festoon and Igor Brunte.

'My own role, gentlemen, must remain in the background for now until I have earned your citizens' acceptance'

He was now insisting that the Council of War was in continuous session. But, he ruled, its meetings should be private and attended by only a very few, for fear that Fyrd spies would report back to Quatremayne what was afoot in the city they were about to invade.

He moved quickly to reduce rancour between the civilian and military forces of the city, with Mister Pike in charge of the former and Meyor Feld the latter.

It was a clever move by Blut.

He had understood early on, because Jack had explained the fact, that the weakness in Brum had been the rivalry between the military and civilian forces. One saw itself as professional and the other amateur; the other saw one as arrogant and insensitive and itself as representative of the true spirit of Brum.

'That has to stop, and *now*, gentlemen. The roles of each must be defined and the objectives clearly stated. I am giving you an hour to sort that out. Now, to other matters: transport . . .'

In this way Blut directed members of the Council to clarify their tasks and work one with the other. At the same time, he worked with Brunte in particular on the question of strategy in the early phase of the coming assault.

'The Fyrd numbers are overwhelming, Brunte, and you cannot meet them equally and head-on.'

'Agreed,' said Brunte. 'We need to focus our defence where it will have most effect . . .'

'You call it "defence", Marshal; may I suggest you call it attack? That will foster proactivity from the first.'

Brunte stayed silent, staring at the impassive face of Blut.

It went hard on him that a non-military should see some things so clearly and state them so succinctly.

'You are right,' said Brunte finally.

'You must understand that I have sat in innumerable War Council meetings in Bochum and been responsible for filing the reports of many more. In any case, war interests me as it did my Lord Emperor Sinistral . . .'

'That is the third time I have heard you refer to him as "my Lord Emperor",' said Brunte.

It was Blut's turn to be silent.

Brunte smiled that canny, warm, avuncular smile of his.

'There is more to this abdication and your accession than meets the eye,' he said.

'Is there?' said Blut softly.

'There is, Emperor.'

Blut flushed slightly, a rare occurrence.

Brunte had seen something others had not.

Their respect for each other was mutual.

'Marshal,' said Blut finally, 'I have a suggestion. I will keep silent

about my contribution to your military thinking if you will keep your
thoughts to yourself about the basis on which I hold this office.
Agreed?'

'Agreed.'

'When the time is right, you will be the first to know the truth. So,
now ... I can tell you what Quatremayne, who has been the most
successful field officer in our time, would do in your situation. He
would gain as much intelligence as he could about the opposing
strategy. Well, that you now have in its entirety. He would realize at
once that militarily his position was hopeless.'

Brunte nodded and said, 'That I now concede.'

'He would then deploy his best forces in one or two places where
they would do most damage and behave as if he thought he was going
to win. The blow would not be a knockout one, but it would give time
for other things.'

'The fullest evacuation possible?'

'Yes. But you already have that in train?'

'We have. We have chosen two sites, to the north and west, both
easily reachable for different forms of transport, both easily defensible,
both with good stockpiles of supplies.'

Blut said nothing.

'Have those evacuations started?'

'In part, but not fast enough.'

'From which areas?'

Brunte told him.

'Wrong ones,' said Blut, 'given where the Fyrd trains are going to be
arriving with troops. And you need four if not five places to send
people. Let me explain . . .'

So the work had begun with the military, and the emphasis on initial
attack, but rapidly moved onto Mister Pike's stavermen, who were the
very heart and spirit of Brum's later defence.

Blut did not doubt they would be doughty and courageous; the
questions he asked were what their objectives were and, from that,
how effective might they be. Only those who had seen the Fyrd attacks
at work knew how devastatingly powerful and destructive they were.

'Tell me, Pike, how are the stavermen organized? Centrally, locally
or not at all?'

Pike had been in charge of the stavermen for twenty years, after he emerged as the city's finest fighter with an ironclad, or metal-hooped stave. He had defeated all comers without much trouble, including in back-alley contests and rough ginnel fights for money, which in the old days were illegal bouts against willing Fyrd fighters.

He had won time and again and had earned that combination of respect and fear which a good staverman needs if he is to control the rougher elements of Brum society.

He was a stolid, grizzled sort of hydden, no-nonsense but good-natured. He had been a particular friend of the late Master Brief and, as such, a protector and supporter of Bedwyn Stort, whom he regarded with affection and awe. He could never quite understand how the thin, freckly youth, as he had first known him, and the abstracted, innocent and obviously harmless adult he had become, had the courage to get himself into the scrapes he did, and the wit to get himself back out of them.

One way and another, Pike was respected and liked by all and there was no better hydden in peacetime to keep the peace.

Blut's skill in handling a hydden like Pike was such that, in a matter of an hour or two, he had made him understand that, in war, things could be very different indeed. The old enmities with Brunte's force must cease forthwith. The organization must be tighter. The tasks given must be clearly defined.

Hence his sharp and pointed questions.

'The stavermen are in what they call chapters, sir, which reflect kinships, streets and where they were schooled . . .'

'Meaning that one chapter may well consider itself a rival to another by family, by locale and by education?'

Pike, like Brunte, fell silent before such inquisition. He considered what Blut implied and saw its truth.

They talked around the problems for some little time.

'So what do you suggest?' said Pike eventually.

Blut shook his head.

'You know the issues now, as you know your strengths and weaknesses as a fighter. It is for you to find a solution.'

Pike frowned and scratched his chin.

Then his rough, scarred face broke into a grin.

'Mix the buggers up into units of fifteen. Appoint new, younger leaders of each. Set 'em tasks for a bit of friendly rivalry. Tell 'em it's demotion or a fight with me if they play the fool with Brunte's boys. And . . .'

Blut held up a hand.

'The fight with you is not a good idea.'

'With Jack then.'

'That's better. And . . . you were going to say . . . ?'

The grin broadened.

'Blame it all on you, sir. Say I'm just following orders.'

'Perfect,' said Blut. 'I'm used to being unpopular!'

Pike nodded and stood up. He could relate to that.

Before he left, he turned and fixed Blut with an appraising eye and said, 'You're not doing a bad job, if I may be so bold, Emperor. Don't forget to get some sleep.'

Blut nodded and said he would.

'And after that . . . if I may be bold again.'

'Yes, Pike?'

'The fighting's going to get dirty and it's going to be street to street, humble to humble. No one knows Brum's ins and outs better than my stavermen. We'll get as many of our people to remain when the Fyrd move in as we possibly can, while the Marshal's forces hold up the advance. Then we'll come back in and fight in ways the Fyrd never dreamed of in their foulest nightmares.'

Blut nodded and remembered Brunte's personal file.

Warsaw.

A city fight like no other.

The resistance there nearly broke Quatremayne.

No wonder he was so savage afterwards.

'I suggest you talk to the Marshal about street fighting. He knows more about it than you might think.'

Pike left – and he left Blut thinking.

In a few short sentences Mister Pike had stated more clearly than anyone else what their overall strategy was going to be.

The thinking was over.

The action must begin.

One last thing to sort out. He rose, stretched, and looked at his chronometer. He had suggested a break in proceedings two hours before. The interviews since had been one on one. He had ten minutes left and no one to see, no one to talk to.

He got up and ambled through the High Ealdor's offices to the main foyer.

The place hummed with activity.

Hydden came and went continuously.

The mood was one of purposeful excitement, nervous but no longer panic-stricken.

He went to the front doors, which were open to the day, and the Square was busy too, with traders, news vendors and folk bustling. That was a clever front devised by Festoon to keep any spies around thinking that the city had not woken up to reality yet. The more amateur Quatremayne believed the defence of Brum would be, the better. As for the notion it might go onto the attack . . . Blut wanted to convey the idea that that was inconceivable.

The guards were under strict instructions not to identify him to others. As he went to go outside and down the steps one came over and said quietly, 'My Lord, would you like one of us to go with you . . . for your safety?'

Blut shook his head and thanked him.

He went on down the steps and wandered anonymously among the citizens of Brum. He heard his name mentioned. He saw people reading his words on the broadsheet. He began to feel the true spirit of the famous city.

You're not doing a bad job . . .

He walked on slowly until he saw a crowd of pilgrims in the centre of the Square and strolled over.

They were crowding round a star of different coloured cobbles that seemed to form the cardinal points of a compass.

A guide was talking to them.

It seemed that even at a time like that, business went on as usual in Brum.

'This star of cobbles, ladies and gennelmen, was made in olden times. You might think it marks the centre of our great city, you'd be wrong. Or maybe the centre of Englalond, wrong again!'

'The Earth?' someone called out.

The guide laughed and stepped onto the star.

'This star was personally laid, I am given to understand, by one of the greatest hydden who ever lived. Anyone know his name?'

'Lord Festoon!' shouted someone.

'Mister Bedwyn Stort,' cried another.

'Not even close and, anyway, they're both alive and kicking and that personage who settled in these cobblestones is dead and gone.'

'The former Emperor Slaeke Sinistral?'

The guide shook his head.

Blut was tempted to correct the impression that my Lord was dead, but wisely did not.

'No? No one knows? It was the hydden who made this Square and the High Ealdor's Residence, who created the famous Chamber of Seasons of which there is a tour once in a while, when permitted, and who was tutor to the aforementioned gennelman, Slaeke Sinistral, who, by the by, was born in this city but for obvious reasons ain't much missed. I refer, of course, to . . . *to*? Does no one know?'

'To ā Faroün,' said Blut, prepared to believe, from the antique look of the cobbles and the old way in which the flat brass plate surrounding the circle was inscribed with places and distance, that they had been made by him.

'Correct! Will that gennelman kindly come here!'

Blut thought it best to do so.

'It is a common belief that any who stand on this fabled spot will, if they face the right direction, be well on the way to becoming a citizen of the Universe!'

'What's the right direction?' someone shouted.

'Now that, one and all, is a secret I cannot reveal!'

The tour was over, tips given, and moments later Blut found himself standing alone on the spot.

He closed his eyes and felt, or thought he did, a shiver in the ground and shift in the air, a brief wobble in things all about.

He heard a running of feet.

'My Lord,' whispered that same guard who had spoken to him a few minutes before, 'they are all assembled, the Council awaits you.'

Blut shook his head but still felt dizzy. He looked at his feet and tried to ascertain which way he was facing. Not the way he had begun.

'My Lord . . .'

'Already? I thought I had only been here a few minutes.'

He stepped off the star and looked at his chronometer. He had lost more than twenty minutes. He stared at the cobbles and the star shape they made. There was something odd about it which ... which ... which did not quite please his sense of order, and how come it was later than it ought to be?

'My Lord . . .'

'I'm coming now,' he said. He looked back again and knew he had left something of himself behind in the 'centre of the Universe'. The city of Brum had taken a little of its newest arrival into its huge, warm, eternal heart.

41

SOMETHING MISSING

By the following morning Blut had matters so well delegated that he was finally able to attend to an item on his continually updated list which kept being put back to the bottom: *Mister Stort*.

He turned to Jack and Arthur, now his advisers and sounding boards, and said, 'I meant to say goodbye to Bedwyn Stort before he left the city ahead of the invasion, but I never did. Not top priority, but important all the same. Is there some way I can get a message to him?'

Jack looked puzzled.

'He hasn't left Brum,' he said.

'Pardon?'

Blut sounded surprised, even slightly alarmed.

'He was at home in his humble this morning when I left.'

'*Pardon?!*'

'Stort is still . . .'

For the first time since he had arrived in Brum, Niklas Blut looked annoyed.

'But . . .'

'He's still looking for . . .'

'Yes, yes, I know what he was looking for. I thought he was about to find the gem. That was nearly a week ago.'

'He has – as good as. But . . .'

'Bedwyn Stort should not be in Brum hours before an invasion by the Fyrd. He should be far away, somewhere safe, where he can continue his work. He will be no good to us dead.'

'He says he can only do his work in Brum.'

'Does he indeed?' said Blut standing up, a touch aggressively, which showed how tired he now was. 'There is nothing to stop him going to . . . to . . . anywhere to do his work and he can take as long as he needs. But if he's in Brum and the Fyrd get him he . . .'

'He cannot take as long as he needs, my Lord,' said Jack, as puzzled by this turn in their conversation as Blut obviously was. 'He only has until Samhain and then . . .'

He too stood up.

Blut held up his hand.

'Why only Samhain? Why not . . .'

Arthur, who had been slumbering, woke up. He had heard this kind of thing before, usually between academic colleagues who were so into their own work that they forgot to ask a few basic questions about someone else's, with consequent wrong understandings and false expectations.

'Gentlemen,' he said, 'please . . . *Jack* . . . *my Lord* . . . both of you, sit down.'

They sat and glowered at each other.

'It is my fault,' said Arthur, 'and mine entirely. I had assumed, my Lord, as I am sure Jack also did, that you understood the nature of the quest for the gem of Autumn. Or rather, as you might put it, its parameters. The gem must be found by the night of October 31st and given to the Shield Maiden by the end of that night, which is, of course, the feast of Samhain, last harvest, the end of Autumn and beginning of Winter.'

Blut considered this, still frowning.

Various things fell into place in his mind.

Lights went on, doors opened, things were illuminated and he was appalled at his own stupidity.

He had been so stuck down in Level 18 of Bochum all these years that he had forgotten the salient details of the legends and prophecies concerning Beornamund, the gems and the importance of their rediscovery and return to the Shield Maiden.

He now realized that since he came to Brum, he had been so involved in directing the work of the War Council that he had completely underestimated the problems connected with finding the gem.

Yes, I have, he conceded.

Finally he spoke, 'I believe I have made a mistake.'

He looked at his chronometer. Time was ticking by, but rarely is anything too late.

'Stavemeister,' he said in a measured way, 'if Stort stays in Brum, how capable is he of looking after himself?'

'Not very.'

'If he leaves, can he do so alone?'

'He could; he often has, but he is inclined to get lost. If he did that before finding the gem it might be a disaster.'

'I had thought that you and Katherine were keeping an eye on him?'

Jack laughed.

'We are, but, as Arthur knows, keeping an eye on Stort, or in any way trying to control how he works is . . . difficult. He does not respond well to pressure. He likes to go his own way. *Many* of us keep an eye on Stort, in fact I would say that the whole of Brum keeps an eye on him as best it can . . . he is the most beloved citizen we have . . .'

Blut looked shaken by his own ignorance.

He said quietly, 'In this matter I have failed and have been less than thoughtful. I imagined it was just a matter of time before he worked out the things he has been thinking about.'

'It is and it isn't. The gems are elusive, this one in particular.'

Jack and Arthur explained.

'So when he talked of finding the gem,' said Blut finally, 'he merely meant finding where it is, not getting it into his hand to pass on to the Shield Maiden. Incidentally, where is she?'

Jack shrugged and said, 'You might as well ask where a storm is. You don't know until it arrives.'

'But I might ask, I suppose, for I never really have, *who* she is?'

'She's my daughter,' said Jack, 'and Katherine's . . . I mean, I thought you . . .'

Blut shook his head.

'It seems I have been so lost in my own world that I closed my eyes to a much bigger one. Well then, we must see if there is anything further we can do for Mister Stort at once. Where is Stort's humble?'

'It's a ten-minute walk.'

'Let's go.'

*

The journey to Stort's was not the discreet affair Blut would have preferred. It seemed his likeness had been made public and he was recognized. The crowd outside, most of whom had never seen him, let out a great cheer. It seemed they recognized him most of all by his spectacles, which they had heard he was always cleaning.

'Whips 'em off his face like a mask off a wolf and hypnotizes people with his eyes,' some in the know had said. 'By the time he's got 'em on again his victims will do anything he says.'

Blut, Jack, and Arthur were followed now by a friendly crowd. The lane where Stort lived had never been so full.

Jack felt it best to observe the formalities now that Cluckett was back from her family visit and knock on the door. She opened it instantly and gazed at her visitor only briefly before she said:

'You're Emperor Blut, I know you from your specs. I'm Goodwife Cluckett who does for Mister Stort. Call me Cluckett, and he prefers Stort. Come in, but wipe your feet, it's been raining. He'll say he's busy but I say a visit's good. I'll make tea.'

Jack went to fetch Stort . . .

'Who? What? *Now* . . . ?!'

'Now,' said Jack.

'But, look, can't you see I . . . am . . . ?'

'Busy?' said Jack.

'That's it! Very.'

Stort was lying under a bench, a pillow under his head, the Embroidery so draped above him that it cut out most of the light. He had been asleep.

'Now!' repeated Jack firmly.

'Who can possibly want me now, at this minute?' said Stort ingenuously, emerging, blinking at the light.

'I do,' said Blut, who had smilingly evaded Cluckett and was now at the laboratory door. 'Ah, is this the famous tapestry?'

'Embroidery.'

'What's the difference?' he asked amiably.

'An excellent question. Let me explain . . .'

Blut was only too happy for him to do so and, as Stort began, Jack left, amazed. Time was passing, he had a lot to do, there was a crowd outside, war was looming, yet Stort and Blut, upon each of whom in very different ways Brum's future depended, were talking technicalities about arts and crafts.

They continued to do so for nearly hour, tea being served in the laboratory, Jack coming and going, Barklice appearing, Cluckett offering scones to the crowd outside.

Jack watched in awe as Blut applied his charm on Stort, who, in his own shambolic way, applied his on Blut. The two were instant friends.

'So . . .' said Blut, finally getting to the point, 'have you got any further with your search?'

Stort shook his head.

'I will say again as I said before, I am nearly there . . .'

They were standing looking at the Embroidery once more, which Stort had now draped at the far end of the laboratory so that Blut might see it more clearly.

'Until recently my attempts to make sense of the Embroidery had been utter failures. But of late I begin to see a few things and understand that the gem will be found not far from a raging shore, after a dangerous battle and, if the wyrd is with us, near some place with a universal view. This may seem something of an advance. But where is that shore? Which that fort? Who the enemy? And why the view?

'All I need is a clue, a key as it were, to unlock these mysteries. I feel sure it lurks in the seeming chaos on the margins of my mind, as it does in the Embroidery before you. Find that last clue and I believe I shall see what I must do!'

'Mountains, sea, a rocky shore,' said Blut, pointing at a spot on the embroidery, 'and is that a castle?'

'An earthwork, I think,' murmured Stort, 'of which there are any number in Englalond, including one here in Brum!'

'. . . a river, a wood, a steeple . . .'

'Half a steeple,' said Stort, 'and a ruined village.'

'. . . and people, different people, a girl here, an ageing woman there . . .'

Stort put his hands over his ears.

'Stop!' he cried. 'I know it all, I see it all, but I cannot see the wood for the trees!'

Blut stepped back startled, but not at Stort's outburst.

'Something in that image seemed to move.'

'Does that all the time, my dear chap,' said Stort matter-of-factly, 'but you get used to it. Never quite the same.'

'You know, it does give the sense of almost wanting to give something away but not quite. I suppose details are one thing, clues or keys another, perhaps. They are more . . . constant. I mean door keys don't change, do they? What's beyond the door does. Just a thought . . . As for not seeing the bigger picture, we are all prone to that. My Lord Sinistral would sometimes step backwards if faced by a problem, to remind himself that he needed a wider view.'

Blut stepped back now, backing away between the benches but still looking at the Embroidery.

'Odd,' he said suddenly. 'I felt a kind of shiver, as if I saw something there . . .'

'That happens too,' said Stort.

'But still . . . I thought . . . I . . .'

'Almost but not quite?'

'Exactly,' said Blut.

He stood, hesitating.

Stort too.

'. . . so many questions come to my mind, Stort, I cannot bear to go! For example, you made a passing mention earlier of ā Faroün as being the creator of this Embroidery.'

'I did and that seems likely. He designed the Chamber of Seasons in Festoon's Residence. Have you seen it?'

Blut shook his head. He had had no time to see any of the sights of Brum.

'He was an interesting hydden . . .'

'My Lord Emperor mentioned him from time to time . . . from the name, I presume he was of Eastern origin?'

Stort shrugged.

'Possibly. Probably. I have read Master Brief's monograph on him but there are no clues about his early life or what happened later.'

Blut's face darkened.

'On that I know something, though it is only a rumour. It is said that the former Emperor, whose tutor he was, murdered him to gain the gem of Spring. When I first knew the Emperor I thought it possible. Later I came to the conclusion it was quite impossible.'

Stort shook his head indifferently.

'I doubt that ā Faroün had much to do with the gem of Autumn.'

Blut smiled.

'My Lord used to say that, when faced by an intractable problem, it is sometimes wise to doubt one's doubts. Now . . . to more practical matters before I go. I would be much obliged if you would agree to leave Brum very soon; I would suggest in the next twenty-four hours. Jack here will see to your safety and it might be an idea if you have someone else who might accompany you on any journey you might decide to make should you work out where the gem is.'

'Barklice,' said Stort. 'He's good at finding routes and does not stop my brain functioning. In fact the opposite. Perhaps Katherine too, unless they are needed.'

'Whatever you need,' said Blut. 'I wish I had had time to talk to you properly before. Most interesting. But now . . . !'

The visit was suddenly over and Blut back at the front door.

The waiting crowd cheered more, he waved, and someone shouted, 'Good on yer, Milud!'

He waved again and they laughed and cheered more loudly still.

'For someone who doesn't like making public appearances,' said Arthur, 'you certainly know how to work a crowd!'

Blut smiled, he waved, he enjoyed being jostled by the friendly Brum crowd and for a little while the affairs of state did not weigh so heavily.

Yet strangely, as he mounted the steps of the Residence once more and turned to wave to the crowd again, it was not these great matters he was thinking about, nor anything of that kind at all. It was of Stort and the Embroidery and the sense that he now had, as he had then, that they were both missing something and it was staring them in the face.

42

WAITING

That evening, as darkness blew in on a front of bad weather, the Shield Maiden sat alone and tired, angry and disappointed.

Her body ached.

Her breasts had known their brief moment and now sagged.

Her hair was grey, no getting away from it. Caught in the night wind, it was a pale tangle of a thing.

Oh, but she was old.

'Stay back!' she commanded her Reivers, who circled on their dogs.

Then: 'Stop staring, I know what I've become without your foul eyes telling me.'

'Mistress . . . you need to eat . . .'

'Leave me,' snarled the Shield Maiden, shivering and wet through. 'Where's that Horse?'

'Wandering, Mistress, across the wide vales and down to the shore. Our dogs are scared of the Horse on nights like this.'

'They should be scared of me,' she said, rising, running at a dog and kicking it off its four feet so that it spun squealing through the air. 'What food have you?'

'Stew.'

'Hot or cold?'

'Greasy.'

'Thick or thin?'

'Glutinous.'

'Near or far?'

'Gone.'

The Reivers laughed at their joke and so did she.

'Give me some.'

'Yes, Mistress.'

She ate, she drank, she stood with her bare feet in mud and her hands in the heavens and she cried out, 'Stort, where are you? Why is it taking you so long? The days are running out until Samhain.'

She was so alone and tired.

So angry and lost and withered within.

Blood used to streak down her legs but that had not happened for days and days, which for the Shield Maiden was years.

Age was eating her.

She felt a woman no more.

She felt the pendant at her neck and the stones he placed there. Spring, Summer; Autumn to come.

'Stort,' she whispered into the wind, 'the gem of Autumn is not so hard to find. Can't you feel it in the *musica*, my love? You're looking in the wrong place.'

Spring, Summer, Autumn: but it was Winter she dreaded, when her body would be old as time and Stort would want her no more.

'Oh, my love, but I'm getting old.'

The sound of the sea roared up from the cliffs; dogs barked down the lane; humans drove by along the roads, the lights of their cars, red at back, white to front: such an affront to the dark.

'Shall we chase them, crash them, hurt them, Mistress?' begged the Reivers.

'No, there's something else we must do.'

'When?'

'Now. Stort, if you were here already this wouldn't have to be. You're not late with the gem but you're not early and Earth is not pleased. It's half your fault and now . . .'

'Where to, Mistress?' said the Reivers, mounting their dogs, gathering behind her.

'Half Steeple,' she said. 'Time's come for the Earth to show her teeth, time for us to get things ready. But I'm aching and tired and age is withering me and I miss what I can never have. I miss Bedwyn Stort.'

'Shall we lead? We know where that place is.'

'Are we coming back here? We like this place.'

'Of course we damn well are, for Mirror's sake and for mine, this is where the gem is. Stort's taking so long.'

'You love him, Mistress . . .'

She screamed her rage at them and said she didn't and chased them with kicks and pokes and bit their ears and shouted so loud her spittle fell on them and they screamed too.

'I don't,' she said.

You do.

43

CLUES

Stort woke after only an hour's sleep, things swirling in his mind.

She was swirling, round and round a single word, which came to him out of the monograph of Brief's that he had read, about ã Faroün.

Brief said that ã Faroün said, 'We all crave to go home and that's the sadness in the music I make and in my lutenist eyes.'

There was a lot in that sentence that woke Stort up, but the word the Shield Maiden was circling, the Reivers and the dogs as well, all angry in his waking dream, was 'home'.

'Home is where,' Bedwyn Stort pronounced as he sat up in bed in his nightshirt, wide awake and excited by the sense that he might have made a breakthrough, 'it's where we all crave to go to at Samhain. The end and the beginning of our year. We start at home as children and we want to end up at home when we die. The bit between is just journeying from and to.'

He got up, very quietly.

Jack wasn't there because of what was happening in . . . in . . . less than an hour. Just enough time.

Very quietly because Katherine was there, and so was Cluckett, and he knew they both had instructions to keep their doors open and listen out for Stort in case he got it into his head to go night walking.

So Stort eased off his nightshirt, winced at the threat of making noise, and eased on his drawers and vest, giggling slightly as he sometimes did. He saw the comedy of himself.

Then, realizing he had no shirt to hand and not wanting to go out without one, he tiptoed absurdly down his own corridor, past Cluckett's open door, into the kitchen – where his hip caught the handle of a saucepan and nearly brought it to the floor – and got a shirt.

He eased that on as well, wrinkling up his face at each imagined nearly noise and tiptoed again, his thin shanks of legs looking as ridiculous as he imagined they did as he reached his room again.

Stort had decided to go to the Library while he still could. He wanted to try and track down the sources Brief used.

He wanted to find out more about ã Faroün because, as that excellent fellow Blut had suggested, or seemed to, it might be the clue to what he was missing. It felt like a great big splinter in his brain which he couldn't quite reach to pull out.

Stort's jacket was over a chair so he put that on. He had no hat except the nightcap that he wore in winter in bed, but that would do. No one was likely to see him in Brum at that hour. All busy with war, and all he wanted and needed to do was to make the ten-minute walk to the Library and check in the stacks to see if he could find out the name and location of the place ã Faroün had once called home.

A lot of material had been evacuated to Wales but not more modern things like Brief's notes on ã Faroün and some of the less important-seeming manuscript scrivenings of the lutenist himself. A mistake perhaps, but choices had to be made and Thwart had made them.

Stort had lit the candle by his bed when he woke. He stepped into his shoes.

Now he used it to light his way to the front door, which presented the challenge of bolts. Great big things which Cluckett liked to shoot at night with relish, and pull back in the morning with glee.

He managed them in silence by easing them back and forth slowly, the house somnolent and dark behind him and his face contorting with the effort of being quiet.

Stort loved liberty and there was a pleasure in stealing into the cold, deserted night with his jacket on against the chill, and his nightcap too, its bobble bobbling.

He realized with a thrill of horror that he had forgotten to put on his trews. His skinny legs were bare to the October night air. But he couldn't go back, not now. He had better hurry on and the sooner he got there, the sooner he would get back. Anyway they would all leave Brum in the morning, after which it would have been too late.

Ã Faroün.

Home.

Samhain.

No problem had ever been as intractable as this one, but for love. That was difficult. Stort stopped, insights came thick and fast. He added 'love' to his list.

Love.

Why had he dreamed the dream he had? Why had he remembered this one, since he rarely remembered dreams?

Oh, but she looked old and sad in his dream and he wanted to be with her and . . . and . . .

But even in his thoughts, which no one else could know, Bedwyn Stort was too shy to put his arms around the one he loved.

'I would like to be with her this Samhain, gem or no gem. Just to be near so she knows I'm not far.'

The Main Square was deserted but for the guards at the Residence. A solitary flame-light flared in one corner and the light was on in the Residence. Across the Square from it was the Library, its windows dark and its great doors, which had never been the same since the earthquake in the summer, loomed.

For a horrible moment he thought he had left the keys in his trews but they were round his neck, along with his Chime. He felt it, as he often did, and remembered Judith's little hand when she gave it him while still a girl and put it round his neck.

And the taste of the small sweet tomatoes which she stole from Arthur's tomato patch as a child, to pop into Stort's mouth.

'Taste them!' she had cried delightedly,

He had done as she'd commanded. It was in those moments that he shared simple joy with another for the first time in his life and his innocent heart began to know the depth of an overwhelming love that, when she became an adult, turned to such torment for him.

He mounted the Library steps, looked round and – *bang!* – there it was again, the certainty that there was something here, right there, that he was missing.

He turned back to the door and unlocked it.

He closed it quickly, lest someone see, and locked it up again.

Now he was free in the dark, free to do what he liked best, which was finding things.

He lit the gas lights down to the stack-room steps which spiralled down and down and led him to other worlds. Stort's pale shanks shivered in the flickering flames but he didn't care.

44

SPECS

Late in the evening of October 23rd, Niklas Blut took a final turn around the Main Square of Brum. He walked alone but for two guards who kept a discreet distance behind. The crowds parted for him, hushed and filled with a dread expectation.

Nobody now doubted that the invasion was about to happen. The intelligence indicated it and Blut's grim face as well.

As he turned back towards the Residence someone shouted, 'Good luck, sir!' and a broken sound of clapping echoed around the Square.

He turned and said quietly to those near enough to hear, 'I will make an announcement very shortly.'

No wonder then that when he climbed the steps back up into the Residence, a rough, blustery, late Autumn wind at his heels, he did so reluctantly and with a heavy heart. The War Council presented a circle of now-familiar faces, silent with expectation.

'We are, I believe, as ready as we can be. Which is as well. The time has come for me to hand over the running of this Council, which it has been my great honour to steer through the historic deliberations and decisions of the last days, to the one among us who is most competent to take us into war: Igor Brunte.

'I can now confirm what many of you already suspect: the invasion of Brum will begin tonight, or, more accurately, at just past two tomorrow morning.'

It was handover time.

Ten o'clock at night and the invasion four hours away. The War

Council was giving way to Igor Brunte's rule. Had it been a war on a national scale Blut might have stayed in charge. But it was a battle over a city, in a city, and it didn't need emperors but soldiers who knew what they were doing, had clear command, and their plans and assets in place.

So over to Brunte.

A steady east wind was driving rain into the sides of the Residence; a staccato sound against its windows.

Brunte took the chair.

'There's a crowd outside, my Lord Blut,' he said, 'and it would be good if you went out and spoke to them. By eleven they need to be gone.'

Festoon agreed.

'You have become popular, my Lord,' he said. 'The right words will be useful at this stage of things. The citizens need a final uplift.'

Blut nodded. He was working on it. But it was hard to think of inspirational words to order, certainly ones which could compete with what he had said spontaneously on the first day he came.

Now they all knew what was happening and who was doing what and why.

The invasion of the city by the Fyrd was due to start with the arrival of a freight train at Lawley Street Station at six minutes past two, half a mile east of where they now sat.

It had been part of Blut's strategy to convey the idea that nobody knew anything about the Fyrd plans and that all was panic and chaos in the great city. He guessed the Fyrd had spies and their reports would be heard and read by Quatremayne.

The advantage to Blut of the Fyrd strategy, and its only flaw, was that it was nearly impossible to change the timings of the trains that would bring the troops in. That element of surprise had been completely lost once the strategy was known in Brum.

But even had Quatremayne thought that Brum knew his plans, and been able to change them, he would not have done so. He had the overwhelming advantage of numbers, firepower and skills. His forces could not be beaten. Resistance there might be, but his victory was inevitable.

As night deepened, the city and its remaining inhabitants stayed calm. Flares had been lit in the Main Square in the expectation that a crowd of those not immediately involved in defence and already in position might gather as a final testimony to the city's fighting spirit. They had, and the flares danced and spat with the wind and rain.

Much was afoot.

A few hundred yards to the north-east, across the Digbeth branch of the Brum Canal Navigation, in the shadow of Old Corporation Wharf, the bilgesnipe were making their craft shipshape, as maritime folk like to do, ahead of the very special role it had been agreed with Blut and the Council of War that they would play. Under the leadership of Arnold Mallarkhi, Old Mallarkhi himself being now too old for such a task, they were to provide transport for forces and supplies during the initial stages of the battle.

Later, when the retreat was sounded, theirs would be the task of getting folk away to fight again in the days or months ahead.

The location gave them instant access in four directions: along the River Rea, which ran north–south, and up and down the Warwick and Birmingham Canal, which went east–west and whose aqueduct passed over the Rea above the wharf.

Meanwhile, in tunnels below, far from the prying eyes of any spies, with only trusted locals in the know, a temporary kitchen had been set up for the duration of the battle. The bilgesnipe would take supplies to all key points while the hefty Fazeley Street porters, renowned for their strength and speed, could load and unload and carry food and arms to places the boats could not reach.

A hundred yards to the north of the wharf, and eight hundred to its west, in the old Cattle Market and Worcester Street Cattle Market respectively, Brunte's forces and Pike's stavermen were gathered, armed and ready. They were well placed to advance at speed and in force on three of the four arrival points of the Fyrd: Lawley Street Goods Station, the Curzon Street Goods Yard and New Street Station.

The fourth arrival point, which lay further off, was Snow Hill Station. A special force combining Brunte's and Pike's people lay in wait nearby for them.

These different groups, which between them contained the best and most skilled fighters available to Brum, would make some of the greatest sacrifices of life and limb. But none of these forces, not even their field commanders, yet knew the exact target against which they would be deployed by Brunte and Feld. There was good reason for this.

On the outskirts of Brum, along the key railway lines, temporary telegraph offices had been set up to alert Brunte's command centre in the room below where they now sat, as to which trains had passed through and what their estimated times of arrival would be.

The intention was to move in Brum's forces, starting with those under Brunte's command, only when those alerts had been given, making it impossible for the Fyrd to know in advance where the strongest defence or attack they might face would be.

These movements would be by foot and very fast. Retreat would be the same – or rather, tactical withdrawal to another point where, combining with other forces, sudden and heavy attacks could be made.

It was a strategy only possible in a complex urban jungle such as Brum. In open country, the Fyrd would prevail very quickly. But in Brum the hope was they would hardly know what had hit them, or from which direction it came, before the attacking force had evaporated into the alleys, conduits and along the canals, to do the same thing somewhere else.

'The aim,' Brunte had made clear to his force in a final message conveyed by his commanders in the field, 'is threefold. First, to slow down and pin down the enemy. Second, to make them think we have much greater forces than they imagine. Third, to sap their morale by making it difficult for them to assess our strength, understand and predict our strategy, and then inflict real damage on them out of proportion to our numbers. A fourth, more general goal, is to leave the Fyrd in absolutely no doubt that Brum is not a place they wish to be – ever.'

No one doubted that a general retreat would be sounded probably sooner than later. When it was, Brunte's forces would then be made subordinate to Pike and his stavermen, whose knowledge of Brum's labyrinthine escape routes was unsurpassed. Their role would be to get the military out as quickly and safely as possible and then go back in to undercover positions long since worked out and assigned.

It was then that different, longer-term tactics would be employed to harass the occupying army.

There were details Blut liked.

One was the decision to pick ten fit youths to act as runners, carrying messages to and from where they might be needed. They were given red and white uniforms to be visible so that when needed they could be quickly found. A risk, but a reasonable one. Their survival, like their usefulness, depended on their speed.

They had been chosen on the advice of Bratfire, the son of Barklice, who laid claim to being the fastest thing on two legs in Brum and could vouch that those he had chosen were 'not half bad too'.

Barklice had been put in overall charge of them, which he did not relish and Bratfire resented, which he let Pike and Brunte know loud and clear.

'Dad finds routes, he don't run 'em. 'Ow's he to know which best to send when it comes to Old Brum and New, Deritend and Digbeth, New Station and Lawley Street? He don't.'

Then, when he was assigned that day by Barklice to Blut, in the mistaken belief that the best of the runners should be with the most senior people, he complained even more.

'Not that yer not important, Mister Blut, but there don't seem to be much happening round the Residence or you. Just folk with bits of paper whispering. No action.'

'Well, that might change,' Blut had said.

'And it might not,' said Bratfire, standing kicking his heels and eating and proving his point.

But Blut was right; things had changed.

When he got back from his visit to Bedwyn Stort he realized that Barklice couldn't do two jobs at once. Standing by to act as route-finder to Stort to aid his escape from the city was a better use of his talents, so on Blut's return to the Residence and before this meeting, he had called Bratfire in.

He felt the dialogue was worth sharing with the Council. War and battles were about strategy and big things. But it was individuals who did the work and it was as well to remember it.

When he had summoned Bratfire he came looking eager but glum.

'You said you knew the runners who your father is in charge of?'

'Yes I do, every one.'

'Is there anyone in Brum they all respect?'

'Meaning?'

'Look up to?'

'Not Dad, he's too old.'

'Who, then?'

'If they don't do what I say they know I'll clobber them, so they do.'

'You, then?'

'Yes. Me.'

'What would you do if you saw a Fyrd?'

'Tell 'im to piss off.'

'Ten Fyrd?'

'Run like hell to the nearest corner, get the lads, sneak up on 'em and . . . and . . .'

'What.'

'Depends where, when, how, time of night or day, what gear we have to hand, if there's an escape route and what mood I'm in and who's with me.'

'I want you to take a message to Mister Barklice.'

Blut wrote some words on a piece of paper, folded it and gave it to Bratfire.

'What's it say?'

'That's not part of your job.'

'I'll only read it when I'm outside. Might make me deliver it differently. There's ways and ways.'

'It tells Mister Barklice that he is relieved of his job immediately and is to report to me at once and that you will take over from him.'

Bratfire shook his head.

'You got to put it nicer than that else I won't deliver it. Dad'd be hurt and I'm not having that, and Mister Jack here would agree.'

Blut rewrote the note.

'What you said this time?'

'I have said that a really important assignment has arisen which only he can do in the whole of the Hyddenworld, and if he's agreeable, and he thinks you're up to the job, he is empowered by me to promote you, his son, to that position.'

Bratfire grinned and took the note.

'That's better,' he said, 'and that's sensible!'

'Off you go!'

Bratfire went.

Blut made the final handover to Brunte formal and had it minuted.

Then Brunte said, 'My Lord, you can hear the crowds. We should all go and appear on the steps before them. Shake hands. That kind of thing. But you do the speaking.'

Blut still had no idea what to say.

'Positive, upbeat, nothing too complicated,' murmured Festoon, '*that* kind of thing.'

Blut felt tongue-tied as the guards opened the doors and a huge cheer went up.

They shook hands, Festoon and Brunte turned to Blut and he found himself stepping forward, no words in his dry mouth.

The flares were magnificent, the crowd huge and expectant, the cheers began to die away and fall to silence but for the wind and the spits of rain.

He could hardly open his mouth; it was dry as bones.

The silence deepened still in a city on the edge of its wyrd, awaiting its fate, knowing that some would die, not knowing where they would be in twenty-four hours time, or even if they would be alive.

There could be disappointment in such moments and there could be magic.

The citizens of Brum were a goodly, warm-hearted crowd, willing to give all comers a break.

Someone did so now.

His voice sang out through the night with a smile and a friendly lilt: 'Milud,' he cried, 'take off yer specs!'

Blut looked up and into the crowd; he put his right hand over his eyes to see if he could see who called. Then he nodded and grinned and, as the silence deepened still more, he slowly took off his spectacles, pulled out a white handkerchief, wiped them as he liked to do, put them back on, hooking first one ear and then the other and he said, 'You know there's nothing, nothing in the Universe, that can defeat us this day and in the days to come or ever, but ourselves.'

The crowd cheered.

'There is nothing to a Fyrd but what you have and I have and Marshal Brunte and the High Ealdor here as well: flesh and blood. That's all they are, same as us. But there's something I've got that you don't have and they don't and you know what that is?'

'Specs!' shouted someone.

'To see the future with,' said Blut. 'To see our families with. To see the harvest of our lives in our young and our city and our time.'

There were more cheers as someone waved a placard and then someone else the same. Then more and more.

It was only when Blut and those with him looked more closely at what had been drawn on the placards that they realized something significant had happened since Blut went out to meet Stort. Something which said more without words than Blut might have said in an hour, though his words were good. Someone had decided to draw on a poster something very simple: two ovals linked by a half hoop. They represented Blut's spectacles.

Someone else had copied it and in the time that Blut had been back and handed over to Brunte, a third citizen, a printer, had copied the image by the hundred.

'Take one, Milud!' someone called out, offering it to him.

He took it, he made great play of examining it, he took off his spectacles and put them on again, and then with a great smile he held it up for all to see.

Then he said one last thing.

'There's no one here in doubt about what to do. Each of you has a role to play, and an important one. But we will finally retreat, the better to fight another day.

'Most of Brum's citizens have been evacuated, courtesy of the orderly help many of you have given. You who remain will fight, or help the fighters, but when the moment comes, you too will retreat.

'We cannot get you far. You will go to Brum's suburbs, to friends, to family, to those who have offered their humbles. You will never, ever, forget what you are: citizens of Brum, with a right to be here and a right to . . . for a little . . .'

Here he smiled again.

'. . . to go on holiday! Not retreat but a vacation! That's what you're going on. From where, with your friends and family, you will fight every second, every minute and every day until the Fyrd leave Brum. Then you will come back and there'll not be a single person in the Hyddenworld who won't be reminded that Brum is rightly as fabled for its sense of freedom and its willingness to fight for it, as it is for the gems of the seasons!'

He held up the image of the spectacles again and so did many, many more.

The Fyrd had not yet arrived but, so far as Brum was concerned, the war had begun.

45

INVASION

Lieutenant Backhaus, in charge of the Brum forces at Corporation Wharf, received the first of two signals he had been expecting, at five minutes to two the following morning.

The first of the Fyrd trains was on schedule and due to arrive four hundred yards north of their position, at Lawley Street Goods Station, in eleven minutes' time. In a great arched underground space lit only by a single candle, he raised a hand to signal for his force to ready itself.

The heavy smoky air was rent by the occasional whistle of trains from the many nearby sidings, the squeal and rattle of shunts, the distant race of freight-train wheels on main lines.

For most of the hydden there, it was their first time in battle.

Many were nervous, a few shivered, or their breathing was fast and irregular. Others were icy calm. One or two felt out of their bodies, not believing they were who and where they were. Dirks ready on belts; staves quietened by cloth; some with crossbows, some with throttle wires, one with a human bayonet.

Two minutes later Backhaus got the second signal.

In twenty minutes' time the other train, the more important one in terms of numbers of Fyrd being carried into the city, would arrive at the Curzon Street sidings.

He let his arm fall, which was the signal to go.

Barely a sound, the quiet clatter of a single stave, footsteps on cobbles, up to street level, and the first force of hydden, grim as the dark night they entered, moved swiftly down Montague Street to their muster point under the same railway bridge which was about to carry the later train in from the east.

Backhaus knew that the Fyrd's first group, fast-moving lightly armed infantry, would move rapidly from within yards of where Backhaus's Brummie boys waited, to provide cover for the troops arriving on the slightly later train.

The intention of Backhaus's men was simple: to pin down the first group and stop them covering the second to enable a near-total disruption of that slightly later arrival. The method for that was one developed by the Fyrd themselves and copied from them. It had never been used *against* the Fyrd before.

Indeed, the Fyrd were not used to counter-attack: they came, they saw, they conquered and the vanquished accepted it.

Not there, not that night, not in Brum.

The night was blustery and the earlier heavy rain had left the cobbles shiny and greasy, a dangerous surface for those not used to it. The area was a complex of ginnels, mews, wharfs and canals, small factories, steps up and steps down to different levels. It was full of shadows and pitfalls. Take a wrong turn and you're in a lethal cul-de-sac.

Take another and you fall six feet into a canal.

No wonder the instructions in Quatremayne's strategy document were crystal clear: stay to the route, avoid any diversion in the area known as St Bartholomew Ward, stay focused, move on to the major targets, do not engage with anyone or anything until the key arrival positions are secure and all trains have delivered their cargo.

Only then start the killing.

It was a tried and tested formula which had worked in all cities the Fyrd had taken, except Warsaw, where Quatremayne nearly got trapped and killed.

Where Brunte's whole family was later torched in reprisal.

Seven minutes after the first signal was received, the Brummie force was in position. Four minutes later, the first of the trains, the one into Lawley Street depot, pulled slowly in.

Backhaus sent off his first runner, a lad of nine, one of Bratfire's best friends.

'Go!' and they heard his feet pattering past the old Cattle Market, south into the night, to tell the boys near New Street Station that the night had begun.

While the force under the bridge waited, shifting back into the darkest shadows, the Rea rippling in the dark behind and beneath them, a bilgesnipe boat already down there in position ready for the next phase of their plan, two of their number scaled the bridge to the line above.

One was raised on that stretch of the line and knew by sound alone which line the train would end up on.

They squatted ready to spike the line, aware of the danger of being seen and heard by the arriving Fyrd below, across in Lawley Street, straining to hear the train on the lines. Hear and feel it.

One raised a hand, the other cocked an ear.

The spot was chosen because it was in the shadows between the lofty rail lamps

'Right side!'

They moved the gear placed there earlier in the dark.

One by one they set four sticklebacks, robust wood and metal structures, in the gap between sleepers. Set in pairs, nine sleepers apart with a band made of fire hose fixed between, on which a string of barbed spikes, two and a half feet long, is set loose and free.

The train rolls over, the spikes spring up one after another, and the poor sods travelling undercroft are stabbed and ripped open before they have even arrived.

But the work was hard and heavy and the two had less than ninety seconds to get each one in place.

Heave, grunt, 'That's it!'

Then heave, grunt again and the second pair of stickles was in place and the train's lights were suddenly in sight, swaying slightly with the bend, and they were off, back down to their mates below.

A minute later Backhaus's group, spying the first Fyrd shadow across the road as someone peered over the wall, moved near. The idea was to wait until they were halfway over the wall, heave them over and knife them as they came, one after another.

Four of them were chosen for that job. They were butchers and they knew their knives.

Then the first Fyrd was taken and the killing began. The Fyrd, stopped almost before they began, had not yet fired a single bolt.

Meanwhile, above their heads, the train they were meant to be covering but now couldn't reach, had just triggered the first of the stickles and, for the Fyrd riding undercroft, a bloody nightmare commenced . . .

. . . You're under a train, you're all fired up, you've never known defeat, you've only ever seen fear in another hydden's eyes and – *thwack!* A spike shoots into your leg, turns and bends and rips right round because the train's moving on and the pain makes you grab and you lose your 'sac and – *thwack!* There's another in your back and you're turning into your own scream in the dark and your mate grabs your hair and you feel his blood in your ear as you fall on the line and he's pulling you along with the other buggers all screaming and the wheels, great, grinding wheels, *Oh nah not tha* . . . and a leg rolls by as your face grinds into the track and . . . the train ground on, its wheels squealing on blood and bone as the Fyrd were stickled one after another and ripped apart.

'*Retreat!*'

The order was sharp, the response rehearsed, this was a ploy that the Fyrd would come to hate.

Sudden silence, the enemy gone, death and Mirror knows what all about; total, bloody, chaos.

The Brummie boys, hyped with success, did as Backhaus commanded, leaving only one of their own behind, a bolt through his head.

'Herey go my lads! Herey down here!'

The lilting bilgesnipe voices came up to them from the watery shadows of the River Rea.

The bilgesnipe lit brief flares to light the way down and then doused them at once. A whistle, a pause to check, screams most terrible from the line above and a warm sticky rain of blood coming down, and the boatyboys are off, skiffing their craft one after another through the dark.

'Where to now, lads?'

'Feld's in charge of the next one,' and Meyor Feld was.

✳

They took a rest and had some grub under the old slaughterhouse off Bradford Street. Another group was already there.

Feld appeared, looking sharp, with Backhaus now at his side. He had blood on his uniform and a look like they'd not seen on his face before: murderous intent.

Feld said, 'Right, you all know where the Worcester Wharf is – behind the Midland Depot. Yes?'

They did.

'That's the Fyrd collecting point for those coming in from the west: troops, arms, Mirror knows what. They're using a building in Holliday Passage and they're regarding it as safe. The whole area's secured, or will be in an hour's time. We're going in hard with the bilgyboys up the basin adjacent and some down the tunnels that emerge at Worcester Wharf. Here's how it's going to be . . .'

The Fyrd arriving over in Snow Hill arrived in a city of the dead.

There was no one about, not even a rat toddling along.

Nothing.

No resistance at all

Their mustering point was St Philip's Churchyard, on the south side.

Not a pigeon in a tree, not a sign of anything except humans, a few, stinking of drink and talking to gravestones and trying to thump a holly bush.

But hydden?

Not a single bloody one.

While Feld was busy on the west side of Brum, the Fyrd on the north side decided to move on at once eastward to St Bartholomew's Graveyard and from there into Park Street Gardens.

More human drunks.

A small gathering of human travellers roasting chestnuts on a brazier in the park, playing a mouth harp of the kind that hurts a hydden's ears, talking in registers too low for hydden to interpret, except for the sibilants, which make them sound like a group of snakes silhouetted against orange flames in the night.

But hydden?

None.

But there were!

Mister Pike and his stavermen, eighteen of them, were sitting twelve feet down in the old catacombs under the 'V' formed by Park Street and the Viaduct.

'They're here, right on cue.'

'How many?'

'More than a hundred.'

'They move quietly.'

'They're Fyrd. Move like stoats.'

'When do we go in?'

'Dawn, so we can see to get away fast.'

Someone chuckled.

'Haven't done this since a boy.'

'I don't think there'll be much laughter in Brum in two days' time,' said Pike. 'This is the good time, when we're the ones with surprise on our side. The bad times will come.'

They were coming already.

Feld's mission had gone awry.

The tunnel was already secured so there were killers waiting for them in Holliday Passage and Feld's killers got killed themselves.

Eight dead before the retreat.

The plan was not wrong, just not fully right. But they had a fall-back.

Half of the Backhaus boys were in craft in the St Thomas Ward basin and the Fyrd, thinking they'd beaten the unexpected attack, were relaxing and getting their second wind.

Backhaus whispered, 'We go on very quietly, very quick, and we come out faster still. Five minutes and I whistle you out. Understood? All of you?'

So in they went again, in the south end of the passage, staves poised ready for the Fyrd laughing over the eight dead lads.

Thump

Thump

Thump and on . . .

A crossbow was drawn, a train slid by, the stars above were still bright though dawn was showing.

Thump and a dirk went into a gut and one of Backhaus's boys squirmed down into coal dust.

Thwunk! And an iron clad crushed his head.

Backhaus whistled them out and they came. But moments later he himself was dead from the bolt that followed them as they escaped.

'Herey go lads, down here boys!' and an oily flame by a bilgy smile showed them the way down off the dock.

'We're away!'

Still, they'd caused disruption and damage and killed more than they lost.

Mister Pike, the best staverman of his generation by far, had an instinct for timing a strike.

Too soon and the blow's weak and leaves the opponent with a strong counter-attack. Too late and you're on the ground spitting teeth and puking bile.

So they trusted him as the Fyrd in Park Street Gardens above had their grub, rested, bided their time, told a few jokes, consolidated their supply line back to Snow Hill Station, saw the first dawn, began to get cold and, well past four in the morning, got bored and restive and slow and didn't know the catacombs were right below filled chock-a-block with corpses and skulls and as sparky a group of stavermen as ever was.

'Right, lads,' said Pike, 'sup up, clear up and limber your fingers on your staves and ready your dirks. The Brunty boys are good but we're going to be a mite better and a mite faster. Peace and cooperation's good but I've said all along that a little rivalry never hurt anybody. So I'll slap any of you bastards who don't do better than his best. We're eighteen, they're one hundred and eight at the latest count.

'You know the layout of this dank place 'cos you were raised here like me. Here's how it's going to be. First, put this gear on . . .'

He opened a bag he had been carrying and pulled out eighteen light shifts, black as coal but for the white luminescent bones of skeletons and skulls.

They put them on, got them right so they didn't obscure vision or movement; standing there, some wanted to laugh themselves silly.

'Right, my lads, we're going to rise from the ground like bodies come to life, using each of the eight exits. Me? I'm taking the exit right in their midst. We move on my whistle, short and sharp, and we move like lightning. In, bash, stab, thrice times but then out, out like bats from a tunnel at dusk, all so fast they don't have time to react. Right?'

Right.

Pike's stavermen rose from the dead at dawn, eighteen skeletons to one hundred and eight.

Oh friggin' hell, was the look on the faces of the Fyrd. *Friggin' friggin' hell. What the . . . !?*

Eighteen in, seventeen out on their legs unhurt and one dragged by Pike 'cos the bugger sprained his ankle in a rabbit hole.

The Fyrd?

Thirty-seven dead, nineteen maimed beyond fighting again in that campaign, thirteen wounded and the rest so scared that some never recovered confidence.

And Pike and his boys were gone in the night, in different directions, except towards Snow Hill Station. Leave *that* well alone!

'*Thirty-seven dead from the Snow Hill contingent and the sun's barely up!*' roared Quatremayne, in his HQ in Coventry, when the message came through. 'How the *hell* is that possible!?'

'General . . .'

'I'm going to Brum now.'

'Sir, they're using sticklebacks. It won't be safe undercroft.'

'And where did they get sticklebacks? And who are "they" if they're not a few grubby townsfolk? And how did they *know* . . . ?'

The day was not going well for Quatremayne and it had barely started.

The force at Lawley Street signalled distress and disarray and total failure of their mission to support the bigger group who arrived a short while later.

That force failed to signal arrival in due time and when they finally did, two out of three commanders were dead, a third had lost a limb, and Mirror knows how many of the best of the best were dead, maimed, injured or dying.

The New Street contingent had better and clearer news, except they too had losses to report.

'*Eight?!*' thundered Quatremayne. 'In a fully secured supply depot?! *How?*'

'We don't know, General. But we killed one of their officers.'

But Quatremayne was beginning to think he did know. That made him more angry still.

No city, especially a layabout place like Brum, could respond like that without two things: perfect intelligence and organization and spirit far beyond the normal.

He had been informed that Blut was dead in the bunker. Though the reports were second-hand they seemed conclusive. The entrance doors were blown up and immovable, all other entrances sealed.

As for the guards, something had gone badly wrong and the bunker exuded the smell of death and putrefaction.

'I want a team to get into the bunker and check every corpse they find and confirm Blut's dead. Because I have a feeling . . .'

'Who shall I send, sir?'

Quatremayne was so angry he might have killed any one of his senior staff on the spot. Instead he said, 'You go, and you and *you*. *Personally*. Do it and report back.'

'But, General . . .'

'Do it,' said Quatremayne coldly, 'while I sort out the mess you've got us into in Brum. First, we're going to have to fall back on all those fronts, regroup and find out what the hell is going on in that city.'

'Sir?'

'Yes, for Mirror's sake.'

'The signals are all down.'

Incandescent is a light that shines very bright. Quatremayne's rage then might have lit up the whole of Coventry.

46

EPIPHANY

As the sun rose on the High Ealdor's Residence, news that all the Fyrd divisions had retreated to regroup was confirmed. Marshal Brunte's commanders immediately wanted to do what so many want who are victorious early on: go in hard after the enemy while the going is good.

But the Marshal had a cooler head and did not intend to depart from the strategy agreed with Blut and the Council of War. Early success by Brum had been expected; later defeat was inevitable.

Festoon said he had no useful view.

Brunte turned to Blut, who was sitting at the table now in a purely advisory capacity, and asked formally, 'Emperor, do you still think we should retreat?'

Blut took off his spectacles for the umpteenth time, cleaned them, but hadn't even put them back on before he said, 'I do.'

In fact, the retreat had already begun, Pike's boys showing Brunte's forces the best ways out, the bilgesnipe boaties doing their bit by way of transport across the whole of Brum.

They had won a signal early victory and bought valuable time to complete the evacuation. They had shaken the confidence of the Fyrd. No need to gild the lily. Time for them all to go.

Arthur had slept throughout at the Residence and woken feeling bright. He attended the Council of War but played no part in it. The day was a fine one, perhaps one of the last before October ended and the dark months of Samhain began.

It was the kind of day that Margaret would have liked, though not here in Brum. She had been raised a country girl and had never moved far from Woolstone all her life, but for brief travel to academic conferences and the like. No, she would not have liked Brum, but how much he would have liked to tell her all that had happened, to share with her things in a way he could with no one else.

Arthur leaned over to Blut.

'Taking a stroll, old chap. Clear my head. That sort of thing.'

Blut nodded, barely listening, except to register that Arthur looked a little wan.

'I'll be here and easy to find,' he said. 'We'll be leaving in an hour or two. No more.'

Arthur nodded, patted the shoulder of the younger hydden of whom, in weeks past, he had grown very fond, and left the Chamber. The plan was for them to leave for the suburbs together and place themselves under the care of Pike's stavermen at a 'destination unknown'.

Dispersal and discretion were the keys to the evacuation and longer-term plan to counter-attack when the time was right.

'Well done, gentlemen,' said Arthur as he left, but the rest were so intent on concluding their business that hardly anyone noticed him go.

Jack had already said his farewell and left for Stort's place to get them all ready to leave. His task was to keep Stort safe and get him clear of the city while he could. He should have gone long ago; if he still had not found the elusive clues he needed to track down the gem it was now too late.

Blut was going with Arthur but not going far.

It had been against all instinct that he originally agreed to leave Bochum. He was not making the same mistake with Brum. He and Brunte would hide out in the suburbs, watch how the resistance led by Pike went, and make their move when the time seemed right.

Pike was going to make sure they were safe.

'Our work here is done, I think,' said Brunte.

'And well done,' said Blut.

They stood up because it seemed likely it was the last time some of them would meet. The Fyrd had arrived; they would not go away for a while. But Brum was its people, not the place, and they had not got their hands on them.

Blut gathered his things, which included his latest list.

He ticked all but one off and eyed the last.

'Lord Festoon,' he said, 'I never got to see the famous Chamber of Seasons. Is there time for you to show me before we leave?'

'There is,' said Festoon.

It was still early morning as Jack hurried through the deserted city. He knew he desperately needed sleep but that it would have to wait. Time to get out now and fast.

When he got to Stort's house he was surprised to see the door was open. Someone was about early.

'Not Stort!' he muttered, seeing his door closed. 'Must be Cluckett, then.'

Astonishingly they were all still asleep.

He woke Katherine.

'Packed and ready?'

She nodded and said, 'All well?'

'All's as expected. We have to go. Rouse Stort and I'll wake Cluckett, unless she's gone out for a moment. The door was open.'

She was not outside but, like Katherine, having been up late packing, was still asleep.

She was up in an instant.

'All's ready, sir, and there's food in the kitchen if we've time for it.'

Katherine came running in, a nightmare look on her face.

'Stort's gone,' she said.

'For Mirror's sake!' cried Jack. 'When?'

'I have absolutely no idea. He went to bed late, like Cluckett and me. Now he's gone and there's no note or anything in his room or the laboratory.'

There were many times in his life when Bedwyn Stort had been utterly indifferent to the world around him or his personal comfort. The problems that interested him were absorbing, his questions often profound. But it was when he had scented success and a solution that his indifference reached grand proportions.

Rarely had that ever been more the case than through that long night and on into the morning when he was on the track, like a predator after a prey, of the truth about the gem of Autumn and what it would mean he must do.

All else was of no consequence.

All else did not exist for Bedwyn Stort.

What is a war in the streets and alleys of Brum at such a time?

Of what consequence an earthquake?

Would it matter if the whole of the Hyddenworld sank into the sea? Not to Stort, it wouldn't.

He had gone to the Library because Blut had asked a question about ã Faroün and he, Stort, had not had a satisfactory answer. Wood for trees! He had seen at once that he must switch his attention to the hydden himself and not the Embroidery he had made if he was to get past his block.

He spent the night trawling through the boxes and boxes of papers concerning the famous architect and lutenist which Brief himself had collected: writings, musical notation, measured drawings, designs – the list was endless. By dawn, and by then cold and hungry but ignoring the fact, Stort had a better picture of ã Faroün than he could reasonably have expected.

He knew what he looked like, from a sketch: dark and saturnine. He was more than sixty when he became Slaeke Sinistral's tutor and he appeared to have died sometime in his eighties, since no record of him except by memory and hearsay existed after that important year.

His lute-playing was legendary and could make 'eagles weep and moles sing', which, thought Stort, was an odd analogy for a contemporary to make.

He had no children nor much interest in wyfkin or anything else in that general department. His passion was his work and his work was making beautiful things in homage to one thing alone: Beornamund's gems.

Extraordinarily one account stated he had made the Embroidery with his own hands in a single night when, Stort was able to ascertain from the documents, he had in his possession three of the gems: Summer, Autumn and Winter.

Spring he did not have because it was lost until Stort himself found it.

Stort discovered that the lutenist saw Slaeke Sinistral as a son, and treated him as such.

He saw the world as beautiful and a thing to honour always.

But he was sad, often sad, because there was something he had missed all his adult life which, Stort began to understand, he could not, or thought he could not, ever find again. It proved hard and took hours for Stort to work this out. It was associated with Samhain, and ã Faroün's darkest episodes of gloom were related to times of seemingly terrible insight about the Earth and, too, what archivists dismissed as his own idle scribblings, made in various languages which included words that repeated themselves over: *choy*, *meindi*, *anath*, *trevan*, *trê* . . .

Stort, though himself a linguist, could not understand these at all. They did not seem to echo ã Faroün's likely Indo-Arabic origins. The words were scrivened as lists, only occasionally alone, and often accompanied by what Stort thought at first were no more than idle doodlings. Which many probably were, but for a certain design which appeared again and again. It was a semicircle with lines radiating up from it, some thin, some wavy. Obviously a rising or setting sun.

How that could be associated with ã Faroün or these strange unplaceable words, he had no idea, though the sun symbol reminded him of something in the Embroidery. But what? He could not place it and had no time to go back home and look. A quick visit to the Chamber of Seasons across the Square was an option, but he did not want to lose concentration when he felt he was so near a result right where he was.

Then Stort asked himself a very odd question.

'Why,' he said aloud, his words echoing among the stacks, 'am I assuming the Indo-Arabic connection? The only basis for it is ã Faroün's name, for which I have found no derivation or genealogy, and material in his archive, which speaks of his interests, not his origins. Supposing he had a different origin and these mysterious words are from a language which . . . might . . . be . . .'

He voice faded away, his eyes widened, he looked appalled as a realization came to him.

. . . might be closer to home.

'Closer to home!' he cried out.

Then: 'I am a fool! Indo-Arabic be damned! These words have a Celtic feel and seen from such a viewpoint there is a far easier explanation.'

He listed the main words again and, treating them as part words, saw at once their common meaning. The prefix 'tre' for example was often used in a Welsh connection to mean 'homestead'. As for 'choy', which he had foolishly presumed must be a phonetic spelling of an oriental word, possibly Chinese, why that was *Cornish*. A language which also used the prefix 'tre' in many homestead names.

Stort tore through the archive, collating scraps and notes and images. They had seemed to make no sense or have no connection before. He did so in conjunction with his confused yet intense memories of his near-death experience with the Embroidery in his humble when the imagery had come alive.

He had seen a raging shore, and here in the archive was an image of one.

He had felt wind in his hair and here were stark illustrations of short poems, depicting stunted wind-bent trees and bushes such as are often found along wild shores with strong prevailing winds. Like Cornwall.

In his own dying state Stort had felt a yearning, a longing, for something he saw now that ā Faroün must also have lost, a yearning deep in the heart of all exiled Celts: his childhood home, his landscape and soul of his beginning.

Choy, meindi, anath, trevan, trê . . . they were all, in different ways, words meaning *home*, something which ā Faroün had missed all his life, Stort now guessed.

Stort's mind was now in total focus. The difficulties and doubts of the past weeks and months were falling away and things moving into their right place.

If the great scholar and lutenist had been Cornish then his name was adopted. It was a disguise and a clever one, for it married his interests in things Arabic to the new persona he seemed to have wished to adopt when he left his native land. Why he left it Stort had no idea. Nor how it could possibly be that the nineteenth-century scholar could have obtained the gem of Summer, which had ended up with his protégé Slaeke Sinistral. How too had he obtained the gem of Autumn and, perhaps, that of Winter also? Those questions must wait, for there were only a few days left before Samhain, when the gem of Autumn must be delivered to the Shield Maiden if she was to prevent her mistress the Earth provoking the end of days.

Stort scrabbled through the papers frantically until he found something he had earlier dismissed. It was a series of images of a solitary rook, cleverly drawn as a study of flight. Seen afresh it was all too plain that the corvid was flying backwards, symbol of the end of days. The great scholar might have feared that *that* time was imminent.

'Half Steeple,' muttered Stort, 'where our wyrd took us on our journey here. That was to be a place destroyed. Mirror forfend that such a thing could happen anywhere, but the time may yet come when that pretty town must pay the price for a devil's contract made in medieval times!'

The images of the rising sun now seemed to speak to him. It too was a clue.

Stort suddenly smiled.

'So, was the form of his name, "ã", merely an affected way of saying "from"?' he asked himself, unsure whether to laugh or cry at the simple yet touching deceit. 'It was impossible for one so homesick as he to invent a name entirely divorced from his home, so he did not. He was telling himself as he now tells me that he was from "Faroün". If we replace the F with a V, to get something more Cornish then our task is simple. We need a place with a name that looks or sounds like "Varoun" and is connected with the rising sun.'

Once again a wild stare came to Stort's eyes and he called himself a fool; memory of his entanglement with the Embroidery returned and he saw again what he had seen when he felt himself upon the raging shore. It was not a sun, it was the flare of a beacon high on a hill or cliff overlooking that shore.

'Varoun Beacon,' Stort cried. 'If there is such a place then *that* is where the gem of Autumn will be. Because he finally went home – and when? At Samhain, when all hydden must, once in their lives at least, return to where they are born and give thanks at the start of the dark time of the year for all their home gave them in their lives since they left it. What better place to hide the gem of Autumn? These "scribbles" reveal ā Faroün's working out of where he should place that gem. But . . . but!'

If Stort's extraordinary night-time epiphany had been like a series of hammer blows in his head, what now finally came was a thunderbolt.

That maddening sense he had had that he was missing something in the Embroidery, which he had shared with Blut, who had sensed it too, now found resolution inside his racing mind.

'Aaah!' he shouted at the shelves about him from sheer frustration at not having seen before what he now saw so clearly. 'Aaaaaargh!'

Ā Faroün might, in a mild way, have been a fraud for changing his name, but he was also a genius.

He had left a clue to where 'Varoun Beacon' was in a very public place and most hydden in Brum, including himself, had seen it a thousand times. But they had not the advantage Stort had had – access to the Embroidery and the Chamber of Seasons as well. For woven into the marvellous imagery of one, and painted boldly across the seasons of the other, was the same image of cardinal points as used in the square outside for the 'Centre of the Universe'. He, like Blut, had missed this now obvious fact because they focused on the more detailed seasonal imagery and did not look for this quite different symbol. Stort was pretty certain he might find a clue out there as to where the 'Varoun Beacon' might be.

He sighed, breathed deeply and mopped his brow.

His work was done. Now, all he had to do was to confirm his findings and make his way to Cornwall. Which, come to think of it as he told himself abstractedly, was exactly the place where Katherine had felt such a strange and seemingly inexplicable urge to go when they first found themselves near Half Steeple in mid-August.

With that, and clutching his notes and the most relevant scrivenings and drawings made by ā Faroün himself, Stort decided that the time had come to mount the stairs once more and return to the light of day.

The moment Jack realized the implications of Stort's disappearance, he knew he had very little time to find Stort, let alone rescue him, and he began issuing commands.

'Katherine, you're coming with me. *Now*. Bring your 'sac and stave because I doubt we'll be coming back here. The Fyrd will be on their

way into Brum sometime very soon and Mirror knows how long we'll
take to track down Stort.'

'But . . .'

'Trust me, this must be. Cluckett! You have to leave Brum now.'

'But . . .'

'*Cluckett!*'

He loomed over her, rather as she wished Mister Stort would do
more often.

'Yes, sir, at once . . .'

'You cannot come with us, I'm afraid . : . But there's something you
can do better than me. There are one or two folk hereabout who were
still reluctant to leave. Round 'em up and get them out into safe places
in the suburbs and don't take no for an answer.'

'Is that an order, sir?'

'*It's a command!*'

'I will,' she said breathlessly, her chest heaving. 'They'll not disobey
Cluckett!'

'He'll be at the Library,' said Jack, as he and Katherine ran towards
the Main Square. 'We can't leave him there . . . Brum is as good as
deserted, the last of us are going now and from all I've heard of
Quatremayne he'll want to claim the prize earlier than later.'

But when they reached the Library doors they were locked, with no
sign of life or Stort.

'We'll try the Residence,' said Jack. 'Quick . . .'

They heard a shout to their left and saw Barklice and Arnold
Mallarkhi coming up from Fazeley Street. Their task had been to wait
for Blut and Arthur at a quay on the River Rea nearby. They should
have gone already.

'This whole thing's unravelling,' Katherine said.

'And fast,' added Jack.

Jack ran over to Barklice.

'We're still waiting for Blut,' he said.

'He's probably still in the Residence with Festoon. Have you seen
Stort?'

Barklice shook his head.

'Nary a sign o' that gennelman,' said Arnold.

'Go back to Fazeley Street,' ordered Jack, 'and be ready to cast off and get going fast. Stort's not in the Library as far as we can see, so he's probably in the Residence.'

They nodded their understanding and retreated back to Fazeley Street.

Jack and Katherine ran towards the Residence. As they reached it they heard the tramp, tramp, tramp of marching feet.

'The Fyrd! Get in, out of sight; if they don't know we're here they won't search for us . . .'

In they went, pulling the doors quietly to as the first of the regrouped Fyrd marched in, the General at their head.

When Quatremayne had arrived on the east side of Brum two hours before, he had still been fuming. But already his forces were recovering from the shocks of the night. In terms of their overall numbers the death toll was not as bad as feared, though it was the worst beginning to any city invasion he had ever been involved with.

The situation report he received was astonishing. After the initial setbacks, and a natural fear of further attacks, the city was deserted, utterly.

'Not a soul about, sir. They attacked us and they left.'

This surprise had been soon confirmed by reconnaissance in the centre and by observers outside it.

The centre of the city had been evacuated. If, as was likely, there were going to be further attacks, they would be by night and the Fyrd were not going to be taken by surprise two nights running.

'Or ever again in this city!' declared Quatremayne, whose rage was now giving way to triumph and relief and a desire for revenge.

Which was why, as he marched at the head of his troops into the Main Square, he was looking and feeling a great deal happier than he had been first thing in the morning.

Indeed, the old levity had returned and his field officers – his staff officers having been summarily sent off to search the bunker near Coventry – were at his side, laughing and joking. The memory of the deaths in the night, horrible though they were, were fading. At least, they were fading in the hearts and minds of those likely to benefit from pretending they had not really happened.

For others, the ranks and junior officers, Quatremayne's image had been tarnished and might never be as bright as it had been before. They would see and he would see. It was now all about image and perception.

So it was that he mounted the steps of the Residence, sent in some Fyrd to check out the building, and turned to face his troops, much as Blut had done the night before.

Like Blut, his mouth was dry – and like him too he sought inspiration. A way of lightening things. Of recovering lost ground by making his troops see him in a warmer light. But he never got started. For it was at that very moment Bedwyn Stort heaved open the Library doors opposite where the General stood and stepped out into the Main Square for all to see.

47

QUICK EXIT

Stort was now obsessed with proving that his suspicions about ã
Faroün's true origins would lead him to work out where to look
for the gem of Autumn.

Once out in the open he was very surprised to see that the Main
Square was full of uniforms, a multitude of Fyrd, no less, all with their
backs to him.

But what of that!?

He had bigger and more important things on his mind than a
military parade. What he wanted to do, and he could not see that it
would inconvenience anyone if he did, was to confirm what the paper
in his hand seemed already to suggest incontrovertibly, which was that
thing which he and Blut had missed.

Stort began down the steps, heading across the Square, when the
tall fellow standing opposite, who appeared to be about to make an
address from the Residence steps, stopped doing so and stared in his
direction and fell into an almost stupefied silence. As did everyone
else. It was as if they saw something so unimaginable that they were
all, at one blow, deprived of words.

Stort looked over his shoulder to see if there was something else
that had had this effect on them, but he saw nothing. So, a little more
slowly lest they behave in some way oddly, he began to wend his way
through their ranks.

Indeed it was true; General Quatremayne could not believe his eyes.

The enemy had disappeared entirely, the citizens of Brum were gone, and the only individual who remained had appeared through the great doors opposite and began to walk in his direction.

'He is not armed, sir,' said one of his officers.

'He has no trews, General, which is very strange.'

'Sir, that sleeping hat on his head is very funny, is it not so?' said another, laughing derisively.

'I can see him with my own eyes,' said General Quatremayne acidly, 'and come to my own conclusions.'

His instinct was to ask one of his Fyrd to put a bolt through this lunatic's heart and have done with it.

But then he noticed something. Some of the men were quietly laughing and looking at Quatremayne for a cue. Others could barely contain themselves, beginning to double up with mirth.

Quatremayne saw a chance to have some fun in the way he liked, at another's expense.

'Gentlemen,' he said with mock grandeur, 'I give you . . . the enemy!'

Up on the highest floor of the Residence, in the famous Chamber of Seasons, Festoon and Blut had lost all sense of time and were unaware of what was happening outside. They had been told Quatremayne was still hours from the centre and had not imagined they would arrive so soon. The powerful imagery, the shifting perspectives and the odd way the octagonal room itself did not seem to stay still had taken them to another world. They had examined the imagery of Spring and Summer and looked with interest at the two doors associated with them, the first of which Festoon had been through two years before.

'It took me, I don't know how, up onto Waseley Hill from where, with the help of Bedwyn Stort, I made my escape from Igor Brunte in the days he was my enemy.'

'Strange,' said Blut.

'Magical,' replied Festoon. 'Mirror knows where you'd end up if you tried to go through one of these other doors.'

They had reached the section of the Chamber concerned with Autumn and were standing by that door, the word 'Autumn' embossed in faded gold paint above it. The door itself was dusty, its brass fittings black with age, its hinges corroded.

'It would be a job opening it, I should think,' Blut was just saying as their musings were interrupted by the rumble and clatter of an ancient lift.

It was Jack and Katherine arriving by the only way to get to that highest level of the Residence. The lift clattered to a stop, the doors were pulled open and the two dashed out.

'The Fyrd are here,' explained Jack urgently, 'and Stort's lost!'

'Well, he's not with us,' said Festoon matter-of-factly, 'and that means we're in an even worse situation. There are ways out of here but we cannot leave without Stort . . .'

'If you mean the basement,' said Katherine, 'we just searched it and then started upwards before taking the lift. The Fyrd were on the steps outside and you can't be sure some of them haven't started searching the building. We can't escape that way.'

Jack looked at Festoon and he at Jack. There was another way, because they had used it before, but it carried risks and might easily not work. They listened and heard no sounds from below.

Jack ran to the lift and blocked the doors open.

'We need to think,' he said. 'Trust Stort! You should have tied him to his bed in his humble, Katherine. Where *is* he?'

The only change Festoon had ever made to the Chamber was to have some slit-like windows cut into one side to relieve the claustrophobia he felt in there. These overlooked the Square and they now went to them.

As they did so they heard the sound of group laughter, deep, loud, male and prolonged. It was guttural and unpleasant.

They looked out and saw forty or so Fyrd in the Square they had just crossed.

'Er . . . I hate to say it,' Festoon said calmly, 'but *there's* Stort.'

The Library doors were open and at the foot of the steps from it, heading towards the centre of the Square, seemingly oblivious of the Fyrd and their General by the Residence, was Bedwyn Stort. Their hearts sank.

He was in a shirt, with a jacket to keep him warm but no trews, and a nightcap, complete with bobble, on his head. It was evidently so breathtakingly strange that he had half-crossed the square before anyone there had reacted or even said a word.

It was Jack who spoke.

'I'm not going to argue about this with any of you,' he said in a low voice, 'and I am going to demand as Stavemeister of this city that in this circumstance you obey my command.'

He held his stave of office close.

It began glowing with an angry, icy fire. He too was changed: in some way looming and large, his eyes intense, his determination clear.

'The only sure way to save Stort is if I go back the way we just came,' he said grimly. 'That's the way I am going to go and I'm going by myself.'

'No, Jack!' cried Katherine.

'Oh, yes,' he said, 'alone.'

'*Jack*,' said Katherine warningly, fearing what might happen, as did Festoon. Blut looked puzzled.

Festoon drew himself to his full height, which was considerably more than Katherine's, tall though she was, and put a hand on her arm.

Jack led them, with Katherine protesting, right up to the door marked Autumn.

'It's the only way, though Mirror knows where you'll end up,' he said.

With that he heaved it open, signalled to Festoon to keep hold of the protesting Katherine's arm and ushered them through, Blut last of all. There was a rush of air from outside which was so filled with Autumn leaves that they could hardly see beyond.

'Go on!' Jack said, giving Blut a final shove after the others and closing the door upon them all.

The leaves had barely fallen at his feet before Jack turned to the lift, his stave very firmly in his hand, freed the doors he had blocked, stepped inside, closed them behind him and turned the heavy brass lever that made the lift descend to 'B' for Basement.

Stort, still in his heightened mood of scientific curiosity, proceeded through the idiotic, laughing Fyrd to that point in the Square where he could test his theory: that ā Faroün, great hydden that he was, was nothing more nor less than a hydden from Cornwall who pined for home.

He peered at the ground and finally, by a knot of Fyrd who were in his path, he saw again the Centre of the Universe, the star of cobbles laid by the fraudster himself, whose design for it he held in his hand.

'Make way!' cried Stort, 'I need to see!'

Laughing, they let him pass.

He was right, the design was the same as that so cleverly 'lost' in the Embroidery.

He went down on his knees and crawled amidst the booted Fyrd, picking dirt from the cobbles to make things clearer.

And there it was, as on the design, a tiny piece of russet-coloured glass, wedged tight between the cobbles, right in the very centre of the star.

Which was not Brum and Mercia, but Cornwall. Not even Cornwall, but a south-western part of it. A tiny place.

'No more than a village, I daresay,' said Stort, 'but it was his home.'

But already he knew its name was something like 'Varoun' and for proof absolute he needed only look at the brass disc set around the cobbles which named the continents and the capital cities and much else that was important.

Smallest of all, in engraved letters almost too tiny to see amongst other more important names, was the name Veryan. From which he made up 'Faroün'.

'And he did return there, don't you see, gentlemen,' said Stort, speaking to the Fyrd as if lecturing them, he went there at the end of his life, but secretly, for he wanted to feel a child again, not a celebrity! And he went at Samhain and he took with him a gem he had as a gift to the place and people who made him what he became . . . yes, that's it. That's where it is . . .'

Stort might have continued in this vein had not the awfulness of the situation he was in suddenly dawned upon him.

He had a nightcap on, he had no trews and he was surrounded by Fyrd who were laughing now but were all armed and might not laugh for long.

Terror caught him.

He turned white.

He stared about in desperate hope that somewhere, someone might

offer him a helping hand in that moment of dire need. He knew where
the gem was, time was running out and forty Fyrd were about to attack
him as one.

'Help!

'Help,' he said again, and help he suddenly found.

Jack's choice of the basement of the High Ealdor's Residence as his
destination was deliberate. He knew its layout and that the access to
the basement from ground level was not immediately obvious. If Fyrd
were already checking the building while Quatremayne spoke to his
officers it was likely they would go up, not down. Jack hoped that by
the time he climbed the stairs to the ground level he might have a
clear run outside.

He did, at least as far as the main doors.

These were ajar and he could see Quatremayne's back. He was
addressing a crowd of Fyrd in the Square. Jack guessed that the one
speaking, who was in a well-pressed uniform and lean, tall and silver-
haired, was the General himself.

He was immediately tempted to strike him down and have done
with him, but that short gain would inevitably reduce what little time
he had to save Stort out in the Square and, perhaps, himself. He
decided on surprise and speed.

He moved silently to the door so that Quatremayne was not more
than a few feet away. The foyer was dark, which meant that Jack could
not easily be seen.

He examined the Fyrd and saw they were relaxed, mostly staveless,
their crossbows and dirks hanging loose from their belts. Those nearest
Stort and laughing at him disbelievingly looked like more senior
officers. There were a few guards armed and ready on the outside of
the group to right and left.

From his vantage point Jack could just see Barklice lurking out of
sight of the Square itself, waiting, no doubt, for a signal or sound that
told him someone was on the way towards him who would need to be
got out fast.

The Fyrd were on the Residence side of the Square; the side
between the centre, where Stort was, and Barklice, was now nearly
empty because they had moved nearer the General.

Jack heard feet on the stairs behind him as he decided on the only course of action he could take: surprise, speed and total resolution.

He moved through the doors slowly so as not to be immediately seen but then leaned forward, took his great stave in both hands in a fighting position and moved very fast to one side of the three by the door and down the steps.

The attention of most of the Fyrd was on the General, waiting to see what command he might give about Stort, for the joke could only last so long. So the reaction to Jack's sudden dash to one side and straight through those in front was, as he hoped, total surprise. It was only when he passed the fourth of the Fyrd that any began to react, with the exception of a single guard, one of those patrolling, on the right side which Jack had taken.

He saw Jack, raised his crossbow, but hesitated. If he missed he would almost certainly maim or kill one of his own officers. As he dropped his bow to his belt to take up a short stave instead, Jack swerved towards him and thrust his stave hard into his chest. Even before he was down Jack was on his way back towards Stort, but now he was on the outside of the group, making his progress simpler.

The guards on the far side could not see clearly what was going on and it was this, and the confusion that now ran through the Fyrd as they turned from Stort or the General to see what the trouble was, on which Jack now relied.

He buffeted two Fyrd out of the way, reached Stort, grabbed him bodily and hustled him past another Fyrd.

He whistled, the frightened face of Barklice appeared, and Jack pushed Stort towards him.

'Run, Stort, and . . .'

'My dear Jack . . .' began Stort, stalling at once.

'. . . don't say a single word! *Run!*'

Which Stort then did, in a manner of speaking, for he was never the athletic type. But even his long gangly legs could carry him along when death was chasing behind.

Satisfied he was on his way, Jack turned to fight off opposition as he himself backed towards Fazeley Street.

The first guard he had hit was still down, the other two running round the group to get clear sight of him, their crossbows at the ready.

One or two other Fyrd were already freeing theirs from their belts, but nearest him were two with staves.

His own stave was now alive in his hand, catching the morning light as he struck the first down and then, buffeting the other to still him, dashed the stave out of his hand.

He knew that the danger was going to be bolts from crossbows, any one of which could instantly disable him. He had no doubt that the Fyrd would then come in for the kill.

He was about to use the officer he had just disarmed as a shield when he spotted an old Fyrd, rather smaller but wearing high-ranking insignia. He moved straight at him, grabbed and turned him and, using him as a shield instead, backed faster still.

The ruse worked. The Fyrd he had hold of was no match for Jack, so he shouted instead for his colleagues and subordinates not to shoot. They ran forward, crossbows cocked, but, apart from one wild shot along the ground, which grazed Jack's foot, and another from the far side, which he felt sting his hip, no one fired.

'This way,' cried Barklice. He could see that Jack dared not look round.

'To your right!'

Jack felt a sudden breeze hit his right side as the hands of Barklice and Stort grabbed him and pulled him round the corner.

'Run!' he said, turning, but now holding the hapless senior Fyrd by the collar as temporary hostage and dragging him as well. 'Run!'

And they did, straight to Arnold's craft, into which they dived without care or caution.

Jack shoved the officer into the water below without ceremony as Arnold Mallarkhi sang out, 'Where to, Mister Stort, my freckly friend?'

'Cornwall,' cried Stort, breathlessly, 'and fast.'

Arnold needed no further instruction. As the main body of the Fyrd charged round the corner from the Square, he pushed off and steered the craft down the river at speed, between buildings and away out of sight.

48
THE ROOK

'He'll come; I'm certain of it,' said Katherine, 'as I am that this is the right place. That's how all this works. We just have to wait and be patient.'

'I suppose she has a point,' sighed Festoon, whose interest in travelling about Englalond had never been great. Brum offered all he needed.

It had seemed that at the same moment they had passed through the door marked Autumn, the three reluctant travellers had arrived, at a place Katherine immediately recognized.

It was on the eastern bank of the River Severn, not far from the town of Half Steeple, which sat where the River Somer joined the bigger river.

It was the same bluff where, in mid-August, she, Jack and Stort had stood after their brief stay in Cleeve.

Katherine had felt a sudden whim then to head south to the West Country. With that feeling there had been some kind of tremble and shift around them, which Stort had also noted. The kind which seemed associated in some way with earth tremors.

The moment had passed and they had decided to cross the Severn and climb the Malvern Hills in an attempt to take the less usual road to Brum.

'Now here we are again, or rather here I am. But I think Jack and the others will soon be too. It was in the wyrd of that strange journey from White Horse Hill that we ended up here and I wonder if, as far as the search for the gem of Autumn goes, we should have stayed?'

'Well, I'm glad you did not just stay here and do nothing,' said Blut drily. 'If you had, I would still be in a bunker with Arthur and—'

'And I, and a great many others in Brum would be dead,' added Festoon. 'But I do not like to be so far from the city that is my life in its time of need. I must trust that the measures we put in place for the dispersal and evacuation of our citizens have resulted in as few casualties as possible.'

Katherine quickly realized that neither of her two companions had any practical experience of travelling at all. She took over at once and insisted they climbed higher to be well clear of the floodplain. That gave them an unrivalled view of the area below, Half Steeple included, where they expected Jack and Stort to arrive.

'How will they come?'

'Barklice will be in charge of route-finding but they have Arnold with them, so I would expect they'll come a watery way. Which will also be safer from Fyrd.'

'How long will they take?'

Katherine hesitated because she was not certain what day it really was.

Both times they had been here time had shifted in an odd way. She knew that travelling through portals did the same thing and she suspected that, though their journey seemed instant, time might have warped.

She soon found it had.

Since there was no way of knowing the day where they were, and none of them had a chronometer that showed the date, she took a walk by night with Blut into Half Steeple and worked it out from a newspaper she found.

Three days had passed. About the time it might take for Arnold and Barklice to get Stort there. The town was crammed to overflowing with humans, many camping on the floodplain between town and river.

'Are all human towns so filled up with people?' Blut wondered.

'This one's special. A miracle happened here once and maybe they think it will again.'

She told them what Stort said about Half Steeple and its strange name and how the town had escaped the Black Death in 1349. Then about the poem, written centuries earlier, which described a place destroyed and its half steeple. Finally about rooks flying backwards.

'Did Stort have an opinion about the significance of this strange and fanciful history?' asked Festoon.

'He thought it was part of the long tradition of prophecy that forecasts there will be an end of days,' explained Katherine.

'And Beornamund's gems, what of those, and in particular that of Autumn? Does this town, which looks very intact and safe to me, have anything to do with that?'

'Ask him,' said Katherine, 'not me.'

'When he comes,' said Festoon. 'Meanwhile I have seen no rooks flying backwards!'

A cawing came to them from the trees Katherine had seen before.

'Yet,' added Festoon.

'How will they see us if they arrive in the dark?' asked Blut.

'I left a white marker at the place we stood at before, which they'll see. Barklice will work out that we moved up here.'

She was right.

That same evening, as they talked by a fire, a lone craft hove into view on the shadowy river below, with four people inside.

'That's surely them,' she said with relief.

They cautiously retreated a little, in case they were wrong, but left the fire burning as the boat's crew hauled in their craft. They watched as they found Katherine's marker and conferred for a while, no more than shadows in the dark.

'They're coming up . . .'

They had come at last, but their reunion was subdued, the events of recent days having shaken them all.

Jack held Katherine tight while Stort, whose late venture to the Library had so nearly caused disaster, even if its outcome had been to show him where the gem was most likely to be and how to find it, apologized to them all.

'We would have been here a day earlier,' said Jack to Festoon and Blut, 'but since you both had to leave the city rather fast, and I guessed you were not nearby, I felt it my duty as Stavemeister to see what the Fyrd did when they took over.

'We spied about a little and made contact with Mister Pike, whose stavermen were in place in their covert hidey-holes and keeping an eye on things. All was quiet. The Fyrd seemed surprised there was no further resistance. There was no attempt to destroy buildings or mount expeditions into the suburbs.

'Pike reported a Fyrd killed trying to remove the drawing of Emperor Blut's spectacles on the Library building. It seems that gets to them.

'But worse will surely follow in time and I hope that none of the stavermen or the bilgesnipe hiding out on the waterways gets caught.'

'They won't, not they!' said Arnold. 'For they'm born and bred to that fair city and knows its guts and innards well enough to hide out fro' they dark Fyrdyones!'

'Oh, and we brought a friend,' said Jack suddenly, when a broad figure loomed up the path from below. 'Dropped him off earlier on the far side of Half Steeple as he wanted to take a look.'

It was Terce, in his robe, looking a good deal fitter and stronger than when they first met him two months before at Abbey Mortaine.

Terce grinned but, as usual, said little, offering no explanation of how he had joined Stort and the others.

'I confess,' said Stort, 'that in the rush to get to the Library I quite forgot about Terce, only remembering after our escape from the Square. Fortunately he was sitting in my kitchen, to which we returned for my things, taking tea all by himself.'

'So here he now be among us, bright as a button and built like a tree!' said Arnold. 'He be handy in a boat and a-hauling out the water, but large, so we found a bigger craft!'

'So,' said Blut, after the new arrivals had been watered and fed, 'quite a gathering! Has anyone any clear idea beyond doomful prophecies about why we're here?'

Stort said, 'We're waiting for a sign, like rooks flying . . . er . . .'

'Backwards,' said Blut. 'Yes, I heard.'

'But not for long,' said Stort, 'meaning, not after tomorrow. We have to travel on . . . a little. Well, quite a lot! We now know, or think we know, where the gem is.'

'Explain to them,' said Jack.

Stort explained what he had discovered in the Library and that a place called Veryan in Cornwall was their destination.

'All that remains is to decide how to get there,' said Stort.

'By road, *I* say,' said Barklice.

'Rail's my preference,' said Jack.

'River and sea, my hearties,' said Arnold, 'safer they be and more certain.'

Katherine reminded them that the West Country was where she had thought they should go in the first place.

But it was late and they were tired and further talk of where they went next had to wait until the following day.

Blut couldn't sleep. The world felt dark and he suddenly missed his Lord Sinistral, whose presence and clear mind seemed needed just then. Naturally Blut had heard of wyrd, and it had never made sense to him to think that things happened for no reason. There was an order to the Universe, a harmony to its *musica*. Things didn't just happen. Wyrd was the Mirror's purpose which, often, was beyond the hearts and minds of mortal kind to understand.

Restive as he was, he was last asleep and first to wake, staring down at the mist on the meadow by the Severn below them to their left and at Half Steeple, which was misty too so that only its church steeple rose out of the cloud.

As Blut watched and the others began to wake he saw a single rook fly out of the mist from the tree where the others had been.

Backwards.

Blut's heart and mind froze. He understood at once the significance of what he saw because Katherine had explained it. It now seemed certain that the end of days was coming.

He thought of drawing the others' attention to it but did not. What, after all, could they or anyone do?

He had thought of Sinistral the night before and now knew he was right to do so. He was needed, needed by them all, needed by the Hyddenworld.

So, too, was someone else perhaps, who had been left behind: Arthur.

'He'll be safe with Mister Pike,' they had all said, one way and another.

Blut was suddenly not so sure.

The rook flew backwards slowly, as if its time had run out. An old bird with feathers missing and grey claws hooked with age who couldn't keep up with life any more, as it disappeared into the mist over Half Steeple.

49

HALF STEEPLE

Later that morning Arnold said, 'The river b'aint herseln. She worn't herseln comin' here and I can tell you straight she be a lot worse now. I'm movin' our craft up a bit to safety. Come and help, lads.'

Jack and Terce went with Arnold and dragged his boat higher, in among trees.

He got a lanyard and tied her loosely, 'so she'm able to move about a bit.'

'After this we go south,' said Stort.

After what? No one knew exactly.

Festoon and Blut shook their heads, thinking they must get back towards Brum.

Terce said he wanted to go back to Mortaine, which wasn't that far.

Jack and Katherine weren't sure but they'd go with Stort to Cornwall. Barklice said the same but, 'It's a long way that Cornwall, a long, long way and I doubt you'll get there for Samhain.'

Only Arnold was certain of anything.

'We'm must and we will, my doubting lads and lady one, and this Mallarkhi will see you right!'

A short while later Jack suddenly shouted, 'The river down there, below the tributary . . . it's flowing *backwards*.'

The sky darkened as they stared, the air stilled and chilled.

Stort took out his monocular.

He confirmed it was.

'Aye, it be,' agreed Arnold, looking away as if he was watching a death.

Jack switched direction and pointed past where the tributary joined the Severn.

'That ... the ... two ... parts ... of the river ... are flowing *towards* each other and ... By the Mirror! Look *there!*'

'Got it, eleven o'clock from the church,' murmured Stort helpfully, 'maybe a shade more.'

'Um ... wow!' said Katherine.

'It looks like there's steam rising from that point of the river ...' said Jack.

'Not steam but a column of spray,' explained Stort.

He studied the odd phenomenon.

'It's caused by the meeting of two flows of water from opposite directions sending fine droplets of water upwards as they flow into the ground and plummet downward into ... into the bowels of the Earth! What we are witnessing is a sudden, localized but catastrophic collapse in the Earth's surface to form a sinkhole into which both parts of the river are flowing. That column of spray is the inevitable result.'

They watched in awe as the pale, swirling column rose higher, until it caught a glint of sun, and a small, intense rainbow came and went at its topmost point.

Their attention shifted to the town itself, which, from their position, looked as if it was going about its normal morning business. Most people seemed not to have seen the drama developing in the river. But a quarter of a mile beyond it, traffic was slowing and drivers opened their windows to stare.

From their vantage point they could see that the church was a very old one and the centre of a medieval cluster of cottages. At that moment, no place could have seemed prettier, no place more settled and secure. Its prosperous past seemed resonant in every stone and kerb, its happy present at every garden gate and turn, and its future ... its secure future soared aloft into the blue sky from the church itself in the form of its steeple.

The church stood on a slight rise, surrounded by a large, well-mown churchyard whose many gravestones, most covered in lichen, a few with thick ivy, others very new from a recent interment, with flowers mouldering, told of the centuries of the thousand-year-old community.

Stort and the others shifted their attention back to the sight of three mallard flying up suddenly from the water, disturbing others along the river and its banks, who flew up as well. The river's surface now grew darker and troubled, its strange flow slowing, the rushes along its bank trembling.

Four cygnets they had seen earlier reappeared, now flapping their downy and inadequate wings as they desperately paddled against a current that was trying to push them backwards, towards the sinkhole. The swans that had been with them had gone.

Then one of the cygnets gave up, turned sideways and was sucked suddenly into the foaming spray. Then another, a third and finally the fourth, clawing frantically at water too powerful for it, squawking for its life before, like a switch turned off, its pale body was gone into darkness.

The sun still shone, the column of spray rose no higher than before, people continued what they were doing, many not yet noticing the plight of the water fowl, the river's peculiar flows and the sinkhole.

They felt they now were witnesses to an unstoppable drama, a horrible thing. But if their instinct was to turn and flee and find shelter, their feet were rooted to the ground.

Then, as suddenly as it had risen, the column of spray fell back and the river's flow returned to normal.

'The hole must have filled,' said Stort, 'and the river's now flowing the way it should again.'

Three of the mallard swung back into view, circled the place where the sinkhole had been and landed on the bubbling water. Cows in an adjacent field, which had stopped grazing, began to do so again.

Finally, a pair of swans appeared high across the fields, heads and necks pointing their way back home. They came in low, circling as the mallard had done, and landed in the field between the cows and the river. They immediately set off for the water's edge.

'They're looking for the cygnets,' said Katherine softly.

One of the church bells rang a solitary note. Just that, no more. A toll of time.

The crisis seemed over; all felt good.

But Stort was shaking his head uneasily.

'Do not be deceived,' he said. 'When the Earth shows her teeth she is rarely so benign as to limit her appetite to four cygnets. This is surely the calm before the storm.'

The surface of the river was now so calm and flat that it reflected once more the light in the sky above. It snaked away into the distance.

A couple more mallard returned to the water.

The swans made their cumbrous way through the longer grass and reeds back onto the river, looking for their young.

'Seems all right to me,' said Jack, turning towards his 'sac to heave it on and encourage the others to move. He felt they were too exposed.

But he took no more than a couple of steps.

'Jack!'

Stort had no need to point, Katherine was already doing so.

No sooner had the swans settled down, ruffling their wings to rid them of excess water, than one of them was suddenly sinking beneath the water, straining its neck, scrabbling its paddles, trying desperately to raise its wings against the weight of water that flowed over them.

Its mate turned its way, stared, and then began to sink as well, but backwards, rump and wings first, feet scrabbling in thin air. Then they were gone beneath the surface entirely, one after the other like stricken ships unable to stay afloat a second longer.

Even as this was happening, the cows in the adjacent pasture raised their heads as one, turned and looked towards the river, and started to run in the opposite direction across the grass, bellowing in panic as they did so. For a moment it was hard to make out what they were trying to do or why . . . but then it became all too clear.

The field was tipping backwards and they were struggling to run uphill in a field that had been flat seconds before. They were running for their lives and failing.

The sinkhole, which had so quickly come and gone, had returned, but much wider than before.

The river and the fields on either side, along with hedgerows and trees, a water butt and a fence, were being tipped backwards and down into it as the first cow lost its balance entirely and slipped into a mixture of water and mud, its bellows stopping suddenly, its front hoofs threshing before they too were gone from sight.

The column of spray reappeared, as the north and south flows of the river crashed into each other once more.

There were flashes of silver and green in the column as if it was shot through with silk.

'Fish,' said Stort.

Then heavier, ragged shadows dark and green-brown. 'Bushes and mud,' said Katherine.

The perimeter of the sinkhole continued to expand, taking in the garden of a house, then another, then three houses.

The water climbed higher in the sky, a swirling mess of spray and foam, detritus and loose green foliage.

Then the roaring began, like that of a heavy sea at high tide on a shingle shore, on and on, unremitting.

A ragdoll dressed in pink spiralled up with legs and arms all over the place.

'A child,' whispered Jack wanting to run down the hill to save it, but it was already too late.

'A little girl,' said Katherine, reaching a hand towards her helplessly.

That was when they saw a man running wildly towards the expanding sinkhole, screaming. The sound of a man losing his child, his home, his everything, before the scream was cut short as he lost his last possession – his own life.

As he disappeared downward into the Earth, the whole church lurched, first one way then another, its steeple wobbling before righting itself once more, masonry falling and people approaching the church-yard sent spinning into free-fall, some smashing into the ground, others turned over and falling on their backs, one grabbing hold of a gravestone for support.

That did not help.

Like dominoes in slow motion, the gravestones began to fall, some onto grass and others onto the stone structure of the grave of which they were part, where they smashed into pieces. Here a shattered cross, there a fallen angel and near the church itself, where a new grave had been dug, the piled earth simply covered with bunches of faded flowers, the corner of something shiny and brown shot into view. A new coffin.

The bells of the church now started ringing at random, and violently.

A sudden donging, then momentary silence, then several bells at once making a clashing of sound, *dong dong dong doi* . . . *nnng!* It was as if a group of bell-ringers had gone mad, their tugging at the ropes frantic and out of accord with each other.

A thump of metal on wood and stone, a shout and a roar as a crack appeared in the square tower that supported the spire, a woman's scream from within the church, shouting men and, over it all, the first howling of dogs.

The crack in the tower of the church widened and shot up the external masonry like a tear in stiff fabric, the sound of it deeper and louder.

The ground beneath them shook. Jack stepped to the side and then in front of Stort protectively as if, even from so far away, he was in some personal danger from whatever was happening to the village below and now threatened them where they stood. To right and left of them the leaves in the trees nearby trembled and the ground shook more, like the subtlest of shivers.

'But . . .' said Katherine, 'it's . . . there's . . .'

It was impossible to say what was happening because suddenly so much was; and all the while the column of water where the river was, or had been, grew broader at its base, its colour darker with the flotsam it carried spiralling round, amid which they saw dead people, living people, dogs and a last cow.

Swirling around before they sank down, lower and lower, into the open, greedy, hole.

Cars had stopped on the bridge beyond, their foolish drivers getting out to lean on the parapet and stare at the wild water below as if they felt themselves immune from its dangers.

The church steeple swayed again, the bells rang and thumped, and the edge of the widening sinkhole neared a row of old cottages. It paused as if looking at them, hesitated as if thinking and then pushed forward straight at them. They swung as one on their axis, as if caught by a flood; someone inside one of them shoved a little window open and tried to look out. Perhaps he had slept late, perhaps risen and fallen, concussed. Whatever his story he was thrown violently back into the darkness of his room now as the cottages tilted high and slid into the hole.

Further off from this maelstrom, people came out of houses to find out what the roaring and shaking was. Those nearest who could see the horror turned and tried to escape. Those further off, their view obscured by their neighbours' houses, made the mistake of coming forward.

As for the bridge, it lurched too and the people staring down began to fall forward, helpless to stop themselves, their cars sliding after them into the water.

The column was now clogged up with mud and trees, cars and people, and it rose higher still as, all around it, dust shot into the air to the sound of small explosions. The sun, briefly bright, became muted, the sky angry grey. As for the sinkhole, it spread ever wider, sucking all that was in its path straight down.

Then the church itself tilted and sank towards the hole, breaking free of the tower at its eastern end, the roof and walls falling away to reveal rows of pews, someone clutching at a Norman column, the top half of someone else's body protruding from fallen stones, a scream on their faces. Then all that dropped away into the darkness, drenched by filthy water filled with things as they went, before being overwhelmed and lost.

The day was overtaken by a cracking, roaring, ripping violence of sound beneath which, like disharmonious bass notes to a terrible tune, came roars and subterranean rumblings.

All the time, the people on the far outer edge of these events who could hear but not properly see made the mistake of walking towards the void and falling or being sucked suddenly to their own frightening deaths.

Further north, another column of water shot into the sky; the ground ripped open and a secondary sinkhole appeared where the bridge had been and was no more. It widened and for a brief moment a man and his wife were caught between the two, facing an impossible choice. They each ran, in opposite directions, and then their ground was gone and they plunged down into chaos, the crushing, suffocating, darkness of a liquid mud filled with the dying, the dead and all the inanimate objects between.

The crystalline dust that rose up from the ruins of the houses billowed higher still, clear of the dirt and catching the dark light. Below the maelstrom of tumbling, breaking, falling, imploding cottages and cars, people and dust, asphalt and vegetation, everything turned and sank, boiled and frothed like the rolling boil of jam in a preserving pan.

The huge void looked like the maw of a great beast whose solitary fang was the spire of the church, rocking back and forth but held in place by the rock on which it had originally been built, like the last incisor poking from a filthy jaw bone.

Half Steeple seemed almost nothing now but its own spire.

It became too hard for Jack, Katherine and Stort to watch, too terrible, utterly incomprehensible. One by one they turned away, as if to look was to do a shaming thing.

Yet further off, across the landscape beyond Half Steeple, the sun was out. A train moved across the horizon, cars along roads, an aeroplane in the sky.

For Stort and the others, time had ceased to be, as initial shock was replaced by a kind of drifting wonder at what they were reluctant witnesses to.

Stort had glanced at his chronometer when the trouble began, but when he did so again, assuming that ten or fifteen minutes had passed, he saw that it was little more than seconds, a minute perhaps, no more than two. What had happened was so shocking, so vast in its scale, so bewildering, that words failed them all. So, at first, did any notion of taking action. There was nothing they could do, together or separately. Nothing anyone could do.

Half Steeple and its people were in the grip of Mother Earth. She, who had given them life and abundance for so many centuries and millennia, was calling in her debt and taking back her own.

Now, wherever they looked, disaster and tragedy were in the making. To the north, coming down the Malvern road, a silver-grey vehicle sped towards what was now a vast hole in the ground in which the remnants of the village were violently stirred about by an unseen hand.

It reached a roundabout as, weirdly, the garage that was there exploded in a ball of flames and black smoke, which prompted the driver to put his foot down and accelerate ever faster to his doom, thinking he was escaping it. His vehicle began to swerve from side to side on a road whose camber had begun to shift, until, too late, the road steepened, broke up and took him and his car into the swirling stew.

To their far left, almost behind them, a flash of colour appeared along the same road from the opposite direction, red and yellow. It was a racing cyclist, then another, then two more.

'No!' screamed Katherine. 'No . . .'

They were too far off to hear and if they saw the rising dust and smoke and plumes of water ahead, they did not show it, their heads down, their feet pumping at their pedals. They rounded a corner, the leader sat up, puzzled by the shaking in the road perhaps, but it was too late.

He tried to stop, turning sideways to the way he was going, right foot on the road, but the ones behind crashed into him and as the road fell away suddenly, they too were all gone into the void, the wheels of their bikes turning slowly as they went.

Then things stilled and silence of a kind fell. Birds and wildfowl, which had first fled in panic and then come back, circled the village high up, in and out of the vast billowing cloud of dust, their bearings lost and their sense of purpose all gone, dark against the sky, like the ashes of burnt paper above a fire.

The air thickened and grew acrid, a slight breeze brought dust over the hill and into their faces. They coughed and turned, stumbling into the wood behind them, eyes streaming, faces drained of colour, words failing in their mouths.

'Stort,' began Jack, 'Stort . . . ?'

Stort sat on the wood floor, his weight against a tree, eyes down, head shaking, as shocked as his friends.

'It isn't over,' he said, 'there's something worse coming.'

The wood darkened and they saw that the drifting dust cloud had obscured the sun, casting a pall of twilight and sudden cold over where Half Steeple had been.

'There must be survivors,' said Jack, staring to the edge of the wood again.

'There may be,' said Katherine, 'but there are some who do not understand what's happened or that there is still great danger.'

She pointed to people who were approaching the village along roads and lanes from all directions, alerted by the dust and rumbling Earth, some in cars, some running, some walking from farms and houses towards the edge of the destruction.

'We stay where we are,' said Jack firmly. 'Go down there and we go to our deaths.'

The others agreed.

He was right and so was Stort; it wasn't over.

The Earth shook again and began to roar and rumble. The edges of the void rose up in a vast circle, a vile raised hole, like something organic, filthy, ulcer-like. The lips of this foul thing pouted horribly and then began to close in towards themselves, a mouth closing.

It narrowed, it moved inward, the hole began simply to disappear. Until what teetered on the edge of the darkness were whole houses, stretches of unbroken grass and the church tower with its twisted steeple around which the mouth was closing.

The tower began to sink into the ground.

Down it went, grass and rubble all around and an occasional gravestone that had survived the sinking earlier.

Down like a sinking ship at sea, upended, clinging on, then shooting down into oblivion. First the tower then the steeple, a third, a bit more, a half, and then . . . it stopped.

Dead, as if it had hit solid rock.

Still.

Vertical once more, but half gone.

Half Steeple was gone, but a half steeple remained.

Stort shook his head in wonderment.

Katherine wanted to weep but her shock was too deep and she could not.

Jack said, 'We had better see if there's anything we can do.'

But his words came out thick as if covered in dust, without purpose or intent. Before such monstrosity there was nothing mortal kind could do.

Arnold said, 'My boat's gone. Stay here, there's some down there.'

He set off before stopping and looking back.

'I'll get you all away,' he said, 'south-westward like Mister Stort says. Where you better find that gem and give it up to her who did this!'

'Who was that?' asked Jack.

'Her!' said Arnold, setting of at speed down the hill. '*Her!*'

It was hard to see what he meant, for it was dark by the river and dust swirled about confusingly.

They couldn't see much.

Just dogs and riders on them and the form of a woman, bent and broken, weeping and wending across the wild waters there. It was Judith the Shield Maiden.

She cast not a single glance towards where Stort stood, but he did at her. Then the dust swirled and fell and she was gone, cursing as she went, and the dogs with her.

'The end of days has begun,' said Stort.

Arnold waved from far below.

He had found a boat drifting, a big clinker-built thing, which he swung with the flow to the shore.

He raised an arm and Stort raised one back.

'We're leaving,' he said, 'all of us together. Rough the water may be but who can trust our Mother Earth after what we have been witness to? Agreed, Jack? Everybody?'

'Agreed,' they said one by one, the risk seeming as great whatever they did. But they were all together now and on their way south and west to fulfil a quest that might be the only thing protecting all life itself from the end of days.

50

GETTING THERE

S tort now knew where they were going, but so did others too.
Quatremayne knew.

My Lord Sinistral knew.

Leetha as well.

And Borkum Riff.

Katherine had a vague idea. When they first stood on the bank of
the Severn discussing which way to go, didn't she turn south-westward
as if hearing a song to her heart? She did.

But she let it go and turned with Stort and Jack and left it behind
when they went the wrong way.

Did Jack know where they were going, even now? He knew what he
wanted but not how to get there. He'd fight for them all, right to the
death, but he couldn't hear *musica* to save his soul.

So Jack didn't know but maybe he would.

As for Arthur, he didn't know where to find the gem.

But Quatremayne did because Bedwyn Stort let his paper drop in the
Main Square when he ran for his life and later they found his notes in
the stacks.

What took him months took them a few minutes. The name of the
place matched that on the brass in the Square; its position, give or
take, was that of the small broken piece of russet glass set fast in the
cobbles.

'I think,' said Quatremayne, his smooth cheeks perspiring and his
eyes as shiny as grease, 'that we may now say, gentlemen, that the

secret is out. The gem of Autumn is in or near a place called Veryan. Since we may safely say that Brum is secure, but for a few insurgents, then we have time to turn our attention to the gem. Why should we bother? Because I can think of no quicker or easier way to secure our position in the hearts and minds of the absent citizens of this city, and lure them back so that we can get it up and running once more, than for us to be seen to bring the gem back to its home. Can you?'

They were on the steps of the Residence once more; the city had now been occupied without incident for several days. Its citizens were nowhere to be seen except in suburbs so widespread that they were impossible to hunt down.

'True,' he pronounced, 'there are some minor irritations . . .'

He said it coolly but he did not fool his new officers.

He was referring to the image that kept appearing overnight in different places all over the city, in every location imaginable: two orbs linked by a half-hoop.

Blut's spectacles.

Usually drawn in chalk.

The worst example was right there across the front elevation of the Library opposite the Residence.

Quatremayne had been forced to look at this huge image of Blut *in absentia* every time he sat at his desk in the building, so he had moved his seat. Then, when he exited by the front entrance, there it was. He was not a hydden to enjoy being pushed into a corner by an image, least of all one that screamed 'Blut!'.

He did not understand it.

Was it a joke?

Whatever it was, it ate away at him.

He said, 'Where is he? That professor whatever his name?'

'Foale, sir.'

'Well, where is the old fool?' he said without respect.

Even they were shocked by Quatremayne. Blut was under his skin and that made him mad.

'Inside,' one of them said, reluctantly. They had better things to do than waste time.

'Bring him here, where Blut's spectacles can see.'

The spectacles gazed impassively across the Square as Arthur Foale was pulled out of the Residence, hands wired tight behind his back, and dropped at Quatremayne's feet.

'Watch this,' said the General, smiling, his minions tittering, 'watch this, Blut.'

He kicked Arthur in the face not once but twice and broke his nose. He kicked him in the gut.

'Can you see, Blut? You cowardly shit you jumped-up . . .'

He kicked Arthur in the mouth and a tooth burst his lip.

And Arthur, in terrible pain and fear, knowing Margaret was dead, called out to the living to help him now.

Jack . . .

Katherine . . .

. . . and you Judith, who knew such pain, you'd know what to do.

'It's enough, sir. "Blut" gets the point.'

The General, after he recovered his humour a little, and breathed more slowly, said, 'We may also say, gentlemen, that Blut is alive, and I am reasonably certain that I know where he will be in forty-eight hours' time, on the last night of October, the eve of Samhain. He will be with his friends.'

His minions nodded.

'I imagine that among them will be that idiot who doesn't wear trews – Stort.'

'Probably, sir.'

'So I have decided, since our job in Brum is done and we have it under control, we may gain much by joining them for Samhain.'

'Sir, I think . . .'

'Don't think.'

'No, General.'

'We will go with force enough to spoil their Samhain and take the gem for ourselves and we'll do it with no more difficulty than our friend Jack and that fool Stort and Meyor Feld stole the gem of Spring from us in Bochum. *Yes?*'

'Yes, sir.'

'By train, nice and fast, in one quick journey. I understand that is possible?'

'Yes, General.'

'I will bring back the gem to this deserted city.'

'Yes, General.'

'I do not like Blut, I never have, but that is not the reason I shall arrest him.'

'No, sir?'

'No, not at all. He is guilty of many things, including – I have good reason to believe – the murder of the former Emperor Slaeke Sinistral.'

They were aghast.

It was a safe lie. Quatremayne had seen Sinistral go off into the Remnants with his own eyes, more or less. He looked as if he was dying then. He was probably dead by now.

'I do not like Brum,' said Quatremayne.

Blood from Arthur's broken face trickled under the General's booted foot.

'General, may I be bold?' said one of his new minions.

'Please.'

'Brum does not like you, my General!'

'Ha ha ha.'

It was a joke and they all laughed, so why did a shard of bitterness stick in Quatremayne's gut?

'And, gentlemen?'

They paused, waited, hanging on his words.

'I think it would be fun to take Mister Arthur whatever with us, to give to Blut, don't you?'

They did, or said they did, treading carefully to avoid the blood.

My Lord Sinistral knew where the gem of Autumn was because he always had.

'I have been there before. It's a windy, lonely, magnificent sort of place.'

'What took you there, my dear?' asked Leetha, her hand to his face. Now he was ageing so fast, and allowing it, he sometimes seemed almost ordinary, just very old. Her love was like a daughter's but her passion for his life and what he was, was that of a fearless lover.

They were sailing in convoy now, having made the crossing from the Channel Islands to Land's End with some difficulty. The weather was foul and not letting up.

From there they sailed to the Lizard and then on along the wild Cornish coast past Falmouth and the Carrick Roads, and then Porthbeor, where rough seas kept them ashore.

'The days are passing, Borkum Riff,' Sinistral complained, 'and once we had plenty to spare. Now time is as good as out, tomorrow's Samhain, so you tell *me* how you get us off this shore!'

No, Sinistral was not happy, nor any of them. The sea takes its toll and at night, on the shore, the waves thundering down and the surf rolling in, their craft looked no stronger than the broken shell of an egg.

Riff was used to this kind of thing but they were not. They were tired and needed better rest than they were getting.

But they were near enough to touch the place now and they knew that on Samhain eve he would insist on making the last stage of their journey, and that Riff would obey, beating to Killgerran Head over water that was nothing but spray and the kind of heavy, violent, seas that break a boat in four.

Riff didn't care, nor Herde Deap, but *they* did.

Meanwhile they hunkered down on the shore and talked, or Sinistral talked and they listened.

'My tutor ã Faroün was a short sort of hydden, with arms and hands like oak roots and a spirit like a raptor in flight.

'He was born of the hydden in a place across this bay called Veryan. From that name, for reasons of longing and because it amused him, he made up the name Faroün. Cornish pronunciation with a touch of the arabesque. The ã was for effect and to get a job. But I saw the beauty of his spirit in all he did and learnt from it. When he was old and dying he talked of his home and spoke of his longing to return.

'"The wind in my hair, the rain on my cheek and the rough falls of ground down to the sea. You cannot imagine it."

'I said I'd bring him home for Samhain. He said no. I said I'd do it anyway. He raged. I said, "Would you take *me*, Faroün, to a place I yearned for as you yearn for home?" He replied, after a time, and more raging, that he would, he would.

'Well then,' said Sinistral, 'now you know why I brought him home. And as for me coming here with Riff and you Leetha ... this is a healing place, and Samhain is a healing time when we celebrate the harvest of our years, whether short or long and however many are left, and we do it at home.'

Leetha nodded.

Borkum Riff looked at their son Herde Deap.

Deap wondered if this Samhain he might ask the question he never had asked.

Slew, his half-brother who had touched the gem and been changed, turned his face to the wind, not sure about Samhain or the thing called home which he had never known. He too had a question to ask since his talk with Riff.

The wind blew hard and cold and washed salt spray into their hearts, where it stung.

'This place I'm taking you to,' said Sinistral, 'has a wind that blows so hard it cleans your body and leaves it pure. Not my words but Faroün's. We all have a need for that once in a while. That's what Samhain does, that's what home should do, that's why tomorrow, whatever the weather, we're going there.'

Arnold Mallarkhi, having used the quieter stages of their journey to teach Terce how to crew, dropped the rest of them at Porthtowan on the north coast and set off at once to round the peninsula to join them at Pendower.

The journey on foot across to Truro was more reliable than sailing round Land's End. They would get there; he might not. They had to; he didn't.

'Fare thee well my lovely ones,' he called out.

Then: 'Terce, listen up, I'm going to teach you a shanty.'

Then he was gone into the surf and they turned inland from the cliff for their long march to the centre of the Earth . . .

It was only as they reached the end of their great crossing of the Cornish peninsula that Stort told them the truth, just as Sinistral told Leetha and the others. It was more or less the same.

'Ā Faroün?' said Stort rhetorically, 'he was a fraud. His name was made up to sound exotic. He was as Cornish as this rough-and-ready land we've had to trek across against the clock. We've been heading for the village where he was born and raised which, I believe, is . . .'

He produced a map of sorts, and a compass and peered about with furrowed brow.

Then he said, 'Not far now!'

They pressed on and crested a rise. They saw as wild a coast as ever was with the sea crashing into cliffs and headlands to right and left, and turmoil of water beyond, as far as the eye could see until it became the sky.

Below them, nestling as sweet as a dormouse in its nest, was Veryan, home place of Faroün.

'Or near enough,' conceded Stort, since the village was human and he a hydden. 'It must be somewhere hereabout.'

'And the gem?' they asked, looking at their chronometers like an inspectorate. 'There isn't much time. Four hours before dark, maybe ten before midnight, when the Shield Maiden wants her due.'

'Humph!' said Stort. 'Let's start looking.'

'For what, exactly?'

'The Centre of the Universe,' he replied.

The Fyrd have a way of making a train stop where they want.

It's a thin hawser with a metal ball on the end which, when let loose under a train bounces along the track and up around the undercroft so loudly that humans think there's damage and stop the train. It's a knack and a skill to get it right, but it works.

Well before dusk, with eight hours left to the start of Samhain, Quatremayne and his force stopped their train at Probus, eight miles inland from Veryan.

The only slow thing about that force was Quatremayne himself, no longer young, and Arthur Foale, broken, shaking, aching and barely able to walk.

'Carry the bugger,' said Quatremayne, 'it's only eight miles and it's a clear night for a march.'

The train stopper was a local picked up in Bodmin who knew the ground from when he was young.

'We'll use moon and stars,' he said. 'We don't trust compasses in these hills or down by the shore; they all go awry like us! Mind you, on Samhain night, everything goes awry. Are you sure this is wise?'

They were, they said, as they shoved Arthur in a litter and started off for the sea.

'You've not said your final destination. Veryan's a human village.'

'Where's the nearest hydden place to it?'

'The Centre of the Universe, where else!'

He stopped and stared at them, these Fyrd from up in real Englalond, this General who had silvery hair and their poor bastard of a dying one who looked like one eye was blind.

'There's such a place?' asked Quatremayne.

'There is but no hydden lives there now.'

'Why not?'

Words failed him and he muttered, 'I'll take you as near as I can . . .'

Across the bay at Killigerran Head Borkum hadn't been able to get their craft past the wind into open water for the long run to Pendower Beach.

Herde Deap the same.

But they were trying, and the Riffs don't give up.

As for Arnold Mallarkhi and Terce, out in the open sea, waves crashing in on all sides, Arnold had no idea where he was or exactly whither he was bound except it was the centre of something or other, which might be the world, but that didn't matter to him just then because he was having the time of his life.

'Old Mallarkhi, if you were here with me now you'd be having a turn and tellin' me it was better in them olden days when you were young, whenever that was! But since you're not and I am I'd better live to tell the tale so I've something to say when I get back home. What was *that*?'

It was a wave as big as the Muggy Duck and more.

He laughed and played his craft in the storm, towards the far and murky coast he saw, which had a light, just one, to show him the way.

The goal of Stort and the others had been Veryan and that had proved not hard to find.

The maps they had were clear and the fingerposts along the way obligingly easy to read. Every road on the Roseland peninsula seemed to lead to Veryan. The landscape itself was verdant but windy, the road and paths set deep between ivy-clad old stone walls, the occasional hawthorn or gorse that grew higher than the rest, hard-bent by vicious sea winds. The air was bracing and tasted of brine and ozone. But having got there more or less they were tired and unsure quite what they were looking for.

It was as they dropped down the folds of the deep landscape towards the village itself, like bugs lost in the folds of a plaid, that there came over them a collective sense that they were beginning to lose time and now going in the wrong direction.

It was Barklice, best route-finder of his generation, who was the first to stop, shaking his head and saying it didn't feel right.

'Going down means we might have to come back up,' he said, 'and if time is of the essence . . .'

'It is,' said Stort rather desperately, 'if we are to find the gem in time to give it to the Shield Maiden when she turns up.'

Barklice stared at him in the strangest of ways, thinking.

Then he cried out, 'What a fool I am! An imposter too! For nobody but a fraud who claims he knows the best routes could not see the blindingly obvious!'

He slapped his face, first with his right hand and then with his left.

He threw himself on the ground and beat it with his fists, as if chastising himself.

Jack and Stort had seen this behaviour before from Barklice, who suffered a sense of guilt and shame if he felt he had let others down.

'Barklice . . .' began Katherine

'Barklice!' said Jack more loudly and commandingly to snap him out of it.

'My dear friend,' said Stort softly, who knew and loved him better than them all, 'whatever is it?'

Barklice reached out a hand from his prostrate position and Stort quickly put a kerchief in it so he could wipe his eyes and compose himself before they hauled him to his feet.

'I am an idiot,' he said. 'If I am not mistaken, Stort, you mentioned a beacon.'

'Indeed I did. This place that ā Faroün dubbed so romantically as the Centre of the Universe is, on the map at least, marked as the Beacon near Veryan. So naturally we are on our way to the village of that name.'

'But, Stort, I have failed you. One does not find a beacon in a valley, least of all one as deep as the one we are now wasting our time walking down into. What would be the good of a beacon lit in such a place as the little village below us? The only people who would see it, were it lit, would be your next-door neighbour! A beacon stands proud and a flame upon it must be seen far and wide, as signal or summons to the world. We turn back now; we find the highest ground we can and we survey this breezy landscape in the hope of seeing some place that is higher than all others. That will be the place you seek. Oh, what a snivelling, loathsome piece of mortality I am to so mislead the High Ealdor of Brum and the Emperor of the Hyddenworld as to cause them . . .'

But Jack shook his head menacingly and Barklice fell silent.

'You want us to go back up the hill?' said Jack simply.

'I do.'

'You want the best view we can find so you can survey the landscape?'

'That too.'

'Anything else?'

'Yes. I will need Stort's monocular.'

They trooped back up the hill the way they had come and stood again at the lonely crossroads where, it now seemed, they had taken the wrong turn.

The wind was getting up, the sky, though bright in its centre, was darkening on the horizon as they glimpsed the sea again. A vast, grey, stretch of flatness on which white horses, running from west to east, broke continually.

'No!' cried Barklice. 'No good going there and down again. We must find higher ground still. Stort, your monocular! Thank you. Jack, you come with me. The rest of you stay here. If I am wrong I shall never forgive myself.'

'Then let's hope you're not,' observed Festoon.

The two found a gap in the fence and clambered through.

The field was filled with beet, the green leaves flurrying in the wind.

'Come, Jack, let us head for the highest part. Over there, I think . . .'

They battled their way through crop and wind, the others watching from the road.

Reaching what seemed the highest part of the field and best vantage point, Barklice slowly looked all around.

'Can't see a thing,' he pronounced. 'I am an idiot but I am not a complete one.'

'What now?' said Jack.

'Hoist me up, my good fellow, onto your shoulders. Wait, I must have the glass at the ready! Right, up I go!'

Jack obliged, lifting Barklice bodily, such that his feet rested on his shoulders, and his legs were held steady in Jack's large hands.

'Get on with it,' gasped Jack, 'you're heavier than you look.'

Balanced thus precariously, the wind whipping at his thin hair and thick jerkin, Barklice surveyed the landscape.

'Turn slowly,' he cried, 'a full three hundred and sixty degrees. Not so fast, I need to study what I see.'

Jack turned slowly, boots digging into his shoulders, his arms straining to keep the verderer upright.

'What can you see?'

'Patience, my young friend, patience!'

Jack continued round a second time, Barklice silent, one eye screwed up, the other open to the monocular.

'Ah! No! Back! Aaah, no! Forward, too fast! Back. No . . . I don't believe it! It cannot, it must not be.'

'What now?'

'The enemy! Now turn ninety degrees to your left. Quickly!'

In that position, Jack saw, he was facing towards the sea.

'A mite more, if you will.'

Then: 'Good, excellent . . . now, a midgekin more . . . I said a midgekin, not . . . yes, that's it. Oh perfection. There it is! Named Carne Beacon on that map, Centre of the Universe indeed! Now, where's my compass?'

He took a bearing, Jack lowered him back down and he said, 'Job done!'

'You sure?' said Jack.

'I am sure,' said Barklice. 'Less than half a mile to the west and we'll be there. However . . . I regret to say . . .'

They hurried back to the others.

'The good news,' said Jack, 'is that Barklice knows where it is and can get us there in ten or fifteen minutes.'

'The bad?' they asked.

'We are not the only figures in this landscape,' said Barklice. 'I saw Fyrd, a whole troop of them, and they are heading in the same direction.'

'How far off?' asked Blut.

'Half a mile,' said Barklice.

'Let's go,' said Bedwyn Stort.

51

PURSUED

The Beacon came into view a few minutes later, a symmetrical hump across the fields, a good deal higher than the surrounding hedges and, too, the slight rise to the east from which they now approached it.

It was in the centre of a huge grass field in which a scattering of sheep grazed, their thick legs, sturdy heads and plump coats set against the south-westerly wind. Stretching away beneath the fold and bluffs of farmland beyond was Pendower Beach, the same which Stort now saw, on which he had imagined himself standing when entangled with the Embroidery.

Jack ordered them to halt in the covering shelter of a drystone wall overtopped by a thick growth of shrubs, hawthorn and ivy.

'Let's study the map, Stort,' he said. 'Lord Festoon, please keep watch. The Fyrd are approaching from our right, probably on this road here.'

He indicated a narrow north–south lane which was plain enough on the map but obscured from view by high hedges from where they were.

'The question is,' Jack continued, 'whether we make a dash across this field now in daylight and gain control of the Beacon or let the Fyrd take it and attempt to wrest it from them in the night. How many were there, Barklice?'

'A troop,' he said. 'Maybe twelve or so.'

'We are no match for such a number,' said Jack, 'not by daylight at least. If we did get to the Beacon now it would become a siege, no better than an exposed prison in a field open on all sides and impossible to cross without being seen by the Fyrd. What's your sense of it, Stort?'

'Dangerous,' he said. 'My vision with the Embroidery was different from this. I was on the beach, the surf coming in, the Beacon aflame in the night, not like this.'

'Katherine?'

'I think we should sit it out until dark.'

'Here?'

'Not sure,' she said uncertainly. 'It doesn't feel right here.'

Festoon and Blut shook their heads at Jack's query, having nothing more to add.

'We'll wait and watch,' said Jack.

He had just made this sensible pronouncement when Festoon said quietly, 'We have been observed!'

There was a dark figure across the fields behind them, on the nearside of the hill they had just come down. He was hard to see against the murky sky but he must have known they were there and he stood in the open as if it didn't matter to him to be seen.

'He has the size and boldness of a Fyrd,' said Jack. 'The other Fyrd may have sent him ahead to scout and now he's seen us.'

As if in confirmation they saw the Fyrd raise an arm and point with the other in their direction.

Jack looked at the map urgently, reading the printed contours and setting them against what he could see on the ground.

'Forget the Beacon,' he said, 'we're going to make ourselves scarce until dark. Then we might have a better chance.'

They hurried to the east side of the field and downslope along its high edge, bringing them to within fifty yards of the Beacon itself, whose massive size now showed itself, for it rose high into the air, dwarfing the few trees on its side and top.

They heard a shout on the far side of the field, where there was a stile, and saw Fyrd streaming over it towards the Beacon.

'Quick,' said Jack, 'we need to get out of this field on the opposite side and away downslope through the village called Carne.'

As they reached the stile opposite to the one the Fyrd had climbed they heard a derisive shout.

Two Fyrd had got to the Beacon and climbed to the top and were staring over the grass at them as sheep scattered to left and right.

They expected to see others come round the base of the mound and give chase, but they did not. Instead more appeared on top and with them someone dressed in civilian clothes it took them a moment to recognize.

'Come and get your friend, you Brummie bastards,' one of the Fyrd shouted.

They froze, horrified.

The civilian was Arthur Foale and he looked ill, broken, in some way destroyed. Two of the Fyrd had to hold him up, but when they were satisfied he had been seen and recognized they let him go and he collapsed at their feet, apparently unconscious.

Their instinct was to run across the field, climb the Beacon and try to rescue him.

'No,' said Jack his voice low and cold. 'No, we stay here. It's what they want and nothing we can do right now will make the situation better.'

'Give Blut to us,' called out a voice from the group on the hill, 'and you can have your friend in time to save his life.'

It was General Quatremayne.

'I'll go,' said Blut at once. 'He has become a friend and I should never have let him out of my sight in Brum.'

Jack exchanged a glance with Katherine and Festoom, who went either side of Blut and stopped him impulsively offering his life for Arthur's.

'I count seven,' said Jack, 'making eight with the one we saw and therefore three or four unaccounted for. They're probably making their way round to us as the others delay us here. We're leaving right now. But we'll be back!'

They climbed the stile with heavy hearts, caught sight of a single Fyrd coming at them from the left and made their way forward into the human village of Carne.

'Carry on,' said Jack, 'the map shows a footpath down to the sea. I'll deal with this Fyrd to even up the numbers a little bit.'

Katherine led them on. Jack waited out of sight for the lone Fyrd to come down the road, and round the corner.

As he did so Jack stepped up to him, his stave fierce and strong, and aimed a blow straight into his face so hard it broke open and turned to blood, spilling flesh and cartilage before he hit the ground. All Jack's anger for Arthur was in the blow and he muttered, 'There's more, much more, where that came from.'

He was tempted to wait and see if any others he had not yet seen showed up, but none did. Perhaps they were further on and trying to cut them off. What was very clear was that, having gained control of the Beacon, it would not be long before Quatremayne sent a party in pursuit.

Jack paused and studied the fields around the Beacon, especially to its seaward side, and then the fields beyond. He focused hard, visioning the ground in the dark, working out the best ways for a night attack. As for the Beacon itself, it was thick with wind-dried vegetation and woody shrubs, a couple of hawthorns, rough gorse and a dead elder tree. He turned about and raced after the others.

He caught them up as they reached the far end of the hamlet and picked up the path he had seen on the map. It ran down the side of a small deep valley, carved out by the stream they could hear but not see on their right.

The vegetation on either side was thick and prickly, so any pursuit, if it was to catch them up, would have to come down the same path they were on.

They paused a moment and he put Katherine in the lead, himself at the rear.

'Don't go too fast, because we're going to divert when we can so we can hide up for a time.'

The light was fading fast and the air cold and dank with little wind in the hollow they were in. There was no visible sign of pursuit behind, but on such a rapidly descending winding path an enemy would be close behind before they were seen. But they could hear heavy running steps and shouted commands.

'We could divert here,' called out Katherine.

They had reached a split in the path, or rather a hollowing out in the bushes to the left past a bluff of rock, used by humans once in a while but exploited by animals. To the right the slope down to the stream had grown steeper still.

'Too obvious a place to stop,' said Jack, 'let's go a bit further down.'

The path turned suddenly and steepened over slippery rocks. Katherine fell, followed by Blut. There was a sickening smell from the river gulley.

'A dead sheep,' said Katherine, picking herself up and hauling Blut upright. His spectacles were spattered with mud but he had no time or inclination to take them off and clean them.

'Here,' said Jack, 'we'll push through the scrub to our left.'

Again Katherine took the lead and the others followed, except for Jack, who remained on the path.

'Carry on downslope through the bushes, find a place to wait unseen; I have a little more business to attend to. Katherine, after a couple of minutes cup your hand and shout upslope the words "Run! They're coming." I have an idea.'

He waited in the shadows through which the others had gone, confident that if the Fyrd coming down were too many he could slip away unseen. If few enough he would take them on as they rounded the awkward corner where the ground steepened and the rank odour was a distraction. Each one he killed or disabled was one less for them to have to fight later.

On cue Katherine's call was heard and his ruse worked.

He heard gruff voices of the Fyrd on the path they had just come down, peered low through the undergrowth to see their feet, a trick Barklice had taught him, and counted three in all. Ideal.

The first slipped round the corner and nearly fell, the second tumbled, and Jack threw himself at him, his stave end into his throat. The other end he shoved twistingly into the groin of the one coming down, who screamed and fell sideways, clutching himself, down into the noisome gully.

He struck in that order because he knew that the momentum of the other would have carried him down a few paces, giving him the advantage of slope and surprise. Jack felt on fire, his stave humming dangerously in his hands, and he had no compunction about maiming for life or killing. None. The sight of Arthur up on the Beacon had leached out any pity he might have had for Fyrd.

He thrust hard at the one below him, who parried well and brought the lower end of his stave up and round very hard. But the slope was such that he could do no more than strike Jack's shin. Jack's second blow was into his knee, the third into the joint of his foot and then the back of it.

He too cried out at the pain, his stave spinning away.

Jack did not kill him, satisfied his foot was broken and he was not going to get far until more Fyrd found him, which was Jack's intent.

He checked back on the others too, one dead, one halfway down the gully and still alive. Jack checked no more Fyrd were on their way, went the few steps down to him and dealt with him as he had the first, a lethal buffet in the throat.

Then he stripped him of his crossbow and bolts, standard weapons of the Fyrd, went back to the path and did the same with the second corpse.

There was a fury in Jack and he looked frightening. The injured Fyrd, lying awkwardly lengthwise down the path below, who now strained and struggled to get round and up, looked terrified.

Jack relieved him of his crossbow too, checked again that he was as good as immobile and retreated into the gap through which the others had gone, slowly and visibly. He let him live because he wanted him to be able to report the way they had gone or had appeared to.

When he caught up with the others for the second time he ordered them to double back in silence so they joined the same path lower down.

'The Fyrd will chase us the way the one I left alive tells them to,' he said, 'giving us a clear, safer run down to the shore. It's no good trying to defend ourselves on a clifftop against superior arms and numbers. Down there there'll be places to hide and we now have three crossbows too.'

They proceeded slowly and in silence, the wind strong in the shrubs and trees above their heads, the sea glimpsed below as the path twisted and turned.

Until at last, the safety of dusk upon them, they reached the stream whose valley the path had been following and picked their way along it through tussocky grass and gorse down to the shore to which it tumbled.

'Take care,' said Katherine, who still led the way. 'These rocks are slippery and dangerous and a twisted ankle now might be a death sentence.'

They finally reached sand, the surf's roar fifty yards beyond them, the breaking waves almost invisible in the gloom.

'What now, Stort?' said Jack. 'What do you remember from your dream?'

That Stort remembered anything at all from his strange encounter with the Embroidery astonished him, but that was Stort. Each had their strengths and the visioning instinct of the seer was one of his.

He gazed back up the cliff they had clambered down and then further along it.

'Not that way,' he said.

The other way, to their left as they faced inland, the cove widened to a sandy bay.

'Pendower Beach,' said Stort. 'Have to go there to get the view inland I think I saw.'

'We'll be exposed,' said Jack.

'But barely visible in this light,' said Katherine. 'Let's do it; the Fyrd will catch up with us eventually if we stay here so it's best we see the lie of the land if we're to go back up to the Beacon and rescue Arthur.'

They waited another quarter of an hour for the dark to thicken, during which time Jack used his torch, hunched among rocks and the sharp smell of seaweed to study the map.

'You saw what you called a fort in your visioning?' he prompted Stort.

'Dreaming, I'd call it. Yes I did, on a low bluff. Not much of one.'

Jack peered closer.

'It must be this. There's a second and bigger stream coming down in the cove, its valley less twisty than the one we've come down. At the top of it is an earthwork called Veryan Castle.'

Katherine peered closer, trained in map work by Arthur.

'Fanciful name,' she said. 'Probably Iron Age. Looks as if it's got ramparts like the ones on White Horse Hill. They would make it easy to defend.'

'My thought too,' said Jack. His finger moved a half-inch to the east.

'There's the Beacon, on this scale not more than three hundred yards or so beyond the fort.'

They saw a light on the cliffs above, on past where they had come down. Their mis-direction had worked.

'The Fyrd!' said Jack. 'Right, time to move on and see what we find.'

They kept near to the cliff until it faded away where the bigger stream came down and across the sandy shore. The shore to their left eased away and they veered along with it, taking them further from the higher ground above. Beyond that was a road, a couple of houses behind it and, nearer the beach, the dark and lifeless windows of a hotel complex. It was deserted.

'It seems the humans have left even this distant place,' said Stort.

'If it wasn't for Arthur,' said Blut, 'those buildings would offer us options to hide. As it is, whatever else may be suggested, I cannot leave him up there by himself much longer.'

They all agreed.

Stort stood and stared up the bigger valley, or as much of it as he could see.

There were trees on either side at the lower end, their branches swaying as silhouettes in the wind from the sea. Further inland the valley had the usual deep Cornish hedges either side, as it rose steeply to the bluff that had to be Veryan Castle.

The torches on the cliff above had disappeared, but moments later they saw them bobbing about as they made their rapid way down.

The sand about them lightened suddenly and they saw faint shadows of themselves.

The wind had shifted and the clouds with it, revealing the moon.

'They've probably seen us,' said Jack, 'but we can't be sure if there aren't more up this valley. But they won't expect us to go back up so soon. If they catch us halfway up it we're done for. If we can get to the ramparts of the fort we stand some kind of chance.'

It was, he knew, a slim one, very slim.

They had done well to get this far unscathed and in different circumstances they would have got clean away by now.

Jack said, 'I'm going up to see what I can do for Arthur, but I don't think you others should all follow. Lord Festoon, you're more valuable alive than dead! Emperor Blut, you are too. As for myself – and

Katherine and Stort – it's in the wyrd of our quest for the gems that we take these risks. You should not take them too.'

Festoon grunted, Blut took his glasses off and wiped them.

'I think I speak for both of us,' he said coolly, 'when I say that we have no intention of spending this Samhain night with anyone but you. Wyrd is a strange thing and in my experience serves justly those who have faith in it and act honourably. Lead on and let us get to somewhere we can stand and fight. Not that I have ever shot a crossbow in my life!'

Jack was about to lead them on when Stort, who had been staring up the darkened valley, said, 'The Beacon was alight, aflame, I saw it clearly in my dreaming. I felt its heat. That is what's needed, Jack, but don't ask me why.'

The wind grew stronger and began gusting about them as a front went over.

The clouds that had parted now came together again and lowered, feathery at their base and picking up the ambient light of Falmouth and Truro off to the north-west to make them lurid.

They set off up the beach to the road and from there found a path with a fingerpost pointing the way they were going. A human house to the right had broken windows and a garage, its doors open and bent by the wind.

Jack stopped them briefly and went to hunt about inside.

'What are you looking for?' someone asked when he returned.

'This!' he said, holding up a red petrol container. He pulled things from his 'sac and put it inside. 'There's another one you could take, Stort. We want a flaming beacon, so we'll have one!'

They passed through the trees on the lower slopes and headed uphill, Jack taking the lead, Katherine behind. The wind roared up the valley behind them, colder now and salty.

They looked back and saw the bobbing lights down by the house. Beyond them the sea was lit by the rising moon, white and shining where the great surf was and the white horses further out. Dark inbetween.

The slope got steeper, their breathing heavier and quicker, chests hurting, legs aching, each silent in their effort to keep going. Behind them the lights came quicker, not gaining fast but gaining. Inexorable.

They reached the bluff where the castle had to be in a final steep climb and stood leaning on their staves, gasping for air.

The Fyrd themselves could not be seen, just their lights, five of them.

'Which probably means there's nine or ten there,' said Jack, 'one torch between two. Now . . .'

He went forward onto the flat scar of the fort, its rampart deepening to their left and on the far side of the flat area presenting a wall of sward.

He and Katherine took off their 'sacs and quickly surveyed the ramparts.

'This is the entrance area, which is why the path leads here. They'll have to come this way too. We could defend it from either side using the crossbows.'

They rapidly discussed the pros and cons; there were very few pros indeed.

'We can hold them back, we might get lucky and maim or kill some, but we're too few to defend this place for long,' said Jack. 'As for heading on to the Beacon, we've seen how tough that can be.'

The lights below were steadily getting nearer.

The moon higher.

The wind stronger.

'A suggestion,' said Blut. 'I do not think I shall do well with a crossbow and I never did learn to wield a stave. Let me take that fuel and see what I may do at the Beacon. No doubt the Fyrd will see me but it takes moments to scatter and light petrol.'

Festoon said, 'I can take one of the crossbows. Can't be that difficult to shoot.'

It was, Jack knew, as risky and crack-brained a plan as he had ever heard. If they didn't get stopped and killed before reaching the Beacon then Arthur would get burnt by Blut or shot by Festoon and all three die unpleasant deaths. But if they stayed at the fort then Arthur had no chance at all.

'You'll do a better job at slowing them down than we can,' said Blut persuasively, taking up Jack's 'sac.

It was too large for him and the weight really too much. Yet he looked as brave and bold as a fighting Emperor should, his spectacles catching the moonlight, his grey eyes sharp and focused.

'In fact, Stavemeister,' he said asserting that same striking authority they had first seen in Brum, 'this isn't a request, it's an order from your Commander-in-Chief. Arthur saved my life, the least I can do is to try and save his.'

Jack had neither time nor energy to argue. In any case, his instinct was with Blut.

'You know which way to go?'

'I can read a map,' he said, 'and I had a good look earlier. My spatial memory is good. Good luck to all of you. Festoon, my friend, let us be gone!'

52

BEACON

Jack, Katherine and Stort had the advantage of darkness and height. They conferred at once.

'If we can get a couple of shots in and fell or hit at least one of them they won't be in a hurry to come forward. We keep it up until they begin to, or look like they're going to try to get round, and you and Stort join me on the high side. That gives us more options and me the advantage when it comes to a stave fight. I will fire first so there's no confusion. I will aim for the nearest to me. Aim for the throat or groin, it's where they are vulnerable. Whatever you do, join me the moment I whistle.'

They spoke in whispers, eyes glancing downslope as the torches got ever nearer until they suddenly went out. The tactics agreed and confirmed, they went to their positions.

Then there was silence.

'They're working out if anyone's here,' whispered Katherine.

The silence continued but for the roar of the surf far below and the never-ending wind in the trees nearby. Their eyes strained to see movement, watering from the wind and effort of staring, the dark forms of the hydden jumping, shifting, hard to keep in vision.

Then one moved, followed by another.

Coming forward up the hill, crossbows glinting in the moonlight.

They walked confidently and easily, clearly thinking there was no one there.

Katherine readied herself to aim at the one nearest to her. She could not deploy the crossbow fully without exposing herself, so she waited for Jack's shot.

The two figures came nearer in the dark, beginning to loom, easy in their upward stride, forbidding in their presence. Katherine's heart thumped, Stort gulped, silence reigned but for the surf and wind and finally the tread of the Fyrd on the steep path. The others below them were a solid, shadowed mass.

She looked from where the throat of her target must be to his groin. That seemed easier but it was lower and she would have to stand up to get her shot in. She decided on the throat.

They came nearer still, Katherine sure that they could hear her short breaths, her beating heart.

Then a soft *thwump!* and Jack had fired.

She rose, Stort's hand on her back to keep her steady, and fired from the hip.

Jack's target had spun round, his crossbow dropped. Katherine's seemed not affected at all, yet he did not fire nor continue walking. He just stood motionless.

'Load it,' she said to Stort, taking up her stave, guessing what Jack would do next.

She was right.

He was up and out and thrusting hard at his quarry before he dropped back to his position. The Fyrd fell back, Katherine's fell to his knees, speechless. She did as Jack had done and thrust her stave into his face.

As he fell back there was a *thwump thwump* from below and a bolt shot past her right side.

But something else happened which made the sound of the crossbows seem no more than soft whispers.

There was a roaring sound on the slope behind them and the low clouds above their heads turned orange-red.

Blut had done his stuff.

The Beacon was ablaze and the Fyrd on the slope below them were suddenly more visible, not from direct light but the ambient light of the clouds above.

Jack watched carefully, counting.

There were six below, so he had overestimated.

He fired another shot, another Fyrd went down, and he signalled to Katherine.

It was time to try to make it to the Beacon.

The hydden folk of Cornwall are like no other in Englalond. Dark, swarthy, strong, good-natured, they can sail a boat as well as till a field, neither gracefully but each with good effect.

They stand together fiercely but, unless threatened, they are welcoming to strangers.

Family matters, land as well; of the seasons Samhain is the most important.

And this was Samhain, the time when families gather, coming from afar.

The yearning brings them home, that same yearning which Stort rightly guessed lived always in ã Faroün's heart.

With the yearning goes a deep, deep sense of duty to their own folk, duty to those oppressed, and reverence to land and sea.

No wonder that if there is anywhere in the Hyddenworld that a sailor would rather go down, if go down he must, it is off the Cornish coast, for help will come more surely than the wind and waves.

So too on the land.

If help is called for, those rough, good folk respond without thinking, for they know that if and when they need it, their people will do the same for them.

None more, in all of Cornwall, than the hydden thereabout the remote peninsula called Roseland, in the centre of which Veryan sits with its ancient Beacon standing on a nearby hill. They help each other on sea and land and would almost kill for the privilege or die in shame if they did not respond to a call for aid.

So it was that on that Samhain evening, when families were gathered close together in expectation of the midnight hour, they paid heed the moment the cry went up, 'The Beacon's aflame!'

The Beacon's aflame!

'It cannot be! Not for three generations has it been lit!'

But it was and they saw it and they knew what they must do.

They put down their cannikins, they set the stewpot to one side, they put the oldest kinder to watch the little ones. Not a grumble from

the males, not a complaint from the wyfkin: the Beacon was aflame
and that was a summons that could never be denied.

From the humbles of Carne and Tregamenna; from the homestead
of Pennare; from Churchtown and Veryan and the deep fold of
Caragloose . . .

Hydden put on their coats and their boots, they took up their staves
and they set off into the night towards the Beacon flames which lit the
night sky and sent a red skirl among the racing clouds.

Hurry! The great Beacon's aflame.

Nor were they the only folk who saw it.

Arnold Mallarkhi, surfing the huge waves into shore at speed, was
very surprised suddenly to see the Beacon light up, even as he caught
sight of two cutters to right and left, racing inshore as he was doing the
same.

His eyes widened and his teeth flashed.

'More sail, Terce,' he called out, 'and sing us a song. They be pirates
on either side and they'll cut us up into little pieces and make a stew
of our best parts if we let 'em. Meaning we must get ashore afore they
do and run like hell! That there Beacon's a signal to 'em to take us
alive!'

Borkum Riff, generally reckoned to be the best skipper south of
Reykjavik, couldn't believe his eyes. Nor could Herde Deap.

Out of nowhere a beacon flared on the hills above. As it did it
showed that in the darkness and foam, and seas like he'd rarely known,
skipping along as if he was on a holiday jaunt, except faster, was a craft
that should be inland. He had rarely seen such seamanship.

What was more, it was gaining and gaining fast, which a skipper out
of Den Helder did not appreciate.

Yet more odd, and it made him think the sailor was a ghost come
early for Samhain, was that the sailor wore a turban, while handling
the reefs was a monk, big and strong, and he was singing a shanty in a
voice so rich it might have come out of the craters of the moon.

'Not havin' this,' said Borkum.

'I was hoping,' said Lady Leetha in the other boat, to Deap, 'that
you might get to the shore before Borkum and Sinistral but it seems to
me . . . is that *another* craft?'

'It's a madman,' said Deap, 'trying to run our fellow boat down and on that tack and against these waves . . .'

His voice gained a sudden urgency.

'Hold on, Ma, we're going to save Pa!'

Then, in the next few waves they all surfed and raced, half-turned, feinted, and set straight on again as if dead heat in a race, and finally came ashore as one, crashing through the breaking waves and running up the shingly sand.

'That was dubious my new-won friends,' cried Arnold, when he realized they were friends not foe and let his sabre fall.

'Aye,' growled Riff, 'what shore you be from?'

'Brum,' replied Arnold, inexplicably. 'Now we've folk to help, and you?'

'We too,' the others said.

'What folk?' laughed Leetha into the wind.

'Ever heard of Jack, of Katherine and Bedwyn Stort?' said Arnold cheerfully.

Slew looked pale; Leetha amused; Sinistral calm.

'Perhaps.'

'Can you guess where they'll be?'

'Up there,' said Slew, 'where the flames are.'

'Searching,' said Arnold mysteriously.

'What for?' wondered Leetha as they set off.

'A gem,' said Lord Sinistral.

General Quatremayne, who had been in the party pursuing Jack and the others, was pleased when the Beacon went up.

Certainly he had lost two more of his best Fyrd with a third wounded, but he saw by the light of the flames that his quarry were in flight and they numbered only three.

The cause of the Beacon burning he did not know or much care. Its light seemed providential and he had no doubt that his soldiers on the Beacon would do as he had ordered if in any way threatened: kill Arthur Foale and await reinforcements with confidence. The force against them was wily but puny and he was sure that by midnight and the start of Samhain control would be his and Blut his prisoner. If he was still alive. If not he did not care.

'Give chase!' he commanded, 'and catch them before they reach the Beacon.'

As he charged on up the hill and made it to the fort, and from there across the easier ground towards the Beacon, he could not but be in awe of the flames raging there.

The whole thing was alight, trees and all, and in the foreground, lit up like sitting ducks in bright sunshine, were three of the hydden who had caused them such annoyance.

The Beacon itself was too much in flame to allow anyone on top of it. Instead, he saw now, two figures stood to one side: his Fyrd, no doubt.

'Catch 'em and do not kill 'em,' he roared at his guards as they ran ahead.

The two figures were Blut and Festoon and they had Arthur lying nearby and were sheltering him from the heat and flames.

They had every reason to feel pleased with themselves.

They had hurried over the hill towards the dark Beacon. Blut had crept to one side, Festoon had walked boldly on the other, calling out, in the Mirror's name, for mercy, kindness, salvation and a chance to see his stricken comrade.

'Are you Blut?' they had called down to him.

'I am,' he lied in his most majestic way, 'and I come to give myself up.'

As he said this he saw the real Blut light a lucifer and throw it unseen towards what looked like harmless vegetation beneath a tree on the west side of the Beacon.

As he did so he dived in the opposite direction, and it was as well he did, because after only a moment's run-around of blue flame, and then a sickening moment of nothing at all, the petrol container glowed briefly red before it exploded in a ball of flame.

Festoon himself fell forward with the blast.

The Fyrd atop the Beacon fell sideways into flames and out of sight and Arthur Foale, on his hands and knees on the further slope of the hump, felt his hair singe as a sheet of flame shot over him.

Weak, badly hurt already, his feet useless, he had the presence of mind to roll down the slope away from the flames, grunting and gasping as he went, right to where Festoon lay.

Blut hurried round, his left hand his only defence against the fierce flames. He dragged Arthur further out, helped Festoon crawl away and searched frantically for the crossbow to use against the two Fyrd when they appeared.

They never did. Their screams were heard as the flames ran through the vegetation round them, a brief agonized silhouette in the light, then nothing but the fire's roar.

It was then that Festoon and Blut saw Jack and the others running towards them, the flames so bright that they might as well have been running into day.

They saw as well the Fyrd behind, close enough now to suddenly stop pursuit, kneel down and ready their crossbows.

One of them looked at Katherine, another at Stort and a third at Jack.

It was no good Blut and Festoon shouting a warning, for the roar of flames, fanned by the wind, was far too loud.

Perhaps Jack and Katherine saw their gaze and guessed what was happening.

As the kneeling Fyrd steadied themselves and took aim and Quatremayne stood next to them with pleasure, they turned about to face them and came together, instinctively protecting Stort who, they felt, was more important than they were.

The one who was aiming at Stort, his view impaired, shifted his attention to Blut behind, whom he recognized from the flashing spectacles.

Quatremayne raised his arm triumphantly. A running fight had turned into an execution. His quarry were perfectly framed by the fire and they had nowhere further to run.

All was still but for the flames.

'Sir?' said one of the Fyrd, for he sensed that his General wished to give the ultimate command.

'I think so, don't you?' said Quatremayne, his words unheard by those he was about to kill.

But the General had taken a moment too long.

From out of the darkness on one side came a rock thrown by a lad from Carne. It arced high through the air and hit the Fyrd who was aiming at Blut in the arm, knocking his crossbow to the ground.

Its bolt shot harmlessly into the ground a few feet ahead of him as Jack sent his great stave whirling from his hand, to catch the bolt shot at Katherine in a shower of blue sparks in mid-flight, before it travelled headlong on to strike the third Fyrd to the ground.

Another missile, a heavy stave, hurled by the strong arm of the spouse of the Pennare wyf, landed bodily on the second of the Fyrd.

There were more Fyrd coming but folk bore down on them from the fields on either side.

Helpers all, fierce and purposeful, the ones they needed to help easy to see, the ones they needed to repel clearer still.

Fyrd!

Folk from Cornwall do not say that name without spitting on the ground.

Fyrd!?

Throw 'em off the bloody cliffs.

Perhaps they did, for the Fyrd were surrounded, every one, and hauled off before Jack or anyone could do much about it, except for Quatremayne, his insignia and uniform torn off and no covering for his upper half but a torn vest.

He was left in no more than his underdrawers.

'What shall we do with him, sir?' someone asked Jack.

'It's not for me to decide,' said Jack.

They came close then, these other folk, bringing food with them and good brew, for this was Samhain and this a fire like no other seen in a very long while. A fire fit to celebrate the last day of harvest-time and welcome Winter in.

They came in large numbers, so that when, a little later, a group of strangers showed up who were tired from voyaging on open sea, no one at first gave them much attention.

Not that Jack and the others were looking.

They were gathered round Arthur, propped up now against a barrel brought over from Carne and filled with good beer.

He seemed well, but he was not.

He could not walk because they had beaten his feet.

Nor see too clearly for they had closed up one of his eyes.

Nor hear as well as he would have wished, for an eardrum was burst from the beatings he had had.

Blut knelt by him in tears.

Katherine held him close.

Jack just stared, appalled.

But Arthur himself?

'I'm glad,' he whispered, 'that Margaret isn't here to see me looking like this. She would not be best pleased.'

He didn't hurt, for the pain was past.

Nor to be getting worse, for how much worse could he be?

'Katherine,' he said, 'it's good to see you on Samhain. And you, Jack, stronger than I've ever seen you. But . . . I . . .'

'What are you trying to say, Arthur?' whispered Katherine.

'I miss my Margaret every moment of my life.'

'I know,' said Katherine.

'And Judith, I miss her too. She held my hand once and showed me how to fly. Is she coming here tonight?'

Stort knelt by him then.

'She'd better come,' he said matter-of-factly.

'Stort!' cried Arthur, coughing painfully. 'Did you find that damn gem?'

'It's here somewhere I'm sure,' replied Stort vaguely, 'but I'll need a little help to find it.'

A shadow fell across them all, long and beautiful, still against the dancing of the light of flames upon the grass.

It was Slaeke Sinistral.

Old and thin but standing tall.

'Who did this to him, Blut?' he said quietly as if being there was the most natural thing in the world.

Blut stood up and the focus shifted as wyfkin came to make Arthur comfortable.

'No, I don't want to move, dammit,' he grumbled. 'I'm in no pain, just tired. Let me enjoy Samhain and this great fire in peace before I fall asleep. Then take me in and tuck me up.'

Blut said, 'Quatremayne did it my Lord Sinistral.'

'Quatremayne,' said Sinistral softly. 'He never did learn that cruelty does not pay. Is he dead? You killed him?'

Blut shook his head and pointed to the edge of the circle, where darkness began.

Quatremayne was tied to a post, like a dog awaiting execution.

'You'll have to deal with him, Blut.'

There was something about the two together that stilled a crowd, even of revellers, even at Samhain.

Folk gathered, circling around Sinistral and Blut. Few yet knew who they were but an awed whisper was going about. And none could doubt that one way and another they were the most powerful hydden there and that the one tied up to the post needed and deserved punishment.

Silence fell but for the flames, now quieter and more subdued.

It was a peaceful crowd, not one seeking blood.

Sinistral was the most commanding figure until he turned his eyes on Blut and backed away a little, Borkum Riff to one side, Leetha to another.

Jack stood by Blut, Katherine too.

Blut stared at Quatremayne and understood that the sentence had to be his.

'Untie him,' he said coldly, 'and make him stand where he can be clearly seen.'

Blut took off his spectacles and wiped them, thinking. There are moments of decision where it is important that the right thing is seen to be done. Sinistral had taught him that.

He might have the General killed there and then for all to see, as Sinistral had done once or twice.

People would fear and respect him then.

He might imprison him, but folk would feel a disappointment.

He might be merciful, but that was not an option that appealed to either his heart or mind.

Or he might be wise and moved from a spirit of compassion, not for Quatremayne so much as the pain he must have in his heart to inflict so much pain on others.

Yes, wisdom was best.

But what punishment was wise?

He put on his spectacles and asked himself what today, this night, right now, Lord Sinistral would do. His was the wisdom of the years and hard old age. His was the wisdom of the *musica*.

He glanced at Slaeke Sinistral but saw no clue in his eyes.

He heard the distant roar of surf and smelt the salt in the air, mixed with the smoke of the fire.

It was Samhain, the end and the beginning of things.

He had seen a township die and that was the beginning of the end of days.

What then was wise?

Death would be just and seen to be strong.

Mercy right but weak.

Blut decided that on this occasion compromise was best.

It was Samhain, and a little mercy at such a time should be shown. But resolution too.

So he ordered that Quatremayne be put in a small boat on the morrow and put to sea where the elements and his wyrd could decide what to do with him. 'The morrow be damned!' cried two sailors from Carne. 'We'll do it right now.'

And that was best of all! They took the General out to sea until they were clear of the surf and shoved him into a skiff. They set his sail for the open sea, wished him well of the night and watched as his craft took him into the darkness and past wild Nare Head.

As for the other Fyrd who were still alive, they were sent packing along the cliff path without a light towards Portloe, where folk don't take kindly to strangers who wander in from the dark and look like Fyrd. Not kindly at all.

53

TO THE STARS

The crowds of locals who had come in answer to the Beacon's flame began dispersing at eleven, an hour before the season's turn, when October became November, and Samhain officially began.

They returned to their humbles and families to stoke their fires, begin their feasts and celebrate the last harvest of the year.

But up by the Beacon, which smouldered still and gave out a pleasant smoky warmth, a very different kind of Samhain began.

It was one dominated by Bedwyn Stort, but very strangely so.

He paced about and around the beacon, restive and uneasy, looking to the stars for inspiration, indifferent and silent to any approach from his friends.

'It's the gem,' murmured Barklice, 'he knows he has less than an hour to find it but I think he has no idea where it is. I have seen him like this before. He is seeking inspiration and it's best to let him be!'

After a while, however, Katherine thought differently.

'This is Samhain, Barklice, time for family and friends. Not a time to refuse to talk to others and wander about on the half-lit edge of things.'

'Even if time's running out for the Earth and all of us?' said Jack. 'What happens if he doesn't find the gem?'

'You've got too much on your mind, Jack!' replied Katherine mysteriously as she turned from the firelight and called out, 'Stort! Stort!'

He might have escaped had she not run out into the shadows after him and grabbed his arm.

'Leave me!' he muttered irritably. 'I have work to do whilst you others . . . you others . . .'

'We others have family and friends,' she said gently, hugging him and not letting go despite his struggles, 'and you think you have not?'

'Maybe,' he admitted.

'We're all your friends.'

'You are,' he conceded, breaking free, 'but—'

'But what?'

'I . . . she . . .'

He stared at the stars as his voice trailed off helplessly.

'You're worried that Judith won't come?'

'Humph! I am worried that she *will* come and that tonight of all nights I have nothing to give her. Added to which, I . . . do . . . miss her.'

'She'll come,' said Katherine, hugging him again.

'Don't tell the others this,' he whispered in her ear, 'but I don't know where the gem is.'

She laughed.

'Barklice has already guessed that! He says you're seeking inspiration. Maybe it's not in the stars but in what Samhain means.'

'What does it mean?'

They turned together and looked back towards the others, caught as they were in the light of flickering flames, the Beacon to one side.

'Family, belonging, love, shedding, the time of darkness and deep thought.'

'All those things,' he said quietly, a new peace descending on him. 'I sometimes think Barklice knows me best of all.'

'He loves you, Stort, as we all do.'

'That's all very well, I daresay, but it is not helping me find what I need to!'

'No? I wouldn't be so sure.'

'Well . . . just don't tell that Sinistral that I have no idea . . . or Blut . . .'

'Sometimes you need others, that's also what Samhain's about. There are things we can't harvest by ourselves.'

'Humph!' muttered Stort again, but happily now. 'Maybe it's like the Embroidery, I just have to stop trying so hard.'

'Very good, Stort! You're learning at last! Now ... I'd better get back to Jack, there's something worrying him and I don't think he quite knows what it is or what to do about it. When you're ready ...'

'I'll join you soon and meanwhile hope that inspiration will come.'

Then he added diffidently, 'Do you really think *she'll* come?'

'She will,' said Katherine lightly, not looking back.

He watched after her, saw her join the others, breathed more deeply and easily than before.

'Where are you?' he asked no one in particular.

Where are you, Bedwyn Stort? the stars replied.

Jack had never really met his mother Leetha, nor her two sons, and at first he did not feel he was ready to do so.

Arthur felt more like family to him than they did, for he and Margaret and Katherine had been the only family he had even known, Woolstone his only true home. The others seemed like imposters and he did not know how to begin talking to them.

Though it was in Leetha's nature to break the ice, that night, with the old man called Arthur that Jack obviously loved near his end, she could not see a way to do it easily.

She looked sideways at Jack, as he at her. He liked the look of her, she of him. It was Katherine who finally saw the truth of things and made things happen.

'It's *time*,' she told him as his lost family stood about not meeting each other's eyes. Adding in a whisper, 'It's all so blindingly obvious, Jack, and quite exciting.'

'What is?' he said gruffly, staying close, terrified she would leave him. 'And it's time for what?'

'Who he is, for goodness sake. *Look* at him.'

But Jack turned away, pretending to tend to Arthur.

He was discovering something that was hard to take in, almost impossible, in fact, and that was the cause of his fear.

But he glanced at Herde Deap again and whispered, 'I don't think so.'

'I do,' she said.

'He doesn't look like me,' he said.

'Oh yes, he does. Come *on!* He won't bite.'

It was strange enough that Leetha his mother was there, smiling a smile he remembered from long before the White Horse came and brought him to Englalond. Now he saw it properly, her smile was like home to him and he was afraid of the emotions it raised.

'You're shaking!' said Katherine.

'I'm not and he *doesn't.*'

But Herde Deap did.

He looked more like Jack than Jack himself: same build, same hair, same eyes, same voice.

Same hands, one of which reached out and which Jack automatically took.

Deap didn't say anything for the first seconds, but when he finally spoke he said everything.

He had Leetha on one side and Borkum Riff on the other and he said, 'Jack, this is your mother and this your father and I'm Herde Deap, your . . .'

'I know who you are,' said Jack, 'you're my . . .'

Twin.

'I know who you all are,' he said, trying hard to feel nothing because to feel anything would be to feel it all.

But it wasn't possible.

What he felt came as a tidal wave and he stood before them, with his eyes filled and a hand reaching for Katherine's until Leetha stepped forward and did what she had longed to do every day since she had to send him away when he was little for his own safety. She held him tight and then tighter, and she wept the tears of years' loss just as he finally did.

'I know who you are,' he said again because right there, right then, for the first time, he did and in saying it he finally knew himself as well.

Borkum Riff smiled his dark smile. Their real meeting could wait. It was enough for them to shake hands and for Herde and Jack to find they liked each other and might find a way to become friends.

A little later Jack went over to Slew, Leetha's other son and so his half-brother, where he stood with Sinistral.

They too shook hands but there was no hope of amity, not then. Slew had killed Master Brief. Slew was the enemy. Jack had beaten

Slew in a fight in Bochum and there was about their handshake the sense that one day there would be a second bout and perhaps a different result.

But Leetha, in the centre of them, ignored all that. She had her boys and the love of her life, who was Riff, by her. If she could have danced in the ashes on the slopes of the Beacon she would have done so. As it was she laughed with pleasure and they laughed too.

This was their Samhain.

Niklas Blut too had rarely been happier in his life. To see his Lord Sinistral up and well and nearly himself again was a joyous thing.

'Old and bent,' said Sinistral, who was thin and stiff these days.

'Not bent, my Lord, but on the way,' Blut replied.

'You always did tell the truth, Blut. That's why I had you come to work with me all those years ago.'

'It was, my Lord.'

'And how is being Emperor suiting you?'

'Interesting, except, as you well know, I am not Emperor, just your stand-in until you are ready again. That was our agreement, I think . . .'

'Did anyone guess?'

'Igor Brunte did. Emperors like you don't abdicate, they die, one way or another.'

'I do not wish to go back to Bochum, Blut. Like Quatremayne, it became corrupt.'

'I have thought of that, my Lord. Perhaps we should move the Imperial Quarters to Brum, city of your birth?'

'Do it,' said Sinistral simply.

'So be it,' replied Blut. 'But first we'll have to remove whatever Fyrd the General left in charge of the city, though I suspect that its citizens are already doing so themselves.'

Festoon joined them.

'Tell me,' said Sinistral, 'will your people like me or loathe me?'

'Both,' said Festoon. 'But it will help if you wear spectacles.'

Sinistral look puzzled and then smiled.

'Ah, Brummish humour.'

'You should know, my Lord, you were born there.'

'Now I shall strive to die there.'

'Perhaps, my Lord Sinistral, perhaps!' said Blut.

Later, as the midnight hour drew near, when much comes to fruition that is sown in the seasons gone by, Stort finally joined them and someone dared say, 'Well, Stort, and what about the gem?'

'I have every confidence,' said Stort, still evasive, 'that its moment will come!'

But he could not hide the fact of his eyes restlessly searching the cloudy night sky as if hoping the clouds would part and an immortal hand proffer the gem that had eluded him so long.

'I confess I am baffled,' he told them. He was at last willing to admit, having thought long and hard about Katherine's comment about needing others, especially at Samhain. 'I know it's here but exactly where I cannot say. I don't suppose, Lord Sinistral, that *you* know anything about the gem?'

'Such as?'

Stort shrugged and said, 'Well, I suppose any scrap of information might help. You did know ã Faroün, did you not?'

'I did.'

'Did you know he was not of Arabic origin?'

'That too. He told me when he brought me here.'

'You have been here before?' asked Stort, surprised and excited.

'On this very spot. Also on the night of Samhain, a great many years ago.'

'Celebrating?'

'Yes.'

'My Lord,' interrupted Blut, 'you are being obtuse. I think what Mister Stort is asking, or trying to, is simply whether or not you know what your great mentor did with the gem?'

'Well, of course I do, Blut, because he did it here when I was standing next to him.'

'He did *what*!?' cried Stort and Blut together.

'Disposed of the gem. He felt the time had come for him to part with it.'

'You saw it?'

'I did.'

'You touched it?'

'Ah ... no ... it is not for ordinary folk to do that. It requires someone rather special, with a heart that is purer than mine.'

'What did ã Faroün do with it?' asked Jack.

'Did he bury it?' wondered Katherine.

Sinistral looked around at them all, enjoying himself.

'No, he didn't bury it.'

He signalled Stort to come and stand by him. The two were the same height.

'He *threw* it,' said Sinistral.

'Threw it?' repeated Stort. 'Where?'

'There,' said Slaeke Sinistral softly, taking his arm and pointing at the racing clouds before them. *'There!* Why not try it for yourself?'

He bent down and picked up a small stone from the earth at his foot and gave it to Stort with a smile.

'Throw it as hard as you can towards the sky, as ã Faroün did, and you will see that it is not so hard to find where the gem of Autumn is.'

They had all gathered round for midnight and fell silent as Stort pulled back his arm to throw.

'Hard,' instructed Sinistral, 'and high!'

The stone was dark and small and they could not see it as it flew from Stort's hand until, by some trick of the light perhaps, its flight began to leave an arc of tiny stars, one following after the other in a myriad that seemed to open up the sky and part the clouds and show that, where the moon shone bright, the White Horse and its rider waited.

The stone's trail of stars fell slowly to the ground as the White Horse, which galloped faster than time itself, flew towards them such that when its two front hoofs touched the ground and the Shield Maiden riding it hauled in the reins, the stone fell between its feet.

They saw that it shone with all the colours of the Autumn and at its core it held the Fires of the Universe.

At once Stort left them where they stood and crossed the field, following the silvery trail to where the Horse and its Rider stood, and he picked up the gem that the stone had become.

Its light shone in the Chime that hung from his neck, and it too held something of the Fires of the Universe and the warm light of Samhain.

'Hello, Judith,' he said softly.

The moonlight lit her hair and the gem her face.

'Hello,' she said, 'where have you been?'

'Here and there,' he said, 'looking for this and finding other things . . .'

'Come closer.'

He did.

She was old and lined, but all that was gone in seeing him.

'You are beautiful,' he said.

'You make me feel so, Bedwyn Stort, you make me feel it. Now, give the gem to me.'

She bent forward so that he could put the gem of Autumn in the setting in the gold pendant that hung from her neck, so perfectly made by Beornamund that once a gem was put back in its proper place with love, it would not come out again.

'There,' he said, 'you have it now. But we . . .'

She put a finger to her lips.

'"We" can never be,' she said.

He stared at her, frowning.

'It *is* a problem,' he conceded good-humouredly, 'but every problem has a solution.'

'This one doesn't, Bedwyn Stort. Not ever.'

'We'll see.'

She smiled.

'You only have until the end of Winter to find a solution.'

'There is one?'

She laughed the laugh he had always loved.

'It's beyond any mortal to find it,' she said.

'Maybe,' said Bedwyn Stort, 'and maybe not.'

She rode among them briefly, all silvery light and fire, and paused awhile with Arthur especially, their words together private. She embraced him and her light seemed to be his own.

Then, as suddenly as she had come, she was gone, over Pendower Beach, high over Killigerran Head, towards where the moon soared and the stars shone.

They all watched after her, who rode alone through the seasons and loved a love that could never be.

Professor Arthur Foale passed away peacefully three days later in nearby Carne.

The hydden made a pyre on the spot not far from the Beacon, where Stort had found the gem of Autumn.

The day of the burning was still and the fire bright and fierce. It died with the coming of the evening, by when Arthur's spirit had returned to the Mirror and his body turned to ash. That same night the first winds of Winter came from the north and scattered his ashes across land and sea and to the four quarters of the Earth he loved; and to the stars above.

ACKNOWLEDGEMENTS

It is a great pleasure to thank Jackie Brockway once again for her support from the beginning to the end of the writing of a Hyddenworld novel. A writer may reach for the stars but, on this occasion, this particular one sometimes needed help getting there. She has given it unfailingly.

extracts reading groups
competitions books new
discounts extracts extracts
competitions reading groups
books new extracts discounts
events books events
extracts books reading groups
new titles reading groups
interviews new
events extracts extracts books
discounts events
new books events interviews
events new new books extracts
discounts extracts discounts
www.panmacmillan.com books
extracts events reading groups
competitions books extracts new